Advanced Praise for Burn It All Down

***

"I sat at the edge of my seat. I yelled at the characters. I could not put it down and literally did nothing for 2 whole days. I also cried and screamed. This is an emotional constant action-packed book." – **Margery, Goodreads**

***

"W.A. Pepper builds a gripping nonstop action story from its opening lines, which also incorporate a flavor of wry humor…As events unfold, Tanto discovers that his team and teachings are fully capable of evolving without him at the helm…Is he even meaningful any longer?

As Tanto absorbs the blame for things he didn't do, confronts emotional backlashes that place him at odds with a wide range of characters, and tackles more than one betrayal when life-threatening events emerge, readers will appreciate the edge-of-your-seat action that keeps the story mercurial and thoroughly engrossing.

Miracles, cyberaction, and powerful evil forces that threaten to take Tanto down with them create a thriller that excels in swift pace, strong characters, and unpredictable atmospheres.

Libraries either seeing popularity with Pepper's prior books or looking for a commanding stand-alone thriller will want to add *Burn It All Down* to their collections.

Packed with accounts of government infiltrations, encounters that are "*as scary as ... brilliant,*" and intriguing contrasts between technology and ideals, the story is quite simply a simmering, event-driven saga that is thoroughly engrossing and very highly recommended:

On the one hand, technology brought me closer to people... On the other hand, my belief in the Bushido Code did the same." – **D. Donovan, Senior Reviewer, Midwest Book Review**

Burn It All Down

A Tanto Technothriller

W. A. Pepper

Hustle Valley Press, LLC

Previously in the Tanto Technothriller Series

After escaping a hidden prison called Hackers' Haven, Tanto is on the run for his freedom (and life). A failsafe installed in him from his tormentors causes him to lose the ability to have and understand conversations. This sets him on a mission to find a cure. Simultaneously, he goes back to his roots and creates a criminal empire with two new acquaintances. Only after Tanto discovers a cure for his disease does he expose the agency that imprisoned him. And, while Tanto has drawn blood, he has also angered two powerful giants.

Current Thrillers by W.A. Pepper

***

Tanto Technothrillers

- DoGoodR

- You Will Know Vengeance

- Running on Broken Bones

- Burn It All Down

***

Rook Thrillers

- One Icy Night

Dedication and Disclaimer

Professionally: This book is dedicated to Sam Esmail and Tom Fontana. Their abilities to create anti-heroic worlds, characters, and powerful, gut-wrenching scenes have helped me create my own. Thank you for letting me stand on your shoulders. I'm sorry I did so wearing golf cleats.

***

Personally: This book (hell, this series) would not exist without the unwavering and vigorous support of my wife, Taddy Pepper. She is the force of nature that encouraged me to bring Tanto to life, to share his world, and to complete his journey in the best way possible. Thank you, Taddy. Without you, this series would be a document on a destroyed computer.

***

W. A. PEPPER

Disclaimer: Adult Content - Reader discretion is advised.

Chapter One

New, Old Friend

Memphis, Tennessee

March 16, 2012 – 2:14 a.m.

Unlike my first abduction, this time there is no ringing of stun grenades in my ears when someone slips the bag over my head. Also, I'm fully dressed and not in my underwear. Instead of getting shoved face down into my stinky sheets, they shove me into the back of a car. Yet as the slamming of the trunk echoes through my brain, one familiar feeling echoes through my soul, reminding me of my first time being captured:

No one can save me.

AldenSong and my lawyer, Ms. Ingrid "Innocent" Vincent, are at the hospital. Penny does not know my location. Even Mr. Judson and Larry are at work, cleaning the floors of MetroMed and covertly smuggling prescription drugs out of the building.

Fumbling in the darkness, I yank off the hood. Each bump on the road tosses me against the empty trunk. I grasp for a latch to pop the trunk, or to snag a weapon, anything.

I find nothing. Not even a spare tire to hide behind.

Three blocks from the police station, a rustle from behind me heralds several unseen hands wrapping me up. I should've known that my outright cockiness at exposing the Mercator Agency, Poseidon United, and even my old covert prison Hackers' Haven would bring the wrath of God down on me.

If I die here, I don't care. We'd made a giant bleed. That win was supposed to fuel my crusade to stop the government from entrapping hackers and forcing us to capture our own.

Now I'm headed to *who-knows-where*. Maybe back to Hackers' Haven.

Or maybe somewhere worse.

It's unclear how much time passes before the vehicle stops. Two car doors open and slam shut. Footsteps crunch gravel. A key enters the trunk's lock. I brace myself.

As the trunk pops open, a garage's work lamp shines from overhead, blinding me. As I raise my hand to block it out, someone grabs my wrist. I ball up my other fist and swing. A hand deflects it, and something stops me from swinging again.

It's not the person's touch, but the smell. Like minty soap, a hint of lemon and rage.

Only one person I know smells like that.

"Well, are you going to sit there like an *escroto* or get out?" asks the Portuguese-American hacker who saved my ass on way too many hacks to count.

"Mane-Eac!" I'm on my feet and I've engulfed her in a nearly back-breaking hug. "Holy shit, you're not in prison!"

"Nope...also...can't...breathe..."

I loosen my grip but keep the pint-sized powerhouse in my grasp as I hold her like she's a figment of my imagination.

"Ah, better. The day the Feds catch me is the day I die."

"Why the hell did you kidnap me?" I ask.

"One, you're an adult, so it's called an abduction." Mane-Eac runs her fingers through her short brown hair. "And two, we had to get you off the street quickly because you're really screwing with what we've been working on."

"Who's we?"

Mane-Eac points her purply painted fingernail to a figure behind me. The guy is probably my age, but he's about fifty pounds heavier than me and three inches taller. There's something in his eyes that is foreign, yet familiar. Somehow, I know him. It is like when you recognize a celebrity, but can't quite place what movie he was in.

"I've been wanting to meet you for a long time, Tanto." My old, new friend with long black hair and full black beard extends his hand to me. "I never thought I would work with the man that saved my life."

As we shake, it happens. I un-age the man with the scruffy beard by a decade. My mind shaves him and puts him in his perp walk outfit that I remember prior to my unfortunate incarceration: wearing a long black leather trench coat with mirrored sunglasses.

"DJ?" I ask, more in shock than in question.

He responds, "We have a lot to catch you up on." A smirk crosses his face as he adds, "Also, since we're going by handles, you can just call me DoGoodR."

Chapter Two

The Nameless

Three Weeks Later

Because I'm working twenty-hour days with Mane-Eac and DoGoodR, these weeks have passed like a fart in the wind. Once I got word to AldenSong through a burner phone and our attorney, Ms. Ingrid "Innocent" Vincent, where I was and how I got there, the big guy couldn't help but join us. Thankfully, he brought my pup, Funk Monster.

Where was I, you ask? Working with the Nameless, picking up where we left off, which helpfully might be exactly what I needed to keep Mercator from taking another bite out of my ass.

Ah, but who are the Nameless, you might rightly wonder? It turns out, Mane-Eac and DoGoodR have been underground. They've been busy since the last time the dynamic duo pulled a fast one on Mercator. It resulted in implementing Guerrilla warfare against Mercator & Poseidon. They're the ones that did their own wiki-leak of Poseidon's internal memo about those shitheads violating human rights with their Indian sweat shop.

As they caught me up on their off-the-grid lives that unfolded, I couldn't help but feel maybe I should have joined them all those years ago. Running until Mercator overtook me and threw me in Hackers' Haven hadn't turned out to be the winningest strategy. Still, it got me where I am today: working with a team again.

Along the back wall of the *S.S. Turing* — what DoGoodR calls this computer-filled safe house — are articles, downloaded classified reports, and more, detailing the relationship between the Mercator Agency, Poseidon United, and the government of the United States of America.

And this relationship is about as corrupt and incestuous as an Osceola ho down. The more we research, the more we discover how powerful this partnership actually is.

With one leg propped on a whining CPU like a pirate standing on a treasure chest with a baseball-shaped coffee mug in one hand, DoGoodR's white-toothed smile peeks through his long, flowing, silk black beard. He puts down his drink and picks up a printout of one of his favorite news reports about their organization.

He reads, "Quote, *the membership of the terrorist cell known only as The Nameless is filled with questionable individuals.* Well, that's pretty damn true. Anyway. *The Nameless organization...* organization, like we have a Board of Directors and membership dues or something. *...is led by a criminal using the hacking handle Mane-Eac. Mane-Eac, whose real name is Nicole Marie Potnik, has led a team that has cost the American taxpayers sixteen million dollars in lost wages and damaged infrastructure.* Fact: just last year, the gub'ment spent ten times that on paper clips. *Psychiatric analysis reports she has a background in skilled technological use, is prone to taking calculated risk, and has questionable morals.*"

From behind a pile of old silver hard drives, Mane-Eac quips, "That last line is not in the article, DG."

"Doesn't mean it's wrong, Sis."

The respect and history between these two is as thick as the smoke trailing from a nearby POS computer. What's amazing is that they spent eight of the last ten years working remotely, never meeting, until eighteen months ago.

"Shit!" DoGoodR grabs a nearby burn blanket, which is a flame-retardant blanket used to snuff out fires. After he smothers the CPU, he blows into the casing. A cloud of black powder plumes back, leaving DoGoodR coughing out gray smoke like Wile E. Coyote after his ACME TNT backfires on him.

"Why do you have to act out when we have company?" he chides the machine, patting it on its metal side. "Drink some coolant and walk it off."

I know that color of smoke. That's the thermal paste melting away from an overheated processor in the motherboard. That happens, even with a pump-out and with crystal clear water coolant and an industrial cooling fan. DoGoodR reinforced the processor heat plates, but these machines are overworked, outdated, and begging for the quick release of death.

Every bit of hardware in this place is about a sneeze away from being classified as obsolete. Most parts are salvaged from pawn shops. Smoke and fire notwithstanding, it's still the safer option. The Mercator Agency monitors shipments of new, or, should I say, more functional, computing hardware. This creepy legal overreach brought to you by the maximum exploitation of The Patriot Act. And few know about the abuse of The Patriot Act like I do.

So DoGoodR overclocks all the systems. They run fast enough to get the job done, but they burn up so fast that their lifespan is that of a mosquito.

A *whirr* from behind me confirms that at least the printer works. AldenSong emerges with a stack of printed code as thick as a loaf of bread.

Aldy drops it on an already paper-swamped folding table, and says, "DoGoodR, you know they have these things called monitors and, on them, you can see and scroll through all the code you could possibly eat up."

"Naw-naw-naw," says DoGoodR as he grabs the printouts and lays page after page on the floor. "Not the same thing. Can't touch the code like that. The only way to understand the code is to tackle the whole thing. The only way out is through. I mean, bro, look at it like it's alive."

"On a screen, it's fluid," I counter.

"Oh, I disagree, old man."

Old man? I think, rolling my eyes but smiling. *I'm only nine months older than you.*

"To find the lies in the code," he continues, "you must first read the truth in the paper. Sometimes you get in the flow with the code in your mind, but only when you hold the paper in your hands, boy, does it sparkle. Sometimes it's a dance, and sometimes it's a drunken back-alley brawl. Often, it only needs finesse, a little encouragement. Other times, you gotta slap it like it owes you money."

"DG would hump a pile of code if it consented," says Mane-Eac, rising to her feet.

DoGoodR raises a finger to protest, thinks on it, and lowers his hand.

"Also, you're being creepy, so..." Mane-Eac plops down a glass jar overflowing with dollar bills and the words *Creepy Fine* written on the side.

DoGoodR chuckles and whips out a dollar bill he already had holstered in his tiny right blue jean pocket. "Worth every penny," he says.

Penny. *Damn.* I'd be lying if I didn't think of her daily. I flat out miss her, and the way I abandoned her to draw out the Mercator Agency wasn't exactly tactful.

However, just because I can justify my actions, doesn't make them right.

I fumble with an empty medicine bottle in my hoodie's pocket — my good luck totem — and Funk Monster sniffs her way around various machines. The last one she flees from like she just discovered it housed a pack of wild bears.

An overcooked smell assaults my nostrils. The odor from the machine is like if someone put a fork in the microwave: metallic, smoky, and dangerous. Usually, I'd take a screwdriver to open its shell, but DoGoodR keeps everything screw-free.

For easy access.

And for our eventual fires.

I don't unplug the machine; any shock like that might short out the motherboard. I know that while it might shock me, it won't kill me. There are too many yellow, industrial strength surge protectors around here to keep that from happening. Inside this machine, I spot the culprit: something jams the heatsink fans that pump out hot air and push cool air through the system.

This little brown and white sucker isn't more than a baby, the size of a half dollar coin. It screams a high-pitched wail when it sees me and pulls at its tail. Instantly, Funk Monster dives into the machine to see what's making that wonderful noise.

"Get back, girl," I say, shoving FM's nose away from the mouse's swipes. With a pair of needle-nose pliers, I spread the fans' fins so that the tiny tail gets free.

Of course, the moment the mouse gets loose, I scoop it up and ease it outside before it becomes Funk Monster's newest chew toy.

It's a cute moment, which comes to a crashing end as an alarm sounds. One that I've never heard before.

Chapter Three

Marching Orders

"Oh, someone's getting cranky," DoGoodR says as he claps his hands and skips in his high-top Converse across the room. He grabs a remote for a classic tube television and presses buttons. Nothing happens. He opens the remote, rotates the batteries, closes the cover, and tries again. Nothing.

After the kid smacks the controller four times and still gets the same result, I stroll over and hit the *On* button on the TV.

"I was getting there," mutters DoGoodR.

After a blank screen shifts from static to a grainy picture of a news report, I recognize the face at the center of the feature story.

"Sincaid Cussh, President and CEO of Poseidon United," says the anchor with way-too-perfect hair, skin, and teeth, "was awarded the Natchez Society's *Person of the Year Award* for his company's focus on improving the environment and for bringing stronger rules and regulations in regards to human trafficking."

"Even the devil gets a medal these days," says Mane-Eac as she and Aldy scoot past me carrying a burned-out monitor to the corner of the room known as The Graveyard. "The bigger the criminal, the higher the focus on the *besteira*," Mane-Eac says, sliding effortlessly back into Portugese.

"We all need our *Ikigai*, right, T.?" quips DoGoodR, referencing our recent conversations about The Bushido Code. He picked up the concepts pretty quickly — like *ikigai,* the Japanese belief around life worth. Sadly, on the back of his own research, he's decided he's more *shinobi,* also known as a sneaky, dishonorable ninja.

"Spoken like a true mercenary," I say.

"It's not like bushis don't have as much blood on their hands," counters DoGoodR.

"Not for anything less than the greater good," I say, knowing that's not the complete truth. Hell, the Mercator Agency captured me, put me in a Poseidon United prison, and forced me to capture others online; I was worse than ninja.

I was a tool that, if not used or useful, was to be discarded.

DoGoodR could bat my comment around like a kitten with a ball of yarn, and he knows it, but he decides to leave it. Instead, he writes the date and time on a white board under a long series of dates and times.

"That's Cussh's third award or press notice this week," says Do-GoodR as his hand dances along the board. "In five workdays, actually."

"They're gearing up, so a storm's a-coming," Mane-Eac states as she glances at the whiteboard and all the other media and printouts along the walls. It's a cross between analytical and obsessive, with lines drawn and strings connecting people, businesses, and deals. "As usual, it's us versus the world, and we're losing...badly."

"Huh, I like those odds," says Aldy as he scoots past me, with large, Samoan arms covered with power and ethernet cables.

Mane-Eac moves as though her bones were concrete. With a lowered head, she says, "And, whatever's coming, we aren't near ready."

"Oh, come on, Sis," counters DoGoodR as he flips through the printed code, marking in red ink certain lines. "We've got this. It's gonna be fun."

She meets his gaze. "You have a strange definition of *fun*, DG."

"I know." DoGoodR hugs himself and adds, "Ain't it grand?"

Mane-Eac cuts the TV off. DoGoodR goes to the corner of the room and takes off his black T-shirt.

"Shit, are you going on a code walk *now*?" asks Mane-Eac, already knowing the answer.

DoGoodR throws on a beaten-up old white shirt with a skeleton in an Uncle Sam outfit. Holes and stains cover it, but not enough to hide the words *Stone Temple Pilots Wants You!* in the center. He plops down in a chair in front of a terminal and hits play on the Winamp audio player.

I didn't have to ask what he was going to play. I'd heard it. A lot. I am quite familiar with the thrashing guitar, slamming drums, and guttural slash primal vocals that make up STP's *Wicked Garden.*

"Headphones!" screams Mane-Eac, and the music stops as DoGoodR straps on a pair of faded, brown 1970s wired headphones, and enters line after line of code. Mane-Eac isn't a fan of this song. Even before he'd played it to death, she'd always been more of a Sonic Youth kinda listener.

We all have our rituals, or totems, that help us code. Aldy's is still a little hula girl, the kind you find on a car's dashboard, bobbing along. His last one got left in a crematorium, so I picked one up at the dollar store for him. Mane-Eac's is her knife, a Tuf-Nut that she flicks open and shut when she's deep in thought. DoGoodR, well, it's STP and his shirt. For me, it's always been the empty pill bottle, a reminder of how my mother abused herself and me.

In his own little world, DoGoodR scans paper, tosses it, adds code through a terminal, then repeats the process. Mane-Eac's hardened facade softens as she watches him.

As DoGoodR headbangs, Aldy waves me over to the machine he's working on. "Tanto, I've been meaning to ask you something—"

"Hey, set the tone, right?" DoGoodR interrupts, yelling over the roar of Scott Weiland's deep, throaty voice in his ears. "Burn Bright, right guys?"

Just hearing those words straightens both my spine and Aldy's. It was part of our battle cry in Hackers' Haven. I taught it to DoGoodR, mainly because I wanted to share some of the good parts of my last decade, however few and far between they've been.

I turn back to Aldy and a black-and-white monitor on a system that we've set up to use *Johnson_TOR*, an open-sourced torrent software that allows us to scour The Dark Web without being tracked. If anyone tries to ping our scrambled IP Address, the only thing they'll wind up with is our protective worm that will shred their hard drive like it's made of tissue.

"A couple of hits came in around three this morning," says Aldy. "The chatter is like what we thought: between Mercator and P.U."

Aldy, in his infinite maturity, always gets a kick out of shortening Poseidon United.

Mane-Eac joins us and scans through the data. "We've got decent packet sizes coming through. They're not software updates, because we know they only do those onsite."

"They're old-fashioned informational updates," I say. "Can you see who sent the most info?"

The clickity-clacks of keys continue for a few seconds as Aldy scrolls and expands our tracking log file. "Most of the big ones are actually coming from Poseidon United instead of Mercator."

"And I bet the Mercator ones are tiny," I say.

"Yep," answer Aldy.

Mane-Eac rubs her temples as it hits her. "The small packets are responses."

"And here I thought you were tired," I say, patting Mane-Eac on the back until she swats me to stop. "They're marching orders. We just have to figure out where to."

Chapter Four

PhauCet

We don't have to wait long to find out. A press announcement about Poseidon United's next business venture. And it is exactly what we feared:

Artificial Intelligence. AI isn't that farfetched; hell, it started after World War II in the mid-50s. However, its power mainly exists in science fiction and horror movies.

Until today.

AldenSong reads the printout, which we're now seeing spikes about from other news outlets and their shared hyperlinks.

"Poseidon United has been working with their engineers to develop PhauCet, an online service that curates news, music, movies, and television resources into one comprehensive, full-service website. Interactive components and the proprietary PhauCet chatbot will offer unprecedented and unrivaled personalization to provide users the exact entertainment they are looking for. A trial version for the public will be available next week. For more details, blah blah blah..."

"Gakunodo wasn't the only software Hackers' Haven was building," I say, even before processing the full impact of my words.

Against my will and under the watchful eye of the Warden of Hackers' Haven, I designed Gakunodo, a software to entrap and capture people searching the Dark Web for illegal things. Mainly underage porn.

Clearly, I wasn't the only one designing programs under duress. It wasn't until I met with Lance-A-Little and his Gogglemen that I even conceived that there were other Double-H prisons besides mine.

There were forty prisons like the Double H, at last count. That means at least forty opportunities for Poseidon United to wrangle similar programs to mine, or others designed to do even more damage, out of literal captives. Aldy reads my lack of poker face and wipes a clean spot on a code-covered white board.

"Man, don't…" protests DoGoodR before he throws his hands up. "Fine. It's not like I needed that."

Aldy sets up a scrum page, half the board with options and the other half with solutions. I wind up a one-minute egg-shaped timer and he goes to work. Once the alarm goes off, I take a spot at the board for a minute. Then Mane-Eac takes a pass, followed by Aldy, and then DoGoodR, after which he promptly returns to his coding station and headphones.

After three rounds apiece, here's our best uneducated guess, from a little bit of leaked code we deconstructed:

PhauCet is free software developed by *engineers*, which probably means prisoners of one of the Hackers' Haven prisons, i.e., Hackvicts. This tool promises to find people what they want, like Google or AltaVista. Maybe more like Ask Jeeves. The difference between it and existing search engines is that this program always runs in the background. It's gathering information about the users, which isn't illegal, just unethical. This particular program will run on a dedicated series of servers away from Poseidon United's headquarters. That means a server farm. The major problem is we don't have access to the full version of the software, and the Beta comes out in five days.

"Someone's gonna have to get into their systems," whispers Mane-Eac.

DoGoodR chimes in, "Me! Pick me! Me-me-me!"

"You're developing code," she says. "Also, these machines will burst into flames if you're not here."

"I'm almost done with the code, and the *S.S. Turing* will sail just fine without Captain DoGoodR at the helm for a day or two."

As if on cue, the closest CPU to me moans in pain.

"Plus," he goes on as if no sound interrupted him, "we know the main upload site is in New Orleans, so...road trip!"

As DoGoodR dives back into his work, Mane-Eac hangs her head. She's diamond-strong, but exhausted. I put my hand on her shoulder and Mane-Eac smiles and conspiratorially points at DoGoodR. "He's a lot like you."

I think he's a lot like I used to be. Before Mercator. Before Poseidon United. And before I spent almost a decade in prison.

AldenSong, cradling Funk Monster like a baby, asks a minor but obvious question. "Why is DoGoodR captain of the *S.S. Turing* when you run the show?"

"Because," responds Mane-Eac, "I don't need to be a fake captain of a fake ship to sleep at night."

She says the word *sleep* with a hint of longing in her voice. She props, no, rests her head up on her left fist as her right hand pecks at a keyboard.

I want to tell her that everything is going to work out, that we will stop both Mercator and Poseidon. This bastardized dehumanization program must stop, and we are the ones to do it. Our friends will go free, and the world will thank us.

And that's when AldenSong hands me a printout that shifts me from *Park* to *Drive*.

"Today?" I ask and show the paper to Aldy.

AldenSong shrugs, picks up a prepacked brown bag of gear, tosses it to me, grabs one himself, and picks up keys from the table.

My big friend hits me on the back so hard that my soul leaves my body before rubber-banding back in. "You and me got some good ole fashioned B&E to commit."

Chapter Five

Ducks

Mane-Eac and DoGoodR hop in her 1986 Honda Accord with enough miles and wear on that poor car to qualify as scrap metal. Also, it always backfires when it cranks. Like clockwork, she turns the key, pumps the accelerator, and two *pops* sound. To everyone else, it probably sounds like firecrackers on the Fourth of July.

To me, it sounds like small-arms gunfire. Like a twenty-two-caliber bullet exploding.

Entering Barca's body.

Again.

And again.

I shake the execution of that monster from my brain and toss my gear in the trunk of AldenSong's 1975 AMC Gremlin, a discontinued car from a defunct company that wasn't even popular the year it came out. It's an odd-looking vehicle: a long hood and short cab with an almost non-existent backseat and an almost comical sleeper-trunk. Most car companies try to make cars that look sleek or sporty; the Gremlin looks like a car a four-year-old on a sugar high drew with a crayon. He was proud of himself for getting it for only three hundred bucks. I'm still scandalized that he wasn't paid for the service of taking that piece of shit off someone's hands.

At the time, he'd laughed and pointed out the eight-track player in the dash. "The owner even threw in some Allman Brothers and Eagles tracks."

What a steal. Now, we're loading it up to break into a warehouse.

Our overall plan is this: Mane-Eac and DoGoodR head to The Big Easy, a five-hour drive. There, they break into Poseidon United's coding division, install the tracer code DoGoodR developed, and get back here. Aldy and I, along with Funk Monster as a cuteness distraction, are to break into the warehouse in Memphis where the CPU processors are being installed, add an extra semiconductor chip to each motherboard, and hightail it out of there.

Once those machines get installed and powered on, the real fun begins. Our software and hardware should gel with their PhauCet software, so we can get the real scoop on what P.U. and Mercator are data mining from users.

It's simple, but simple enough plans often complicate themselves. Unlike my last case with Mane-Eac, this warehouse isn't in the middle of nowhere; it's in an abandoned building sixteen blocks from MetroMed in Memphis, Tennessee. If this building were off the beaten path, breaking in would work like this:

Get there at night when security is at a minimum.

Get through the gate.

Take out the exterior cameras.

Install the chips.

Get out.

Unfortunately, this building is at an intersection between Webster and Main. With this much consistent traffic, and no other entrances, there's no opportunity to do this under the cover of night. That means

I've got to do my least favorite type of hacking: social hacking, also known as acting and speaking with humans I don't care to know.

That's why AldenSong and I are now in the gift shop lobby of the infamous Peabody Hotel, a historic hotel in downtown Memphis, grabbing touristy items. We each have roles to play for this game, and if we don't play them perfectly... well, the threat of going back to Hackers' Haven is always on the table.

I've bought a green shirt with three ducks on it and the words *Give 'em something to quack about: Visit the Peabody*. Aldy has grabbed a tourist map from the hotel's concierge and marked a coffee shop near Poseidon's warehouse. I'm stomping around the white marble floors looking for the last piece of the puzzle: a room key return box.

"Got it," I say, more to myself than Aldy. He's off watching the hotel's ducks and ducklings swim in the fountain in the middle of the hotel.

Can't take the big kid anywhere.

I examine the lock. Basic two-prong locking mechanism. I can pick it in a minute, maybe two. The problem is that it's maybe ten feet from the front desk, which means I'll need Aldy to distract the clerks.

The good news is that it's almost 11 a.m.: checkout time. Three lines of tourists with luggage block a lot of sight of what we're doing, but I'm certain that could change in a heartbeat.

"Man, those ducks live the life," chuckles Aldy as he saunters back to me. "So, you got the key yet?"

"No," I answer. "I need about two minutes of distraction to pick the lock—"

Aldy sighs and asks, "Why do you have to complicate everything?" Then he lifts the box.

"No, don't..." I say as Aldy shakes the box, and two cards fall out on the tile floor.

Then, nothing bad happens. No one sends security over. There's no alarm as Aldy picks up the cards and hands them to me.

I pocket them and smile at how easy that was.

"Man, I've missed you," I say to Aldy as I affectionately punch him. His clear-headed thinking is a refreshing relief to my consistent paranoia.

As we leave the hotel and walk back to the car, I think that *this went way too easily*.

It's only when we arrive two buildings down from the warehouse do I see that someone has already beaten us there.

Chapter Six

Really Bad Idea

Two undercover cars flank our target and they're too obviously Mercator. First, it's the obvious extra tint on each vehicle's windows. Too dark to be legal. Second, the tires. Government agencies exclusively use Goodyear on their cars. No clue why, but that's what Aldy says he saw when he strolled by them holding his tourist map as cover.

Those two don't guarantee federal vehicles, but the license plates also don't match traditional ones. They don't blatantly have a *G* for *Government* like most official vehicles. They have yellow tags, like the kind you see at the dealership. From my spot on a city bus bench, I can barely make out that there's an official State of Mississippi inspection sticker in the driver's top left corner of the windshield.

People do inspections on *sold* cars, not cars *for sale*.

Our current problem is how to get those vehicles away from our target. The agents have their orders, and it will take something pretty major to get them to abandon the base.

"I'm open to ideas on how to get them to move," I say over a sip of coffee.

Aldy chuckles, "I have a really, *really* bad idea."

My gut doesn't turn, as much as quake, when I ask, "This is going to be bad for me, isn't it?"

Aldy sips his tea and concedes, "Oh, you'll be fine as long as you've got your running shoes on."

Chapter Seven

Recruited Chaos to My Side

To say this is a horrible idea is an insult to horrible ideas.

In any case, two hours, two purchases, and one mile walk later, I'm doing the dumbest thing I've done in the past, well, twenty minutes.

Once the security is gone, AldenSong will break into the warehouse, solder the chips into the motherboards, and meet me at the rendezvous point. He gets the productive part of this caper; I'm the distraction. And I'm gonna have to make it a grand one.

I am in an Internet Café called *Cup of Joe's Fire Down Below*. This coffee shop slash BBQ pit has a couple of computers in the corners. One sign on the door reads *Free S'mores Fridays are Back!* Another sign reads, *Keep your four-legged friends on a leash and your misbehaving two-legged ones as well.* I didn't want to put Funk Monster in more danger, but Aldy made a good point: people trust someone with a dog. So, here I am, with a small dog and a backpack full of mayhem, about to set off an alarm and bring down the wrath of God on myself and this ten-pound dog.

It has the same feel as any internet café, even the one where I met Kilroy: a few working computers with a bunch of people punching away on their own laptops and cellphones. This place sells more coffee than computing time because the old CTX machine I power up moans when I cut it on. Luckily, unlike DoGoodR's babies, this one doesn't cover me in a smoke screen.

I count eight customers and two employees. Two entrances. And lots of glass for visibility to and from the street. In the middle of the shop, they have an open-air fireplace that goes one story deep, and every Friday you can cook free s'mores . . . with the purchase of a large custom coffee, of course.

I log into the Dark Web, on an intentionally unsecure line. I go directly through the cafe's router. No encryption. No VPN. There are headphones plugged into the CTX machine, so I put them on, pretending to listen to some jams, or whatever kids call music these days.

Then it starts. First, as a ripple on my screen that most people might mistake as Internet lag.

I ain't most people.

I close out that particular window, however, before I can yank off my headset, a blast of static smacks my eardrums. Through gritted teeth and clenched eyes, I keep the headset on. A voice I know all too well fills the headphones.

"There is feedback...static on the line. Cut outside chatter...monitor just spiked. Please consider...target spooked. Happy Hunting. Over."

Agent Michelle. The person whose career I almost made slash ended when she tried to trap both Mane-Eac and myself a decade ago.

Michelle fooled around and found out what happens when you go after an underage techie such as DoGoodR.

And then she caught my ass eighteen months later. But a victory is a victory.

Good. In my gut, I knew it would be her. One of the lesser tenants of The Bushido Code eases my panic slightly as I unclench my hands. Sense your enemy.

The problem is that there are enough unknowns in our plan to fill a sporty-sport stadium. I must assume that the Mercator Agency has requisitioned slash hijacked satellites with thermal imaging, ways to record sudden spikes in heart rates, and more.

That's why I move to the front door quickly. I don't open it, though. I just give them visual confirmation of the target because I need as many of them here as possible for this to work.

The blood in my ears pounds like a bass beat at a rap concert. I dart side-to-side in the store, giving the satellite a show. Several people hold their cellphones high in the air, searching for a signal. Mercator has locked down the Grid. No calls, no info, in or out.

Three black SUVs skid to a stop in the block over from the cafe. They're keeping their distance, not wanting to spook anyone. From what I know about their tactics, these assholes are the back lines of defense. They only made themselves known after someone identified me from the window a few moments ago. Next, they will send in squads to cover any known exits.

I left enough of a digital footprint that Mercator has a damn good idea it's me they're after. Now, with visual confirmation, they're bringing, as Aldy calls it, the entire House of Pain, my way. Agent Michelle knows me, knows I'm not violent, but she still wouldn't risk injuring civilians with a haphazard breach on the building. At this point, she's hoping I'll look out the window one last time; then they'd have my current attire and profile for confirmation.

I've screwed up her plans so many times she's the human equivalent of a corkscrew.

But she did get me that one time.

And then I spent eight years in a hellhole.

Sirens squawk from outside, which means the average person goes to the window to see what's up. I'm not average. They're probably watching infrared to see who is fleeing. It's just as much about who they can see as who they can't. Still, I give Agent Michelle this present and lean against the glass in my black hoodie that covers my head with just enough of my face visible to guarantee identification. As I do so, ten SWAT officers exit their vehicles.

Now that they've got a view, I turn back to the cafe's crowd. A quick scan of the room gives me two possible stunt doubles. One is a guy in camo pants and a Memphis Grizzlies hoodie. The other is a girl wearing a Hello Kitty one.

I choose the girl, partially because girls love dogs. I hope. Again, I'm going on gut instinct here.

This girl's probably eighteen, nineteen, with long auburn hair. She sips an iced coffee and only looks up when she sees Funk Monster in my arms.

"Oh, look at that fur baby!" she exclaims, putting her coffee down.

"Would you like to pet her?" I ask the rhetorical question.

"Yes, please!" As I put FM in her arms, I knock the coffee on her hoodie.

"Shit!" I exclaim, taking off my mine and handing it to her. "I am so sorry, it should come out. Take mine until it gets clean."

Then the girl looks at Funk Monster, then me, and responds, "Um, no."

"Excuse me?" I ask, counting the seconds until SWAT breaches the damn door.

"Um, I don't know you."

Well shit. The self-awareness. The confidence. Her head's on her shoulders better than the average human being. On the one hand, good for her, but this puts some piss in my Cheerios. I don't have time for this. I snatch up Funk Monster and head straight to the dude wearing camo. He looks up from his *Sports Illustrated* and gives me this dead-eyed look.

He's stoned.

Out-freaking-standing.

I snap my fingers in front of Shaggy from *Scooby Doo* and he focuses on me, then the dog.

"Oh, cool dog," he mumbles and reaches for FM. I swat his hand away and toss my hoodie at him.

"I'll give you fifty bucks to wear this."

He rolls it from hand-to-hand before cracking a stoned smile so big both of his eyes shut. "Um, make it a hundred."

Mother—

One big bill later, I've got my decoy. The guy, a little confused but clearly money hungry, pocketed the cash, put on the hoodie, and strolled up to the deli counter.

With the easy part of this taken care of, I dump my backpack on the coffee counter. Before the barista can even protest, I hand her a twenty as I sort through my chaotic collection of electronics. I attach my custom-built keyless entry code grabber. It's a remarkable invention that cycles through all possible RSA or lesser encryptions in a matter of seconds. It's also a great tool to hook to a small booster antenna, punch the *Randomize* button, and press *Loop*, like I just did.

You see, most cars are susceptible to code duplication. Particularly when it comes to their alarms. My goal is simple, more or less: I need a dozen pissed off cars within radio distance to think someone is breaking into each one. Granted, I've never tried this, but it should work.

I just hope my luck hasn't run out.

For a few seconds, nothing happens, and it appears luck has abandoned me.

Damnation, what did I do wrong?

Then a chorus of car alarms fills the air.

Without time to celebrate, I snatch a homemade radio jammer. I fire off a similar barrage to distort communications. At least I am following Bushido Code: *even in the midst of possible death/incarceration, use every weapon at your disposal and leave no arrow unfired.*

I have successfully recruited chaos to my side.

Now for my next trick: getting out of a building with all the visible exits covered.

Chapter Eight

Dive Into the Darkness

In a matter of moments, the place will explode with federal agents. Maybe they'll serve an appetizer of tear gas, followed by a full-on breach for the main course. It's possible someone prepped SWAT with a floor plan of the coffee shop.

However prepared they were, it's unlikely they took the time to also look at the original blueprint of the building.

Like I did.

That's why it took me ninety-seven minutes to get here. I stopped by the City Planner's office, paid the right clerk for both copies of the blueprint, and had my shitty plan's Ace in the Hole. Before converting into a caffeine distributor, this place was a bankrupt auto body shop.

That is why they could have a fireplace for s'mores in the middle of a quaint little cafe. Most auto repair shops were actually two stories: a top level for customers and a bottom where employees worked on the underside of the cars.

I grab my empty backpack and leave all my incriminating gear. Then I snatch up Funk Monster and put her in the backpack like a little Yoda to my Luke. She gives my face a lick and snuggles down into the bag. Now, like I have done many times in my life, I dive into the darkness.

Chapter Nine

Supply Up

At the bottom of the pit, through the gray light trickling in, I spot a service door down a hallway. This is probably where they empty the ashes from *Joe's* weekly fires. Using the light on my burner phone, I scurry to the end and emerge in an alley next to a row of storage units. Before exiting, I smash the burner against the concrete wall, just to be on the safe side. I lean out and, from around a corner, I see the agents swarm the coffee shop.

There are now mere seconds before Agent Michelle realizes I am not the stoned hippie in the hoodie.

I make it a half a block strolling nonchalantly in the other direction before two police cars roar my way. Instead of running or hiding, I lean into a community bulletin board next to Merrick's Magic Shop and yank off a flyer:

This Friday only, see the Mysterious Norman levitate, eat fire, saw a woman in half, and MORE at the Scott-King Convention Center before the National Speakers Bureau's Annual Meeting. Free to the public. Note: The Mysterious Norman is not associated with the NSB or compensated by them. Finally, attendance at this show is in no way connected to the NSB Annual Meeting.

I've always respected illusionists. They're a lot like hackers: both work around your established defenses in ways that you never expect. Plus, they, too, like a challenge.

Whether by luck or a higher power, I get an extra layer of legitimacy as a blue-haired lady scurries out of her parked Lincoln Town Car next to me and fails to shut her car door all the way. There's enough jewelry on her to give Mr. T a run for his money. She slams into my shoulder, even though she clearly sees me standing in her path.

"Watch where you're going!" she snaps at me with some serious audacity.

Funk Monster barks back for the old crone to mind her own business, though I doubt the walking raisin speaks Mutt. She gives me the finger as she pops into the *Kurl Up 'n Dye Hair Salon.*

When the cop cars blow past, I dart into the magic shop. In the store, I spot more capes than you'd see at a comic book convention. I have two minutes, tops, before someone SWAT-related enters the store.

Funk Monster growls at a statue of the Wicked Witch of the West, and I take that as a friendly reminder that I have ninety seconds until capture. From floor to ceiling, it is not just full of prepackaged magic tricks. It's full of crap. I mean, fake vomit and blood capsules are next to the edible magic wands level of crap. It's horrible, but it'll do, because I can't hide out here.

But I can supply up for a really terrible idea.

Chapter Ten

Moths

Inside Merrick's Magic Shop, which is also a convenience store and tanning salon, I head to the lone employee. I hold up the flier from the community bulletin board to the guy with a glazed-over look working behind the counter. *Norman,* his nametag reads and my brilliant observational skills suggest this might be the *Mysterious Norman* referenced on the flier.

He spreads his hands and says, "Hey, man, that's not cool. I only printed a few of those."

"Where are your fire fingers?" I ask, ignoring his protest.

The acne-covered dude peers through his narrow, pretentious glasses, and kicks his head back like I just insulted his God. "They're called Finger Flashers."

For the love of—

"I need all you can find. Plus, all the fake blood you have, now!" To highlight my urgency, I throw a wad of cash on the counter. Norman gets a lot less *mysterious* as he follows my less-than-subtle hint and leaves the counter. Out the window, a SWAT team enters a building down the street. A normal criminal might take this as a sign to flee.

And, while I am certainly a *criminal*, no one ever called me *normal*. Between my gut and my Bushido training, I have everything I need to get away clean in this store. I breathe and reassure myself that I have time. The police will always focus on the largest threat in the area.

Unfortunately for them, that won't be me. But it will be *because* of me.

As Norman digs around for my order, I snag a stack of electric mini smoke machines, two piles of AA batteries, a handful of cheap promotional digital watches with *Merrick's Magic Shop* on them, a roll of duct tape, and enough Bubble Tape canisters to piss off Wilford Brimley. I also unwrap a Slim Jim, take FM out of the backpack, and present it to her. She snatches it away and curls up against the counter to snack.

As FM gobbles up the prepackaged meat, I yell to Mr. Mysterious, "Also, watch after my dog for a sec."

From behind a stack of boxes and capes, he says, "I'm not sure I am trained to dog sit."

Asshole. "Does twenty bucks get you qualified?"

"Man, I just love learning."

I pet Funk Monster and dart back to the rude lady's Lincoln Town Car. SWAT has locked down the perimeter, but their sweep hasn't hit this area yet.

Fly, Tanto, fly. If I were more of a religious person, I might be pinging the Lord's inbox instead of urging myself on. Anything to support this half-baked plan of mine. The good news is that ever since I downloaded the banned *Anarchist's Cookbook* when I was fifteen, I've known exactly how to make explosions and chaos.

Lucky for me, the lady in her rush to get her hair done neglected to close her door properly and it opens without effort or alarm. I slide into the driver's side and open the glove compartment. In it, I find a binder with her insurance documents, all of which appear to be up-to-date.

Good. Miss In-A-Hurry is going to need her auto insurance sooner rather than later.

I reach under the steering wheel and pop the trunk. In there, under piles of old blankets and clothes, probably meant for donation at one point in time, sits a roadside emergency kit: jumper cables, a car jack, and a flare.

Apparently, Christmas came early.

I grab the car jack and use it to raise the back-right tire. To any prying eyes I'm fixing a flat. Under the car, I find the fuel line and clamp the alligator teeth of the jumper cables down on the dirty cable and twist.

After four shredding turns, the harsh fumes of gasoline hit my nostrils. A steady stream of yellow oozes out. The river of fermented dinosaur remains trickle down mostly empty parking spaces. I let the fuel pool before striking the flare against the concrete. As the red phosphorus smoke fills the air and stings my eyes, I drop it and run like hell.

By the time I get back into the magic shop, the vehicle explodes. This chaos will bring customers and clerks flooding out of their respective stores, as well as the full attention of police and SWAT. Like moths to a literal flame, they'll want to know what's going on.

If this was an average police perimeter, Funk Monster and I could slip past the unaware crowd and escape the area with ease.

But this is the Mercator Agency. And they're more relentless than a junkyard dog with a bone. That's why things are about to get not just worse, but damn weird.

Chapter Eleven

Least Risky Part

The clerk, excuse me, *magician*, follows his curious human nature and runs out of the store to find the source of the explosion. That doesn't matter; I no longer need his help because he'd put all the supplies I requested in two large plastic bags. The next part of my plan will cause more havoc but less property damage. I already had the fire department in the mix. Now, I need to get all the emergency services involved.

And that's much easier than you'd think.

I snatch up the bags, put Funk Monster in her backpack, and take a breath. *Here we go...*

We dart out of the fire exit in the back of the store. An alarm sounds, but the car fire will keep the crowd and law enforcement's attention.

I hope.

We emerge into an alley. At the end, I spot police and SWAT surrounding the burning Lincoln Town Car. It looks clear. However, just because I can see my enemies on my right doesn't mean that there isn't an army to my left.

I take a second and open a can of Bubble Tape. I shove the entire wad of sugary candy in my mouth. It takes all the effort my jaw can muster to chew it like *Mr. Ed* on TV pretending to talk. As a cop car with its blaring siren shoots past the opening on the left, I slink out of the alley.

Police are on both sides of the city streets about fifty yards away. Two squad cars block off the street to my left, which is about the best outcome I could have hoped for given the circumstances.

I crouch in a nearby doorway and load up one of the smokers with batteries and fuel. As I ignite it, oily plumes of gray trickle into the air. I sneak behind a Mini Cooper stuck at the end of the standstill traffic and duct-tape the smoker just above the bumper. After a few more gum chomps, I yank the massive wad of Bubble Tape out of my mouth, cover the exterior of the smoker in it, snap the band off a watch so that only the face is visible, and shove the watch on the gum.

The icing on this fake bomb cake is the load of fake blood vials I bought from Mr. Mysterious. I pop an entire package of the high-fructose-filled capsules and dribble them along the edge of the trunk, making it look like someone is trapped or dead inside.

Not far off, the rude lady from the hair salon is screaming at a police officer and several people wander over to watch the blaze from a distance. I casually nudge one guy in the crowd with my shoulder, not enough to piss him off, but to get his focus to shift.

"Hey, man, watch..." The guy's eyes go big like Frisbees and he yells, "Yo! There's a freaking bomb!"

And, just like one of The Mysterious Norman's illusions, wouldn't you know it that a dozen cellphones went to people's ears like someone magnetized them as the mob runs in the opposite direction? Of course, at the sight of a chimney of smoke coming from a *bomb* on the back of a car leaking blood, well, even the most cynical bastard would call 911 and flee the scene.

But that's not enough to guarantee my escape. That's why I scurry one block away and repeat my Unabomber tribute again. And again. And two more times, for a grand total of five threats.

In a matter of minutes, the situation shifts from *Contain and Capture* to *Defuse and Evacuate*. As a police officer waves a mob past the perimeter, I thank God, Buddha, hell, even the great Spaghetti Monster in the sky, because this is still the least risky part of today's plan.

Chapter Twelve

The Mountain

Even with multiple distractions and calculated chaos helping Funk Monster and me sneak past SWAT and the Mercator Agency, we still must take side streets and a zig-zag pattern from *Explosion City* to our rendezvous with AldenSong. After four hours of moving, hiding, crouching and sneaking, it's past midnight by the time I catch up with Aldy in his shitty Gremlin, pumping *Low Rider* by War on the radio. The big guy's sipping Starbucks and eating a deep-fried chicken on a stick.

"Oh, how'd it go?" he mumbles through a mouthful of batter and dead bird.

"Well, neither of us is in jail, so that's how it went."

Aldy turns down the radio. "You coulda just said *good*."

"How'd it go on your end?" I ask.

"Man, it was awesome." Aldy smiles wide and continues. "I don't know what you did, but not only did the undercover cars take off, but so did the security here. I just walked right up, used the flipper to scramble the door codes and found a smudged fingerprint of the security guard on a coffee cup which got me right through the fingerprint analysis lock. Then I just soldered in our chips into each motherboard, between the hard drive and monitor settings so that no one got curious, and amended the software on each system's BIOS to detect our chips. Coulda done it in my sleep. Oooh-oooh-oooh, there's this cat in the warehouse that kept bringing me a mouse. Like a computer mouse. I'm like, *whaaaat?* We played fetch, and—"

"Aldy, I'm exhausted and a little shellshocked, so are we set?"

Aldy bats his eyelashes and says, "Oh, we're so pretty."

I remove Funk Monster from the backpack and we both collapse into the passenger seat.

"Hey, you know anywhere to eat around here?" Aldy asks.

"I know just the place," I say and steer him toward Woo's Diner, the 24-hour Asian cuisine place I frequented with Larry and Mr. Judson, my Daimyo, from MetroMed. They specialize in Seoul-Food, a food fusion that mixes soy sauce into Memphis BBQ, and has a brisket and kimchi dish with okra that I've thought about for weeks.

We're the only folks in the diner at this time of night, or morning. Dealer's choice of which part of the day it is, I guess.

"Morning, y'all. Hungry?" greets Mr. Chan, the restaurant's owner and a pleasant Asian man with long hair and a Southern accent so thick it comes with gravy. Funk Monster splays out on the pleather booth and Mr. Chan gives her some pats waiting for our orders.

I point at the Seoul brisket and a side of kimchi on the laminated menu. Mr. Chan doesn't know I've regained the ability to speak, and I'm too tired to deal with the subsequent questions that would come after I utter my first word. Aldy orders a dish listed as *The Mountain*, informally known as *The Heart Attack* by regulars. It's hashbrowns covered with grits, then a layer of scrambled eggs with cheddar cheese, and then a row of cooked sausage, topped with redeye gravy and a little toothpicked flag with the words *Climb the Mountain* on it.

When Mr. Chan leaves, I joke, "Aldy, you're always eating…"

"I only eat when I'm nervous," Aldy sighs.

"You're the coolest cucumber in the drawer," I say with a smile.

"If you ever gave your head a breather and took it out of your ass," Aldy chides with a wag of his finger, "you'd know better than that."

We sit in silence as my body processes all the spent adrenaline and pent-up cortisol. A taste like old vanilla floods my mouth. *That was too close*, I think. I want to drop my guard completely, but I must remember one of the best pieces of advice for a Bushi after a battle: *after winning the battle, tighten your helmet.*

When our food arrives, Mr. Chan places my plate in front of me gently but lets AldenSong's heavy plate and calories drop with a *thud*. Mr. Chan points at AldenSong and says, "I normally have customers sign a waiver before they take the first bite, but any friend of Vice's is a friend of mine."

"Vice?" asks Aldy right before I kick him under the table. "Ow! Yeah, Vice's my boy."

Mr. Chan's eyes dart between the two of us. "You know, I ain't seen you, Vice, in a minute. Your boys keep coming in here, though."

I nod. I'm not sure how much Mr. Chan remembers about my recently addressed disease, whether I could nod or shake my head to yes-or-no level questions. In any case, he continues.

"Though there are a lot more of those guys these days."

That catches me off-guard. And, from my face, Mr. Chan clearly noticed. *What could've happened at MetroMed?* I think.

"I'm sorry if I'm telling tales outside of school, but I thought y'all were close," adds Mr. Chan.

Well, since we're only three blocks from the building, it's about time to find out how close my *friends* really are.

Chapter Thirteen

My Damn Business

As AldenSong, Funk Monster, and I stroll through the early morning air on an empty street, something catches my eye. Correction: someone. I'd already felt an immense sense of déjà vu as we approached the small hospital near to the downtown of Memphis, Tennessee. It had been a recent target of mine, when I thought all I needed was medication to keep my seizures at bay. But my planned heist uncovered a potential Pandora's Box of corporate corruption and revealed a Death Star-sized vulnerability that I exploited. In the end, I did it for more than just myself. I did it for Mr. Judson, a man who saved my life.

Now, it appears MetroMed is someone else's target. I can't make out too well what this guy is wearing, or any real details, because he's sandwiched between two bushes near the back *Employees' Entrance*. My gut says this stranger is planning to break into MetroMed like I did. If so, I can't blame him; it was the perfect target. This place left me like a hacking Cookie Monster given the keys to the *Chips Ahoy* bakery: fat and happy. It would be a tempting target for anyone who noticed it.

But something about the shadowy character doesn't ring the bell of *thief* to me. Maybe I'm stereotyping, but the guy's too fidgety, like a colt at the starting gate for its first race. He's nervous, maybe jonesing for his next fix.

Maybe he's not trying to break in, but to get someone coming out, I think. After glancing around, I lower my voice two notches and whisper, "Aldy, we have to consider this guy dangerous, and possibly not alone. I can't tell if he's Mercator or maybe even from one of the rival gangs that I pissed off over the years. Maybe Russian, or part of Kingfish's group..."

A slight grimace, quickly suppressed, grazes AldenSong's lips before he asks, "Why don't you just go ask him?"

"Shit, Aldy," I respond, "What if he's armed, or he's just a lookout or—"

"You overthink every damn thing," grumbles Aldy as he stomps toward our stalker. By the time I scoop up FM and get to Aldy, he's spun our Peeping Tom around and pinned the dude's arms to his sides.

"Now, hold up, bro," AldenSong says to his captive. "We aren't mad that you're out here. We just need to know what you're doing."

The five-foot-ten guy probably weighs as little as I do, so he's like a puppy in an adult's arms.

"I need...to get in there, man," the guy says in a heavy Memphis accent, his *man* sounding more like *main.*

Aldy reads our new friend as a non-threat, so he lets go of the guy's arms. Maybe letting go of him will work more like a bees-and-honey maneuver than a vinegar-beatdown one. Our stalker shakes his arms, getting feeling back in them, then turns his head.

That's when I see it: a tattoo on his neck. There is a gray and green man-fish on his neck: The Gill Man, commonly known as *The Creature from the Black Lagoon*. That classifies him as a Memphibian, even though that gang got absorbed into Penny's gang recently.

Unless his isn't part of Penny's gang, and he's here to retaliate for his gang going tits-up once he gets inside.

As the guy pulls down his sleeves, he says, "They've got the best paying job around."

"Job?" I ask. "You mean custodial work?"

"Yeah, let's call it that." Even scared out of his wits, the guy laughs at me. "Look, since Kingfish went away—"

"Hold up," I interrupt. "Kingfish is gone?"

"Uh, yeah." The dude snickers and points to the street. "Some big Fed sting took him and his crew down. Dude went ten toes down and didn't rat on a soul. Respect."

The dude taps his chest twice, so Aldy and I do the same.

AldenSong's eyes dart between our stalker and me. "Is anyone gonna fill me in on what's going on or shall I just sit here with my thumb up my ass?"

"Kingfish was my, um, our buyer, maybe retailer, if you will," I say. "Now that he's gone, I wonder who's picked up the slack."

"Man, where you been?" asks our stranger with a snort. "Now it's Agon's world, and we're just living in it."

As Aldy talks to his right thumb and mutters, "Well, I guess you're in for a ride," I pull out my MetroMed RFID badge and march us to the door.

Now who the hell has taken over my damn business?

Chapter Fourteen

The Lights Go Out

As we three musketeers enter the EMPLOYEES' ENTRANCE of MetroMed, the light from the bright overhead fluorescents and gleaming white walls narrow my eyes and gives me a slight headache. Two custodians mop the floor along the far wall. The problem is, neither of them is Larry or Mr. Judson. One, a white guy with a shaved head stops and addresses us.

"Y'all here for the meeting."

He doesn't ask, more states.

I nod, and he points his mop's handle toward the cafeteria. Aldy thanks him and the other new janitor pets Funk Monster on the head and we move on. We enter the corridor, and two more custodians clean the windows of offices with rags and cleaner. I brace for the harsh fumes of ammonia to hit my nose, but nothing but the smell of a clean, spring meadow fills the air.

It's brand-name Windex, ammonia-free, and one of several advanced cleaning tools in the cart.

They've even upgraded their cleaning supplies since I was last here.

When we reach the cafeteria doors, two big bouncers stand in front of them. Both look like they could be our Russian enforcer's brothers: big, intimidating, and unmoving. That Russian not only had a ton of family in The States that worked with him, but he's as connected as any Kennedy.

Aldy smiles, waves at the giants, and steps to the doors. A hand the size of a personal pan pizza plants in his chest.

In a thick Russian accent, the blond one says, "Password."

"Um…" AldenSong glances my way. I shrug. So does our new friend.

"Please?" Aldy asks in a voice that squeaks like a twelve-year-old boy.

The dark-headed bouncer reaches for his radio.

The last thing we need is the new drug lord Agon to know we're here. Historically, they don't like someone showing up unannounced, and this isn't the way to become their friend. The tension in the room is like standing in quicksand: thick, suffocating, and one wrong move will sink us to the very bottom.

I take a wild guess just as Bouncer Number Two hits his radio.

"Vice," I blurt. It's a calculated gamble: if there's a chance that Thugly or Mr. Judson are still part of this empire, saying my fake identity might get us in.

The bouncers exchange a glance.

On the other hand, since Vice is slang for the police, I may've bought each of us a permanent stay in a tiny box six feet underground.

I tap Aldy on the shoulder, signaling that he should be ready for anything, though I doubt either of us could do much more than muss these Russians' hair in a fight.

"Eh, older password, but checks out," says Bouncer Number One dubiously.

"You know what they say on the *Golden Girls*," quips AldenSong. "Better late than pregnant!"

Both bouncers stare at Aldy like he's from Mars. Then, a small laugh creeps up Number One's chest until he chuckles. Number Two tentatively follows suit.

Warriors make friends with those that are brave, just, intelligent, and influential. As the old Bushi saying goes.

Let's add humorous to that mix, shall we?

"You, funny man," Number Two says shaking AldenSong by the shoulders and whipping Aldy's head like a bobblehead. "I see why Moscow likes you."

"And it is good to be liked," says Aldy proudly as the bouncers open the door.

Then, just as we enter, all the lights go out.

Chapter Fifteen

Thugly

It takes only a moment for my eyes to adjust to the darkness. A cacophony of conversations melts together into Charlie Brown's teacher's voice: garbled and useless to interpret. At the front of the cafeteria, several shapes take form: people behind a table, facing our way. Possibly studying us. In front of them are rows of folding chairs, mostly filled. A few silhouettes turn our way and a hand goes up. Our stalker shoots past me and takes a seat next to the raised hand.

AldenSong and I, with Funk Monster in tow, grab two seats in the back of the room. Something crinkles under my butt as we sit. A pamphlet for one Ms. Ingrid "Innocent" Vincent. It's too dim to read the text in this light, but even in the dark, there's no mistaking the image of my powerhouse lawyer.

"Alright, children, shut up and let's get going."

As the crowd silences, it's not the speaker's words that get to me. It's who says them:

Larry.

A projector lights up from behind me, illuminating Larry. Instead of his evenly sorted dome of cornrows, Thugly's hair is straight and slicked back against his head. Gone is the custodial attire, replaced by a jet-black suit with matching tie against a pressed white shirt. He's Memphis own drug-dealing Gordon Gekko. His fingers are pressed together, barely touching his lips, like a Bond villain eager to monologue his evil plan.

"Everyone in this room has purpose," he begins, his eyes staring at a spot on the ground as the words filter through his hands. "Also, everyone here has a past. I'm not one to judge it. Hell, I've done my fair share of...questionable things, right?"

The crowd responds with chuckles, head nods, and one guy claps, then quickly stops when he realizes he's the only one doing so.

A squawk hits the air, and every criminal sits up like a teacher just called on them.

Someone's got a police scanner.

Larry glances back at the table, leans over, grabs a glass of water, and takes a sip. He lets everyone's ruckus die down before continuing.

"Raise your hand if you've got an active criminal record or you are currently out on bail."

As a few hands slowly raise, several *oh-oh-oh pick-me* noises fill the air.

"We don't care what you did in juvie," comes a deeper voice from the table.

Mr. Judson.

"Also, anything acquitted, expunged, or dismissed doesn't count. The here-and-now is the focus, people."

I can't make Mr. Judson's face out, but his voice sounds steadier. More in control than the last time I saw him, when this little drug empire was just three men and a baby, er, Russian.

Hands continue to raise. By the end, about a third of the room has their hands up.

"I thank you for your honesty and, for everyone else that's lying, we will find out." Thugly reaches into his pocket and pulls out a roll of hundred-dollar bills in one hand and something small and silver between his fingers. He tosses the money from hand-to-hand while he scans the crowd. Then Thugly takes the silver device, a laser pointer, and runs the light along a row in the audience. He stops at one guy with spikey hair straight out of a Yahoo Serious movie.

"You there..." starts Larry. "Your hand went up and down. What's your deal?"

"Um, I just wasn't sure what you meant, and maybe I could just explain my situation to Mr. Agon..." says the guy with a Southern accent so strong it could play linebacker. After an initial glance, he breaks eye contact with Larry and stares at his feet.

"I see." Thugly and Mr. Judson both leave the stage. The spotlight follows them as they take slow, deliberate steps toward the guy.

"Do you want Agon here?" Mr. Judson asks wryly as his narrow, suspicious eyes study the man. Mr. Judson puts his arm on the guy's shoulder before he speaks further. "Do you really, really, want Agon to take time from his day to come and coddle you? How's that going to look?"

The guy stammers and stutters as Judson returns to the stage. However, Larry stays behind, staring at the criminal, and shaking his head.

"I can make it simple for you, if that would help," says Larry. "But first, what's your name?"

"Will," the guy answers.

Larry asks, "Okay, Will, do you have an active criminal record?"

"Well, that's not a yes or no..."

Larry makes an error noise that sounds like when a contestant chooses poorly in a gameshow. "It is a *yes-or-no* question. But, since you're going to be difficult, I'll make it easier on you, Will. How about that? How about I spoon-feed you what you need to know, like you're a toddler or an infant? Unless you are an infant. Are you a baby, Will? Do we have a little bitch-baby here?"

This man, this bully, is not the Larry I left behind.

Wiping his brow, possibly from the stress and spotlight combination, Will stutters and stammers before saying, "I've got a court date next week, but it's alright."

Larry sucks his teeth and gives a little *tsk-tsk-tsk* as he leans over Will.

"See, that's not what we're looking for here. You're bringing unwanted attention, and that's not how we operate. You stupid, stupid son of a bitch. Let me ask you this, Will. Next week, are you going to be found not guilty?"

"I hope so..."

"Wrong again!" Larry snorts before he continues. "We don't *hope* here. We *plan*. Anticipate. But we don't run on hope." Larry points to the door. "Get the hell out of here, Will. If you ever set foot back in here, you won't set foot anywhere else."

As Will zips up a jacket, mutters, "Eat a dick," and heads to the door.

"Wasn't looking for feedback or a snack, thanks." Larry returns to tossing the money between hands. "Now, for the smart people in the room, even if you've done dumb shit in the past, if you have an active criminal record or you are currently out on bail, you will get five hundred dollars for your discretion about tonight and to not come back here. Hold 'em high if this is you, people."

At this point, three-fourths of the hands shoot up. Part of me wonders if that extra half of the room that joined in is only doing so to get quick, free money.

Is this a preventative tactic? I think.

Thugly motions for those with hands raised to line up. From a shadow in the room's corner appears Moscow, still looking like the result of when an eighteen-wheeler and pro wrestler have unprotected sex. Larry tosses the roll to Moscow, who peels off five bills for each person. As soon as each criminal gets their stack, another big Russian escorts the convict out of the side exit. Only when the room is clear of those elements does the blinding overhead light cut on.

Larry undoes his tie with one hand and takes off his jacket with the other.

"Now we can get down to it." He turns a chair backwards and straddles it as Larry looks out into the crowd. We make eye contact. Neither of us breaks it as Larry leans to Moscow and points. Instinctively, the remaining ten people in chairs turn to me.

I freeze, unsure what to do.

Aldy, ever proactive, pageant waves, turning his wrist side-to-side and smiling. "Thank you, thank you, but I only sign autographs on Tuesdays," he quips.

The crowd loses interest and turns around.

"Now that we've thrown out the trash," quips Larry, "let's get down to it."

Just as Thugly starts, a hand loops under my arm and pulls me up.

"We've got to talk," says Mr. Judson as he escorts me out of the room.

Chapter Sixteen

Easy Peasy

"**W**here the hell have you been?" asks Mr. Judson. He's whisked me away to an empty ICU room. Well, not completely empty: drinking an RC Cola and reclining on a foldout sofa is the crazy-haired, semi-con Will.

He doesn't look nearly as pissed as I'd be if Mr. Judson and Thugly had just torn me a new one.

"Shit, forgot..." Mr. Judson's hands go to his pockets, past a police scanner on his belt.

That's probably where that squawk came from earlier.

He shifts seamlessly from a tight, accusatory expression to a *hold on* eye roll as he snatches a pen and pad from a bedside table. "Gotta write all this shit down..."

"No, you don't," I say.

The words dance through the air and slowly kick Mr. Judson's brain as his writing slows. Then slows more. And finally stops.

He places the pen down with a *thwack*. A look of hurt crosses Mr. Judson's face. His eyes halfway glaze over, like there was little-to-no shock in finding out I can speak. As if he always knew I was a liar.

"Well, ain't that just a kick in the pants," he mumbles pulling an envelope full of cash from his pocket and handing it to Hairy Will. "Good job out there, Reggie."

"Easy peasy, mate." A playfully light British accent replaces the deep, mucky Southern drawl we heard earlier. The guy flips through the bills just as Larry enters the room.

"Well done, Reggie!" Larry's refined posture is now replaced with Thugly's classic, lean, almost Fonzie- relaxed stance.

Of course, neither posture prevents Reginald's right fist from slamming into Larry's crotch.

"You're still a bit of a mean twat, but that performance was just full of beans, Lare-Bear," says Reginald. He extends his hand to a hunched over Larry, who takes it and painfully reaches a full standing position. "Warn a fella when you're about to get all shirty, okay?"

"Uhrm..." Larry coughs and clears his throat before he continues. "Can't...needed to sell it...too many doubters in the crowd...uhrm...plus, the last time felt corny."

"I trained at The Globe, and spent six years as various understudies at Royal Court Theatre." Reggie stands and flicks his fingers as if he'd just washed his hands and couldn't find a towel. "Specifically, as understudy to Chiwetel Ejiofor, for the role of Boris Alexeyevich Trigorin in Chekhov's *The Seagull*."

"I'm pretty sure you just made up most of those words," Larry mumbles through gritted teeth. After another cough, Thugly turns his full attention to me.

"V-man!" he yells, and gives me such a deep hug that one of my ribs makes a weird pop. It wasn't too long ago that a mercenary named Dendro gave me a hell of a beating. I'm not completely healed up, but I don't have time to slow down and heal like I should.

Larry sees the notepad dangling in Mr. Judson's hand. He reaches for it, but then Mr. Judson sighs and moves it out of reach.

"Our Nell here has gained her voice," quips Mr. Judson.

Technically Jodie Foster's *Nell* could speak, just not coherent English. However, starting this battle when I'm losing my friendship war isn't worth the ammo or potential blowback, so I let it slide.

"Huh?" asks Larry.

Apparently, he's no film aficionado.

"I can speak *now*," I say, stretching the word *now* out.

Shock, concern, elation, and disbelief tag-team Thugly's psyche. He's about to speak when he catches the flat expression on Mr. Judson's face and tones back his joy a few notches.

"Well," says Larry. "That's a good thing, right?"

"That depends," counters Mr. Judson. "How long have you been able to speak?"

I take a moment and think through my answer. It's at moments like this that adhering to the Bushido Code makes living my particular life a challenge. The tenant of *Makoto,* or Honesty and Sincerity, are hard to pull off in my line of...work. Part of me wants to tell them I never faked my disability or illness, but I also purposely avoided Larry and Mr. Judson because I knew that, with a new ability, comes new questions.

"I had surgery less than a month ago," I start, my eyes moving between Larry's and Mr. Judson's. "I've been recuperating, and since then, I found some of my old crew..."

"Ah, there we have it." Three thunderous slow claps blast from Mr. Judson's hands. "Once we served your purpose, you left us out in the cold."

"Now, hold on," I say, pushing Mr. Judson's hand out of my face. "I sent word through my friend..."

"I have a name," AldenSong says from behind me. He leans against a white wall and picks at the dirt under his fingernails with a wooden tongue depressor. "And, if you'd listened to me, you'd remember that I told you I tried to talk to them, but they didn't know me. I met with Moscow only."

The realization hits me like a Reggie punch: I abandoned them.

I clear my throat, take a deep breath, and continue.

"Look, I don't know what I've missed, or why Kingfish is gone and why you brought in someone named Agon to captain this ship, but I want to make sure you are okay." After another breath, I ask, "Are you actually okay?"

To my surprise Mr. Judson breaks the silence before the normally chatty Larry.

"You don't get to disappear, then show up, at your own damned convenience, and check in on us like we're some pets you left in the yard," says Mr. Judson. "We were worried sick about you, then we went to war. Without you, Vice. Or Tanto, or whatever name you go by now. When the shit hit the fan, you weren't here. If it wasn't for Moscow and Penny, Kingfish would've wiped us from existence."

I thought I'd figured everything out in advance. Moscow covered protection, both at MetroMed and through the right political and bribery channels. Penny handled some of the local muscle on the streets. Ms. Ingrid "Innocent" Vincent set up our business to handle the cash inflow, and our CPA Leonard Frey turned that corrupt wine back into pure, taxable water.

But it wasn't enough.

Mr. Judson's eyes bore through me. "Do you know what you put us through?"

I have no words. How could I possibly respond?

Mr. Judson shakes his head. "Not just me, Vice. My wife. My child. Even Mama. We looked everywhere." Judson closes his eyes and pushes his thumbs into his temples.

His *sick* wife and mother, two of the countless people whom the American healthcare system's benefits weren't quite enough to make whole. A system that keeps them down, functioning, but not thriving.

"I can't tell you the number of shelters, hospitals, hell, even morgues, we checked with to see if you were...alive." He forces down a lump in his throat. "And then there was the great chance that the bastards that were after you finally caught up to you."

"Well, the bastards did," I interject, this time holding my finger up to keep Mr. Judson from speaking. "I really wanted to reach out to you, but it wasn't safe."

"*Safe*?" the lone word leaves Mr. Judson's throat like projectile vomit, covering me inside-and-out. "Safe? Because of you, we started a multi-million-dollar drug dealing business. I have ulcers on top of ulcers. And then you don't even have the decency to let us know..."

"I was in trouble!" I erupt, my words spurred by years of pent-up frustration. It is a tsunami that isn't intended for Mr. Judson. He's just gonna get caught in its path. "And I left you, you two, a functioning and profitable empire. I'm out here fighting a crusade, and you're here becoming rich."

"So that's it, huh?" He leans forward.

Instantly, I want to apologize. But whatever he responds, no matter how hurtful the words, I know I deserve it.

"Is that how little you think of me? That it was only about the money?"

I open my mouth to speak, but nothing comes out. It's not like in the past, where my body stole my speech. This time it's shame snatching my words. My pride, my arrogance, just burned my relationship with these two to the ground.

As Mr. Judson steps away, he looks me dead in the eyes and says, "You're not listening to me. If you're not going to listen, I'm done. I wash my hands of you."

Before I can respond, Larry puts my head in a headlock and drags me into the hallway. He says, "Well, it was absolute shit, but we survived."

I break free and pop my neck. It is nice to see that at least Larry still has my back. It's more than I deserve.

"The short of it is we had a shipment go missing. Kingfish blamed us. Brought his entire empire down on us. Penny's troops kept them at bay, and Moscow called in a favor through his brother. Next thing we know, Kingfish and his minnows get taken in by the DEA. Boom! That left us all alone with the product AND the distribution."

"But how does Agon work into this?" I ask.

Then Larry answers a question with a more powerful one. "Well, how about you meet him first?"

Chapter Seventeen

Agon

Strolling through the halls of MetroMed to meet the mysterious Agon, something occurs to me: there are no patients here. In fact, there's no staff, except for my fellow criminals.

"Larry, where is...everyone?" I ask. Then, as if my question summoned him, Moscow appears from behind me.

"The hospital is...under renovation," he offers. Part of me wonders if the pause is his mind translating an answer from Russian to English. But a larger part of me thinks he's doing this to emphasize a point. Or for me to hear what isn't being said.

"For how long?" I ask, knowing in my gut what the answer is.

"It's...complicated," says Moscow, his thick Russian accent drawing out *complicated*. If there ever was a word that explained my life, that's it.

Moscow continues, "You see, the board of directors made a...bold choice to shut down the facility until someone removed all the asbestos."

"Huh..." The United States stopped installing and using asbestos in buildings back in the 1980s. This building, which I studied deeply prior to breaking into it the first time, is only five years old, which means they built it in the early 2000s. "Real shame about that."

"Yes. A very delicate matter." Moscow opens a door that reads *Private* and holds it as we walk through. "Sadly, there were questions from previous members of the board of directors. That is why they are...previous."

We enter a storage area near the middle of the building. Zero windows or cameras in here. That's when I see the industrial sink against the far wall. They converted a janitorial closet into a completely private office.

"What about our night pharmacist?" I ask. "Doesn't he still have to approve all the arriving meds?"

"Our night pharmacist has to do his work from home, because of the...asbestos. He blesses all shipments over tele...how you say, telehealth video."

Once we've all packed into this room, Larry screams, "Ta-da! Meet your offspring, Vice!"

I glance around, but the only things in the room, beside the sink, are folding chairs and an old IBM desktop computer with a monitor, keyboard, and mouse.

That's when it hits me. I cross my arms and smile. "Agon is your database."

This should've occurred to me. A basic definition of the Greek work is Agon means *contest*, or more specifically *the people behind the contest.*

"Bingo, son!" Larry's enthusiasm comes back full force as he jumps in place. "So, we still follow your system, though this CPU doesn't even have any of the parts for internet access. We just move everything over with one of those flat little drives that I can't figure out how to shove into a machine. Anyway, we order, duplicate, then delete orders.

However, now we take those scripts, pair that info with the areas of town that have the most consumption, and then assign those areas to our technicians..."

"Technicians?" I ask.

Larry chuckles. "Weren't you the one who told me that, even though our nametags read *sanitation*, that no fancy title would change that we scrubbed toilets?"

I nod. I also note his use of *we*. It's not much, but it's a start.

"So," I say, "You created a supply chain algorithm for incoming and outgoing inventory, but instead of using convenient nodes for easier logistics, such as starting the work day near the dealer's, excuse me, *technician's* home, you're deliberately starting them as far away as possible, yet still within the distribution radius."

"Well..." Larry crosses his arms and squints as he looks at me. "When you say it like that, you really sound like a smug dick."

"Don't be fooled," adds AldenSong as he slips out of the room. "He actually *is* a smug dick."

"So, why keep everything recorded here?" I ask. "Why keep any paper trail at all?"

When everyone still in the room looks at Moscow, I get it. He's gathering information on everyone involved in this caper. I guess it's less of a *caper* at this point and more of a full-blown criminal empire.

In any case, Moscow's the man behind the algorithm. He's gathering info on our inventory, workers, clients, and who knows what else.

Which makes him the most dangerous man I know.

However, before I can put any more thought into it, a high-pitched chime goes off. To everyone else, it probably signals a shift change or something. However, to me, it brings me to one of the darkest times in my life.

Chapter Eighteen

Not Her

Y EARS AGO

A good five months passed after Mrs. Lin and I helped a rich kid who had more money than sense, Jedediah McIntosh, wander into bankruptcy. Through some creative maneuvers at the blind auction on my part, we now owned our apartment complex. Despite my role in acquiring the building, this five-foot-nothing powerhouse worked my ass like I owed her money. And in many ways, I did owe her. At the very least, I owed her for saving my ass from a dude that got a little peeved when I gave him a light stabbing.

I was sixteen going on sixty, and Mrs. Lin was every bit of five hundred when fall in New Orleans rolled around. For a non-smoker, she coughed up a lung every day when the warm air mixed with the night breeze. We rose before the sun, fed the chickens, then worked on other people's property, the OPP that kept our income, well, coming in: me on electronics, and Mrs. Lin on watches. Then we would wind down by reading tales of Bushido warriors and their noble quests.

It was a basic routine, but it was ours. We were happy and didn't have a care in the world.

Unfortunately, the combination of those two feelings never bodes well.

One morning while feeding the chickens, I caught the slightest movement out of the corner of my eye.

Mrs. Lin stumbled.

To the average person, it might look perfectly ordinary. Old woman, uneven ground. Hardly a dire situation. To me, it was a slap to the face hard enough to clear my nostrils.

Mrs. Lin moved like a Bushi walking on rice paper: each step so deliberate that not a single mark or tear existed. I often joked that ants left bigger footprints than she did.

But now was no joking matter. By the time I got to her, sweat covered Mrs. Lin's wrinkled skin. She brushed my hand away when I tried to lift under her soaked armpit.

"I'm fine, Tanto..." The words left her throat, but not without a battle, as if her lungs weren't strong enough to push them past her lips. "You worry...too much."

"Mrs. Lin, you need to sit down and drink some water." It was the only thing I could think of. Isn't that the remedy for everything? Rub dirt on it, walk it off, drink some water? The dirt and walking options seemed unapplicable, but surely water would help.

"You think I've made it these eighty-six years by not knowing my body?" she asked, more sass than statement.

She turned, and there it was: a second stumble.

"Maybe we should go to the hospital?" I asked, my voice cracking.

"I don't like your tone, Fanboy." She only called me fanboy *when she was mad or losing an argument.*

"Well, you can bet I don't enjoy asking it, but here we are," I replied, half expecting a slight slap for my smartassery.

"I need no hospital," Mrs. Lin ordered, a hint of a threat lingering in her voice. She straightened her back and looked toward the sky. "I am where I should be."

And that's when something took Mrs. Lin's legs right out from under her. Even though I was right there, I failed to catch her. I mean, I tried. It was as if her bones turned to rubber because she slipped right through my arms and collapsed into her flowerbed.

"Mrs. Lin!" I cried out.

"Don't touch me, I'm...fine..." Through fluttering eyes and a series of deep, raspy coughs, she tried to push herself up.

And failed.

Again.

And again.

After the third attempt, I headed toward the back door to call the ambulance. With her rubber arm, Mrs. Lin caught me by the sneaker. As I turned, the look on her face wasn't anger. It wasn't even fear.

It was stoic, cold acceptance.

"Tanto, do not...call for help," she began, through wheezes and gasps. "Just get me...inside."

I crouched, snaking my head under her arm, lifted with my legs, and carried her. Once we got indoors, I put her on the couch and covered her with a blanket. She was sweating, but it was what I'd seen in the movies, so it's all I knew to do.

I must've watched her sleep for no more than five minutes. It felt like a lifetime. Next to her head was one of two portable phones in the house. I had to call an ambulance.

If not for her, then for me. Because I couldn't lose her.

Not her.

Chapter Nineteen

Moscow

This painful memory skitters away like a cockroach when the lights come on, ready to re-emerge when the darkness returns. I shake my head and come back to reality as Reggie and Larry all straighten up for another presentation. Reggie untucks his shirt and starts a routine of saying *periwinkle perry's wrinkle pudding pops peppering the pond*. I guess he's getting into character. Moscow takes a big swig of black coffee and Thugly turns back into *Larry the Motivation Guy* and adjusts his tie in the mirror.

"Okay, Round Two," says Larry as he slicks down a wild hair. "Vice, you coming? You could even do the presentation."

"I need our friend for a few minutes," Moscow says, catching me off guard.

Everyone vacates but Moscow and me — and AldenSong, who makes it clear he's not going anywhere.

Moscow gives me a questioning look.

"AldenSong can stay," I say, answering his unasked question.

He nods in agreement, studying both of us intently as gauging whether the big guy and I pass some unwritten evaluation or metric that only Moscow knows how to score.

I bet he's wondering if having Aldy here is going to hurt his chance to bully me into whatever he's about to do, I think.

"More the merrier," he finally says, rubbing his chin and taking the lone chair in the room. "What have you learned about Mercator and Poseidon since we last spoke?"

Shit. I totally forgot that part of my deal with Moscow to secure his protection and logistical support for our little drug empire.

Before I speak, I think about how this drug dealing business grew without me. I'm less proud, but more hurt: this was my doing. Now they even went with the idea of gathering data on a secured database. Still, I can't help but notice how shitty DoGoodR's makeshift computers are in comparison to this operation. Moscow might just have a way around Mercator tracking parts that we can't access.

I give Moscow both barrels of info. Everything from our upcoming hack to my attempted capture-turned-assassination by Dendro, to Ms. Ingrid "Innocent" Vincent and AldenSong stuck in the interrogation room. How we went from detainees to seconds away from getting a strictly lead diet. Had Kilroy not come through, I'd be having this conversation from the other side of a Ouija board.

I relay this, but leave out Kilroy. Sharing any knowledge of another hacker goes against the Bushido Code virtue of *Chū*, or Duty and Loyalty. And I owe Moscow details about Mercator, Poseidon, and the Double-H, the last thing I need is someone as powerful and power-hungry as Moscow getting his hands on that administrative flash drive that I gave to Kilroy.

I mean, through it one has access to some of the most powerful computing systems available. I cannot imagine what someone like Moscow would do with it.

"Now that you know where we are," I ask, "is there a way you can get us some tech that is fast yet not traceable?"

"I can get you anything up to and including Big Blue," casually suggesting he could steal the computer at the heart of the IBM company.

"It has to be in twenty-four hours," I say, preparing for a whistle or *tsk-tsk-tsk* of doubt and disbelief from Moscow. Instead, he opens his Palm Pilot. I'd heard that the company for that personal database went out of business, but that might be why Moscow still uses it. Just like Agon, there is some security behind unwanted tech.

"Best I can do is two, three days," he says matter-of-factly. "But I will place an order for a dozen worthy machines. Just in case."

Now there's something I wasn't expecting: a contingency plan.

Or is Moscow more of a threat to this upcoming hack than I could've possibly imagined?

Chapter Twenty

Song of An Old Friend

"**I** will have your mega-machines wired and set up in one of my empty storage buildings," Moscow says, referring to one of his family's many real estate ventures into 'distressed' assets. "Maybe they become necessary."

Necessary. There's something in the way Moscow says this word that I'm sure this request will come back to stab me square in the ass.

Moscow is hungry, possibly because he will never reach enough power. I can see it in his eyes: the way they light up at any possibility of expansion, dominance, or control.

Something in my gut tells me that there's a better-than-average chance Moscow helped Kingfish's shipment get *lost*. He's also the type to play both sides against themselves with only Moscow coming out as the winner and force Kingfish to retaliate and expose himself to a DEA takedown. It made sense. And Moscow has always been the type to know how the last punch will land before someone throws the first one.

"Do it," I say, knowing damn well the machines will not help this hack. A bug in my gut scurries around telling me we might need these machines later. For what, I'm unsure.

"I like you," Moscow says, and chuckles as he enters something into his PDA. "You remind me of my grandfather. He, too, determined son of bitch."

Moscow, AldenSong, and I stroll down the hall only to be stopped by Ms. Ingrid "Innocent" Vincent, our perfectly coiffed lawyer in a perfectly loud powder-blue suit.

"Tag out, you big lug," she says to Moscow. "I need to speak to my clients in private."

I guess that's lawyer speak for piss off.

As Moscow opens the door to the cafeteria, he glances back. The stone-faced look on his face appears content, not insulted, by Ms. Vincent's dismissal. From the other room, Larry rails on poor Reggie, er, Convict Will.

The show goes on...

As Ms. Vincent's black stiletto heels click against the white floor tiles, she leans into my ear mid-stride. "Don't speak until we get out of the building," she says, a whisper laced with a threat. "This place is more bugged than the KGB."

We exit the *Employees' Entrance* as the Memphis sun blinds us two ways: from the sky, and from its reflection off the Mississippi River. Once the door shuts behind us, Ms. Vincent punches me in the gut with her non-broken hand.

"You don't leave your lawyer out of the loop," she says, a rage building in her voice. "If it weren't for Mr. Pese here, I would've had the Big Russian dredging this damn river looking for your body."

Aldy used his real name? Ne'igalomeatiga Pese. In Samoan it means *forgetting song.* Someone saddled my uplifting friend with a name that basically screams *loss.* Which is why I'm glad he landed on the handle I know him by. Alden means *old friend* in Scottish, so combined with the definition of Pese, creates a perfect name for my friend.

The song of an old friend.

Ms. Vincent, still peeved, takes a breath, and mumbles, "I'm on retainer, I'm on retainer," a few times before straightening her back. "So what fresh hell are you about to get us into? I can see it in your face."

Then, before I utter a word, she puts her perfectly manicured fingernail to my lips.

"Remember, just like before, vagueness is our friend."

Ms. Vincent is referring to her *surprise* arrival when the Mercator Agency took me into custody. I'd barely prepared her. I didn't tell her about Kilroy leaking some names of Hackers' Havens' captives through the Amber Alert service. All I told her was, *I need you waiting.*

I bite my tongue, crafting an obtuse answer. "I think my drug addiction is impeding my work."

Ms. Vincent sweeps the blond hair from her eyes and chews her cheek, sizing up my comment. "Well, I guess it's going to be nice that there is a very reliable check-in, check-out rehab facility that you're going to be paying two hundred bucks a night starting tomorrow...plus my booking fee, of course." She reaches into her purse and adds, "Luckily, they never check IDs at the door."

I nod, because she catches what I'm throwing down: I need an alibi. I might even stop by and sign into the clinic for evidence. The joy of *reasonable doubt.*

However, we're both thinking about this from a trial point of view. If the Mercator Agency catches me, they won't try to take me alive.

Ms. Vincent's cellphone rings. Crime's favorite lawyer never sleeps.

"Yes, I'll accept the charges...Deja de hablar. Ahora. Lo último que dices hasta que llegue es la dirección de la comisaría...bien. Nos vemos en veinte." As she closes her flip phone, Ms. Vincent sighs, then looks me up and down. "Your girlfriend has been asking about you."

Before I can answer, she turns her back and heads away.

As Aldy and I stand outside of MetroMed, I look at the building and think about what's going on inside. The criminal empire I helped start no longer needs me. Joy or relief should flood my heart; instead, emptiness and uselessness creep in.

And, just like the big miracle he is, AldenSong puts his arm around me and says, "If we start walking now, I bet we can catch Penny and the kids."

I don't respond. I've jerked Penny around more than a dog jerks around a new toy. *Would she even want to see me?*

As we put MetroMed in our rearview, I wonder if Penny's greeting will be as hollow as Mr. Judson's.

I wouldn't blame her; the last time we saw each other, Dendro almost killed both of us.

Chapter Twenty-One

You Say Paranoid

The morning's coolness keeps me from sweating as AldenSong and I go straight to the facade of Penny's decoy home. I jab in the digits from my last visit. A maybe pleasant *buzz* lets me know we're in.

"She gave you the code?" asks Aldy.

"Hang on," I say. "You're not impressed yet." I hold the door for Aldy to enter the building. We stroll through the dimly lit, torn-wallpapered hallway. Quarter-sized green and white tile squares squeak under our shoes. Instead of going up the stained, carpeted staircase to our right, we head out the back door marked *Exit*.

With narrow, cautious eyes, AldenSong follows me into the repurposed alley-slash-community hangout. AstroTurf catches my foot, but not enough to stumble. Someone must've moved around the white wicker couches and chairs to be closer to the grill in the northeast corner.

Aldy asks, "You gonna tell me what the hell is going on?" Instead of answering, I take us to the end of the alley. There, a plain wooden pallet about a foot taller than me covers Penny's actual door. AldenSong sighs and shakes his head. "Only you would date someone as complex and paranoid as you."

"You say *paranoid*..." I knock on the door and step back so that Penny can properly see us through the keyhole. "I say *prepared*."

The one thing I'm not prepared for is for Penny to *not* open the door. *Maybe she heard Aldy say the word* date...

It's not like we are dating, or that Penny would even consider dating anyone like me, but I didn't exactly deflect AldenSong's quip either. For so long, she was the girl in the photograph I found at Hackers' Haven. Now, she's all I can think about.

I check my watch: 7:20 a.m. "Shit," I say and move the pallet cover back into place in front of the door. "I forgot it's a school day."

After I re-cover the door with the pallet, Aldy and I dart back through the fake entrance. We turn the corner on the street. There, across the street at the bus stop, are Penny, her daughter Hazel, and her son Liam. The still-rising sun illuminates Penny's pinkish hair. She looks up, sees me, and her eyes go wide, a variety of emotions moving across them. Hazel sees me but just shrugs and turns away.

Next to Hazel is Liam, in his little-old-man outfit, a tucked-in button-up shirt, tie with Looney Toons characters on it, and ironed khakis. His look is more like it's a dress-up day rather than an average school one. As Liam pushes his oversized glasses up on his nose, he spots me. I wave.

And then he dashes toward me.

Across the street.

Straight into oncoming traffic.

Chapter Twenty-Two

The Darkness

I want to say that, when something bad happens, the world shifts from a real-time speed to slow motion, the way you see it in the movies. That everything slows down so that I can think, or react, or do *anything* to save this kid's life.

Instead, the world speeds up. Liam ignores his mother's yell, already three steps away from her. By the time Penny is off the curb, he's ten of his tiny steps away. The joy I see on Liam's face vastly contradicts the open mouth and screams of his mother.

Penny's fast.

But she's not fast enough.

Move, Tanto, move.

I sprint. I don't even have time to look at the traffic. But I hear it. The roar of tires on the road. The blaring of a car horn. The screech of brakes. As I speed toward the tiny human, the one with a smile the size of a slice of watermelon, instinct takes over.

My right ankle turns. My heel catches the edge of the curb as my toes hit the road. I use my stumble to crouch and push forward. In my peripheral, a silver grill of a black Cadillac sedan reflects the morning sun.

I've never stretched my hands out as hard or intently as I do right now. I will my arms to stretch like a comic book character.

I can't tell you which hit me first: the grill of the car, or the body of the boy. It's like the two came together in perfect synchrony: as the grill bent my right knee, causing my ass to land on the car's hood, my hands pull the boy up. His tiny, brown penny loafers bounce off the car's crest of a hood ornament.

I pull him close. Close enough that I feel the air in his lungs evacuate. Close enough that the hardback book he still holds tight jams into my ribcage. I wrap my arms around Liam as we roll up the hood.

Across the roof.

Down the trunk.

Until our human cocoon slams into the concrete.

Everything — and nothing — hurts. I'm certain I'm dead. My body won't move as my vision fades in and out as I stare at the hardback of Jules Verne's *Twenty Thousand Leagues Under the Sea* torn in half from the impact.

But it doesn't matter. Right now, all that matters is Liam. I have failed so many times in my life. But, God, please don't add this failure to my tab.

That's why, when I hear his cry, I let out a breath I didn't know I was holding, and let the darkness envelop me.

Chapter Twenty-Three

The World Shifts

It's like I've always been here. This reminds me of the scene in *The Matrix* after they plug Keanu Reeve's character Neo into a simulation. And, just like in that movie, for as far as I can see, there is nothingness.

Except for two figures in the distance seated at a table. In a flash, I'm standing over them.

At one end of the small table is Mrs. Lin, stoic and poised as ever, and dressed in the flowery green dress she wore when we won the auction for our apartment building.

At least, I *think* it's Mrs. Lin. Her face is hard to make out, somehow. It's a moving blur, like there is a sheen of water over it.

Across from her is a man in steampunk-looking goggles. Even seated, he is a good foot taller than Mrs. Lin. His slumped, almost defeated posture speaks volumes. A shimmering substance covers his face as well. A lone line of blood trickles down his nose from under his goggles and drips to the white floor.

Lance-A-Little, my mentor from Hackers' Haven.

A marble chessboard rests in the center of a crystal-clear glass table. Instead of a traditional square board, this round one has half of the board white and the other black. Upon further review, it's not a chessboard, but a yin-ang symbol, the meeting of conflict and the inevitable binding of life's harmony.

Mrs. Lin sits on the black side, the Yin. That doesn't make complete sense to me; if memory serves me, some of the Yin's forces include femininity, darkness, passivity, and absorption. While feminine, no one would ever call Mrs. Lin *passive* or *dark*. I only lived with her for half a year, so maybe I didn't know her at all because the ferocious and feared Tiger also represents the Yin.

Lance-A-Little's position follows the light side of the board: the Yang. It represents masculinity, light, activity, and perception. This, too, confuses me, because Lance's vision, his perception, was skewed to the point of lobotomizing his team. Plus, if anyone had darkness in them, Lance did. What happened to us in the Double H still makes me shudder. However, the one part I do agree with in matching the Yang is that Lance-A-Little is the Dragon. This dominant mystical creature serves two different masters: protection and destruction.

Apparently, they are mid-game, because several pieces line the side of the board, warriors lost in battle. The pieces aren't traditional chess pieces with their horses, castles, and royalty shapes. Mrs. Lin's pieces are various historical Bushido warriors. The pawns are small helpers of Bushis, the *Gokenin*, or warriors in training. The rooks are farmers, the *Goshi*. The knights hold banners because they are the highest rank of Bushido warrior, *Hatamoto*.

Her bishops are *Chukanbushi*, defenders of their queen and king. Speaking of which, I don't see her royals anywhere on the board. They are all lost in battle.

Lance has a strangely fitting collection as well: they are all various parts of a computer. His pawns are memory chips, each standing on its rectangular end. The rooks are cooling fans. His knights are graphics card and power supply, respectively, and his bishops are hard drives.

And, just like Mrs. Lin's pieces, he, too, is without his queen and king.

"But doesn't that mean the game is over?" I think-ask as the opponents stare at each other, arms crossed, waiting on something. "What are you—"

Their game resumes at my words. Yet when they move, it is to put chess pieces back on the board, not take them off.

"You're playing in reverse," I say, catching myself off guard. "Why am I speaking my thoughts?"

"If there were no thunder, men would have little fear of lightning," Mrs. Lin responds as she places a pawn on the board.

"They have ears, but hear not," Lance adds, moving a rook backwards.

"I like things better done than about to be done," says Mrs. Lin as she moves her bishop backwards.

Lance places a memory chip on the board. "I am not what you call a civilised man! I have done with society entirely, for reasons which I alone have the right of appreciating. I do not, therefore, obey its laws, and I desire you never to allude to them before me again!"

While their cryptic speech makes no sense, there is a familiarity with it I can't quite place. It's tickling the back of my brain-brick.

The game continues, or I should say, reverts.

"Am I dead?" I ask.

"Your dead sleep quietly, at least, Captain, out of reach of sharks," Lance quips, adding a pawn.

"Yes, sir, of sharks and men," returns Mrs. Lin as she moves her bishop.

A flash of lightning skitters through my battered brain.

It's *Twenty Thousand Leagues Under the Sea.*

"I read that as a child and thought it was about exploration. But it's also as much about imprisonment and fear," I think-say. "Liam had that book under his arm," I add before blurting, "Oh, God, is he okay?

"Everything has an end, everything passes away."

Mrs. Lin scratches an itch on her blurry face. Since her actions reverse, it's as if she's flicking a fly from her nose.

"Dammit, answer me."

Lance opens his goggles and studies the board. Both of his eyes blaze crimson fire. "Complaining doesn't have to do any good—it's enough all by itself." He replaces his goggles.

"Is the boy alive?" I ask.

Mrs. Lin reaches beneath the table and puts a piece on the board: a tent.

But not just any tent.

"Gakunodo," I think-say the name of the tent that Bushis rested in. It is also the name of the AI software Cyfib forced me to create while imprisoned. "But I don't need the software anymore. It shouldn't even run anymore. Not without the core code I stole."

"We may brave human laws," Mrs. Lin says, "but we cannot resist natural ones."

Lance puts a piece on the board as well. And, like before, it's something I know all too well: a single cylinder with a button on top of it. It looks like the kind of button that hospitals give patients so they can give themselves morphine injections, but that's not what it is.

"That's the escape button to the LODIS," I think-say. The *Liquid Ocular Display Interface System,* the defensive system that I learned to operate to keep attackers away from Hackers' Haven's servers. "I had the blueprint for that as well, but lost it."

Now, all the game's pieces are together. The pair stand, shake hands, and turn away. Yet, they do not move. As I walk around them, Mrs. Lin balls her hands up into fists.

Her shimmer-face tilts my way. "That terrible avenger, a perfect archangel of hatred."

I don't ask what that means and proceed to Lance-A-Little. Underneath his black goggles, pulses of red and green light alternate. Unlike Mrs. Lin, Lance's prayer hands catch me off-guard. Even though he's pressed them together, there's something in the middle of them that keeps Lance's hands from closing.

"What gamblers regret the most isn't the loss of their money so much as the loss of their hopes."

I slide my fingers between his icy hands and something falls to the ground. As I kneel to pick it up, the mysterious object morphs into a black blob. The blob spreads to my feet, slithering up. I claw at the blob, but it covers my hands. As it slides up my nose and pushes on my brain, the world shifts from white to black.

Chapter Twenty-Four

A Choice

I scream awake, my face on fire. Finding myself under a harsh light that hurts my eyes so much it's almost a laser, I close them tight. I try to cover the light with my hands, but something holds down my arms. Harsh cotton sheets scratch my arms.

"There, there," comes a familiar voice.

My eyes won't focus and the light is still painful.

"Someone hit the dimmer," the man says, sensing my distress.

The laser becomes a lesser white light, and my eyes finally adjust. I'm in a hospital room. Instantly, I tear at my restraints. Two leather straps hold me to the bed. An IV bag hangs to my right and connects its fluids to my right hand.

They've got me.

My thoughts jump to forced hospitalization where they tucked me away in the land of forgotten patients. The Epilepsy and Neurological Disorder wing, also known as The E.N.D.

"Hey now, Mr. Vice, stay with me."

Even though I'm acting erratically, the voice keeps even, calm yet authoritative. As the blurry cloud over my eyes dissipates, the man shoves a fresh bit of lit hell into my left eye.

"Follow the light."

For the first two passes, I do nothing out of confusion.

"Mr. Vice, please follow the light."

I grumble and oblige. After I follow the first light, the man moves the light to my right eye. We repeat the same dance.

The light clicks off, and a hand touches my shoulder. "You gave us quite a scare, Mr. Vice."

As the last of the spots fade, I recognize my *protector*, Dr. Brent, the man who has already healed me once.

I ask, "Doc, was it the Union or Brooks city bus that hit me?"

"Oh, you big baby, it was only a Cadillac."

This answer doesn't come from Dr. Brent, however. From the corner of the room, Penny Lee. Her usually perfectly cut hair hangs all over the place. The bags under her eyes are puffy and swollen enough to classify as *too large to fly in the overhead bin*. And, even though she's just hit me with a quip, now she chews on her fingernails.

Blinking away all other thoughts, I swallow hard. "Is Liam alright?"

When Penny turns her head, my stomach drops.

Dr. Brent taps on my head, and I turn my attention back to him. Dr. Brent chews his lip. My every instinct is to jump up and hold Penny.

"The boy should be fine," he says.

These words form a warm tidal wave and wash over me, yet I get stuck on the word *should*.

"The MRI shows no cranial hemorrhaging. He does have a concussion and a minor laceration just above his right eye that we fixed with stitches. Once we're done monitoring him, he'll be able to go home. I'm prescribing him rest for the next couple of days, so no school."

"Well, that'll suck," says Penny as she kicks her white Adidas against the wall. "If that boy ain't learning, he ain't living."

"Where's Aldy?" I ask her.

"Once you were out of the woods, he said he had to *get back to base* for something," Penny answered. "You know, that dude loves you more than you love being a martyr."

Dr. Brent clears his throat. "Mr. Vice, while what they tell me you did was extremely brave, you're also extremely lucky." He flips a page on his clipboard and continues. "Oftentimes, I can tell when patients aren't taking their meds. Clearly, you're still taking them because your body more absorbed and redistributed the car's impact instead of tensing up. It's like how when a drunk driver gets in a wreck, he is so loosey-goosey that he walks away unhurt."

Yay to the drugs that make my brain itch and make me go pee every hour, I guess.

"However, like little Liam, you, too, have a minor concussion. And on top of it, you have at least one broken rib, as well as bleeding under the skin consistent with ecchymosis and contusions. Normally, that would be a cause for more immediate concern, however it appears to be an older injury..."

"Those are from getting my ass kicked a few weeks ago," I say.

Dr. Brent chews his pen and turns his head. "So, she's the lucky Penny and you're the unlucky one." He flips back to the first page on my chart and says, "We're gonna keep you a few hours, just to be safe, so lie back down and rest. As long as you can keep from throwing punches and clawing at your face this time, we can avoid strapping you down again.

Thoughts about my dream flash before my eyes. A chess match of balance. Unique pieces either helping or mocking me. A cryptic Mrs. Lin and Lance-A-Little correcting the board.

And, finally, a piece I can't quite remember covering, then invading, my body.

The last time I had a dream like that, Barca killed Quidlee. *What could this mean?*

"I had an itch," I lie, keen to avoid a psych evaluation if I can.

Dr. Brent pats my shoulder and says, "Oh, and before we dismiss you, I'd like to follow up with you about your existing condition."

"You mean the *no-talkie-talk* now *too-much-talkie-talk*?" asks Penny as she angles her right thumb toward me. "I'm worried he won't shut up now that you've crowbarred open Pandora's box here."

Dr. Brent undoes my straps, removes my IV and slaps a bandage on my hand before nodding and leaving the room.

As I sit up on the edge of the cot, Penny keeps her distance. I've never known what a woman was thinking, and right now I couldn't hazard a guess if my life depended on it.

I take a shot at breaking the ice. "Why'd you bring me here and not MetroMed?"

"Like I'm taking a wanted felon, who got hit by a car in the middle of a populated street, to get medical treatment at the place where we're running a multi-million-dollar drug empire." Penny snorts and adds, "I didn't eject from my mama's hootie-hoo yesterday."

While a smart move, I notice the emphasis on *we* in *we're running a multi-million dollar empire.*

Everyone has moved on, even improved what I helped set up, without me.

I attempt to clear my throat but apparently a bunch of razors slid down it while I slept. I reach for the glass of melting ice chips, but they're too far away on the side table. As I stand, I stumble. Penny's arm slips under mine, and she helps me back to bed.

"What part about *lie back down* did your monkey brain not follow?" she asks, fluffing the world's shittiest pillow to hold my head up. She grabs the small Styrofoam cup with ice chips in it with one hand and a plastic spoon with the other. "I've got you."

The spoon full of ice bits on my tongue gives a slight reprieve to the desert in my mouth. The minor cooling and quenching relief is only temporary, because the moment I swallow, my throat is hit with Sahara heat again. Part of me should feel degraded; someone extremely attractive is spoon-feeding a grown man who has two perfectly functioning hands. Yet I cannot help but stare at Penny's Mona Lisa smile and sea-green eyes as I eat two spoonfuls in silence.

"You know why they give patients ice like this in hospitals?" she asks.

I shake my head and Penny chuckles before answering her own question.

"Because only in a hospital would they itemize the spoon, cup, and the free frozen water for your bill."

I crunch ice and quip, "Too bad I don't have health insurance."

"Oh, Tanto doesn't." Penny grabs a tissue and wipes away the water trickling down the corner of my mouth. "But Eric Vice does."

Penny addresses my questioning glare and answers, "Don't look at me like that. Ms. Vincent decided that your *temporary* insurance that someone must've forged through MetroMed was too much of a risk, so you've got good coverage through Smith & Sons, LLC."

Ah, our fake corp. Got it. I smile and respond, "Allegedly forged, my dear."

"Oh, of course." She doesn't flinch when I call her *my dear*. I don't know why I did it. Scratch that. I know *exactly* why.

"How's HydraCash holding up?" I ask, swallowing an icy mouthful. Over the past month, I've done everything I can to not dive into the Dark Web and scrounge around the money laundering system I set up to compete with the Russians' hopefully defunct KronosPay. I'd set Penny up as an admin; the others are faceless hackers that I only know from their reputations.

"Well, let me see..." Penny takes a mouthful of ice for herself and crunches a few times. "We're still filtering our clients' money though non-FDIC-insured banks, yet politely covering any wire or transfer fees, then paying out money so clean — through multiple mom-and-pop type outlets — that you could perform surgery on the stacks we distribute."

"But what about—"

She shoves a heaping spoonful in my mouth. "I wasn't done talking."

I chew the mouthful wide, like a horse eating a carrot.

"You keep that up, I'm gonna treat you like one of my rugrats and put a sheet over your face..." After saying this, Penny stops, placing the cup and spoon on my rolling table. She reaches to the back of her neck and unclasps a necklace I've never noticed before.

"You know how people get gifts and wear them out of respect?" she asks. I nod, then Penny adds, "Well, I got this for myself because I respect myself." She stares at the heart shaped pendant and rubs the gold locket between her thumb and forefinger. "I didn't use to. Respect myself, that is. It took...it took a lot to get to where I am."

Penny tosses it to me. I fumble at catching it. But once I do, I notice the button on the side.

"May I?" I ask.

Penny answers, "I didn't hand it to you to get it appraised."

"You didn't exactly hand it to me."

"Oh, shut up, you dumb little bastard, and open it." Penny smirks as she says her insult. I remember that's the first thing she called me, back when the Memphibians tried to kill her. I mean, I fought one guy, poorly, while she took down the rest like she was more Bruce Lee than Penny Lee.

I open the locket. Inside are two pictures. On the left is Hazel. It's an old photo, a school photo from probably kindergarten or first grade or some class where they eat paste and don't learn cursive anymore. She's in a school uniform that would probably embarrass current-aged Hazel to no end.

The second photo is of Liam. His glasses take up three-fourths of his head. A giant smile covers the rest. Of course, he's wearing a white shirt and tie with Care Bears on it. And he's rocking some sweet brown braided leather suspenders with Liam's thumbs behind the straps, pushing them forward.

"I never wanted to become a mother. However, I knew the life I created required risks that might endanger others." Penny rubs something in her left eye and clears her throat. "But apparently the universe said it needed me two times for the job." Penny extends her hand. I give the necklace a little kiss, ball it up in my hand, and extend it over Penny's outstretched one.

For a second, I don't let go. I hold it, this precious item, above her tiny, open hand. Our gazes meet, both in this moment, together.

I drop the necklace. She catches it and puts it back around her neck. Penny glances toward the door, then back at me.

"You know, I really hated you. I mean, really, really, hated you." Penny lets out a sigh between her teeth that sounds like a balloon losing air. She pushes the rolling table away and sits on the edge of my bed. "You were...instrumental in my brother's incarceration. His torture. His..."

Her voice shrinks like a shadow in the morning sun.

"Ahem, I, whew, then I screwed up and thought about how you felt. About what you went through. How you weren't given a choice—."

"Everyone has a choice," I interject. "And I chose me."

It's the first time I've said those words aloud. Sure, some of my captures, my *kills*, were the scum of the earth. Pedophiles. Rapists. Monsters.

And some were kids like Quidlee who made the wrong choice at the right time. The right time for me, that is.

Penny climbs into the side of my bed and drapes her arms and legs over me. Even though her limbs carry weight, it is a welcomed touch. Her unblinking, unflinching eyes bore into my soul as she strokes my arm hair. Unfortunately, this caring touch means I'm praying away an erection like I'm a boy at Catholic school who's been riding the bus and now has to slink off with a tent in his pants.

"Anyone would've done what you did," she says.

"I'm not anyone."

"No, you're not." Her lips part in a smile, a hint of lemon on her breath. "Tilt your head up."

I do, and then she kisses me. Firm yet smooth. Our lips part and I jerk away.

"Y-y-you don't owe me this for helping Liam," I say, fumbling over my words.

"Then maybe I just owe this to myself."

Then she turns down the lights.

Chapter Twenty-Five

No Time

I've had sex before. I've done the deed. Knocked boots. Clapped cheeks. Whatever you want to call it, I've enjoyed it. Though, the last time I got laid was so long ago there were dinosaurs.

It starts with a squeeze on my left arm, right above the elbow. She rips my hospital gown from my neck producing tiny rope burns that bring a dash of joy and excitement with them.

At first my meds and my injuries slow things down, especially a stress headache that puts a nine-inch nail right in the center of my brain. But Penny is patient, by shifting between intercourse and foreplay. I guess this makes this *actual* play, even when my body refuses to do what I need it to do. She never shies away. She just lets me be me, in all my brokenness and healing.

Her patience pays off and slowly my body responds in line with my mind and heart. My throat dries as the blood and attention in my body shift, and I do more than feel her. I watch her. Her expression as she straddles me. The way her hair bounces until some moment hits her. She drives for both of us, and she is a *good* driver. As her sweat mixes with mine, her hair whips across her face like someone on the Coast just opened a window and let the ocean air in.

I've never experienced anything like this. Hell, my back pops during orgasm. It's like waking up on a planet with multiple suns. A place that doesn't allow doubt or darkness. A place where comfort and risk ride together, and where every zenith, every peak, is possible. This private world of ours, where wet, rhythmic sounds accompany quick breaths and stifled moans on a roller coaster of excitement, lasts forever. Our bodies morph. Our minds ease. And all of our efforts result in this intoxicating, dizzying journey of ours that culminates in one final primal and passionate roar.

As I wipe the stars from my eyes and pretend my chest isn't about to explode, Penny's breathing is calm. Well, calmish. Her right leg's pulse on my left one tells me that she has a pretty rapid heartbeat.

"When was the last time you had sex?" she asks after we finish.

Part of me wants to lie, but I won't. Not to her, so I say, "Well, thankfully, we'd just fixed those Y2K problems..."

Her laughter is deep, yet kind. She pulls her head up onto my chest and lets out all the air from her lungs. It's like she's expelling something else. Maybe she'll tell me. But probably not. And I'm okay with that.

"I've been thinking," she starts, to which my spine instantly straightens. "You...you didn't kill my brother."

Even spent, I jump into argumentative mode. "I am the one who trapped him."

"Stop." Penny punches my side, not hard enough to hurt, but enough to get her point across. "You shut up or I will slap the white off you. And there's a lot of it. What do you think you prove by taking on weight that isn't yours? Tim, *Quidlee*, was my brother. He made a bad choice. No, he didn't deserve what he went through, but stop trying to make a Saint out of a Sinner, dude." She buries her head in my armpit, sighs, and comes up for air. "I know there's something in you, something that feels unworthy or unnecessary, that you must live some perfect purpose—"

"It's called Ikigai—"

"I'm gonna punch you right in the dick if you say one more word," says Penny. Now, unlike her playful tone a moment ago, this is a tight response. I chuckle but keep otherwise silent.

"You can't save everyone. I know we don't know each other — well, I guess we know each other better now. Look, you've got more issues than a subscription to *US Weekly*, but I also want you, Tanto, or Vice, in whatever capacity works for *us*. Now. And always."

Even if I could respond to this act of kindness, I doubt anything I could say would be more important than the only two words I have. "Thank you."

Penny rises from the bed and removes the chair that kept our private time private. Opening the door, she is greeted by Dr. Brent's flat smile.

"Well, shit..." Penny says.

I have no idea what the good doctor heard, but he avoids eye contact as he hands me my medication. "Take these with food and follow the directions. Also, given your family history of addiction, I must ask that you do not, I repeat, *do not*, under any circumstances, snort this medication. It will hit your heart like a bullet."

I nod. Dr. Brent takes a seat on the corner of the torn-up bed, changes his mind and makes a beeline for the gallon-sized container of hand sanitizer. Then AldenSong shoots through the door and points at me.

"No time for love, Dr. Jones," he says, quoting Short Round from Indiana Jones. "We might have a window."

Chapter Twenty-Six

Burn Bright

In thirteen minutes, AldenSong got us through heavy midday traffic. Even on little-to-no sleep, the big guy got us to the *S.S. Turing* in record time, cutting down alleys and taking back streets.

Not bad for a dude that grew up without a car on an island about the size of this very city.

We get back to the *S.S. Turing* and rush into the building. Twice as many POS machines fill the already-cramped room. It stinks of hot exhaust and desperation.

"DoGoodR, one of these days, we're gonna get you machines that aren't old enough to drink," I say, thinking of the machines Moscow will have waiting for us in just a few days. "Okay, someone hit me with a status report."

"Oh, you can't disappear and then expect us not to tear you a new one," counters Mane-Eac. Her sunken eyes look worse.

I bet the last time she slept, DoGoodR couldn't grow a decent beard.

"Lucky for you, AldenSong there came by when you were in the E.R. But since you're being *extra*-Tanto today, I'll give you the bullet points. DoGoodR and I got the software uploaded in NOLA."

"Did you have any problems?" I ask, secretly wanting to vent about the shit I went through as Aldy waltzed into a warehouse and played with a damn cat while he installed our microchips in Poseidon United's machines.

"Did I say we had problems?" Mane-Eac hits me with her *teacher-didn't-ask-you* look: a squint and a finger pointed my way.

I shrug, frown, and look away, aka my *what the hell did I do?* look.

"Anyway, the trucks holding the new machines you and your better hacker-half jury rigged were on the move. The tracker Aldy placed is still active, but they're not moving anymore."

"Someone is offloading them," I say.

"Good, you're paying attention." Mane-Eac aims a laser pointer at a map on a large monitor. "We're getting some consistent pings. I don't think this is an early release of PhauCet, but it could be the Alpha test."

My puffed-out chest and radiant smile give away my thoughts. "We have the chance to shut this down before it even comes into contact with the public."

"Bingo," agrees Mane-Eac. Then she lowers her head. "But we haven't moved all of our machines to the designated war room two clicks south from here. That one has six exit points and a clear line of sight for a quarter mile. If we hack here, we're easier targets than the ducks in Duck Hunt."

One CPU at the far end of the room screeches, then a small bit of fire shoots out.

"Shit!" yells DoGoodR as both he and I grab fire extinguishers.

"You're just ready for anything, ain't ya, T?" asks DoGoodR as he slaps me on the back. He grabs a pair of screwdrivers, and we both go into the machine.

"What's with that?" I ask pointing to one of his tattoos, a dotted line that starts at his index finger's nail and snakes up.

"Oh, we got tats after a hack one day," DoGoodR says, like getting a tattoo is as easy as getting a pizza. "Mine runs all the way from my fingertip to here." He points to the line I've noticed a million times: dots that go up his neck and connect to his temple. "Connecting my thoughts and actions. Sis got a tattoo on her upper left shoulder of a Phoenix fighting its way out of a cocoon. It's sick."

"I'm sure," I say, impressed with their comradery.

DoGoodR looks around and whispers, "Did you see where Poseidon United is looking for a Chief Information Technology Officer and offering over a million a year in pay?"

I chuckle. "I think they're looking for someone less...criminal-ly than you or me," as I undo two screws and toss them across the room. "My wanted ass showing up for a job interview might not be what they expected."

"True, and, oh, you could tell them how you and your prisoner buddies—"

"Hackvicts," I correct him.

"Right," he says, slightly irked at the interruption. "But y'all did some good. Like the time y'all stopped the assassination of Secretary of Defense David Masterson."

Wow, The Nameless track everything. I hadn't thought about that win in almost a year.

"In a perfect world, someone could join these bastards and fix them. But we don't live in a perfect world. We only live in one that we get to try to make perfect," I say.

This POS's motherboard just ran its last cycle, so DoGoodR and I turn it on its side to scavenge any salvageable parts.

"Speaking of DJ," says DoGoodR, "you never met my classmate JJ, did you?"

"Nope." I jam a flathead screwdriver in the docking bay and start popping loose the RAM chips. "Should I have?"

"He's the one who showed me how to get into the NASA databases."

With that comment, I stop and give DoGoodR my full attention. "Wait. You broke into those servers and everything you did went national, so that's how we knew about you. What happened to JJ?"

"They got him," answers DoGoodR, his eyes and hands working on the CPU's fan. "Served some time, and then they got to him again."

"So, he's possibly one of the hackvicts?" I ask.

"Naw," he answers as the fan pops out, burned to a crisp. "He took his own life because of their obsession with him."

My gut hurts as if DoGoodR just punched me. I would be lying if taking myself out of the equation hadn't occurred to me. Especially with everything I went through this year...

"Well, you can't save them all..." he says flatly, popping the hard drive loose. "Hold up, y'all..." Our Bearded Boy Wonder dusts off his gray shirt. "If we move our mobile transport and there are fiber optic cables already laid just below the surface we can splice into them and harness them for our own personal bandwidth."

Mane-Eac rolls her shoulders and shakes her head. "It's too risky...especially with the faulty machines."

"Hey, don't go insulting my work without buying me a drink first," says DoGoodR. "I can bounce between the two spots if anything goes down."

A series of pings sound from a nearby terminal. Mane-Eac goes over and refreshes her tracking code with a few keystrokes. "Ninety percent online. Nope. Now ninety-seven. Dammit..."

Mane-Eac blows out two breaths as our eyes meet. "Tanto, what should we do?"

I rub my chin as I glance around the room. The odds of us getting another shot this clean at Poseidon United and the Mercator Agency are nonexistent. By the time PhauCet goes into Beta or partial-live version, they will have fixed most glitches that we can exploit. However, if we wait, Moscow will have set up his power machines and we won't have to rely on scavenged parts.

By then, it might be too late.

I study the faces of my comrades. AldenSong's big smile and jovial attitude cover his nervousness. Mane-Eac has so much stress it's coming out her ears. And DoGoodR is just a kid at Christmas, ready to open his presents and hack the world.

And yet something feels off. This was easy, but not too easy. Hell, they sent a freaking SWAT team after me. Yet Mane-Eac and Do-GoodR got in and out cleanly.

Or maybe that's what Mane-Eac told me, worried I'd think less of her if they didn't do everything perfectly.

I go over to one of our chalkboards and erase the handwritten code, despite DoGoodR's grumbling protests. I write two words.

Burn bright.

Chapter Twenty-Seven

A Good Sign

We have our marching order and go into techie overdrive. If this works, our software and hardware gels with their PhauCet software, and we can get the real scoop on what P.U. and Mercator are data mining from users. AldenSong gathers up our laptops, wireless routers, a spool of Ethernet cable, and a few other computing odds-and-ends. He also snatches up Funk Monster in the process. DoGoodR boots each machine in the *S.S. Turing*, sweet talking each one as it whines for the sweet release of death over more work. And Mane-Eac gets on the Dark Web and contacts the few other members of The Nameless. She'd told me she had some feelers out there for people we'd worked with, but never wanted to give too much away. That's how secrets get out.

My focus is on the chessboard in the center of the room. Mane-Eac and DoGoodR's game is close to finished. I think her Ghost Pinky is two moves away from taking down King Mario — if DoGoodR moves his mushroomed Rook the way I think he will.

I can't stop thinking about my dream with Mrs. Lin and Lance-A-Little and the LODIS piece in the chess set. Why was it there? We don't even have access to its blueprint anymore.

And what the hell was the last piece? *Why can't I remember?*

"Hey, Silly Caucasian Samurai, you going to join us or not?" Mane-Eac asks, her tone light but with a serious, *get-your-ass-in-gear* emphasis.

"Sorry," I mutter, grabbing gear. "DoGoodR, how much are you overclocking these systems?"

"They're about to be so hot you could grill a steak on them," he answers and aims a giant oscillating fan at the stack. "One last burn, little ones." He salutes them and grabs another fan to set up as well.

"Mane-Eac, are we alone, or do we have allies?" I ask as I run a battery tester over our extra batteries.

"Got four, maybe five. That'll cause interference." She points her nail at the black screen covered in white code. "They're gonna hit Poseidon and Mercator's Human Resources servers at the same time. Those machines don't matter to us, but it'll be enough to force their automated defenses to focus on those attacks. It will be up to us to deal with human determent."

And that includes some of the best hackers on the planet countering us with the best tech and their own LODIS.

"Will that be enough of a distraction?" I ask.

"Oh, their pentests are actually penbreaks, designed to cause greater damage instead of making a tiny hole." She glances at a monitor next to her and adds, "Hence, our boys are bringing sixteen gigs of noise and traffic down on those sons of bitches like the backhand of God."

I'd have taken a simple *yes,* but the answer of *backhand of God* is much more reassuring.

"Aldy?" I prompt my right-hand man.

"Locked, loaded, and ready to bring the rain." He's talking about the Star Craft van we bought from a junkyard. "Yanked the seats, minus the front, of course, to make room for our gear. It's got two computing stations that run on six car batteries and a jack we can use to connect to some hijacked fiber optics. Plus, port scanners, worms, both Trojan horses and byte eaters, pentests, penbreaks, malware, portalware, and keyloggers. If it makes noise or causes damage, we've got it, as well as nets to catch everything that we run through sifters to see if any of the data has value."

And even with all our tools, we might not do a damn thing. We're David to their Goliath, except our sling will toss pebbles at a fortress, not a behemoth with a glandular problem.

"How're the shields, Mister Scott?" I ask AldenSong, in a butchered Captain Kirk impression.

"Aye, Captain," Aldy responds, putting me to shame with an impeccable Scotty, "she'll hold and be ready. Those blasted Klingons aren't the only ones that can cloak."

He's referring to the package on the van's roof. It looks like a storage bag for clothes and such. In truth, it's packed like a pressurized parachute, except it's a weighted Faraday bag that will completely cover the van. Prior to explosion, it serves as a damper for any satellites trying to search for spikes in bandwidth, power consumption, or Internet traffic. Of course, it'll stop all our digital work in its tracks if we use it. All of this works, in theory. And theory has bitten me in the ass more than Funk Monster having a bad dream.

One click of the remote that's strapped to the van's dashboard and the bag will explode outward, covering the entire vehicle in a preventive mask from any and all digital surveillance. Too many people think that disconnecting from a network or pulling a wire will stop a trace. That's not completely true. Yes, it will, only if the tracker doesn't know what he is doing or just doesn't care. We're dealing with the best of the best. Even dropping this bag might not work. That's why we've got one more Ace in our hand.

"You got the CYA?" I ask, about our final, emergency-use-only contingency.

AldenSong answers, "The Anti-Holy Trinity is set to light the world on fire." Good. AldenSong refers to the emergency kill kit we rigged in the van. Complete with a pull string that will rip open the trio of evidence erasers: acid, bleach, and ammonia. The acid kills living organisms, such as DNA, that we leave. The bleach sullies fingerprints and causes a general mess of a crime scene. And the ammonia, well, when it mixes with the vehicle's gas tank, the van shifts from a shitty vehicle to explody bomb.

Better to have it and not need it, I guess...

"Are you sure we can't spray paint *Free Candy* on the side of the van?" asks DoGoodR.

Mane-Eac slaps him across the back of the head, which saves me or Aldy having to do it.

As I look around the room, I know there's still time to call this off. But we're ready. I mean, *really* ready. Even with this quick turn-around, there's no one I'd rather use than this team to take down the biggest bastards around.

We load into the van. Mane-Eac takes the wheel. Forget your base-less stereotypes about drivers; it's a proven fact that women get pulled over less than men. Plus, since this van looks shadier than Cyfib in a hoodie near a playground, we need all the help we can get. I take the spot against the far wall in the vehicle. Funk Monster climbs into my lap. AldenSong takes the spot next to me, and DoGoodR climbs in and shuts the door.

"Ready?" asks Mane-Eac.

In response, FM lets out a howl. DoGoodR is the first to join our tiny tyrant. Then Aldy adds his baritone voice to the mix. I kick my head back and let out something primal. Finally, Mane-Eac lets out a small bark to add to our wonky chorus.

Mane-Eac puts the van in drive, pulling out onto an empty road ahead.

That's a good sign, right?

Chapter Twenty-Eight

Snowden

Even though we're only driving a quarter of a mile away from our base, the *S.S. Turing*, Mane-Eac clocks four miles on our odometer using side streets, doubling back, and taking a sudden, yet legal, U-turn. Anything to lose a potential tail. Once we're as safe as we can reasonably confirm, we pull up to a chained fence in front of a radio tower. Aldy hops out and picks the lock in under a minute. He yanks the chain off and Mane-Eac backs the van flush against the building. To the naked eye, it looks like someone doing maintenance.

Crooks pull straight up to their mark; repairmen back up.

The van's slide door pops open. Funk Monster darts out first. She's either doing a perimeter check or about to poop. In any case, I grab a handful of cables, a few other odds-and-ends, and look for the closest manhole cover.

Sure enough, there's one on the west side of the building. "Crowbar," I say as I finish scraping away the weeds and growth around the round lid, and DoGoodR places the hunk of metal in my hand. Even with both of us, the lid stays shut.

"Let me show you how it's done." AldenSong's cockiness is rare. He leans down and, with one shove, pops the lid free. As he holds the lip in front of us, AldenSong drops it off to the side like it's a frisbee. "Y'all need some mass."

"Hey, I'm one-thirty-five," quips DoGoodR.

Aldy sticks his tongue in his lower lip, looking like he has a dip in his lip, and responds, "Boy, I crap bigger than you."

"Did you just quote *City Slickers*?" I ask, knowing full well he did.

"Don't know what you're talking about..." says the big guy as he hands me a flashlight. "It's just one thing..."

DoGoodR snaps his fingers and says, "Okay, now *that's* definitely from the movie!"

Aldy walks away whistling, and I descend the rusted ladder rungs. The stench is unbelievable, like a used, water-logged diaper that some-one left in the sun. It only takes a few seconds to find the junction box. Some cities with large sanitation pipes run their fiber optics through those routes. Luckily for us, I'm staring at exposed wires.

"Mane-Eac, you're a better installer than I am," I say, and we both know it's true. "How about you get down here and help me out?"

"Sem inglês," she quips, refusing the invite. A laugh escapes my chest. I'm almost done with the hookup. I just wanted to see if she'd willingly jump into a sewer for me. I bet if DoGoodR asked, she'd do it. The bond they've formed over the last almost decade bleeds into everything. I bet the last eighteen months physically together has only increased it. DoGoodR's the ragtag little brother slash son Mane-Eac never knew she wanted, and she's the big sister he didn't know he needed. They've dealt with more shit than a NOLA janitor cleaning the bathrooms during Mardi Gras. Without the work they've done and the risks they've taken, we wouldn't be about to take down the biggest assholes I've ever known.

Maybe one day I can repay DoGoodR and Mane-Eac. There is no telling how many people these agencies have destroyed, and The Nameless are granting me the chance to expose the bastards that ruined my life.

Once I return to the surface world, everyone else is already in the van. Everyone except Funk Monster, who's hovering over the sewer's entrance, tail wagging.

"You miss me, girl?" I ask. Then she tries to scoot past me and go down into the nastiness. I snatch her before she dives in. "It's not the goodness you think is down there."

In the van, Aldy's got his laptop set up on the driver's seat as he sits cross-legged on the floor. Mane-Eac stands above her workstation, chewing a wad of gum the size of Delaware. DoGoodR's stretching.

I'm just about to take the workstation next to Mane-Eac when DoGoodR takes off his shirt and reveals a back tattoo that drops my jaw. He's midway through putting on his torn and stained Stone Temple Pilots shirt when I grab the bottom of the shirt and lift.

"Is that..." I start, unable to finish my question because my brain refuses to compute what my eyes see.

"Damn right it is," boasts DoGoodR. From the bottom of his neck to the top of his butt crack is a tattoo of Edward Snowden's head. From the hair cut that parts on the left and swoops to the right, to the rectangular glasses, to his stubble-ish goatee, it's all there. "Pretty badass, ain't it?" asks DoGoodR, a snicker in his voice.

Mane-Eac never looks up from her keyboard. "I think you should focus on how *bad* it is and what an *ass* it makes you look like."

"Oh, you're just jealous," retorts DoGoodR as he undoes his belt. "Y'all should really see the quote just below the chin."

With that, DoGoodR lowers his pants, and I whimper, "Please, don't."

The kid ignores my plea and shows me one more tat: *When exposing a crime is treated as committing a crime, you are being ruled by criminals.*

"At no time has that quote been more needed than right now," I blurt out.

"Damn straight," he says with pride.

"Hey, DJ?" I ask.

"Yeah?"

"Would you please get your bare ass out of my face and get to work?"

AldenSong's laugh is so deep it shakes the van. DoGoodR finishes getting dressed and takes his seat.

Around the van, everyone finishes their pre-hack rituals. Aldy pets his little hula doll, her hips rocking side to side. DoGoodR's headphones already blast the same Stone Temple Pilots song, *Wicked Garden*, as he pops his neck. Mane-Eac flips open her Tuf-Nut pocket knife, the one her father gave her, and jams the blade into the van's wood trim.

I stare at the empty orange pill bottle. My reminder of where I came from, and where I never want to return. While I hold the bottle, I close my eyes. Eight breaths fortify my body and mind. When my eyes open, I ask, "Aldy, you want to start us off?"

"That's on you," he responds, "but I'll second."

I kick my shoulders back and yell, "Burn bright!"

"Burn fast!" Aldy pumps in.

It's DoGoodR that blasts, "Burn down!"

And, just like that, the attack begins.

Chapter Twenty-Nine

They Know

People think all hacking is the same: nerds in their mama's basement log onto laptops to break into servers, get stuff, and blitzkrieg everything along the way. Wrong. Dead Wrong. Hacks, as well as the location of the hack, vary according to the desired outcome. If your boyfriend cheats on you, you break through his firewall, find his search history, and release it on the socials. But you don't cause any physical damage, because that hack was about gathering info, not destruction. Not to the computers, that is.

Now let's say you do like I did a decade ago and try to impress a girl you're dating by destroying the server that houses the Ku Klux Klan's website. That hack wasn't about gathering info, though thinking back, I should've leaked everything. Finances. Membership. Dark, dirty secrets. But, no, I was there to destroy. Anything and everything.

And that choice inadvertently killed people. As I load up my tools on this POS laptop, the giant chess piece tattooed on my arm stares back at me. A Rook. I can still read the names of those that died because an outsourced medical database was also on that KKK server.

When I crashed that server, I never thought about what other companies used it. It didn't occur to me that a hospital outsourced their organ transfers on it. Two hearts, three livers, and a kidney expired.

So did their recipients.

I'm ten lines deep in code when an alert hits my screen. Poseidon's proprietary firewall just fired a warning shot my way. It hit back at our own firewall, and just ate up forty percent of our computing power.

"Did anyone else just get slapped across the face by a giant digital dick?" asks DoGoodR, five times louder than he needs to.

Mane-Eac pulls DoGoodR's headphones down. "Gross and, yes. I just sent a battalion of bots in, and something disintegrated them in seconds."

I check the monitor on the wall. Poseidon's firewall power shifts from green to yellow.

"We're only pissing them off," I say.

A *wheep wheep* alarm interrupts my thought.

"Shit. What'd they fire at us?"

"Something big and ugly," AldenSong mumbles, leaning further into his computer screen.

On a hunch, I ping our own servers. Since we're under our own firewall, nothing should come up.

Emphasis on *should*.

"Sweet baby Jesus, they just crashed our firewall."

DoGoodR says what we're all thinking.

"They know where we are."

Chapter Thirty

Long Thought Dead

I respond to the trace with a blast of digitized flak — basically gibberish computer code that'll slow a trace — and Mane-Eac jumps from her seat in the van, dashing to the Faraday blanket ejection button. The way we set up the explosive, it'll cover the van, stamping out any signal.

And, while I understand her urgency, I get between her and it.

"Move, Tanto," she orders, pushing my chest hard enough that the air leaving my lungs brings a small cough with it. Still, I stand my ground.

"We only get one blast of camouflage," I say. "Now is not the time to waste it."

"You dumbass, they know where we are," she says, and tries to finagle her way past me. "You don't know what they can do to us when they get here."

Our eyes meet. Neither of us speaks; we simply sit in understanding of the pain that these monsters put each of us through separately. For me, it was imprisonment, torture, and abandoning what I hold dear.

For Mane-Eac, it was a decade on the run. That probably brought its own kind of abandoning.

Mane-Eac reaches for the button again, but I put my shoulder against hers and brace.

"I know what fire from the sky they will send. I've seen it. Felt it. And lost people to it. But we only get one shot here."

"We need to abort." Mane-Eac gets nose-to-nose with me. "It's like they were expecting us."

She shoves me against the van's wall. As Mane-Eac's hand grazes the button, DoGoodR speaks up.

"They didn't take out our firewall," he says, his nose in his work.

That one sentence is enough to stop both Mane-Eac and me in our tracks, though her pink manicured fingernail taps the button lightly.

"The *S.S. Turing* has a leaky hull," he clarifies.

AldenSong scans the screen and points. "Tarnation. The kid's right. We're only operating at sixty percent." Aldy snatches his laptop up. "Look right here. I can see everything up and running on the chips we installed into their machines."

Mane-Eac sucks air between her teeth so hard my hair moves and asks, "Is our implanted software still functioning?"

Aldy flips open a new screen and nods.

"I saw the damaged nodes," I say, "so we all know that Poseidon sent a dambreaker to kill our firewall. They don't know we weren't fully powered. We can set up our firewall to filter it out before the next one hits. It's like diverting a punch by rotating away from it. Then, we can reboot and add the *Turing's* power, and hit them so hard their mamas feel it."

Then, something in the pit of my stomach turns confidence into a slice of doubt.

"DoGoodR, how's our system's health?"

"No worms or trojans trying to eat our guts, T," he responds as his eyes light up with an idea. "Look, I'll hop on my rocket bike, get to the *Turing* in two, three minutes tops. Y'all reboot and keep the wheels turning and we can do some real damage."

"We don't split up," orders Mane-Eac. "We can't protect each other if you do this. Aldy or Tanto can go with you."

"Sorry, señorita, but the bike only holds my scrawny ass."

"Then you don't go," she says through gritted teeth.

The bearded boy gets off the floor and puts his arm on Mane-Eac's shoulder. She twists away, but he holds firm.

"We need that power," says DoGoodR, "and no one knows our systems better than me."

The pair share a look with a history to it: it's like they're reading each other's eyes and having a discussion that no one else in the world is privy to.

"Well, then I'm not going to make this call," she counters.

And, like before, all eyes go to me. Unbidden, the words of the great Bushi Yamamoto Tsunetomo float through my mind.

A wavering warrior is worthless unless he rises above others and stands strong in the midst of a storm.

My answer to DoGoodR is from another wise philosopher. Freddie Mercury.

"Get on your bike and ride."

DoGoodR snaps shut his laptop, a giant smile on his face, and gives Mane-Eac a kiss on the head. She doesn't even look him in the eyes as she stares through the van. At what, I can only imagine.

"See you old people later," DoGoodR quips as he opens the door and snatches the rocket bike from the back of the van.

Just before he floors it, Mane-Eac snaps out of her trance and yells, "Radio and helmet!"

"Yes, mother," he says, giving a crooked smile from under his black beard and snatching a blue-and-white walkie-talkie from Aldy. Then he shoves a black helmet with red flames on his head.

"Radio us when you get there," she says, tightening his helmet. "Also, if you hear three squawks from us, but no words, run. You hear me? You run."

"Girl, I only run if I'm being chased or cake is involved," he quips tremulously.

As DoGoodR speeds off in the distance, a new alert hits our screens — a deeper *wok wok*.

Any hacker worth his salt knows, the deeper the alarm, the darker the danger.

"Is this part of their trace?"

"Negative, they've stopped since we halted our attack," Mane-Eac says, chewing on her nails. "Shit. We just lost two of our five allies." Her pager chirps. "X_Marks_Da_Hot's system just crashed because his pentests went from annoying to threatening. He thinks Poseidon's locked on him, so he's running."

It warms my heart that one of my Hackers' Haven hackvicts is out and helping us, even if he's had to make a run for it. "Who else did we lose?"

"PT Zeus."

I didn't even know Part-Time Zeus was still hacking. *Shit, how old would he be?* I mean, he was around when DISRUPT slapped around the US Department of Defense servers in the '90s like they owed a pimp money.

"PT Zeus's last transmission said that he was almost through the firewall, but they got a fix on him, so he bailed." She checks her watch. "All systems off until we get the signal from DJ." She locks eyes with me and points to the van exterior. I feel like a kid called into the principal's office as we step several paces away from the van.

"We should stop this," she says.

I raise an eyebrow. "What about DoGoodR?"

"He'll be fine, especially when we try this later," she answers. "We could consider this a test, especially since we only have three allies left still pecking away at their shields." With narrow, dead-serious eyes on mine, she says, "We're losing this battle."

A breeze hits my face as I pull my shoulders back and say *exactly* what Mane-Eac doesn't want to hear.

"No."

"Excuse me?" Mane-Eac asks, no, demands. "We're exposed, ill-equipped, and already behind. Now is not the time."

"No, that's exactly why we need to hit them hard. Right now," I say. "Look, once PhauCet gets up and running, it'll be worse than anything any of us have ever seen. Innocent people will get hurt."

"And what about us *not-so-innocent* people?" asks Mane-Eac. "The last time you risked my life so lackadaisically, you wound up in prison and I never stopped running." She flaps her hands wildly like she's washed them and couldn't find a towel, then Mane-Eac adds, "What the hell is wrong with you? When will you listen to anyone other than yourself?"

I can't even meet her gaze. "We stay on target."

Mane-Eac lets out a grunt that would scare a black bear and goes back in the van.

"DoGoodR's on the horn," she says flatly after a moment.

I enter the van as she squawks the walkie-talkie.

"Mama Bear to Disobedient Cub, go ahead. Over."

"Sorry, Disobedient Cub is not available right now," comes Do-GoodR's voice, "but if you'd like to leave a message…"

"Fine. Choose whatever handle you want. Over."

A few seconds pass in silence before DoGoodR responds.

"Mama Bear, this is Courageous Cub standing in for Disobedient Cub. We've got power. Over."

"Rebooting in ten seconds. Over," she commands.

Before I reboot my computer, I study the difference between X_Marks_Da_Hot's attack pattern and PT Zeus's. X is using the latest worms, the ones that feed off each other, as well as a few heavy-handed dambreakers.

It's Zeus's attack that clears my nostrils and dusts off a part of my brain I long thought dead.

Chapter Thirty-One

Headwig Handshake

One of the first books I *extremely borrowed* from the library was a book about hacking written by The Knightmare. This was in the mid-to-late 90s, so cybersecurity and cyberterrorism were still mostly hypothetical. But The Knightmare taught me the basics: Social engineering your way to a person's password, creating dummy accounts for entry level access, stair-stepping your way into convincing admins to grant that account greater authority, and so on.

And that's when I remember the benefit of being an old hacker, because we've been using modern tools to crack a modern firewall. In my experience, sometimes a modern tool can't compete with a good old-fashioned brick through a window.

After we reboot, I open up a folder I keep of old-school C+ code, the building blocks of today's modern software. "Y'all keep hitting the glass walls with our spears. Keep them focused."

"What're you gonna do?" asks Mane-Eac.

I respond, "Clean up an old, dirty, and possibly unstable bomb."

"Can you please not speak cryptically?" Mane-Eac asks, sending a salvo of worms at the firewall.

"I'm attempting a Headwig Handshake."

The clickity-clacks from my comrades slow to stop as they process my response.

"Damnation, T," says Mane-Eac. "Would you like us to drop the connection and let you use dial-up? Why don't you just go right up to their servers and punch them? That might work better."

I snort. "Don't threaten me with a good time."

To my knowledge, no one has attempted a Headwig Handshake in the last three presidential elections. Which is exactly what I'm counting on. I pop open my command prompt and open up two other screens. It's a gamble, but I bet that Poseidon's firewall build is not a legacy one, meaning it runs on the most modern code only.

And that sends the Hallelujah Chorus straight through my brain. You see, when you're dealing with a modern firewall, you also have to consider Border Gateway Protocol, or BGP. This includes a network's layout, design, host names, ports, op systems and, most importantly, firewall guidelines and rules generated in that code.

And their code is so fresh you can still see its paint drying. I send a ping at the firewall that gets rejected generating an error message that will in turn generate a log file. Exactly what I need.

Error: user does not have access to servers. For further assistance, please contact our help desk during business hours. PS1.4.

That *1.4* means that this firewall is indeed a first-generation, though with four updates. In a perfect world, we'd hit a wall that is a *1.0*, but hackers can't be choosers.

Usually, a legacy build, one that is fortified on top of an existing program, would present opportunities to get through. Historic weaknesses that get improved upon and reinforced until the firewall's own commands and code work in contradiction to each other. Hence, a new version doesn't have those details.

It's like how when a person gets exposed to flu season every year, their immune system gets stronger. Without a legacy or historic firewall, it might be vulnerable to an old-fashioned case of Spanish Flu.

Or, in my case, a dambreaker built out of outdated code.

Our radio squawks. Mane-Eac gets to it before the noise even fades. "Mama Bear here. Go ahead. Over."

"We're pumping juice like we're about to compete in the Olympics," radios DoGoodR. "Over."

Mane-Eac's eyes bore into the back of my neck. "I need thirty seconds," she tells him.

Meanwhile, I put the finishing touches on this ugly-ass thing of beauty. I've got a file that won't split into smaller data packets because it's built before digital compression existed. That means it's loaded with pure, unfiltered, and conflicting code from back before cellphones were common. Before Google. It's even got a series of bar codes that I just stole from products that Poseidon United sells to the public: voice-over command devices, such as weather and music devices.

That's the handshake part: convincing software that your intrusion is not only allowed, but welcomed.

It's a poisonous brick wrapped in pretty wrapping paper.

I signal Mane-Eac to join me. "Bring the radio." She plops down next to me, brow furrowed and shoulders drooped, confirming that this idea is as crazy as I think it is.

"Dear God, did you write this using an abacus?" she asks, skimming the code.

"That's too advanced for this," I say as Mane-Eac punches the talk button. "I'm gonna need all the bandwidth you've got, DoGoodR," I say into it. "Over."

"Oh, all fly-by patterns are clear. You can drop your load when ready. Over."

My finger hovers about the *Enter* key. Only the hum of machines fills the air.

And then I punch it and drop the bass so hard it blows a hole in Poseidon's ozone.

Chapter Thirty-Two

A Growing Rumble

In the movies, there'd be some giant explosion on our monitors as the audience watches the anti-heroes smash through a firewall. Some screen would show a protective shell around a CPU just before the screen faded away to nothing. Cheering would blast and gunshots and fireworks would fill the sky.

In reality, we sent code, so we got code in response saying that we knocked the firewall offline. While anticlimactic, it's better than magical; it's practical.

"YAHOO!" Aldy screams triumphantly into the van loud enough to make me cover my ears.

"How'd you know you'd overload the firewall?" asks Mane-Eac.

I answer, "Because it's not what I'd ever expect."

"T, if you were my type, I'd kiss you."

"I'm spoken for," I quip with unwarranted swagger.

Mane-Eac snorts. "See my previous statement before bragging."

The monitor on the side of the van flickers. Excitement fades as pragmatism takes the wheel.

"Shit," mutters Mane-Eac. "Okay, we've taken care of the firewall, but something is off. Like really, really off. I can't get my mapping bots through…trying to read this is as frustrating as trying to zip up a jacket in a snowstorm."

On her screen, I see the problem. I take that back; it's more like a flood than a problem, and we just broke the dam.

"Holy shit," says AldenSong, his face glued to his screen. "They've got the entire perimeter full of log files, jpgs, gifs, temp documents…"

"So, it's like our flak?" asks Mane-Eac.

"Worse," I say. "It's a damn digital moat. Instead of purging their cache, they use it as a barrier to keep people like us from getting to the secure files."

I grab the radio and hit up DoGoodR. "Do—Cub, whatever your damn name is, can you switch pull a *Spaceballs* move with their junk so we can overload them with their filth? Over."

After a moment of processing, DoGoodR radios back in my native tongue: smart ass. "Going to suck, then gonna blow, son! Over."

On the monitor, the cached files download to our laptops. Meanwhile, I run a check on Poseidon's temp folder capacity. Four hundred terabytes. *That's more hard drive space than NASA!* I shake off the thought and focus. Their hard drive space remains the same. That means the system is drawing other cached files.

Which means what we're doing should work when DoGoodR reverses the download and shoves the shit files back down Poseidon's throat. As I'm reading error messages that duplicate files are entering their system, I bet every alarm is pumping. For once, things are going as planned.

"Okay," says Mane-Eac, "I can see the directories, but they've got something, scratch that, someone, taking out the second cluster of bots I just sent in as a scouting party."

"Damn, okay," I start. "We still need to try to map their system, and your code just got bounced from this club faster than I did when I was fifteen and had a shitty fake ID made on a dot matrix printer."

"Damn, grandpa, I forget you grew up with fax machines and quaaludes," says Mane-Eac. "Well, it's certainly not a printer that's kicking our asses..."

And our culprit kicks me in the teeth.

"They're using a LODIS to take out your bots," I say. I recognize the spray pattern: erratic, missing bots at times. Extremely human.

"Saying random words doesn't help," Mane-Eac says, clicki-ty-clacking away.

"Liquid Ocular Display Interface System," I say, scanning the data on my computer. "It's basically a dude in a *Star Wars'* bacta tank playing *Asteroids* with his eyes."

"Details later," mumbles Mane-Eac. "Because unless you know how to *stop* your gamer, T, that's about as helpful as speedbumps on a handicap ramp."

"Aldy, the human element just came in earlier than we thought," I say. "What's the ratio of our bots to theirs?"

"We're rocking sixty, maybe seventy percent to theirs," Aldy says, "but they've got a fresh wave coming."

"Concentrate half of the bots on the firewall's borders only. Have the other half suck up five megabytes of data, any data, then cease operations."

"T?" AldenSong's voice cracks when he speaks. "That'll deplete our pre-programmed viruses."

"I'm counting on that," I say. Aldy shrugs and hits the command. "The goal is for you and DoGoodR to get us a clear shot at mapping the directory. We need to know what to target if, and when, we've got the window."

AldenSong switches between command windows, enters new parameters for our bots, and sends them off to fight our war. In ten seconds, error messages fill his screen.

"Well, they're dead or dying, but what good does..." That's when Aldy sees it. "You're using those bot corpses as a barrier to slow their attack."

"You're building a body bunker!" Mane-Eac chimes in with a snap of her finger.

"Their bots will attack enemy bots, whether or not they're functioning. Poseidon's anti-virus is working overtime on the files."

Joy hits me. I sit back in the driver's seat and pound on the steering like a happy gorilla.

"Firing mapping torpedo," says Mane-Eac. "Boom."

I abandon my drum solo and pace. "Mane-Eac, which Nmap 4.0 program are you sending?" Part of Mane-Eac's toolbox includes mapping software, a tool that will tell us about the structure of Poseidon's network.

"JasperX," she says. I remember that one: it's like sonar for computers, one long *pong* and we've got a layout.

"That's fantastic," I say. "Alright, load it up on our monitor here to —"

A sound cuts me off. One I can feel in my bones. One that I remember all too well.

A growing rumble, followed by a deep bass hum.

Then Mane-Eac says exactly what I'm thinking.

"They've locked a missile on us."

Chapter Thirty-Three

Drone

"**S**hut it down! Everything! Go!" The command leaves my chest as I'm yanking ethernet cables from our machines.

Mane-Eac dives toward the Faraday blanket ejection button and smacks it as if it just called her a bitch. A loud *pop*, like someone just opened a giant soda, fills my ears. A clear blanket covers the van. AldenSong pulls the cables from the car batteries just in case they're tracking power as well as bandwidth.

And now, all we can do is wait. With all the contingencies fired, each of us remains motionless, just in case the drone or satellite or freaking evil paper airplane hovering over us has motion sensor tracking. Hell, Aldy even stopped his little hula dancer's hip-swaggering. Any motion, any screw up, means we're seconds from having the worst sunburn of our lives.

The sweat dripping down my palms makes little *splick-splick* sounds on the laptop beneath me. Mane-Eac eases her head slightly to the windshield, but thinks better of it and holds off. Aldy's breathing so hard I wonder if his lungs are part vacuum.

If this were a movie, now is the time someone would try to stifle a sneeze.

My mind is flashing back to the last time Mercator found one of our hacking bases. To Dendro, who convinced everyone at Lance-A-Little's base that he was a good guy and volunteered to drive me away from their hack. To the attack where the vibrations came from above. When time stopped before the projectile destroyed our base. My ears popped as the nearby explosion sucked all the air from our vehicle right out the open windows. The shockwave knocked that vehicle up on two wheels, cracked the windshield, and obliterated my only allies.

Now, I'm in the same damned position. Except one of my crew is stuck at the base, unaware of the sword of Damocles dangling above our heads and may return any second.

At a snail's pace, I gently pick up a pencil.

Mane-Eac sends me a wide-eyed, disbelieving look.

I write on top of the laptop three letters, hoping that this minor move won't register on any orbital tracker. *DgR.*

I point my finger at the clear Faraday bag covering our windshield and vehicle and she catches my drift: we have to contact him because, if we don't, he might rocket bike back here and blow our cover *and* get himself killed. Somehow, someone needs to get outside of this shield so that we can establish contact with DoGoodR.

I point to the van door. AldenSong leans over, his body extending, more like stretching, while he's deliberate about his movements. He twists the handle. A slow creak comes out before the locking mechanism releases. I grit my teeth and my eyes instinctively close as the door slowly cracks open.

Mane-Eac steps toward the door radio in hand, but I put my hand up.

Her eyes shoot daggers my way. *What the hell are you doing?* she mouths.

My plan, I go, I enunciate silently and extend my hand.

Mane-Eac mouths what I can go do to myself.

I don't budge, demanding she give me the radio.

Reluctantly and none too happy with my wonderful leadership skills, she places the radio in my hand like she's passing off a Fabergé egg.

Mane-Eac and AldenSong place their hands flat against the door. They inch it open until the gap is just wide enough for me to slip through. When my right shoe crunches against gravel, everyone holds their breath, waiting for the worst. When nothing happens, I leave the vehicle.

Once outside, I push my back against the van's side and angle my head up. My breath catches as the Faraday bag clings to my face. I look skyward.

Through the clear Faraday bag, I can't see anything but clouds against a blue sky. A flock of birds in a V-formation go east to west, yet suddenly change their flight plan and go back the way they came. Then, a hundred yards above us, I see the reason.

A flicker in the sky. It probably looks like something caught in the wind. Or, to the normal eye, the remains of a dissolved cloud filtering into the rest of the sky.

It's a drone.

The sky blue and metal machine is almost undetectable. Its virtually motionless hovering holds, waiting for a command from its operator or its AI code.

Plus, I can't tell if it is scanning for motion.

I press my back against the van even harder, willing, demanding my body to morph with the van's exterior. I press the call button, but the radio's LED status light is red.

I'm going to have to get away from our protective cover to use it. Cautiously, I lower myself to the ground and lay flat. The hot day's gravel burns my face, but I can't risk even the slightest of raises.

I lay the radio on the ground, buttons face-up. With one finger, I slide it one inch away from the dangling cover.

The radio's light stays red.

Shit. It's still too close.

Something in my gut turns. Yet another bad idea crawls into my brain, just itching to be tested out. I rotate so that I face up. Now that I know the general area of the drone, I watch the drone's location and I angle one finger out to push the radio further away from our shield.

The moment I do, the drone moves and a red light appears on it. My asshole puckers like I just took a dip in a barrel of dill pickle juice. I don't need a background in drones to know that's not good. My every instinct is to rip my hand back. Instead, I gingerly move it back.

Once my hand returns to the Faraday's cover, I take a breath.

And that's when DoGoodR's voice screeches over the radio. "Hey, what's going on?!"

Chapter Thirty-Four

Damned If We Don't

I shoot my hand to the radio and snatch it and all the gravel under it up. As I look at the sky, the drone is gone.

Oh shit. It's gone higher or just out of my view. Either way, we're in trouble. I turn the radio's volume down as low as possible, push the radio back to where it was, and hit the squawk button three times. As I leave it on the gravel, I climb back into the vehicle.

The moment I hit the van's nasty, fake fur carpet, I nod at Mane-Eac and Aldy's questioning looks and say, "Sent."

A deep rumble answers the second question on their minds.

"Crank it and go!" I shout at Aldy through chattering teeth.

The big guy moves like he's a hundred pounds lighter as he dives into the driver's seat.

I know there's no way we can survive the blast. I've seen its power. But I'll be damned if we don't try.

Chapter Thirty-Five

STP

With no time to spare, Mane-Eac blasts her right steel toed boot through the passenger side window to grab the Faraday bag. Glass shatters, but her leg gets caught in the jagged remains. She screams; luckily, I'm able to lift her sliced jeans up and over the glass's sharp edges.

As I do, sticky, warm crimson covers my hands. I go to put pressure on the wound, but Mane-Eac waves me away. I reach through the window and pull in the Faraday bag from our van because, even if we outrun the blast, we still need to freaking see where we're going.

Aldy goes to crank the vehicle, but all that comes out is a *whirr-whirr-whirr* from the engine.

"You're flooding it!" I yell.

"You have to prime it!" he yells back.

"It's primed! We just drove here!"

At this moment, we're dead; we just haven't experienced the explosion yet. In the distance, I hear a familiar rock song playing. Or maybe it's just my imagination.

Mane-Eac grabs my shoulder. I look her dead in the eyes and say what I think might be my most useless, yet last, words.

"I'm sorry."

Mane-Eac looks around the vehicle and asks, "Why aren't we dead now?"

"Maybe that drone is more of a recon one," I say, looking out the window. There aren't any approaching SWAT vans.

That's when I recognize the song playing outside. Without a word, I dash out of the vehicle.

"What the hell are you doing?" asks Mane-Eac, climbing out, the blood turning her blue jeans purple.

Even AldenSong leaves the driver's seat and joins us.

We look skyward to nothing but blue skies. There is no drone acting like an Old Testament God about to smite us with a death projectile. The sky doesn't split. The ground doesn't swallow us up.

All that remains is that song, faint yet nearby. As we look around, AldenSong creeps over to its source: the handheld radio.

It's Mane-Eac that leans down and picks it up. She turns the volume up.

"That's *Wicked Garden*."

And there's only one hacker that listens to that STP song on loop. *What has DoGoodR done?*

Chapter Thirty-Six

Wicked Garden

Mane-Eac is holding down the radio's squawk button and yelling, "DJ, what the hell are you doing?"

Something in my gut shifts, spurring me beyond doubt and into action. "Aldy, get us cranked and out of here!"

The big guy shoots to the driver's seat. Mane-Eac repeats her question into the radio. I put a hand on her shoulder. "He can't hear—"

"Shut. Up." Her flat, decisive tone tells me that the potential drone strike isn't the only possible explosion. Still, I reach for the radio, but Mane-Eac jerks away. "Dammit, DJ, can you hear me?" she pleads.

Even though the handheld's speakers are crappy, I feel the *thump-thump-thump* of DoGoodR's favorite song blasting through the radio's collection of plastic, circuits, and wires.

"He's got the squawk button stuck."

"No shit," she snaps, fear and anger flashing in her eyes like emergency road flares on a pitch-black night. As the song reaches its chorus, Mane-Eac puts the radio up to her lips, hands shaking, to try one more time. A voice comes in over the pumping rock music.

"Hey, can you old folks hear me, or do you need me to turn it up?" says the ever-plucky hacker. "Because I'm all home alone and using no headphones, girl! I'm blaring it loud enough to wake the dead! Call the HOA, because I'm gonna get fined, sucka!"

"Yes!" Mane-Eac's voice trembles with relief. "What happened?"

In place of a response there are only the song's lyrics.

After a while DoGoodR's voice rings out again. "I don't know why I asked, because I've got the send button taped down. I didn't want to argue with y'all."

My stomach quivers like I just won *and* kinda lost a hot wing eating contest. Weiland's crooning says he's gonna burn us, but not to death. To life. A life we're afraid of living, and away from our chosen chains.

Mane-Eac bites her lip, and she tries several *squawks* to get his attention. The song switches to questions; the ones that the band wonders if we have the courage to ask ourselves. The last query, about being alive, stretches the word several measures.

Ali-lie-lie-lie-lie-live.

Mane-Eac punches the radio's buttons so hard and frequently the plastic casing cracks. Ice fills my body. A lump enters my throat, then my stomach clutches tightly around the rock I'd swallowed.

"I saw on the drone on the radar, so I gave it a better target."

The world fades and my stomach turns into a knot. Fear pulls that knot so tight my back bends.

"Sorry about the noise," says DoGoodR. "I'm kicking my babies, so they keep working."

I know what he's about to say. And I cannot stop him.

"If Poseidon or Mercator notice a lag in the bandwidth draw, they might send the drone back your way. In any case, to guarantee y'all got away, I dropped my firewall."

Chapter Thirty-Seven

Ten Years, Ten Minutes

I try to force reality away by shoving my thumbs hard enough against my shut eyelids that stars flash before my eyes.

The van cranks and Aldy yells, "Get in!"

However, fear glues my feet to the pavement in dread and disbelief. Mane-Eac's appear to be made of rubber as she sways side-to-side. She holds the radio between two fingers, dangling.

Then, from the radio, comes, "Hey, Tanto, if you can hear me, I want to thank you."

Tears swell in my eyes and I reach for the radio which Mane-Eac relinquishes limply. I hold it like a baby passed between us. As we stare at it, the Stone Temple Pilots chant *burn burn burn* repeatedly.

"T, you gave me ten years."

My body evicts all the air in my lungs and refuses to let any other tenants enter the building.

"Ten years away from the hell you went through...stuff I can't possibly imagine."

Tiny, invisible ants attack my fingers and toes as my chest caves in, crushing my heart.

He clears his throat and says, "I'm sorry we couldn't do this your way."

A flash pops in our peripheral, but we're lost in the radio.

"The least I could do is give ten min—"

And that's when the shockwave from the *S.S. Turing* exploding knocks us on our asses.

Chapter Thirty-Eight

Baseball

I hit the ground headfirst. Gravel embeds in my face and the palms of my hands. The only thing louder than the ringing in my ears is the thump of my heart trying to eject from my ribs as I breathe in dirt. I push myself to my knees, and the wind blows even more dust into my open mouth. I try to spit, but a desert's dryness overtakes my tongue.

Mane-Eac grips me under my shoulder and yanks me to my feet. "We have to go get him!" she says and hops in the van's front passenger seat. I can't form words. It's not dirt that's stopping my voice. It's pain-wrapped sorrow covered in damned barbed wire sliding down my windpipe. Still, as I shut the sliding door behind me, I try to say what we all know.

About DoGoodR. About our friend. But I can't.

Thankfully, Aldy is stronger than I am. He says, "Mane-Eac, he's not—"

"Shut your goddamn mouth and drive!"

The big guy looks at me. Although it's the worst choice available in a long list of bad ideas, I send him a simple nod. Whether we're going into a trap or a tomb, we do this together.

As we drive toward the smoke cloud, my psyche overwhelms me with this new, broken reality:

Our friend is gone.

Our base is gone.

And it's only going to get worse from here on out.

Aldy takes a right, slowly, driving smart, unremarkably, even though there's not another car on the road. I think he's steeling himself, and us, for the inevitable.

Funk Monster crawls into my lap and balls up, and I give her some pets, more for me than for her. The tires on the road make a weird whining sound as we head down the short stretch to the *S.S. Turing*.

Or where it used to be.

It's like when you see a photo of a building after a tornado or hurricane hits it. If you knew the building, maybe you lived, worked, or schooled there, well, it seems like a dream. Or something you'd see happen on the news, maybe in a foreign country or something.

But this happened to us. To DoGoodR. To DJ.

AldenSong avoids concrete and steel debris in the road about thirty yards from the battered shell of the *S.S. Turing*. Without even waiting for us to stop, Mane-Eac swings open her door and dashes out.

"Mane-Eac! Stop!" My request falls on grief-filled ears, but I try. Instead, she runs head-first into the smoke and fire.

I do the only thing I can: I follow. I follow her to the center of the smoldering command room.

The south and east walls are completely gone. The west wall halfway stands, broken at an angle, a jagged sliver of former support.

And, for some reason, the north wall looks untouched, like the bomb chose to leave it as a memory to remind people this building existed.

There are no computers.

No upright tables or connected wires.

And no body.

Just desolation.

AldenSong joins us, atypically somber as we soak in the despair.

Then, among the silence, the crushing gravity of the situation, comes a roar. It's primal, like one that doesn't come from the body, but straight from the darkest part of the soul. Like it is layered with pain, history, and crushing regret and loss.

I know that banshee's yell because I've popped the lid on my boiling kettle before. I can't help but think of Quidlee, in my arms while we laid on the cold tile floor in the latrine of Hackers' Haven. How my arms burned after hours of CPR on his long-dead corpse. How AldenSong held me from hurting myself more, calming me. And how I wailed on him. On my friend. Because Barca's murder of Quidlee did more than wound me. It broke me, and that monster did it just because he could.

This time, it's not me who's broken. It's Mane-Eac. She's on her knees with her back to me and there's something in her clutched hands. As much as I want to comfort her, ice water fills my bones and then freezes my body in place. I'm terrified to find out what she holds. If it is tearing her apart, how much of my soul will it take?

I step to her, running on pure instinct. Mane-Eac doesn't even notice my hand on her shoulder. The tremors that run through her body fluctuate between rapid and steady.

Bits of burned and charred paper float around like thin ghosts taunting us, and I reach for her balled-up fists. Something is dripping between her fingers; a red line forms from the bottom of her hands to the broken concrete below.

Without saying a word, Mane-Eac opens her hand, revealing a broken portion of DoGoodR's coffee cup: the yellow baseball handle.

It's no longer yellow. Maybe the blast, the heat, the explosion, darkened it.

No, I realize, it's not the blast. It's covered in red. But Mane-Eac's hands have no open wounds.

And then I notice the last thing, the diarrhea icing on this shit cake.

Stuck to the bloody handle is something black. Charred black hair.

The kind you find in a friend's beard.

As she takes my hands in her icy ones, Mane-Eac chokes, the words fighting to stay in her chest as long as possible. She tries again and, as she flicks her head to the right, Mane-Eac says, "Look...over...there..."

I don't want to. Whatever Mane-Eac wants me to see, I *know* it will sear into my soul hotter than any burn ever could.

Even though it will destroy me, I tilt my head.

At first, it seems to move and I mistake it for a sign of life. Maybe DoGoodR didn't vaporize or melt or whatever happens at a bomb's ground zero. For a moment, that dollop of hope hits my tongue before life's bitterness overtakes me again.

DoGoodR's tattered hacking t-shirt. The one with a skeleton dressed as Uncle Sam that points at the viewer and says he wants you to listen to Stone Temple Pilots.

It's not the whole shirt. Only the skeleton part. It's upside down over a pile of rubble, caught on a jagged piece of metal. Flapping in the wind like a flag at half-mast.

And, just under the upside-down flag, the international sign of surrender, is a lone hand, barely visible in the rubble.

Unlike my hand, this one lacks skin.

Chapter Thirty-Nine

Roadblock

The world wobbles. I catch myself on the edge of a smoking computer desk. The orange-hot metal singes my hand, though not enough for me to want to remove it. Maybe this little taste of pain will keep me in reality.

A tightness builds in my chest, seeming at first like a panic attack. Then, without warning, comes my wail. It's a cry that starts like a train whistle rising in the background, forcing its way between my clinched teeth. Before it reaches its crescendo, already-flowing tears race down my cheeks.

"I-I-I can't breathe," I stutter. Instead of getting the air I desperately need, I cough. As my body fights the wails and coughing, a damned laugh shows up out of nowhere, bringing with it hiccups. It would be disrespectful if it weren't so real.

Luckily, my hiccups abandon my body when Mane-Eac punches me straight in the gut. "You did this!" she snaps as I crumple to the floor. "Every red flag was flying high, but noooooo, *The Almighty Tanto* just had to complete the mission! You just had to keep pushing and, like always, you didn't give two shits about who it hurt!"

Mane-Eac turns her anger from me. She plants a foot into a fallen piece of rubble. Her steel-toed boots take the damage, but the shock of the impact must've sent lightning up her leg because Mane-Eac grabs at her boot. Her rage returns when we make eye contact.

She rears back her boot and I don't even close my eyes. Part of me wants to comfort her, but what good will that do? DoGoodR is gone...now he's just another name to get tattooed on my arm. Whatever happens to me, I deserve it. And more.

It's Funk Monster who gets between us, taking turns barking at both of us.

"Look, the dog is right," AldenSong says joining the pup's Sanity Parade. "And more importantly, we have to go!" As if on cue, a siren builds in the background. Aldy isn't waiting on us though. He scoops me up and wraps his other arm around Mane-Eac. While I'm as limp as one of FM's toys in Aldy's arms, Mane-Eac breaks free.

"Don't. You. Touch. Me." She pushes Aldy so hard he stumbles backward. Rage steams off her the way body odor does the rest of us. The pain in Mane-Eac's voice is heavier than all the elephants in Africa. And she's not done with me. "And you! You!" She points the tiny, stubby, blood-covered miniature bat at me and screams, "You *killed* DoGoodR."

Those words would hurt if I didn't already have them tattooed on my heart. "You're right...but so is AldenSong, because we have to run."

At that moment, she scans the room. Mane-Eac darts to the torn T-shirt and yanks it from its makeshift flagpole. She snatches up Funk Monster and darts outside toward our van. Then, something in my gut screams the opposite of our *glorious* plan. Knowing words will not stop her, I sprint and get between her and the open door to the van. She points the bloody bat at me and flatly says, "Move."

"We can't acid wash the data because then this was all for nothing," I say, no, plead. "Aldy, we still have several megs of expelled cache from Poseidon United, right?"

"Tanto, it's probably all trash," he says calmly. "Downloaded photos and visited websites and the like."

Mane-Eac reaches under my arm and grabs the burn rope. With one little pull, everything in the vehicle will melt away. She wraps her hand around it as if it's a ripcord and she's about to jump out of a plane.

I look her in her eyes and say, "if there's a chance there is something, anything, in those files, we owe it to DoGoodR—"

"No!" Mane-Eac slaps me across the face with one hand while keeping her other firmly wrapped around the cable. "You don't get to say his name, his handle, ever again."

The words sting more than the slap. "Look, I don't know why I'm pleading over scraps of damning data or broken hyperlinks," I start, with virtually no clue of how I'll end this sentence. "And if we get pulled over with the data, it damns us. I know that. But we have to try."

Mane-Eac's rage settles from rollercoaster level vibrations to small shakes. She is about to let go when Aldy shoves both of us from behind. Thankfully, Mane-Eac lets go of the acid wash as we tumble to the van's shag carpet.

"What the hell is—" is all Mane-Eac gets out before AldenSong tosses Funk Monster in on top of both of us and slams the door behind us. As the three of us scramble off each other, Aldy hops in the driver's seat and floors it.

"We're two blocks from the getaway cars. You can both have your feelings later." Aldy heads down the same empty road that we took in. The problem this time is, at the end, I spot a police roadblock.

Chapter Forty

A Lot Like Today

Instead of flooring the van's brakes, AldenSong speeds up. Against the pull of inertia, I crawl up and take the front passenger seat as the van's speedometer goes from thirty to forty.

Fifty. Sixty. And keeps going.

"Aldy?" I ask tentatively. "What are you doing?"

Two standard po-po cars and one SWAT van line up to block the rest of the street.

"Hang on," Aldy says. His tan knuckles whiten as he grips the steering wheel. "I saw this in a cartoon once."

"Please say it didn't involve an angry coyote and a roadrunner."

"*Meep-meep,*" he says drily, making me shit my pants.

A flicker of something shiny on the road catches my attention.

"Aldy, they have tire strips."

As a Cheshire cat grin crosses his face, AldenSong laughs. "Not on the sidewalk."

And with that, he yanks the wheel left. The driver's side mirror shatters against a storefront's red brick and sparks fly. The van barrels toward the rest of the barricade. The distance between us and it drops to sixty feet. Fifty.

Forty.

Aldy angles the vehicle back toward the last tire strip.

"You're still going to hit the spikes!" I yell, panic rising in my voice.

"That's the plan," he retorts as the van's right-side tires scream and then pop. The van tilts right, and we turn left. The sound of metal rims scraping concrete assaults us.

Then, impact. The van's passenger side slams into one empty police cruiser. Somewhere in the cacophony, it dawns on me. The one thing the barricade was missing.

Cops. People. *Anyone.*

Maybe they're in the SWAT van. Or maybe they're storming the remains of the S.S. Turing.

Like a game of bumper cars, the van's momentum shifts as we enter a narrow alley adjacent to the barricade.

"Aldy, we're running on rims, and our getaway vehicles are hidden past that barricade."

"Yeah, we're not going that way," he says as the alley empties onto a busy one-way street. Unfortunately, we're not headed the one way.

As he swerves around an on-coming eighteen-wheeler and two Toyotas, AldenSong overcorrects the van, sending us headlong toward a fountain in the middle of an intersection.

Aldy hits the brakes. Nothing happens.

Mane-Eac buckles up and wraps up Funk Monster in a bear hug. I try to buckle myself in, but the latch won't catch.

We slam headfirst into the fountain. Everyone lurches forward. My head hits the dash and stars fill my vision. A slight trickle of blood forms on AldenSong's temple.

"Is everyone...okay?" I ask, my voice heavy with pain and hollow from my crushed lungs.

"Define...okay..." mutters Mane-Eac as she rubs her neck.

"I'll live," Aldy says and hops out. "But not if we get caught."

I jump out of the vehicle and take the Faraday bag with me. I don't know why, but we might need it. Then I pop open the sliding door and Funk Monster pops out with the biggest smile on her face.

One creature's near-death experience is another's joy ride, I guess.

Mane-Eac can't get to her seatbelt because she's clutching her ribs. I dart in and pop her loose. She crawls out to AldenSong's outstretched arms. I grab the two laptops and wrap them in the Faraday. Then I pull our acid wash button, getting rid of our DNA.

A light spray of the acid hits my cheek and burns like a sunburn, at first. As the burn deepens, I clutch and claw at it, but the pain continues to grow. Meanwhile, our Anti-Holy spray does its job and destroys our getaway vehicle.

AldenSong gathers us up, pointing to a city bus fifty feet away. We hurry to it and dive through the closing doors.

I plop down in an open middle seat near a drunk frat boy. Yes, there are other open seats. I sit next to him so that the casual observer might think we're together. He's holding his head between his legs, so it looks like I'm taking care of my little brother. AldenSong sits next to an older lady, while Mane-Eac and Funk Monster take the seat behind me.

The adrenaline leaving my body sends a chill up my spine. A massive headache smacks me between the eyes. And my cheek still feels like the devil just branded me.

Then I feel a tapping on my head. I tilt my head back and see AldenSong's wide eyes as Mane-Eac points forward.

On the bus's small TV monitor at the front, a Breaking News Report flashes across the screen. I would say I'm thankful the *Closed*

Captioning is on, but reading this bad news doesn't make it any less of a poison pill to swallow.

Reporter: *This just in: the cyber-terrorist group The Nameless has attacked a Memphis, Tennessee building. There are reports of several dead, including one of the terrorists.*

Several? The building was empty.

Except for DoGoodR...

Reporter: *Two police officers, Timothy R. Wendig and Charleen N. Zahn, were killed while trying to apprehend these individuals.*

Two photos of officers I've never seen in my life flash on the screen. One is a white man, and the other is a black woman. Both are in full police attire, with the American flag hanging in the background.

Reporter: *If you or anyone you know has any information about the following individuals, please contact the station or call 911.*

A distant shot of Mane-Eac that looks recent flashes across the screen. Then AldenSong's mugshot follows. Instead of his usually jovial eyes, sunken and hollow ones accompany bruises around his face.

Finally, my mugshot pops up. Dead eyes and a busted lip. I remember that day over a decade ago; the day they caught up to me and all of my running was for nothing.

And that day felt a lot like today.

Chapter Forty-One

A Little Hope

In the last thirty seconds, I bet everyone with a smartphone probably got a message like an Amber Alert about The Nameless and our terrorist attack. Without uttering a word, our team enacts our Worst-Case-Scenario plan.

This means no contact with anyone we work with or know. No Penny. No Mr. Judson. No cellular or Internet use. And, no matter what, we don't let people get a good look at us.

We're already dodging glances when AldenSong takes out his ponytail and drapes his long hair over his shoulders. Mane-Eac shoves her hair under a collapsible baseball cap. I hide in my hoodie like a kid under the covers.

We need to get the hell off this bus that is blasting our photos everywhere. But we can't all leave at the same time. Getting on the bus at a popular stop was one thing. People just move on like cattle entering the slaughterhouse: blank stares and dead eyes. Getting off is where you get noticed, because everyone is watching to make sure they don't miss their bus stop.

The electric sign at the front of the bus shows two things: the route and the next stop. *Route 30: Westbound - Brooks. Next stop: American Way.*

Something in the back of my brain tickles like two ants fighting. This area reminds me of something, but I'm too exhausted to place it. Then, as the vehicle slows, what I see out the window smashes those pesky ants flat.

It also demands that I violate the first rule of our Worst Case Scenario.

I turn and tap Mane-Eac. "Get us a table," I say, pointing at the restaurant.

"How can you eat right now?" Mane-Eac more mumbles than asks, those busted ribs and cut leg catching up with her. "T, they killed DoGoodR..."

"And they're blaming us for it and more," I counter. If we had more time, I'd put on kid gloves and handle the situation properly. As it is, I'm ham-fisting the shit out of our emotions.

All on a hunch.

"Please, just go," I say, pointing at Aldy and myself. "We will Hot Potato this, hop out the next two, and meet you in an hour."

The bus stops. The doors open as a robotic voice comes over the speakers. "Current Stop: American Way. Doors closing shortly."

Mane-Eac's eyes dart between me and the window. She closes them, shakes the thoughts from her battered brain, and says, "Well, I'm keeping the dog."

I nod, and she slips out.

After Mane-Eac is clear of the bus, AldenSong and I abandon our seats to sit as far apart as possible. He takes the front; I take the back of the bus next to the *fragrant* toilet.

AldenSong hops off at the next stop, Airways Transit Center. I take his seat at the front of the bus and hop off at Third Street at Eastman.

Also known as the end of the line.

I scan the perimeter. The only other vehicle around is a beat-up white school bus that reads *Third Church of Poplar* idling in the parking lot. My guess is it will take me fifty minutes to make the trek to the restaurant.

Then someone calls my name.

My first instinct is to run. But then I recognize it and a little bit of hope sneaks into this epically shitty day.

Chapter Forty-Two

Huddle

I scan the horizon for a trap. Camera. Snipers. I find nothing, so I stroll up to the bus's door. It creaks open, and someone who I thought had kicked me to the curb decides to pick my ass up off of one instead.

"Get in, Vice," says Mr. Judson. I crouch and sneak in the open door, taking the first seat behind the driver.

"What are you doing here? How'd you find me?" I ask as we lurch forward and enter traffic.

He's chewing on his cheek, probably gathering his words. "You always loved taking the bus. Plus, when I heard over the scanner about someone driving a car into a fountain, I just knew you were involved. Vice, is...is what the news says about you true?"

That should sting. That someone I once thought of as a friend, a mentor, a Daimyo, would ask if I'd killed innocents. But, then again, this wouldn't be the first time my actions cost lives.

I reply, "No," and he continues our drive. "It was a trap, and I walked my team blindly into it."

As if on cue, Mr. Judson's police scanner squawks. Luckily, it only has to do with a motorist's car trouble off of Union Street.

Our church bus stops before crossing a railroad track, opens its doors, closes them, and then continues forward. "Vice, I've thought about our last...discussion..."

I start, "Mr. Judson, I—"

"Stop," he interrupts with a monster-sized sigh. "We both said some things in anger, and some things my wife calls *barbed truths*. It can be hard to compose your thoughts and...feelings...following such truths, so, please, shut up until I finish."

I allow my silence to be my affirmative. Mr. Judson takes it as such and continues.

"With the funds we've made off our...taco business, my life has gotten significantly better."

In the distance, a police siren grows. And, even though his police scanner doesn't squawk, Mr. Judson turns us onto a side street.

"My wife, who you call Mrs. Cher, and she loves that, is the healthiest she's ever been. She can actually live without pain," he says with a small, private chuckle. "Even Mama's able to move around without coughing up a lung. And Little Timothy. Woo-wee. He's in the *gifted* program. I mean that boy's taken to learning like weeds take to a garden..."

Even though we are away from the highway, the police siren continues to get louder. "Vice, do you know what we've done with the money, besides improve our own lives?"

Before I can answer, Mr. Judson jumps back into it.

"Six community day care facilities. Three addiction clinics. Four laundromats. And two community kitchens. All free to the public. All because of what you made."

"What *we* made," I counter. "We did this. I just wanted the best for you."

"Is that because you owe me a *life debt*?" Mr. Judson asks, turning his head my way. I can't believe he found out about that. I can't meet his gaze, because I did initially do this because of my dedication to The Code. The man saved my life.

"Yeah, ole Moscow told me that came up during one of your little *chats*," he says, putting air quotes around the word *chats*. "Look, if this was all over me killing that snake that tried to bite you, consider the debt paid."

The words slap my brain, like forgiving a life debt was as easy as saying *the cup of coffee is on the house*, or something. "You can't do that," I argue.

"If you say that you are honor-bound to me as your Daimyo, then I control that bond, right?" he asks.

I reluctantly nod in response.

"If that's the case, I release you from your bond."

"It's not that simple, Mr. Judson."

"Yeah? Why not?" he asks, his words more kind than biting. "If you live by a simple, yet firm code, then I get to respond in a simple, yet firm way. You, you just feel so sorry for yourself all the time. Somehow, you think you don't deserve happiness, that you are the eternal bad guy. You're as loveable as you are frustrating, Vice."

A police car blasts its siren behind us. My blood runs ice cold as Mr. Judson pulls us over all cool and collected. There's not a drop of sweat on his brow.

"Let me handle this, and then we'll get you out of town," says Mr. Judson as he opens the door and walks to the officer. I'm prepared for the cop to draw his firearm, or pepper spray Mr. Judson for leaving the vehicle without permission. Instead, the two joke like old friends before the officer pats Mr. Judson on the back and drives off.

When Mr. Judson reenters the vehicle, he says, "Just one of my fellow parishioners reminding me that Alverez's Autobody will give church buses oil changes for free." He closes the door but, before we drive off, Mr. Judson turns to face me. "I don't want you to owe me. I'm not that type of person. What I want is a friend, someone that has my back and I have his. If we're gonna be in each other's lives, it has to be on equal footing. Do you understand?"

I nod, and Mr. Judson extends his hand. We shake, and then he asks, "So, the tank's full. How far do you want me to drive you?"

When I tell him we have to go back to that Huddle House for the rest of my team, Mr. Judson only hangs his head slightly before a smile crosses his lips.

"Even when you're on fire, you're still not the *stop-drop-and-roll* type guy, huh?" Mr. Judson adds, "If this vehicle goes back that way, it'll stand out too much. I can drop you a couple blocks away. Then, if you need me, you call."

I nod, knowing full well I won't risk his freedom or his family's. We don't speak again in the five minutes it takes for Mr. Judson to get me to an empty parking lot. I hop off the bus, we tip invisible caps to each other, and he drives away.

The entire walk to the restaurant, I question my impromptu plan. If I were to bet on this plan, it might have a twenty percent chance of working. *Who am I kidding? Ten percent. Five.*

Maybe I should have Mr. Judson wait with his church bus for us and we all escape together. No, that's too risky.

As I enter the Huddle House, I say a little prayer, hoping Alden-Song and Mane-Eac are there. In the back booth, I find them. Aldy with the Big House Breakfast set out before him, three eggs, hashbrowns, biscuits and gravy, and three strips of bacon. Bacon Funk Monster is eying.

Mane-Eac sips an orange juice, her head low.

I grab the seat in the booth behind them. I ask for a menu and work up the courage to speak to my devastated team. The back of Mane-Eac's head touches mine. I put a hand on her shoulder. I can't tell who is colder, me or her. Then her hand touches mine, and she gives it a little squeeze.

Outside the window, my longshot, my Menthol miracle, comes into view. I tap on the glass, getting her attention.

"What're you doing?" asks Mane-Eac as she yanks her hand away. I shush her, knowing full well she'd knock my teeth out if Mane-Eac had the energy.

The bell on the restaurant's door *chings* and my nostrils clear. I'm jumpy, but hopeful.

In a worn Ramones T-shirt and with teeth the color of the sun, my old lab partner takes the seat across from me. The smell of baby oil and Chanel Number 5 fills the air.

"Aren't you a sight for whore eyes?" Rusty asks.

Chapter Forty-Three

The Magician and the Whore

I mean no blasphemy when I say Jesus Christ was spot-on when he made friends with and followers of prostitutes. Or, in my case, I pay to help me relearn to speak while strapping my ass to a medical board and interrogating me to the point of seizures.

Rusty already saw the news about the terrorist attack, so she's already tossed a handful of crumpled bills from her bra on the Huddle House tables and ordered us out of the restaurant before we do more than greet each other. In ten seconds, AldenSong, Mane-Eac, Funk Monster, and I are out on the street. In under a minute, Rusty flags down a trucker she knows, and he loads us into the back of his cattle truck. It's empty, though the smell of the last haul is still present. And, in twenty minutes, we're south of Memphis at Rusty's house.

Though the word *house* is an insult to this dwelling. This house reminds me of the monstrous McAllister's in *Home Alone*. It's two stories tall and ten windows across the luxurious front. I think we left Tennessee and entered Mississippi, just south of Memphis. My brain spaced a bit, or maybe I passed out from exhaustion on the ride over. The stately red brick on the mansion fits the other homes in this neighborhood, each of which sport perfectly evenly cut grass. Sure, it's odd to be on the run from the government and dwelling on the rules of Rusty's homeowners' association, but maybe that's my brain decompressing.

Rusty opens a tiny, wrought-iron gate and motions us down her long walkway. I'm the last one through, so I shut it behind me. As the latch catches, the clink of the gate echoes in my brain.

How long before the next clink I hear is of jail doors slamming shut?

Rusty goes to the door and opens it without a key. Inside, the foyer goes up almost fifteen feet tall and a curved staircase greets us, but Rusty ushers us to her right. We cut through a reading room straight out of *Home & Garden* with a pair of white leather L-shape couches in front of a wall-to-wall mahogany bookcase. In it, leather-bound books marked in gold lettering rest evenly on the shelves.

"I didn't know John Grisham's books came in leather," Mane-Eac says, running her finger along the titles.

"They do when your husband golfs with him." Rusty grabs one, *The Pelican Brief*, and hands it to Mane-Eac. "I've got an extra one, so please enjoy."

As Mane-Eac opens the leather bestseller, the book creaks like an old, weathered door. On the inside, there's an inscription:

To Ron and Mal, thanks for the memories, John.

Funk Monster fidgets in my arms as she holds her nose high, sniffing and wanting to explore. I can't blame her; *we're not in Memphis anymore*, Funk Monster.

"Where's your TV?" Aldy asks, his eyes saucer-big. Every once in a while, he jumps to try to touch the ceiling.

"We rarely use one," Rusty says, simply. Sure enough, there are no wires or cables around the outlets. She doesn't even have a landline set up.

Rusty puts a hand on Aldy's shoulder, keeping him grounded, and points up. "The crown molding we had before was older than the house. We had it shipped in from Sussex. It was a shame to let it go, but it just clashed with the French doors. We had the ceiling coffered instead," she says, referring to the octagonal grids against the recessed panels.

We all look up, and Rusty smiles and adds, "Did you know that coffer literally means an *indentation*?"

A buzzer on the wall goes off. She holds up one finger and presses an intercom. "Hey, dear, we have company."

A winded British-sounding voice comes through the intercom. "O-o-utstanding, Dah'ling! I'll be down momentarily...finishing...the elliptical."

"No rush," she replies, punching the intercom. "Don't lose your streak on my account."

We enter a chef's kitchen, if that chef was Julia Child. In the center of the room are double cooking islands surrounded by white marble, white cabinets, two sub-zero fridge/freezer combos, and a view out to a lush, green, sprawling backyard.

"Tea?" asks Rusty, grabbing a small box out of a kitchen drawer. Initially, I think it holds tea bags, but as she says the word *tea*, in walks a woman in a white maid's outfit. She grabs a pink and gold kettle from a cabinet, fills it with sink water, puts it on one of the many burners and ignites the fire.

"Everyone, this is Claire," says Rusty. "Claire, these are friends that were never here."

Claire fetches porcelain and gold teacups from a deep brown china cabinet. "It's a real shame I was so busy in the laundry room when they dropped by."

"A shame indeed," agrees Rusty, reaching into her mouth and removing her fake yellow teeth to reveal pearly whites so bright I need sunglasses. She puts her fake teeth in the small box, then Rusty grabs a handheld mirror and runs a silver brush through her hair. "Had a hair puller, not mean enough to mace, but I'm worried he got a chunk." Rusty looks at me, grabs a nearby pen and pad, and asks, "Check me?"

I get behind her and find nothing, so I tell her so.

As she examines other parts of her hair, Rusty asks rhetorically, "And now you can talk?" I nod and she puts the pen and pad up. "Always could or learned again?"

"The latter," I say.

Her eyes tighten, then she winks.

"So, all of this," Mane-Eac starts, boiling over like our kettle, "and you're a..."

"Whore?" asks Rusty, as she chuckles to herself. "Or would you prefer the term prostitute? Woman of the night? Skin trader? Juice collector? You name it, I've been called it," Rusty says as she stretches her arms wide. "Because I am it."

Aldy's hand shoots up like a kid in class.

Rusty smiles and nods.

He points at everything he can and says, "But you're..."

"Home early!" announces an older gentleman dressed in a red and white tracksuit and covered in sweat. His silver hair plastered to his head gives the man a sleek, stockbroker look. "What a pleasant surprise, darling. And you brought guests!"

"I did," starts Rusty as she shakes her head, "but I also didn't."

"Say no more," he says as the man briefly puts a finger across his mustachioed lips before kissing Rusty on the lips. As his blue eyes connect with mine, he says, "We know a thing or two about discretion in our family."

"If you were here, well, you'd have met my husband, Ron," she says, slapping Ron's ass as he bends into one fridge and grabs a steel bottle.

Ron unscrews the top and takes a gulp and slinks out of the kitchen.

From the reading room, Ron says, "Well, maybe I'll meet them next time."

The high-pitched squeal announces our tea. Rusty pours the four cups, but lets us doctor them with cream and sugar as we please.

"He's nice," says Aldy as he heaps spoonfuls of sugar into his tea. "And what's he do?"

Rusty stirs in a dash of cream and a spoonful of sugar. "He's sort of a magician," says Rusty as she blows steam from her drink. After she takes a sip, Rusty adds, "He makes people, or problems, disappear."

Unprepared for that answer, because Ron looks like a banker to me, I choke on my hot tea. Then I cough hard enough that Funk Monster, resting on my chest and held up by my left arm, slaps my face.

"The Magician and the Whore," Mane-Eac says with a smirk over a sip of tea. "Sounds like a children's book."

Everyone else laughs, though I'm still recovering from choking.

After I get my wind back, I ask the only reasonable question.

"Is the magician available for private parties?"

Chapter Forty-Four

Scalpel

"I'm assuming you young'uns were smart enough to leave all cellular devices as far away from here as possible," says Rusty as we leave the kitchen and enter the hallway. After various affirmatives to her query, Rusty ushers us through a door in the center of the house, leaning into the reading room and saying, "When you have a minute, hun."

"Certainly, darling," says Ron as the crack of a book snapping shut echoes against those high, coffered ceilings. "I'll be down in a jiffy."

In contrast to the grandeur of the rest of the house, what is behind the wooden door is merely a set of plain wooden stairs heading down. Rusty, Mane-Eac, Aldy, and I, with Funk Monster under my arm, descend to a basement straight out of a '90s horror movie.

The basement's triple-plastic-lined walls make me think that Rusty and Ron have set up multiple Faraday bags to keep out all signals. An array of surgical tools line a metal table nearby.

We are peaking behind the magician's curtain. The kind of magician that, when he saws a woman in half, she stays that way.

Something in my gut encourages me to look down. As I do, I spot two, no, three industrial-sized drains built into the concrete floor. I crouch to examine one, and the combination of the smells of antiseptic and bleach fill my nostrils. I stand up and walk over to the surgical tools.

They, too, emanate a freshly cleaned smell.

"So, what does—" starts AldenSong, but Rusty covers his lips with her finger.

"Not yet, dear boy," she says, kind, yet definitive. The door opens, but Ron stays at the top of the stairs. He shuts the door and hits a button that is recessed in the wall near the light switch. From the floor above us, music plays. It might be the Beatles, but I can't quite tell. Ron takes a breath, then heads down. His footfalls on the stairs are a cross between energetic and deliberate, a quick step with thunderous pacing. He joins us with a large yellow legal pad in one hand and a basic Black Warrior No. 2 pencil in the other.

"Sorry, everyone," says Ron as he joins us. "Even with the reinforced walls, it always helps to ease the nerves to have some background noise prior to...sensitive discussions."

Ron goes over to the surgical instrument table but, instead of grabbing any tools, he opens a small drawer and grabs an instrument I'm highly familiar with: a digital sniffer, AKA a listening and tracking device finder. This isn't our first rodeo so AldenSong, Mane-Eac, and I all prepare to let Ron run the wand over us like we're about to board a flight to Miami.

Even though I know we're clean, something worries me. I mean, I trust everyone in this room more than anyone else in the world.

But what if one of us is crooked? What if one of us is a spy? It wouldn't be the first time. Hell, during the DoGoodR case, Squirrel_Lord betrayed us, and I'd worked with him a dozen times.

No, I can't think like that. The gig went south and Squirrely had as much honor as a cartoon villain. Gigs screw up. It happens. This recent failure wasn't someone betraying us.

Still, something feels off. Even so, I'm the first to volunteer for a TSA-search level of treatment. Ron starts at my head and works his way to my feet. All the while, I'm terrified that something will cause the detector to beep. Fortunately, after the wand reports nothing, Ron pats me on the shoulder and my sphincter unclenches from its death grip.

Mane-Eac steps up to the digitized plate to the same result and Ron moves on AldenSong. He starts at the top of Aldy's head, sweeping lower to his T-shaped arms, and then to his belt buckle.

Nothing beeps.

Until he reaches Aldy's boots.

Aldy quips, "I think they have some metal in the toes," although his voice trembles as if he's riding on a bumpy road.

Ron sighs and says flatly, "It's not detecting steel, my friend."

And that's when he jams a scalpel into Aldy's throat.

Chapter Forty-Five

Spy

Everything happens so fast, neither Mane-Eac nor I can stop the attack. For a senior citizen, Ron moves with battle-tested swiftness. His strike and his countering stance keep all of us in his sights, and AldenSong a hair from death's door. By the time I realize what's going on, Rusty stands between Aldy and me, shaking her head and aiming a silenced Glock at my gut.

Aldy clutches at Ron's hands, but then Ron presses his free hand into the muscle between AldenSong's neck and collarbone, forcing the big guy's hands and arms to go limp. It's like this serial killer's version of a Vulcan nerve pinch, except instead of the victim falling unconscious, the touch freezes AldenSong like a statue.

"The neck is a remarkable area because it has some of the most elastic skin on the body," says Ron, his voice as steady as his hands. "That is why I'm able to slip my little surgical buddy in and not cause any long-lasting damage. Yet any twist or turn from here, well, our...guest...will go from needing a stitch to requiring a coroner."

My eyes dart between Rusty's gun and Ron's scalpel before I chance a glance at Mane-Eac. She's waiting for some signal, some action from me. No matter my choice, she'll follow me into the mouth of Hell.

"And before you striking young'uns get any heroic ideas, I need you to listen," says Ron, as if reading our thoughts. "If this instrument is removed incorrectly due to your interference, it will be you, not me, that ends your friend's life."

Ron holds a deadman's switch: a tool of mutually assured destruction. I grab Mane-Eac's shoulder, and mouth the mantra AldenSong has said to me many times, especially when I didn't want to hear it:

Be still.

Mane-Eac eases off her throttle, rocking back on her heels, but still geared to go. We step away from Rusty and put our backs against the far wall. There's no way to derail this train, so it's best to take a seat and follow the route.

"Splendid, chaps, but I need the lad's assistance," says Ron, his eyes on me. I step to where Ron can see me clearly. "Unlace this man's boots. And please, be a dear and do this slowly."

I take a knee on the cold floor under the bright white lights. Then I undo the white laces on the old, weathered boots AldenSong has worn since our incarceration.

"Dear boy," starts Ron as he takes a breath to suck his teeth. "I said unlace, not untie."

Now corrected, I grab the strand on the right foot and pull it through the sneaker's holes. Each pull goes *thwip* as the lace slides through and out. When the last lace leaves its hole, I present the lace in front of my face to Ron as if I'm a child that just captured a baby snake.

"Now, the left," says Ron. "You're doing marvelous."

When I repeat the same process to AldenSong's second boot, something different occurs. When the very end of the lace goes *thwip*, it catches on something.

As I lean closer to examine the end of the lace, I find it actually connects with the interior of the boot.

"It's hooked to something," I say.

"And there's the rub," says Ron. He lets out a groan that I can't quite tell whether it means he is disappointed, disturbed, or destructive. "Darling…"

Rusty lowers the gun and joins me on the floor. Rusty is not as gentle as Ron is, because I hear a muffled cry escape Aldy's clenched teeth as Rusty raises his foot and peels off his shoe.

Inside of the shoe is the worn and warm innersole. AldenSong's body temperature has the sole reeking of months, if not years, of old sweat. Rusty reaches in and yanks the innersole out and tosses it across the room. Then, between the sole and the heel, recessed in the shoe, is a small battery pack.

My stomach plummets and my head spins. My closest friend, my one true ally in life, is a spy.

Chapter Forty-Six

Doors

Alfred Hitchcock's movies changed cinema forever. Not only did they introduce you to villains that stand the test of time or show how ordinary people overcome killers and psychos with sheer force of will, but his cinematography changed the way we watch films. And one of the most famous effects Hitchcock came up with is one where the camera lens zooms in on the subject, like the hero or heroine, while someone moves the physical camera backwards. It creates an effect so dizzying, disorienting and popular, they named it after him. Seeing the Hitchcock Effect on the big screen is one thing.

Living it is completely different.

My head swims in a lake of static. I want to yank the scalpel from Ron's hands and hold it in front of AldenSong's face myself. I want answers, and I want them any way I can get them.

I also want to vomit and shrink down so small no one can see me.

AldenSong is a spy.

Then Rusty puts her hand on my shoulder and shows me what else is in that shoe. Where the sneaker's toe should be is a smooth, black radio transmitter. And, even though I don't know squat about spy-level transmitters, I do know that the transmitter works best when it's not shattered into a million pieces.

"Dead soldier, my dear." Rusty clears her throat and continues. "If anything is coming out, it's only the battery pumping."

"What…is…going…on…" AldenSong squeaks the words out. He doesn't moan or cry, but his eyes close tight and a lone tear slinks down his face.

Ron chews on his tongue as his shoulders take the slightest shift downward. "Now we are in a quandary. When someone reaches one of those, it is best to take a quantitative approach. In doing so, we will only express facts, not opinions, understood?"

While none of us reply, our silence is clear in our unanimous affirmative.

"My wife picks you up and brings you here because of her prior…relationship with the skinny lad. Upon entering our home, you smuggle in a concealed transmitter in…"

"B-b-broken transmitter," interrupts Mane-Eac as sweat trickles down her right temple.

"That may be inconsequential at this time, but it is a fact, so kudos to you, my dear," responds Ron as he runs his eyes over and through our faces. He's studying, running kinetics, the study of human emotions and tells, behind his eyes. I know the same tricks.

But he's also running other scenarios in his gray matter. There's no real way to tell what mental boxes he is checking. They say, in war, *it's the unknowns that get you*. Ron's wheels are turning, and I'm terrified of what will come from their rolling thunder.

"Soon, I will open the floor to feedback," says Ron. "But first, I would like to share what I believe are our options moving forward in this…discussion."

My body clenches every muscle between my stomach and my sphincter as if I just dove into a frozen river.

"This reminds me a bit of Monty Hall's *Let's Make a Deal*," Ron starts, though I can't tell if he's talking to us or himself. "Now, unlike that show, you're going to know in advance what is behind each door. For example, if you choose *Door One* and choose to charge me or my wife, she will gut-shoot the two of you while I twist Monsieur Scalpel on Mister Goodbody here, and then my wife and I will deal with the mess after we go to Red Lobster."

Without missing a beat, Rusty says, "Hun, their Endless Shrimp promo ended last week."

"Curses." Ron sighs and shakes his head.

I don't know what bothers me more: that he considers the taking of our lives a trivial affair, or he's more focused on a meal than murder.

"I should've written that down...fine." His *tsk-tsk-tsk* sounds more annoyed than life-and-death worthy. "Ah, we can hit the Olive Garden next to Red Lobster. Back at it. *Door Number Two*: the lad reaches into the middle drawer in the silver desk over there, grabs some gauze and a quick clot bandage, and I remove the scalpel while he applies it to the wound as the lady stays put."

I open my mouth to answer an immediate *we choose Door Two*, but Rusty wags a disapproving finger in protest, somehow having trained her gun on me again without my notice. Apparently, there's a third option.

"Or, *Door Three*." Ron clears his throat and shuffles his feet. "Now, unlike *Doors One* and *Two*, it's an option available only after you go through *Door Two*." Sweat stings my eyes, but I'm too nervous to wipe it away. "Let's say that after you apply the bandage to our well-fed friend here, you two decide to take that shot at me that you've got gleaming behind your eyes. If you make this choice, I will...gladly...respond in kind." Ron sends me a flashing sideways glance, his eyes sparkling with a hint of madness and a Joker-worthy smile. "I would say you can trust me, but I'm a firm believer that my actions will answer any unasked question. And, depending on what you do in the next few seconds, I will answer in the best way I know how."

I keep in Ron's eyeline as I go to the drawer, grab the gauze and quick clot bandage, and remove both from their individual packaging. And, while there's a calm look in Rusty's steady eyes after choosing *Door Two*, Ron's disappointment is apparent as the fire in his eyes dies down a bit. He removes the scalpel with the precision of a surgeon. AldenSong's face tenses, but he keeps steady as I hold pressure with the gauze, then promptly remove the crimson-soaked pad and apply the quick clot over the wound.

Once this is done, Aldy's body goes from the stiffness of a wooden board to silly putty, loose and without shape. I catch him, not fainting, but as all of his muscles unclench and exhaustion overtakes him.

"Oh, dear," gasps Rusty, the only time she's acted emotionally. I don't even take time to glance at AldenSong as I shove both Aldy and Mane-Eac behind me.

I have zero idea why Rusty acted this way and, as I said, it's the unknowns that get you.

Rusty tosses the Glock on the table. It bounces several times as she heads upstairs. "I forgot to offer our guests cookies with the tea."

Chapter Forty-Seven

Are You Hurt, or Are You Injured?

AldenSong, Mane-Eac, Funk Monster, and I sit on the basement's concrete floor eating the best tasting cookies I've ever had. Of course, everything tastes the best after you've almost died.

Ron and Rusty are sitting in folding chairs, sipping out of their fancy cup-and-saucer combos. And, as dry as my mouth is, I can't lift my cup without my shaky hands spilling it everywhere.

Ron lets out a yawn as he leans back in his chair and raises his arms above his head. "Whew...okay...now is the time when I apologize for being accurately suspicious and you rage about our violent, yet effective, tactics, and we go back and forth with insults over pleasantries." He checks his watch and says, "Though in the manner of full disclosure, I'm only free for another thirty minutes..."

"Oh, did nothing cancel?" asks Rusty, her tea-holding hand as steady as a rock.

"Joyfully, the payment ultimately came through," Ron replies as he steals a cookie from a brown-and-black clay platter. "The Patriot Act slows so many transactions that are just clear cut."

With the word *cut* in the air, AldenSong scratches at the patch on his neck.

I think, *if the Mercator Agency had that tracker active on AldenSong when they released him, why didn't they snatch us up earlier?*

"So, let us examine the crushed elephant in the room," says Ron as he dangles the broken transmitter in front of our faces, this *magician* trying to hypnotize his audience with a swaying pendulum. "Young man, do you know how this wound up in your boot?"

"Erhm, uh, no idea." AldenSong's words fight through his damaged neck to reach us. "I've had those shoes on since Agent Michelle and that dickhole threw me in that interrogation room with the lawyer and Tanto."

"Hrmm..." mumbles Ron as he leans back and rests his head in his hands.

"When did you not have them with you?" asks Rusty as she grabs the tracker and pulls it close, squinting.

"Well, when they yanked me from Hackers' Haven," answers AldenSong.

"And no one checked him or his gear for a tracker?" asks Rusty as she reaches for something near her neck, but comes away empty. Seeing this, Ron reaches into his pocket, opens a black glasses case with the words *Washington, D.C.,* on it, and hands her his reading glasses. She smiles, puts them on, and leans into her examination of the transmitter.

"Traditionally, they insert our trackers into our legs," I offer, rolling up my pants leg to show my scar, as does AldenSong. "When we took his out, we thought we were being thorough."

Ron continues to stare at the ceiling. "And you never checked his clothing?"

"We did," counters Mane-Eac. "We always do. But nothing was transmitting or emitting power."

"Until recently...hrmm..." Ron checks his watch, but keeps his head back.

Rusty rotates the transmitter and says, "It's clearly American. You can tell by the soldering marks. The Chinese and Indians use a higher temp. Beyond that, the transmitter is unlike anything I've ever seen."

Part of me wonders what a whore and a killer know about international welding and soldering standards. However, that question is mighty trivial, considering they almost killed us with ease a few minutes ago.

"May I?" I ask, extending my hand to Rusty. I'm not even sure what I'm looking for, but I'm desperate to do something, anything, to help. Both Ron and Rusty nod, so I get up and hold the transmitter under the light.

"It's a jack-spread," I say.

"Young man, I think that's a sexual position," says Ron with a glance at the sexpert in the room. Rusty nods. "What's that mean to the rest of us common folk?"

"It means it is an open-sourced transmitter that is, or was, constantly scanning for ways to send limited data out, such as longitude and latitude," I start. "It'll latch onto any open or non-passworded router, carrier, even RFID system. I just wish we knew when it broke, and how much the assholes who put this here know."

Rusty finishes her tea and asks, "Is it broken or destroyed?"

AldenSong asks, "What's the difference?"

"It's like how you Americans ask each other, *are you hurt, or are you injured?*" asks Ron as an alarm goes off on his watch. He silences it and says, "If it's fixable, that's key."

Mane-Eac speaks up and asks, "Why would you want it fixed?"

Ron leans forward, a wide smile crossing his lips, "Because, only then, will this thing buy you the one thing you do not currently have: time."

Chapter Forty-Eight

The Airplane Model

For a contract killer, Ron sure has a lot of technical tools at his disposal. From a coffin-sized green-and-yellow storage bin, Alden-Song and Mane-Eac scrounge up some electrical wire we can use as replacement tank coils for the busted transmitter. From a clock radio upstairs, I snag a key jack, power button, and RF output connector. And, from an upstairs nursery, I snag a baby monitor that we steal a decent transmission antenna from.

The plan is simple: the battery in the shoe is our working power supply. Power pumps from it through the oscillator, our repurposed wires, to the modulator, which creates the actual signal. And the antenna broadcasts our final product out to whatever, or whoever, is tracking us.

Granted, all of this ragtag work takes up the entire inner part of the shoe, but AldenSong probably would never wear them again. Especially knowing someone used him as a human GPS. Thankfully,

Rusty has already given AldenSong a pair of Ron's flip flops, a feeling I'm sure Aldy has missed since he left the islands.

Ron takes the completed shoe device upstairs and yells down, "Claire, I need you to go grab some flour from our friend at the market."

"Do I need petty cash?" she yells back.

"And two changes of clothes, please, dear," Ron responds.

"Well, then I'm packing a suitcase and taking my vacation while I'm there," she says. "Y'all know I deserve it…"

"Have a lovely time," he says.

Now it is just us and Rusty in the basement. I don't know if it is my nerves, or that the person most likely to stab someone just left the room, but I rise to my feet. I throw my shoulders back and, just as I'm about to shove my finger in Rusty's chest and yell at her for this whole *almost-shot-almost-stabbed* situation, she embraces me in a hug.

"Sorry," Rusty says as I squirm. It's like she's an aunt who hasn't seen her little nephew in a year and I'm a kid who just wants to go play Nintendo. I initially push away, but she holds firm. Then, after a few seconds, I embrace it, and squeeze back.

"We had to be sure," she adds. For once, her breath smells like peppermint tea, not menthol cancer sticks. Rusty gives me a light kiss on the cheek and lets go, a glint of tears possibly in her eyes. She turns too quickly for me to be sure.

This hug, however, doesn't deter Mane-Eac who is up in Rusty's face in a heartbeat.

"You were going to kill us!" cracks Mane-Eac, her voice angry but not shrill.

"That…was an unfortunate possibility," responds Rusty, her gaze matching Mane-Eac's. "Though, that wasn't our preference—"

"Oh, forgive me for not believing you," Mane-Eac spits out. "I think if there was a single doubt about what we'd done or if Aldy here was a spy, you'd have killed us all. Am I wrong?"

Rusty's head tilts, her nose only slightly higher than Mane-Eac's. She answers simply and directly. "You are indeed correct."

Mane-Eac's arms go wide and she turns around to face me. "And *this* is who you thought would help us?"

I open my mouth to respond, but Rusty cuts me off.

"Sweetie, we live the airplane model here," starts Rusty.

Hearing her call Mane-Eac *sweetie*, both AldenSong and I exchange a glance reserved for servicemen who hear the high-pitched whistle of an incoming missile. Mane-Eac takes one step towards Rusty, but Rusty holds up her hand and lowers her head.

"What I mean by that is, if the airplane has lost cabin pressure, we make sure we secure our oxygen masks before we help others." Rusty sweeps her hand out at the three of us. "I invited you to my home. Ron and I acted in accordance to protect ourselves, meaning ensuring you and your device were not threats. We're ready to help slip your masks on now."

And, with that said, Rusty goes to the far wall, unclips a section of the protective plastic covering, and presses on a section of the wall, opening a small door. From inside, Rusty brings out a handful of passports.

"These are blank," she says as she drops the passports on the table in front of us. "We have the software for not only inserting your pictures but also matching the latest printed holograms and imprinted code. Also, we have a backdoor into the passport database, so any scans or imaging of these babies will come up as real people, not just false identities. These will get you across the border."

"Mexico?" asks Aldy, his flip-flops popping as he shuffles.

"Wrong way," Rusty responds. "That is the current destination for your tracker. Claire knows the drill: cut the tracker on for ninety seconds every hour, then power down for an hour. She'll go north for an hour, then south for two. Give the feds a nice long tail to chase. The drive to Mexico would run about seventeen, eighteen hours, from here. It'll take three days the way she's driving. During that time, we get the three of you north, let this die down, and regroup."

From the little tote, she grabs several sealed Ziplock bags. She pulls out a barber's electric razor and flips it on with a smile.

"Time for a trim, everyone."

Chapter Forty-Nine

Brady Bunch

Even though he has, excuse me, *had* a beautiful head flush with long, black, silky hair, AldenSong rocks the bald look well. Of course, he almost cried when Rusty snipped off his ponytail and handed it to him. Shaving my head didn't take nearly as long. I guess having balding genetics is good for something. Rusty dyed Mane-Eac's dark hair a bright red and shortened it from shoulder length to right above her ears. Both Rusty and Mane-Eac say it's a pixie cut. To me, it's a bowl cut, but to each their own.

Once we've got our trims, Rusty pulls a string from the ceiling and down pops a blank backdrop.

"Who's first?" she asks. AldenSong volunteers, and Rusty waves him up. He kicks his shoulders back and a smile spreads across his face.

"Nope. Look constipated," she says as she adjusts the camera's focus. "Better yet, you've been in line at the post office for this photo and passport service since 7a.m. It's now noon and you haven't had lunch. Show your DMV face."

At first, AldenSong tries to not smile, but in every photo he takes, there's still a glint in his eyes. Finally, I sneak his non-transmitter boot under his nose just prior to a photo. The smell provides the expression Rusty needs.

Mane-Eac is next. She's all business, stoic yet pissed. On my end, I just think about how we got where we are right now, and the picture basically takes itself.

Rusty stares at one of the florescent bulbs in the ceiling, gets directly under it, and takes three steps west. Once there, she lifts a seamless piece of concrete up and grabs three totes from inside.

"Grab one and get accustomed to its contents," Rusty says as she hooks her digital camera up to a laptop and printer hidden under the plastic in the southeast corner of the room. "Each bag has five K, basic medical, some MREs, a tracking tag that is not currently active, and one...COA thing."

"What's COA?" asks AldenSong.

"Something that will *cover our asses*, if you choose to use it." Rusty keys a few commands in the laptop, hits *Enter*, and smiles to herself. "I'll work on the ride north while you three get ready to go. The sooner you're in the land of hockey, the safer you'll be."

Now, apparently on the same page as Rusty, Mane-Eac says, "Are we taking the same transport, or separate?"

"Different vehicles, times, and routes," Rusty says. "Splitting up is key. One of you will go up through St. Louis to Chicago and cross over in Mackinaw City, while another will go the long way around through Kansas City to Bismark and cross over just past Grand Forks. The last—"

"You'll only need two transports...because I'm not going." The only thing more shocking than hearing those words is saying them.

"Are you shitting me?" asks Mane-Eac, clearly not understanding my statement. "With the entire damn country looking for us, you're going to stay and do what? Take down an untouchable corporation and a clandestine agency who has the backing of the US of A government?"

"I don't know, but I can't run," I say, my voice cracking slightly. "Not anymore, and not again."

"You self-righteous little asshole," says Mane-Eac, venom filling her throat. "We just got our asses handed to us! We have no support. No infrastructure. All we have is some shitty laptops with even shittier cache and junk files. We have nothing. We have *less* than nothing, we lost...we lost..."

Where Mane-Eac's words trail off in exhaustion, AldenSong speaks the name of our unspeakable loss.

"DoGoodR."

"Mane-Eac, you and AldenSong didn't sign up for this," I say. "I want you two to get north, regroup, and then—"

"Don't you start," she counters, putting a finger in my face. "Don't you damn well start with your needy savior complex. You think because you were part of this *Hackers' Haven* that you were the only one *fighting the good fight*?" Mane-Eac keeps her eyes locked on mine. She crosses her arms and says, "DoGoodR and I were fighting this fight while you and Mister Positivity here were coming after us."

And there it is: the hidden war none of us ever speaks about. The thought had crossed my mind that, when us hackvicts kept hackers out of our systems, we were keeping out The Nameless. While Cyfib tortured us in his prison, I never thought about a team of hackers on the outside trying to take down Poseidon United and the Mercator Agency. Trying to win our freedom. In all honesty, in my heart, part of me sure hoped there were hackers trying to stop us.

Still, like a good little soldier, I fought their crusade every chance I got.

I break eye contact with her, staring at a drain on the concrete floor. "I'm sorry."

"Are you?" she asks, rage forcing Mane-Eac's body to tremble as she snatches up her gear and bug-out bag. "You know what? Screw you. You want to stay? Do it. But I'm not busting your ass out of jail again."

My left raised eyebrow asks my question for me.

"You didn't know?" Mane-Eac asks, leaning against a desk.

"Wait," starts Aldy. "I contacted Mr. Longfellow, and he got the IDs, the body doubles, and the disposable vehicle."

"And who took out the external cameras?" asks Mane-Eac.

I want to argue. I escaped by skill with a dash of luck. But the way I got out of Hackers' Haven with no lasting alarms or security tazing Barca and myself...

"How did you do it?" I ask.

"You mean, erhm, how did DoGoodR do it?" With closed eyes, Mane-Eac shakes her head. "He got access through Poseidon's main servers, recorded clean, non-escaping footage, and ran it on loop."

Mane-Eac runs her hand through her dyed hair. When a little of the red coloring comes off on her hands, she stops and rubs her hands together.

"It wasn't the first time we tried to get you out. The other time, well, there were...complications..."

At this point, my brain can only handle so much bad news, so I grab the laptops that are wrapped in the Faraday bag and shove everything in my bug-out bag.

A chime on the laptop goes off, and my nostrils clear as Rusty leans over it. She glances around the room and says, "Printer is upstairs, so how about Marcel Marceau comes with me and gets the hologram adhesive for the passports?"

I take the hint and join Rusty upstairs. Once we reach the top of the stairs, Rusty closes the door behind her and says, "Up here, we can talk, but nothing specific, understood?"

"Vague is my middle name," I quip, though my heart isn't in it.

Rusty reaches into her pocket and grabs a pack of nicotine gum. She offers me a piece and, even though I'm not a smoker, I take her up on it. Upon my first chew, a numbing sensation covers my tongue and the inside of my cheek.

"So, where's the printer?" I ask, glancing around.

"Better yet, where's your head at? Because it's not on staying alive and staying out of jail." She drags me by the hand into the kitchen, turns on the microwave, turns on the faucet, and flicks the switch to the garbage disposal.

Rusty goes to the fridge and pulls out a pitcher of water with slices of cucumber and lemon floating in it. She offers me a glass, but I shake my head. After she pours herself one and takes a swig, Rusty looks me over.

"If you don't go north, you get caught," she says. I watch the water; the condensation on the outside of Rusty's glass forms and drips droplets on the counter as I assemble my thoughts.

"Rusty, I can't remember how much I shared with you about my life during our...sessions..."

Rusty sips her water, then responds, "I know enough to say calling your life complicated is an understatement."

"True, true," I say, drinking straight from the faucet. After a gulp, I cut it off and wipe my face on my sleeve. A *ding* comes from the pantry, so Rusty opens the door, opens an oversized breadbox, and takes out a small laminate printer. She snatches three hologram adhesives from the printer's tray and holds the first to the overhead light. She repeats this two other times, and some printing criteria meet her internal expectations, so she returns the printer to its box and shuts the pantry door.

"You remind me of my kids," Rusty says, her eyes not really looking at me, but through me. "They went into the family business, but they did it their way. And kudos to them. At first, their father and I didn't want that. It's got its ups and downs, and I don't just mean sex or magic shows. I mean, part of it is about working with family, and that's a beast." Rusty takes in a long gulp before she adds, "And that bunch you've got down there is anything but Brady Bunch right now. So, if you're going to go it alone, this breather might be the refresher you need."

"Where you go, I go," comes a voice from the basement stairs.

You know, for a big guy, AldenSong sure can sneak his ass into a plan.

Chapter Fifty

Hella Dangerous

I wait a good five minutes before I cut on the guest shower, letting Mane-Eac and Aldy use the water pressure in the main shower. And, just like I predicted, my crew used most of the hot water. For once, I'm thankful for the cold shower. It reminds me of the Memphis hostel I stayed in prior to this fuster-cluck which never had hot water. Danielle, the girl who dog-sat Funk Monster, told me this was intentional because *you can't cry in a cold shower.*

She was right. As I immerse myself in the cold, I shiver, but don't crack. *There'll be a time for it,* my gut tells me. But not now. Now is a time to compartmentalize this really shitty day and keep moving.

After I dry off with the softest towel I've ever felt, I find a change of clothes on the guestroom's bed: plain white socks, Wrangler blue jeans, and a gray T-shirt for the Memphis Grizzlies. Checking myself out in the standing mirror in the corner, I realize I look like a tourist.

The perfect undercover ensemble.

A knock comes from the closed door. By the time I say, "Come in," Mane-Eac's already in the room. She's dressed in a similar getup: white jeans and a Graceland shirt. Her eyes meet mine, but then she looks at my clothes.

"You look like a sad store mannequin," she says. "Like one they discontinued, but the store is too cheap to drop you in the dumpster."

I respond, "Yeah, I would've gone for *Obsessed Elvis Fan*, but I think you've got that market cornered."

"Aw, we could've been twinsies..." she chuckles and lets her sentence trail off. And then the awkward silence we were both desperately trying to avoid engulfs the room like someone just yanked a cord on an emergency flotation device. We both owe each other apologies for so many things, not just for what we said earlier. The very thought of listing them might make me break down. The only thing that stops it is that I'm still chilly from my shower.

"If I were trying to pull the shit you are, would you try to stop me?" she says, breaking the silence.

"One hundred percent," I reply without hesitation.

"But would you ultimately let me do it?" she asks.

The words carry enough weight to pull my head down. "I...I don't know..."

"Rusty told me about your conversation." Mane-Eac steps closer to me. Someone once said that the only pain worse than your own is seeing the pain of others. That's what I find when I meet Mane-Eac's gaze and her eyes well with tears.

I clear my throat and say, "If you're worried about me getting caught and ratting, I already found the COA in the bottom of Rusty's bug-out bag." I pull out the sealed, little dime-sized Ziplock and put it in my palm. The lone pill in it almost glimmers from the window's light. Mane-Eac and I completed enough suicide-run level hacks to know what this Ziplock really contained: the only way to keep everyone else safe if you're caught.

"I've got mine as well." Mane-Eac closes my hand and wraps both of hers around mine. "But I'm saying this out loud, so it makes it real. I'm speaking it out into the universe." She looks me dead in the eyes and says, "I'm not burying another friend."

"Mane-Eac, I'll be—"

"You're not hearing me," she interrupts. "Like you, I'm prepared to do what it takes. If necessary. But we're not letting it get to that point. Just because we're willing to go to greater depths than our enemies doesn't mean we openly choose those deep dives. All it means is that we're fighting like we've already lost. Maybe we have. Maybe we're just circling the drain. But we're going to take out as many of those sons of bitches as possible before we go down for good."

I snicker. "Because it's not *if*, but *when*, they get us, so we've got nothing else they can take from us."

She squeezes my hand and says, "And that makes us hella dangerous." When our eyes meet, Mane-Eac takes her right hand and strokes the left side of my face. Then she stretches back and gives me a light tap on the chest as we release. "You tell anyone I care, I'll feed you your testicles." She smiles and points back at me as she leaves my room. "And, just because I'm in the land of maple leaves and maple syrup, won't mean I will not bust my ass trying to figure out how the Mercator Agency and Poseidon United got ahead of us."

She heads out the door. I wonder if this is the last time I'll see Mane-Eac without prison bars between us.

As I brace myself to leave as well, the hair on my neck stands up. Maybe it's sensing the strong winds coming from inside, a natural disaster brewing. From inside my room, a clock dings, signaling the hour. The tone is a higher register than I expected, like the beep you'd hear in a hospital.

And that's exactly where my mind takes me.

Chapter Fifty-One

Tai-Atari

Y EARS AGO

Since I called 911 for Mrs. Lin's collapse, her six days in ICU passed as quickly as a thought and also dragged on like a midday summer sun. Over this time, we'd met with a half dozen doctors, taken countless body scans, and come up with a doozy of a prognosis: Lung Cancer. Stage Four.

What's worse was that I'd never seen Mrs. Lin smoke. Maybe it came from one of her old work environments. Or maybe it was genetics. Hell, maybe it's Maybelline. Whatever it was, it's got the worst diagnosis on the menu: terminal.

Since we got to the hospital, the staff went above and beyond to take care of us, like we're gonna tip them or something. Mrs. Lin hadn't missed a snack or had an empty juice glass since she checked in. Everyone here worked like clockwork making sure Mrs. Lin got attention, updates, and twice-a-day assisted walks around the fourth floor. Throughout all of this, Mrs. Lin didn't once chide me for calling that ambulance. For violating her instructions and her trust.

In the early morning light, I held this blowing ball device for Mrs. Lin. It had a tube connected to three cylinders complete with ping-pong looking balls. The goal of this torture device was for Mrs. Lin to get her lungs strong enough to lift all three balls in the air. Yesterday, Mrs. Lin got the third ball to wiggle in its base. Today, she struggled to get the second ball to raise.

I wonder what tomorrow will bring.

I sat down next to Mrs. Lin on the hospital room's couch that turned into a foldout bed. I'd tried sleeping on the bed part, but I wasn't the biggest fan of jagged springs stabbing me as I slept, so I'd taken to sleeping on top of the pleather monstrosity. When your friend is dying, you don't complain about poor sleeping conditions.

One of the machines in the corner was what Mrs. Lin called the vacuum from hell. *This particular torture device pumped gas into her lungs where it caused uncontrollable nausea. She'd wretched up, from her lungs, enough green shitty-looking tar to repave Bourbon Street.*

The beeping of machines had increased since yesterday. When she was admitted almost a week ago, it was just a heart monitor. Then a breathing one. Now, I think they're just grabbing spare Nintendos and plugging them up because this beeping guarantees restless sleep.

Exhausted from her physical therapy, Mrs. Lin closed her eyes and leaned back on her scratchy sackcloth pillow. She removed her coke bottle glasses and dropped them on the bedside table. Despite drinking juice and rubbing Vaseline on her lips, they'd still cracked. The hospital air felt like it was sucking the moisture straight out of my pores. And the cold hospital lights sapped Mrs. Lin's usually glowy skin.

Deep down, I knew the reason for Mrs. Lin's decline wasn't from the air or lack of light. These were the lies I gladly told myself. It was easier than accepting the hard, punishing, and penultimate truth: Mrs. Lin's failing body wasn't something anyone could fix.

Including me. I shook my head like an Etch A Sketch, hoping to dissolve the bad thoughts. Instead, they settled into the crevices of my brain and became all I could think about. It'd been, what, five, no, six months since Mrs. Lin took me in. Why did it feel equally like it was yesterday and that we'd always lived like this?

"Oh, dear, I know that look," Mrs. Lin rasped. "You've got to poop."

Not ready for a joke, I attempt a comeback, but my body needed the laugh, so I choked on my words and embraced the moment. So did Mrs. Lin. We laughed like we'd just watched the funniest skit ever.

And then her coughing returned to steal the little sliver of joy we'd just made for ourselves. I rubbed her back which through the thin hospital gown felt like paper-thin ice. Mrs. Lin's body's slowing its internal warmth. The doctors warned us about this.

Mrs. Lin was a CPU whose motherboard had already overheated. Her system was just running through the motions until the final crash. Until her blue screen of death became a genuine one. And there wasn't a damn thing I could do to stop it.

"Tanto, I'm sorry," Mrs. Lin started. "I've put you in a predicament..."

"Hush it, Mrs. Lin," I said, my tone more serious than playful. "We're going to get you out of here and home in no time."

"Oh, my little dagger," Mrs. Lin said. "I may be going home, but not the way one would hope."

Invisible fishhooks snared my eyelids and sealed them shut. My legs lost their usefulness, and I sat on the bed's edge. The beeping of machines seemed louder now. That's when Mrs. Lin rested her heavily IV'd hand on my neck. The slightest heat emanated from under her cold fingers.

In that moment, I was no longer a hardened sixteen-year-old who'd run away from home. I wasn't the screwup who stole, robbed, and scammed people to stay alive. I was a boy about to lose his mama, and I wasn't ready for that.

"Lay back, little dagger..." Mrs. Lin's words, though sweet, almost hypnotized me. I crawled into the space between Mrs. Lin's right arm and leg. She wrapped one arm under my head and the other over my body.

And I cried. It wasn't even a good cry, like the ones you see in movies. The ones where you rage, wail, and throw punches in the air. This cry was like the safety drain on a bathtub: my body was too full of pain, and I needed to let a little bit out to keep the tub from overflowing.

"Let me tell you a story," said Mrs. Lin. I'd learned that when someone ever started a sentence with a preface like that, you were going to hear that story, willingly or not. "I was born in Ogimachi, Japan. My father was a surgeon and my mother was a nurse. I had one brother, but he was much older than me. I was, how do you say, an Oopsie Baby." Mrs. Lin chuckled, coughed, and caught her breath before she continued. "Japan had entered the war the summer of '37. Against my father's wishes, my brother Haruto joined up. The Nippon military tested the...aptitude and skills of all applicants. My brother passed with literal flying colors — they selected him for the aviation academy."

With what could've been a shudder or a swallow, Mrs. Lin continued.

"My mother and father tried to talk him out of it, but Haruto felt the call from his warrior ancestors, whatever that meant. The day my family snuck aboard the, curses, I can't remember its name, large boat headed to America. Unfortunately, we had one suitcase more than we had passengers in our party..."

I'd read those requirements in some World War II book: every passenger brought only one piece of luggage.

"We'd hoped Haruto would surprise us, that he'd come to his senses," Mrs. Lin said, her voice raising an optimistic octave at the end of her sentence. *"I remember staring out at the dock, straining, willing my eyes to focus in on every person watching the boat leave. And not a one of them looked like my brother."*

Mrs. Lin ran her fingers through my shoulder-length dirty blond hair before she continued.

"When we got to America, my father went to work in the steel mill and my mother cleaned houses. It wasn't the life we had back in Japan, but what we had, well, it was ours. I remember listening to those great radio shows, like The Shadow, *with my father. We loved following a vigilante that knew the system was broken, and only he could fix it. We lived in San Diego, and it was a tough time to be Japanese in America. But we made it work. Until the camps."*

This time, I knew the shudder came from me. I'd seen the documentaries on the Japanese camps and, while the internment camps that our government set up for the Japanese weren't what the Nazis had, they also weren't necessary. They were optional horrors that this great country chose to do to its huddled masses.

"My father was allowed to leave the camp and go to work, since the mill was helping the war effort," said Mrs. Lin. *"Then, one day, a support beam gave way under the section my father worked in. Witnesses say he pushed two men out of the way, but couldn't get himself clear."*

Something wet and warm hit the back of my neck, and I patted Mrs. Lin's hand as she sniffled and cleared her throat.

"It was easier for the doctors to tell us which few bones weren't shattered than list what were," she said, her voice small yet determined. *"My mother and I huddled around a cot in a hospital. There were no machines, only the march of time keeping track of how soon he would pass. My father's eyes were always open, always scanning that room. He*

had one eye in this world, and one in the next. Then he started talking about lights and family and he really scared me. I remember grabbing his shoulders and shaking him. Then, right before the light left his eyes, he looked at me. I mean, really looked at me. And said one last thing."

The back of my neck was now coated with warm tears. I didn't wipe them with my hand; they were part of this moment.

"He said, It's going to be okay...and then, like that, he went from just seeing us to seeing everything."

The blood pressure machine followed its timed inflation routine and filled Mrs. Lin's cuff tight enough that I felt her heartbeat, as shallow as it was, thrumming against my back. When the machine released its death grip, Mrs. Lin continued.

"Two days later, my mother read an article in the paper about the success of the Shinpū Tokubetsu Kōgekitai pilots, the Special Attack Unit. Americans would know as Kamikazes... that's where the pilots used the planes as tai-atari..."

"A body attack machine," I said. I couldn't tell you how I knew that translation. Maybe it was in a book Mrs. Lin read me.

"Yes, little dagger," said Mrs. Lin. "I...knew my brother died in the war. Even though we received nothing about his death. I don't know if the Americans shot his plane down, or he was successful in his tai-atari. All I do know is that my brother lived to kill and that my father died so that others may live. I've lived my life as best I can. Tanto, get me out of here and take me somewhere peaceful."

That afternoon, when the hospital staff changed shifts, I powered off Mrs. Lin's machines without setting off any alarms, unhooked her, and wheeled her out without a hitch.

It would be our last time together, and it's something I wouldn't trade for all the seafood in NOLA.

Chapter Fifty-Two

Dog

AldenSong and I stop at the closest gas station to fill up. There's no one else around, so I let Funk Monster out. On the ground, I find a switchblade. Correction: a switchblade comb that I flick open and chuckle about.

"I always wanted one of these as a kid," I say, shoving it into my belt loop. Sure, it has germs and who knows what else on it. Lice is the last concern for my bald head.

AldenSong is whistling away as he pumps. Something in the air, besides the gas fumes, tickles my nostrils.

It starts with a growl from Funk Monster that I wrongly ignore. Then, as AldenSong's soft eyes meet mine, something happens. He winces and turns his gaze toward the sidewalk away from the door. When he turns back, Aldy's gaze goes soft. His eyes roll up, and he mumbles one word.

"Run..."

I'm on my feet the moment Aldy hits the ground. A dart protrudes from the side of his neck.

That's when I feel it: a sharp pain, as if the world's meanest hornet just stung the hell out of me. Even though I know what's happening, I still have to touch the metal dart sticking out of the side of my neck.

And then I turn to face the figure that, even though the world wobbles and my vision fades, I'd recognize the shape of that son of a bitch anywhere.

As I hit the ground, the bastard holsters his dart gun, walks over, and leans over me with his long, blond hair dangling across my face.

As his pointy nose nicks mine, Cyfib merely greets me as the darkness overtakes my body.

"Hello, dog…"

Chapter Fifty-Three

Coffin

Wave after wave crashes down on me, thick and clingy, like syrup or molasses. I think it's nighttime, or at least the sun hides behind a suffocating black sky. I look for land or a ship. I find none. Only an oddly shaped rectangle in the distance, which turns on its end and sinks into the sludge.

A sliver of gray light cracks the sky. It doesn't show me land; it shows me what I'm actually swimming in.

Blood. Red currents slam into me, knocking my head under the crimson. And there's something floating in the goo. I scoop up a handful, hold it near the gray light, and see the oddities: tiny ones and zeros, the size of matchbooks. These basics of computer code swell in the blood like evil sea monkeys. They go from matchbook size to playing cards. To VHS tapes. To loaves of bread.

Then, from underneath, a magnetic pull yanks me down. Somehow, I'm able to keep my eyes open in the crimson and code. I spot a coffin below, its door open and its interior beckoning me.

I break the surface and my burning lungs scramble for air. All around me, the dichotomous code grows as my ability to take a deep breath diminishes. By the time the code is the size of a movie poster, I'm gasping as it crushes me.

When the binaries reach the size of automobiles, they overtake me. Submerge me. Pushing me deeper and deeper, until they shove me in a coffin as its lid closes shut.

Chapter Fifty-Four

Zero

I'm freezing. It's not from the dream of drowning; it's from a bucket of ice water that the world's biggest bastard just doused me with.

There's a tightness at my right love handle that I can't quite place, like there's something jamming in there. I try to move my arms, but they're pinned behind me with plastic zip ties.

While handcuffs can be picked, zip ties can be broken.

"Hello, princess..."

Shit. I glance to my right. Seamlessly morphing in and out of the wall is Barca. I can't tell if it's his damn ghost or my meds and concussions uniting to fight my psyche.

I toss my bald head back and spit a mouthful of water in my captor's face. He doesn't even flinch. Instead, he grabs my T-shirt by the collar, yanks hard enough for it to rip and to give my neck a rope burn, and wipes his ugly mug.

"You are a hard little mutt to track down," says Cyfib, his gray eyes focused in on me. "But, you are not as smart as you think you are, and you are as predictable as the rising sun."

"Where's Aldy?" I ask. I can't see him anywhere in the room. "Where is my dog? If you've hurt either of them, I'll kill you."

"Your threat is cute," begins Cyfib as he straightens up and walks over to one of the room's two double beds. On the farthest one is Funk Monster, hiding in the pillows. "She is an obedient dog, and you know that I only correct dogs when they misbehave." Cyfib reaches out to pet her, but Funk Monster buries herself deeper in the bedding, out of his reach.

"As for the large one, he is not my mistake. Someone else let that pup out of its kennel. But you..."

"Tell me where he is, you asshole," I order, though I have no leverage or power to make this cocksucker answer me. "Please..."

No harm in letting him think I'm broken, or at least breaking. The lightest of smiles crosses the face of my former warden before his stoic demeanor returns. "Even though he took the same dosage as you, that dog is still asleep in the hotel bathtub."

I master any indication of the relief I'm feeling. I guess I have more of a tolerance to drugs than Aldy. However, I'm also not giving this robotic bastard that satisfaction. I pretend to stretch my neck as I examine the other double bed. On top of it, Cyfib has laid out all of our gear: Passports. Money. Cyanide pills. Even the laptops, two USB flash drives, and the torn Faraday bag.

My gaze must've lingered too long, because Cyfib picks up the closest laptop. "What is on here?" From the illuminated green light on the side of it, I know my old warden already powered it on. I bet he's even cracked my encryption.

He's not asking, he's confirming.

"Junk," I respond.

"Obviously," counters Cyfib as he turns the screen away and punches keystrokes. "But this is not your junk, so it makes it your treasure. That makes it...interesting."

I take the time to really look at Cyfib's appearance, beyond the cursory glance. For the first time since my incarceration, he's not in a pressed white dress shirt. His wrinkled and stained clothes do not fit the *all-powerful warden* I remember. The bags under his eyes and two days of facial stubble do not fit this man who believed that all of us *dogs* needed more *cleanliness,* more *sterility* in our lives.

Cyfib is just like us: on the run.

He's unplugged the television, as well as the telephone. The smoke detector dangles from the ceiling, its battery missing. Cyfib has even unscrewed the wall sockets. And he's not only drawn the shades to keep prying eyes out, but sealed them with either glue or staples.

The enemy of my enemy is my friend.

Most people credit Winston Churchill with saying this about the Axis Power Germany choosing to fight a two-front war against their then-ally Russia. If I remember correctly, many cultures have a similar saying, but it was young and imprisoned Bushi Yoshida Shōin who said it best after he befriended his rival in prison:

When bitter rivals unite, their fortitude triples, not doubles.

Of course, the same rival later betrayed Shōin, which ultimately led to his decapitation, but I'll deal with that executioner's sword when I'm out of these restraints.

"It's the excess cache and junk files from Poseidon United," I say, meeting Cyfib's gaze. "Our hack...didn't go as planned."

"Naturally," says Cyfib, smugness covering that lone word. "Have you sifted through the data yet?"

"No, sir," I say, as the word *sir* bitters my tongue. I need Cyfib offguard. Plus, I need to know what he knows, so I slip back into *docile prisoner* mode. "We haven't had time."

"We all have the same number of hours in the day, dog," snipes Cyfib.

I've missed his smart mouth like a slug misses salt.

Cyfib reaches into his pocket and pulls out his own flash drive. It looks just like the one I stole from his office when I escaped. The one that Kilroy has in his possession, complete with the names of several prisoners, the complete schematics of the LODIS, and my Gakunodo software.

This gives me an idea. "They let you keep your administrative key when they cut you loose?"

"Those short-sighted fools did not even leave me with the clothes on my back," he starts, turning the flash drive around and around in his hands. "They only left me with my life because they needed a scapegoat. Simple as that."

"So, they paroled you...sir?" I ask. The tightness in my waist returns with the word *sir*, so I move my zip-tied hands to that side when Cyfib looks away.

"Ah, parole..." Cyfib shoves his flash drive into my computer and enters commands I cannot see. Probably transferring all of those stolen, yet useless, files to his drive.

What's he expecting to find? Though it's not like I knew what to expect to find on there either.

Cyfib paces the room before he runs his fingers through his long hair and says, "Parole was a concept that Cussh came up with."

He knows Poseidon's CEO personally?

"You've met him before?" I ask.

Cyfib snickers. He keeps his gaze away from me, like he's studying the far wall for answers. That suits me well, because I've realized what is causing that jabbing pain in my side: it's the found switchblade comb.

If only it was a real blade.

"How well do you know him?" I ask, trying to keep him thinking as my right finger grazes the comb. "I bet he's a powerful ally to have."

Unfortunately, this last question produces the opposite of what I wanted: Cyfib's full attention. He turns and stands over me. His right hand grasps my throat and squeezes, with eyes blazing. Stars burst before my eyes as the trapped air in my lungs starts a fire of its own.

"Sincaid Cussh owes me everything," Cyfib says through gritted teeth. "Everything!"

From the bathroom comes a muffled, "Wh-what's going on?" Clearly, the warden's yell has awakened AldenSong. Cyfib releases me and reaches into his front pocket. From there, he withdraws a syringe.

"This kennel is getting loud," says Cyfib as he turns toward the bathroom.

I need Aldy awake if we're going to survive this, So, I do the one thing I can: I trip Cyfib. Unfortunately, my foot intertwines with his scuffed dress shoes. We fall together, Cyfib on his face and knees, and me over in the chair. The comb falls from my waistband as I hit the ratty carpet.

Blood trickles from the warden's nose as he says, "Bad...dogs get put down," and turns toward me with the syringe. My scrambling fingers find the comb, though I still can't get a grip.

Cyfib's eyes dart between me and the drop of fluid dripping from the open syringe.

"On second thought," he says and drops the needle on the wooden dresser. He rotates my chair so that my back is on the ground. I kick at him with my feet, but he scoots around my flailing legs. With one black shoe, he puts weight on my throat. I jam my chin toward his shoe, hoping to stop his foot from cutting off my air. He's just faster than I am.

Forget the air. It's like mastering breathing: an empty lung and a full lung both desire what the other already has. Focus on the comb...

Ignoring the slow burn in my chest, I spread my fingers wide like they're a giant spider using its legs to search for prey. Seconds pass, and still nothing. My chest demands a cough that I can't provide, so my body trembles.

Then, for no apparent reason, Cyfib lifts his foot. I suck in enough air for me and three other people. As I do, my fingers find the comb.

"As much as it would please me to end you, I need something from you," says Cyfib, his tone slightly optimistic.

I cough and say, "If it's a foot in the ass, I've, ugh, got two willing volunteers."

The warden chuckles as I scoop up the collapsed comb and extend it. Then I place it in the zip tie and twist using my fingertips. Again. And again.

"I will politely decline that offer and make a counter of my own," he says.

The tension of the comb/zip tie combo increases as my turning slows.

"Give me HydraPay, and I will let you all live."

And there we go. He needs the most basic of human requirements: money.

I don't even need to lie. "I no longer control it." I can't turn the comb anymore. A numbness spreads to both of my hands because the tension has cut off the circulation.

Cyfib leans over me. "I know," as he reaches into his pocket and pulls out a burner phone. "But she does."

It's a distant shot of Penny with Liam and Hazel in tow. Today's date is at the bottom of the picture. The implied threat is just the motivation I need to get the final push out of the comb. My numb hands break free, and I punch Cyfib straight in the nose and get to my feet.

He blows a blood booger out of his right nostril and wipes his bloody face with his white sleeve.

From behind him, the silhouetted ghost-Barca slow claps...

"It was always going to come to this," Cyfib says.

I go for the gold and swing for his jaw, hoping to knock his ass out but Cyfib easily dodges it. Hell, the Pony Express could've delivered that punch faster. Then my ribs explode from two body shots. I toss my right elbow up, a Hail Mary, but Cyfib catches it. He uses that momentum to spin around, putting me in a sleeper hold.

All hearing ceases as the thump of my trapped blood fills my ears. My face flushes as air eludes me. I scramble to reach anything, even shifting my weight to grab at the disconnected landline phone. All I manage to do is get a small *ching* sound out of the phone.

For some reason, that's enough to freeze both Cyfib and me for just a moment. It's unexpected but I'm not wasting the advantage. I reach up to gouge at Cyfib's eyes, but he turns his head. Instead of eye, I grab his long blond hair and pull.

"No!" he screams, releasing me.

In my hand is a blond wig.

This whole time, he was as bald as the day is long. On his head is the most vicious raised scar I've ever seen starting in the center of his head, spreading to both ears, and returning at the back of his head. A circle of keloid scarring.

Cyfib answers my unspoken question.

"Now you know just who Prisoner Zero was."

Chapter Fifty-Five

The Idea

In every medical case, there is the story of the first infected, but no one ever calls this person Patient One. They are always Patient Zero, because all the other patients' symptoms, ailments, and even deaths are linked to this individual. Oftentimes, Patient Zero contains not only the disease, but a way to the cure.

What the hell kind of cure did they try to come up with by cutting into Cyfib's brain? I think, staring at the man who I only ever envisioned as a monster, never a victim. Never in my wildest dreams did I think that the Mercator Agency had once incarcerated Cyfib.

What in the world did he do to go from prisoner to warden?

Cyfib extends his hand for his wig. The motion is slow, pleading. Even though I hate him one one-thousandth less, we're still not simpatico by a long shot. He's still the man who tortured me. AldenSong. Quidlee. I toss the wig on the far bed. As far as I'm concerned, it's Funk Monster's newest chew toy.

"Go and get my hair, dog." Cyfib doesn't move toward the bed. He's off-balance but not defeated. I keep my expression stone-faced, though I hear Aldy's feet thumping around in the tub. I want to go help my friend, but now is not the time to turn my back on this cyborg.

"What did they do to you?" I ask, wanting to hear the horror from the monster's lips.

"My hair," commands Cyfib.

"Answer me, or I let the pup go to town on it. And she's in heat."

A flash of rage floats through his eyes before Cyfib takes one of the two plastic chairs in the room. His eyes meet mine, then he does something I didn't think he was capable of.

He cries.

He could be acting. His goal is the data, the wig, and control. Always control.

Still, I take the other chair across from him. A car alarm sounds outside, but stops after a yelling match starts and finishes between two unseen men. In this time, Cyfib's eyes bore into a spot on the stained carpet, probably preparing his story.

Or building his lie.

"With two others, I created DISRUPT," he begins. Wrecking ball hackers that terrorized the DOD at the start of the commercialized Internet. Way before The Nameless. Before the infamous hacktivists Anonymous. DISRUPT were the digital boogeymen, and every hacker wanted to be one of them.

"We were...betrayed by one of our own," Cyfib says as his focus shifts to the ceiling. I can't tell if his eyes roll up to the right or left. If I could, maybe I could tell if he was telling the truth or producing a lie. "Cussh."

"Poseidon United's CEO," I say.

"He...does not deserve that job," counters Cyfib as his eyes float over to the closed blinds. "My other...comrade was incarcerated along with me. They... experimented on us. With the first surgery, I drew the short straw." After a hard swallow, Cyfib continues as his fingers trace his scar. "They installed my discipline chip a little deeper than yours."

A wave of nausea hits; I choke it down.

Cyfib continues. "The brain does not feel pain; just regulates and reports it. That was their theory. What...they did not...predict was how the chip would react to submersion and long-term gestation in a living brain."

I think about my own two tracking and discipline chips: the Tic Tac that later became a Skittle. The pain it applied to my body with just a push of a button still haunts my dreams.

On the other end of that button, was Cyfib.

"Who thought about opening your head up and putting a chip?"

"That bastard, Adam Kissiah," answers Cyfib.

I know that name, but I can't place it.

Cyfib correctly reads my confused face. "In the '70s, Kissiah was a mostly deaf NASA engineer. Coupling that with his background in telemetry, electronic sensing, and sound, vibration sensors and NASA's tech, Kissiah developed the first cochlear implant using digital pulses to transfer sound and stimulate auditory nerve endings."

I'd read studies about implants before, but never in the brain. The average body temperature is 98.6, though the brain's internal temperature can get as high as 104 during times of stress or effort. That means Cyfib's implant not only was a tracking and disciplinary tool; it's possibly an infection that's been cooking, rotting, and corrupting him for over a decade.

Maybe this tiny computer in Cyfib's head changed him into the hardened bastard before me.

On the other hand, once a bastard, always a bastard.

"Look, I'm not one to ever suggest animal test subjects, but what made them think this would work on a human?" I ask.

Cyfib chuckles bitterly. "When the odds are against a patient's survival of a radical procedure, you cannot ask for a better guinea pig than a person without human rights."

Even though he says this and my heart aches slightly, this is still the mega-bastard that violated our rights. Every. Single. Day.

"One day, another prisoner and I decided to escape," says Cyfib. "We figured that, if we made it out of the prison's perimeter, the implants would not have a source to lock onto. So, one night, we made it out of the prison, much the same way you did…"

"Hold up," I interrupt. "You used something to climb the fence?"

"No, dog," chides Cyfib. "The door that you and that dead dog used on the south end when you were practicing your escape."

My sinuses clear when I hear Cyfib knew about our practice run. "How'd you know about that?"

"Because I'm the one that gave you the idea."

Chapter Fifty-Six

Tsunami

I shake my head, refusing to believe what I've just heard. I have close to a photographic memory, so I close my eyes and run every conversation I can remember with Cyfib. None of them even closely resemble any type of prison break.

Something still feels incredibly off, like I'm trying to shave my face while looking in a fun house mirror, so I just retort, "You're lying."

"Oh, if you only opened your eyes, dog, you would see we are not that different." His statement actually stings my eyes and also brings back my desire to vomit.

Outside the window, a girl chats on a cellphone. As she passes, Cyfib shudders, then twitches, and resumes talking.

"My chip...reacts badly to electrical transmissions..."

Without thinking, I ask, "The rage?"

Cyfib opens his mouth, then closes it, and merely nods. In this moment, I'm not Tanto. I'm not a former prisoner in front of his evil warden. No, I'm a little boy, watching his Bushido stories on a grainy VHS tape, sitting way too close to a shitty television. I'm watching *Yojimbo*, the Kurosawa flick, starring Toshirô Mifune as a Sanjuro

Kuwabatake, a Ronin who works for both sides of warring Yakuza crime families.

I might've been seven or eight when I first watched it. I remember realizing there were no heroes in it, only villains. And then I felt terrible because, if we live in a world of only villains, then the need for heroes is gone. And that's a world I never wanted to see happen.

Cyfib is no Sanjuro Kuwabatake, nor is he some innocent corpse that someone made into Frankenstein's monster. He's a man who made bad choices, but for which his punishment exceeded his crimes.

"What happened after you escaped?"

"Oh, that was only the goal of my fellow prisoner," starts Cyfib. "No, I met with the...someone higher up prior..."

There's something about the way Cyfib spits out the words *higher up* that makes me realize this isn't just about the person who ran the prison. It's also more than the man behind Cyfib's surgery. It's personal.

"Your warden was Cussh, wasn't it?"

Cyfib turns his gaze to the window. "Worse. He was Director of Prison Security, over my technology prison and several formal ones. But I told him the day he put me behind his bars, *you betrayed me for your position, so if I can escape your prison, I get to run it.*"

I know ambition when I see it, and there's something more here. I ask, "Why didn't you just escape?"

Cyfib snickers. "Because I knew other prisoners would arrive, and someone would need to look after them."

Look after them? Like some kind of guardian angel? Rage fills my body. This bastard's benevolence tank always ran empty. No, he's lying. He has to be. If he is anything like Kuwabatake from *Yojimbo*, it is in this line:

I'll get paid for killing, and this town is full of people who deserve to die.

"And what happened to the prisoner who tried to escape with you?"

Cyfib answers, "He was...disciplined..."

"You needed a fall guy for the jailbreak," I say, as the puzzle piece snaps into place. "You traded Kilroy's freedom for a promotion, didn't you?"

Cyfib's brow furrows. "Who is...ah..." A sliver of satisfaction dances across his face. "So, you know poor, gullible Leonard?"

Unbidden, a memory of my first meeting with Kilroy comes to mind.

'I know a lot, okay? I know about the missing hackers, the abductions, the torture...If I could ever get my hands on Prisoner Zero...'

"He's also not your biggest fan," I say, thinking back to that conversation.

"He is as harmful as a bug in a jar," retorts Cyfib.

A noise from the bathroom interrupts us as AldenSong stumbles out, eyes groggy, confused and, landing on Cyfib, furious. Seeing his best friend and his torturous warden chatting in a fleabag motel must've kicked Aldy's psyche like a mule. He stumbles, shakes his head, and stomps our way. "You son of a bitch..."

"Heel, dog," orders Cyfib, slamming the unplugged landline against the wall. The chime that comes from the phone echoes Cyfib's damned spurs, rocking me back unexpectedly. It clearly does the same for AldenSong.

In any case, Aldy shakes his head, ducks it, and charges, slamming into Cyfib and pushing both of them into the drywall.

Cyfib doesn't scream. He isn't fighting back.

He merely laughs.

Then Aldy balls up his fist and slams it into the warden's pointy nose, screaming, his voice full of rage, pain, and tears. He yanks Cyfib from the wall, slamming him to the carpet. The phone, too, drops. Its chime brings a painful blink from me, but I shake it away.

Aldy raises his fist high.

"This is for SweetThree!" One of our fellow hackvicts who Cyfib pushed to suicide. In the end, all that was left of him was a bag of ashes and his noose: a bloody Ethernet cable.

Smash.

"That's for letting Barca destroy what we built!"

Smash.

"And this one's for Quidlee..."

After each blow, Cyfib cackles, though the blood in his mouth muffles the laughs more and more.

AldenSong raises his arms high, winding up for a two-handed haymaker.

Cyfib grabs the landline, pulling it up to block the blow. Aldy smacks the phone, and a deafening chime fills the room.

In an eerily calm moment that follows, Cyfib says two words. Two words that every hackvict in Hackers' Haven knew were part of a celebration. Comradery. Flat out hacking.

"Burn bright."

And then everything I've known — no, everything I've *forgotten* about my time in Hackers' Haven, hits me like a tsunami.

Chapter Fifty-Seven

Jericho

*I*mages, sounds, even smells, pop before me in an overwhelming flood. *I'm in this shitty motel and I'm also back in Hackers' Haven. I know this is the past, but right now, I'm living this flashback. It is as real as the air I'm breathing.*

I'm in the War Room, our command center in Hackers' Haven where us hackvicts hunted others, protected some, and attacked those that threatened the servers and organizations under our protection. To my right, PoBones, our Cajun comedian, works away on his terminal with his tiny New Orleans Saints helmet on his workstation, probably setting up some bait and tackle to lure in our prey. To my left, AldenSong is clickety-clacking away, possibly initiating a dam-break, all the while his little hula girl totem sways her hips side to side. And, in front of me is my terminal and my totem: an empty orange prescription pill bottle.

"I was midway through my second bottle of rum, when I realized, doing shots of it on an empty stomach was gonna ruin my Mardi Gras," says PoBones.

"Why were you shooting rum?" asks AldenSong.

PoBones responds, "Because it was my favorite type."

"Bacardi?" asks Aldy.

"Free!" cackles PoBbones.

The hackvicts laugh, and that's when I hear the war drums chiming in the background:

Cha-ching.

Cha-ching.

Cha-ching.

Those damned spurs of the warden rise from behind me. Just his presence in the room is enough to tighten my sphincter. When you add in those cha-chings, my asshole could well crush a diamond.

"Dogs," says the warden, stomping his spurs, the ringing overtaking any other sounds. "Burn bright."

With those two words, I am blasted from a vivid, well-known mem-ory into something new. Like how after a night of drinking you don't remember that you took a dump in a urinal until your friend reminds you. That's when your brain dusts off and everything becomes clearer, though not crystal.

In this memory haze, my eyes glue to the monitor as my fingers rest on the keyboard. My eyes refuse to blink as various code zooms on the screen.

"Dogs, who is knocking on our doors?" asks Cyfib.

"I'm attempting a trace," comes a voice, almost as robotic as Cy-fib's. It's PoBones, who never spoke without some Coastie-Meets-Daquiris twang in his dialect.

"Work faster, dog." Cyfib paces as cha-chings *follow in his wake.*

"Sir, I have a possible contact," says AldenSong, his voice also zom-bie-like. "It is AES-encrypted."

"Tell me the level," demands Cyfib, his voice flat and a bit annoyed. Aldy answers, "256-bit."

"Impressive," says the warden. "Someone spent the big dollars to pre-vent our counter-hack. Time required to break through?"

"Full team effort, sixteen hours, nine minutes," answers AldenSong.

I can't turn my head, but I feel the warden's sigh.

"That is acceptable," he says. "You have your orders. Burn fast."

At this point, my hands fly over the keyboard. I hear the conversations geared only on the hack. I even participate in some, whether or not I have a choice.

Time has passed, but I can't tell how much. Cha-chings *announce that the warden has returned.*

"Burn bright," he says after he stomps. My hands stop mid-keystroke. "Report."

"We're through, sir, and have a latch on the assailant."

Those words don't come from Aldy or PoBones.

They come from me. And I have zero control over them.

"Alright, dogs, is the TPS report ready for my review?"

"Yes, sir," my ghost self says.

"Good," states Cyfib as he walks away. Then, as he stomps a cha-ching *from the stairs to his office, he says, "Burn down."*

"So, I was midway through my second bottle of rum, when I realized, doing shots of it on an empty stomach was gonna ruin my Mardi Gras," says PoBones.

"Why were you shooting rum?" asks AldenSong.

PoBones responds, "Because it was my favorite type."

"Bacardi?" asks Aldy.

"Free!" cackles PoBones.

Like a TiVo rewind button, everything has reset by thirty seconds. Everyone laughs, and several people yawn. Others mutter about being tired unexpectedly.

And, in my gut, I remember, this is one of the few good moments.

***

I'm a statue in this motel room. So is AldenSong. Everything, every molecule in my body, thrums. Every nerve, ever fiber in my body demands that I step forward. That I do something. Anything. But I can't even blink.

All we can do is watch as Cyfib crawls up from the shitty ass carpet and dusts himself off.

"You dogs certainly choose violence first," he says, sarcastically. "You have probably noticed a...sensitivity to bells and chimes. That is on us. I cannot fully condemn your proclivity for violence though, because it is certainly part of the...programming."

Programming. Holy shit. A thin needle of crystalized pain shoots through my brain, its barbed ends tearing at my precious memories and letting me know I've been living a lie...

AldenSong and I stare at our warden. I'm coiled, ready to act, like a dog anxiously awaiting its owner to throw a ball.

"Let us try this again." Cyfib grabs a hand towel from the bathroom and wipes his bloody nose as he points at me. "How do I gain access to HydraPay?"

"There is an FTP backdoor accessible using the early 2000s version of AppeFTP," I blurt out. I want to stop these robotic words marching from my mouth, partially because HydraPay is not just about me; it's about the people that aren't following the law *to a T,* but aren't bad people.

People like Penny.

"Why would you use such an outdated format of technology?" asks Cyfib.

"Because no one is looking for it, sir." The words that are mine, yet not-mine, bring a bit of bile with them.

"Ah..."

The approval in his voice is enough to turn my stomach.

The paralysis reminds me a bit of when I lost the ability to speak. I cannot speak about all pain, but losing the ability to converse, to share, to connect with another human being is a hell I wish on no one.

Except for this puppet master asshole in front of me.

"Username and password?" asks my puppet master.

"Username: Kurosawa," I say, with my mind and gut trying but failing to throw a *coup de grâce* against my throat. "Password: Iron-Monkey."

"Good," mutters Cyfib. "Good dog."

I want to explode. I want my body to turn into ball bearings going a hundred miles an hour and take this sucker with me upon eruption. Knowing now just a sampling of what he has done to us, makes me want to stop him from ever doing this to anyone ever again.

Cyfib strolls in front of us, then settles in front of AldenSong. "Dog, plug your ears." Aldy shoves his digits in his eardrums and Cyfib says, "Burn down."

I blast from my statuesque position to a full-on pissed-off croco-dile-on-crack attack. I'm on a mission of pure destruction. Any good-will or sympathy I have for Cyfib evaporates into the ether.

And this bastard waves me on like he is freaking Morpheus in *The Matrix.*

I slam into the sucker with all of my weight.

And he laughs.

I punch his kidneys over and over with everything I've got.

And he laughs.

Every single body blow I land, this masochist soaks it up.

"You really think you're the hero here, do you not, hero dog?" he asks, taunting me as he slaps the phone, produces a chime. "Were you a hero when you could not protect your dead friend from my replacement?"

***

I'm in The Hole, one of Hackers' Haven's disciplinary rooms right after that monster Barca ended Quidlee's life. The Hole brought a series of seemingly sporadic tortures: confined quarters where the oxygen was randomly pumped out. Unpredictable loud music. Eye-piercing lights. I remember all of that like it was yesterday.

I sat up from my corner on the concrete floor as the warden entered. His wavy blond hair and perfectly clean and pressed attire suiting him. I remember that.

What I don't remember is having damned company.

With one cha-ching *and a, "Burn bright," I'm seated at attention like a soldier waiting to respond to the drill sergeant. My new memory forms before my eyes. After the warden enters, so does Barca.*

Big beefy bastard Barca. He squats and waves his hand in front of me as if he's testing if I'm blind or something.

"Damn, man, you've got them trained like circus seals," he says.

"You will learn to what extent soon enough," Cyfib says, standing next to the crouching giant, resentment in his eyes. "Unless you care to contact Cussh and tell him you do not want the assignment."

"Ha!" roars Barca as he slaps my face. A fleshy fire runs across it, yet I don't react. Not don't — can't. "You've done an...adequate job so far, but I cannot wait to see what this crop can do under my leadership."

"Leadership..." He says the word as if it has a toxic taste. He points at me and says, "This dog excels at the LODIS, but is mouthy."

"Don't I know it?" retorts Barca as he slaps the other side of my face. "Oh, little dagger, I'm gonna do so many wonderful things to you and yours."

His breath smells of his favorite snack, Corn Nuts. Sweat drips down to my frozen lips. It catches on my stubble and itches like the blazes.

Yet I cannot scratch.

"Why did you kill the newest pup?" asks Cyfib.

"You give me too much credit," responds Barca. "I just gave him the incentive and the ingredients. The coward is the one who made the choice to mix the batch and cook it himself."

Like lightning hitting a clock tower, my body shakes, even under hypnosis. I never thought that Barca's mind games were the reason that Quidlee died. I always assumed it was Barca himself.

If only I'd been there for Quidlee instead of following my own foolish pride.

"You know, this little bastard thinks he can break out of here," says Barca as he sticks a finger in my left nostril, just to see if I'll react.

"I know," says Cyfib. "I recommended it."

"No shit?" rhetorically asks Barca. "Why'd you do that?"

"Because it will show management that we need more funds for security," he says. "Also, if any dog can get out of this pen, it is this mutt. There is a willfulness to this one that I...recognize."

"Aw..." says Barca as he stands and heads toward the door. "Y'all are just two peas in a pod."

Monster 2 leaves me with Monster 1 and Cyfib stares into my dead eyes before speaking.

"And that is just one reason I hate him...Burn down."

***

Back in reality, I'm a ball of rage and pain. My internal world shatters as I question everything that I know about myself and my life in Hackers'

Haven. It was only a few weeks ago that I thought I made the whole thing up; the flawless cover-up of the Double-H facility hit me right between the eyes.

"This has gone on long enough," Cyfib says, pushing me away and punching me in the gut so hard I taste my breakfast from two weeks ago. I collapse into a ball on the shitty carpet. He grabs the complimentary motel pen and pad, writes one word, and crumples it in his hand.

"You...released yourself from my custody just prior to the latest...updates to prisoner programming..." His measured words equally scare and piss me off as he drops the crumpled ball to the carpet. "On this paper is the only way to stop him. Do not forget the bell..."

"I don't understand," I say.

"Oh, you will," he says, with a smile that lets me know exactly *who* he is talking about.

I try to get to Cyfib before he unleashes Hell. I really do. But I'm not fast enough. He picks up the landline phone and slams it against the wall. And I'm not smart enough to cover the warden's lips before he utters a command that forever decimates the best friend I have in this world.

"Jericho."

Chapter Fifty-Eight

A Miracle

The primal roar of carnage that blasts from AldenSong's throat is not that of my friend. His enormous arms smashing the shitty particle board table are not at all the actions of my pacifist partner.

The fire in his eyes is equal parts anger and fear. My friend is in trouble.

Funk Monster buries herself deeper into the bed as Cyfib grabs his flash drive and heads to the door. AldenSong swings at him, but Cyfib dodges the punch and then slams the landline phone against the wall. This stuns AldenSong just long enough for this Hawaiian Hulk to turn his attention to the only other human in the room.

"Aldy…" I say, approaching the human wrecking ball. "It's me. Tanto."

A growl straight out of a werewolf flick rumbles from AldenSong's chest. He bull-charges me, knocking me straight through the thin motel wall, covering me in plaster and pain as I land on the bed in the next room. I cough dust and probably asbestos in the air as Aldy pins my arms to my chest with one hand and throws punches with the other. They're wild and inaccurate, so he misses my head a few times.

It's the accurate ones that ring my bell. A catcher's- mitt-sized fist pummels my face as caveman-level grunts erupt from Aldy. I dodge where I can, but he's too strong, too fast.

From the gaping hole in the wall, Cyfib watches us *dogs* do what he wants us to do: obey...and destroy.

"You don't have to do this!" I plead to Cyfib. "We can shut down Poseidon! We can expose Mercator!"

"That is not how the world works, dog," says Cyfib as a chunk of plaster falls onto his shirt. He brushes away the dust, a frown crossing his face. "They are unstoppable. If there was a way, all it would do is create another monster in its place. We are merely their tools, to be used and discarded."

After the next swing, I get one hand free and turn into Aldy's punch, leading with my forehead. Something pops in AldenSong's hand; the impact probably broke a couple of his bones on my hard noggin.

He doesn't even flinch.

Somehow, I get out from under AldenSong enough to dart toward the hole in the wall. Before I get there, AldenSong's arms wrap around my waist.

"You do not have to be what they made you into!" I scream at Cyfib right before Aldy chucks me across the room. I bash into the far wall, not hard enough to go through the drywall, but enough to get stuck in the sucker.

Yet even though Cyfib is clearly done with me, he stands exactly where I left him. When our eyes meet, he says, "There are no heroes left in this world, dog," as he swallows hard and checks his watch. "Only us ordinary monsters...do not forget to use the bell."

Cyfib opens and shuts the door to the shithole. Aldy's animalistic panting fills my ears as his bloodshot eyes zero in on mine. AldenSong rotates his Sumo-worthy body my way and squares his shoulders.

I can't take him, but I can stop him. To do so, I need two things.

Number One, the codeword on that crumpled pieced of paper.

Number Two, the phone's chime.

Actually, make that three things.

Number Three, a miracle.

Chapter Fifty-Nine

Kill

Everything in my body feels broken, jagged, and heavy. I'm a sock puppet that a pissed-off chihuahua just found under the washer and took out years of aggression on. Needless to say, I'm in damned pain.

AldenSong charges me again. Unlike all the other times, I'm counting on this one.

When he ducks his head, I sidestep him, but still catch the impact of his passing left arm. I turn Aldy's left wrist behind his back and touch his right ear with it like he is made of taffy. Aldy's shoulder slips out of socket, but he doesn't scream. Instead, he pushes me away, grabs his dead-ass arm, and shoves it back into the socket without effort.

It's enough time for me to get to the landline. I yank it into my chest as Aldy wraps his arms around me and spikes me into the carpet. Every trace of wind abandons my lungs like it owes me money. There, balled up against the metal frame, is the codeword. I extend my hand and snatch it up.

Before I can look at the word, AldenSong catches my arms and lifts me like I'm a ragdoll, nothing more than cloth. He dangles me, holding both my arms wide.

And I let this all happen because I only have one shot to do this right...

I drop the landline phone. Upon impact with the floor, the mountainous noise rattles both AldenSong and me. Luckily, I'm a split-second faster at getting my thoughts back to reality because, from my right hand, I uncrumple the paper that may just save my life.

"Lazarus," I say, with the ringing of the phone's chime still echoing in the room.

And just like that, AldenSong returns to normal. The skies part, and the sirens play harps or whatever they played when they weren't enticing sailors to crash their ships. Aldy and I hug and Funk Monster comes out of hiding. Then the three of us leave without any issues.

That's what I expected. And that is what I deserved.

What actually happened, well, was as opposite as oil and vinegar.

That asshole. That asshole Cyfib told me that the word on this paper is the only way to stop him.

The warden never told me it would kill Aldy.

Chapter Sixty

Saves the Day

How do you prepare yourself to answer the last question from your best friend? Do you go at it from a pragmatic point of view, weighing the situation and its literal meaning and address him like a human being at the end of his life? Do you take the high road and go all buttery optimistic and sugarcoat your lie?

Or do you lay down the cold, hard truth?

Before I answered AldenSong's question, it had to be asked. That's why Aldy's question, his last utterance, was not really a question; it was a shock. A plea. And, God forgive me, one I was not nearly ready for.

"T...?"

I should've known the truth before I said the code word. Because, deep down, I'm a coder. Coders understand the rules because the rules in life and the rules in computing can overlap. I mean, why wouldn't a hacker like me expect this? The Mercator Agency and Poseidon United took human beings, exploited a government loophole, and turned them into tools without human rights. They destroyed lives for an increase on a profit-and-loss spreadsheet.

Why wouldn't I assume two groups so overflowing with hackers wouldn't work some computing code into their hypnosis?

I say this because there are many common computing commands that are crucial for programming. No matter what happens, no matter how many steps or how grandiose the program becomes, there is always a final bit of code. This stops the program. Ends the procedure. Stops the sequence. And, whether or not the program succeeds in its purpose, this bit of code always has the final say.

End - Kill the program.

If Cyfib had told me the truth, that uncrumpling that ball of paper would give me the command to end my best friend's life, yet save my own, I'd have eaten that paper then and there.

But life doesn't present you with the question *and* the answer. It serves up a half-cooked plate of unknowns, makes you choose the seasoning, and then you get to chow down on a course of your own making.

And that's where I'm dining. Right now. I'm watching the life leave my friend's body as his brain hears my command and follows it. It starts with Aldy's eyes rolling back in his head. Followed by a foaming mouth. Then shakes as AldenSong collapses in front of me.

"Aldy? Aldy!" I equally question and scream at the writhing corpse of my friend. A stream of foam escapes from his mouth as I roll him onto his back. I take my fingers and jam them at various pressure points on his body, searching, begging for a heartbeat.

I find none.

"No..." the word escapes my thoughts and enters my vocals as it crawls from my throat. I shake my head and focus.

I-can-do-this-I-can-do-this, I think. But it's a lie. *The last time I did this, I failed. I failed Quidlee. I failed myself.*

After a self-slap so hard I taste pennies, I put my fingers in AldenSong's mouth. I rake out the foam and place my lips firmly over his and blow two breaths.

His chest refuses to rise.

Something is blocking the airways...

With my left hand, I pop his jaw as open as it gets. With my right, I shove my index and pointer fingers into Aldy's windpipe.

There's nothing there...

I take the deepest breath my bruised and broken ribs can handle and expel it into my friend's lungs. Two breaths in, and then five chest compressions out as my balled-up fists press down on Quidlee's hairless chest.

No, not Quidlee; Aldy. Keep your head in the game, T.

I repeat the process. As before, I no longer breathe for myself.

A breath in for me.

A breath out for him.

Push.

Pump.

Pump.

Pump.

Pump.

Do not fail.

Unlike Quidlee's death, time does not elude me. This time I'm acutely aware of the lack of oxygen getting to AldenSong's heart. I know his brain is dying.

And I keep pushing.

A breath in for me.

A breath out for him.

Push.

Pump.

Pump.

Pump.

Pump.

Do not fail.

My hands cramp as a fiery river shoots up into my already burning shoulders. And nothing is working.

The last time I did this, I wasn't completely beat to high hell. Even then, I failed.

An overpowering shadow engulfs me. Others in this situation might think this is a visit from the Angel of Death. I know it's just my own personal devil soaking up my misery.

"Hey, what's with fat boy?" asks the giant.

He asked me that very question after I asked Aldy to help me and Barca escape.

"He's…not…fat…" I say to no one. "He…just…stress eats…"

The crackle of crunching Corn Nuts floods my left ear. "If y'all just want to smash one out, I'll look away."

That, too, is from when AldenSong hugged me, knowing he might never see me again after the jailbreak.

And now, I'm battering his lifeless body, struggling for one heartbeat.

"You had to complicate things, didn't you?" asks ghost-Barca.

Then, a little growl comes from the other room, and that's when Funk Monster saves the damn day.

Chapter Sixty-One

I Hear a Voice

As if she can see my very own vindictive Casper, Funk Monster barks at Barca's ghost. The big bastard tries to shoo her off, but she stands her ground.

Then, she disappears into our original motel room, only to emerge with a bottle of my anti-seizure medication. She drops it in my hand.

I'm a little past needing these, FM.

Then comes AldenSong's voice in my right ear, subtle and kind: *Be still.*

"Screw your mantra, Aldy," I mumble. "I'm trying to save your life and..."

Be still.

A sense of calm covers my body. I want to yank this invisible blanket off, to keep fighting, but I stop. I look at my friend's body. And then I look at the pills in my hand.

After this, a second voice dances through my eardrums. It is of Dr. Brent, and it is a warning I'm going to now ignore.

Do not, repeat, under any circumstances, snort this medication. It will hit your heart like a bullet.

I could really use a helpful bullet right about now. I'm trying to solve today's problem with yesterday's failed practice. Yes, the CPR will work, but I need something else. These bastards caused Alden-Song's full-body shutdown. I need something more powerful than ups-and-downs on a chest...

We need some *better living through chemistry.*

Blowing the dust and debris off a chunk of the busted drywall, I dump a dozen pills on it, crush them into powder with the plastic bottle and pour them into each of AldenSong's nostrils...

And nothing happens. I've got to get them into his lungs. I lean over his nose, cover it completely with my mouth, and blow, ingesting some of the powder on my own. A taste of paint chips and aspirin covers my tongue, which I bet is gonna burn like a bitch in AldenSong' nostrils.

If only he'd breathe...

I start CPR again.

A breath in for me.

A breath out for him.

Push.

Pump.

Pump.

Pump.

Pump.

Do not fail.

I hear the crunch of Corn Nuts, but still keep going. Ghost-Barca taunts me, even dances in the background. He wants me to fail, to lose another ally.

I keep going.

On my ninth, no, tenth round, I'm spent. I have nothing left.

My hands feel like they are full of broken glass. Every second hurts. I push from my abs now. There's no way to keep going. All is lost. Aldy is lost...

"I...can't...do...this...alone..." the words come out during each pump. I'm running on automatic, and my tank is way past empty.

"It's not working..." Barca says, repeating the same taunts he used on me when we tried to walk in unison out of Hackers' Haven's security gate. "You better not have screwed this up, you little runt."

I push. I pump. And I fail. So I go again.

At one point, the powder I ingested takes hold. Or maybe it's the lack of oxygen in my lungs. Either way, it feels like I'm breathing fire and choking on smoke. The world spins.

But I can't stop.

"You ain't got no Plan B," grunts Barca, a phrase he said when I failed to get us out of the prison the first time.

Think, Tanto, think...

"I...need...help..." Those words heave from my throat as Barca's laugh echoes in my brain. "Barca...messing with...my head."

And that's when I hear a voice I haven't heard in over a year.

"Nah, man...he's just being friendly."

Chapter Sixty-Two

Beautiful Sounds

Reality just took off without me. Maybe it's the concussions, the meds, or the trauma, because my brain is a seven-layers-of-shit dip. Something clearly shifts in my head because, lately, I've grown accustomed to seeing one dead man.

Not two.

And, technically, I can't see this new one, an old friend who shouldn't be here, helping me. Especially because, the last time I did CPR, it was on him.

All I know is I feel Quidlee's presence in the room. Right next to me as I push up and down on AldenSong's chest, pumping, praying for the big guy to take a breath on his own. I want to say something to Quidlee, the Rookie or Rook of Hackers' Haven. I want to apologize for failing him when he needed me most.

I also want to tell him I respect his *Yu*, the Bushido Code's Virtue of Heroic Courage. Quidlee stood up to Barca before I ever did. His life, and his death, gave me the strength to do what had to be done.

However, instead of a conversation or an answer, a translucent hand joins my efforts. No longer does Quidlee have the junkie scratch marks or scabs on his fingers. He's not wearing the bandage on his wrist from where I popped his thumbs out of socket.

He's whole. And he's helping.

I push. Quidlee pushes. And Barca leans over Aldy's face and says, "Hey, fat boy—"

"Get out of our way," interrupts Quidlee.

He said the same thing as he stood between Barca and me, a tiny Chihuahua facing off against a Great Dane. Speaking of which, in walks Funk Monster with my bloody, torn T-shirt in her mouth. She drops it in front of Ghost-Barca, then growls at the big bully, so Barca moves off into the corner.

The bully of an elephant is scared of a little mouse, I think.

As we push, a new, translucent hand joins the stack. This one sports a tattoo I'd never forget: a single dotted line that goes from his pointer finger up to his brain.

"Sometimes it's a dance, and sometimes it's a drunken back-alley brawl," says DoGoodR, quoting himself from just yesterday. "Often, it only needs finesse, a little encouragement. Other times, you gotta slap it like it owes you money."

DoGoodR. DJ. His frankness, even in tough situations, is, no was, the living embodiment of *Rei* or Respect. Respect for the code, the systems, and for his team. Even at the end, when DoGoodR sacrificed himself for us.

Six hands push in unison. And nothing happens. We're just pushing away on a body that is getting colder by the second.

I still feel my hands. The biting pain goes up past my elbow. From my left side, a rugged hand joins ours. I know who is part of this miracle, even before he says, "Took you long enough."

Lance-A-Little.

"But...Lance...I'm so...tired..." I say.

He responds with the same answer he gave me when he said I needed to shove an ice pick through my skull. "T, this is the only way."

DoGoodR and Lance shared some of the same traits: both would bust your balls while also patting you on the back. Lance-A-Little was more than just my mentor; he was my friend. He lived honestly and sincerely, a life of the Virtue of *Makoto.*

I duck my head down, and together, ten hands push. It's still not enough. Yet we keep pushing.

Ghost-Barca emerges from the corner when Funk Monster curls up between Aldy's arm and chest.

Get away, you big bastard. You won't get another friend of mine.

Then, a new-old hand joins us. It's weathered. Worn. Tiny. And belonging to the strongest woman I ever met. Mrs. Lin repeats the first thing she ever said to me:

"Damnation, someone is throwing away perfectly good white boys these days."

"Mrs. Lin," I say between pushes, "he's Samoan..."

She ignores me and continues our first conversation as if it is happening right now.

"You fanboy?" she asks.

"No," I say, keeping my answer the same.

She leans into my ear. "Then what are you?"

"I'm a...warrior," I respond through gasps of air.

Mrs. Lin repeats her question as something in my shoulder burns. I slow my part of the chest pumps. Everything is failing, and I'm not just spent; I'm hollow.

"Mrs. Lin, I can't...we...can't...I'm...so...broken..."

"That's okay," she says.

I tear up, knowing the next part like it is my own mantra.

"I like to fix things."

"I'm a warrior…" the words grow in my chest and trickle out.

"Because, if you want to be more than a fanboy, you must learn to live all of the Code, not just some."

I push with a resolve that is not mine. Through gritted teeth, I say, "I…am…a…warrior…"

"You are a little dagger,' Mrs. Lin says. "You will conquer many a giant, and they will never see it coming."

"I…am…a…warrior…"

"You are Tanto," she says and fades into my peripheral. Mrs. Lin, the epitome of *Gi*, the Virtue of Integrity, always kept me accountable. Made me believe in full commitments, not *fanboy* tourism.

She joins the push. As we do, one last hand joins ours. It's larger than the rest, but lies on top in the way only a gentle giant could.

"Where you go, I go," he says, as he said a few hours ago. AldenSong is here, by my side, but also not here at the same time. Part of me believes he knows he must join our fight to save his life. He combines his strength, his *Jin*, the Virtue of Compassion, to our push.

And I'm the *Chu*, the Duty Virtue. I chose this life, it did not choose me. I was a tool; now I am its wielder. Where I was once used, I'm now repurposed. No longer will I make excuses, only changes.

As much as any born and bred Bushi, I am a warrior. I have trained, focused, and honed skills. Now, together, hands over one body, we push. As we do, our hands morph into a round shape, almost like a small sun. Through the brightness, I recognize that our unison produces one last symbol: *Meiyo*, or Honor. All of the other Virtues combine to strengthen this last Code, one that summarizes all of the other virtues.

Everything you do becomes who you really are.

With one last push, AldenSong's gasp of air and subsequent scream are the most beautiful sounds I have ever heard.

Chapter Sixty-Three

Every Crisis, An Opportunity

Within an hour of Aldy's resurrection, I find a neighborhood kid with a cellphone, give him twenty bucks for one phone call, and send for the cavalry: Moscow. From the same kid I get the phone from, I find out we are in Covington, Tennessee, halfway between Memphis and Jackson. The big Russian gets a team of *cleaners* into the destroyed motel rooms and gets us the hell out like he's being timed. The first wave of workers includes former military medics, parttime EMTs, and back-alley docs. They get AldenSong stable enough to move to MetroMed.

When we leave, the second wave arrives. It includes contractors, men and women who bring sledgehammers, drywall, and all the odds and ends to remodel a couple of rooms. I'm also sure Moscow paid off the motel's owner, and everything about this incident is now very *hush-hush*. The mobster can take it out of all the money I've made him in the last few months.

I refuse everything from aspirin to air splints. Ice and rage are all I need. With icepacks taped to the top of my hands, knees, ribs, and back, I look like I went ten rounds with Mike Tyson. I'm more than hurt; I'm pissed, full of bile and rage. And I'm holding tight to this sensation like a damned grudge.

One of the first things Moscow did when he saw me was hand me a burner phone, so I put it to use. I call Ms. Ingrid Vincent who instantly takes the call, always there for her clients...especially the well-paying ones. Once she realizes it's me, she tells me to *shut up and hold tight*. Then hangs up. Twenty seconds later, my line rings. Even though it's a crappy burner, the Caller ID shows about twenty numbers. Scrambled ID, not hidden. Means it won't get caught in an NSA listening filter. *Smart*.

"Okay, what hornets' nest have you tossed up my skirt?" she asks.

"One that's about to get a whole lot bigger."

She sighs and mumbles, "And I was having such a good day...do you know you and the rest of your Lil Rascals are all over the news? I mean, you can't step one foot on the street. You'll get more attention than Charlize Theron walking down Poplar in her birthday suit."

"I've changed my appearance," I say.

"Oh, I bet you shaved your head, right?" asks Ms. Vincent as I instinctively rub my chrome dome. "You do realize the police are smarter than a barber?"

They have less training, I think, but don't dare say.

"I know how to stay in the shadows," I say.

"Good," says Ms. Vincent, which is the opposite feeling than she's about to get when I say the rest of my sentence.

"Which is why I'm going straight into their searchlight."

I'm sure Ms. Vincent thought that covering the mouthpiece on her phone was more effective than hitting the *Mute* button. It wasn't. It's been a minute since I've been called so many colorful words.

"Okay, numbnuts, why isn't this the worst idea since they allowed smoking on the Hindenburg?"

I stall, gathering my thoughts. "I heard what you just said about me."

"Good," she snaps. "At least your ears work." And, instead of hitting *Mute*, she exhales and says, "You're just too much sugar for a damned dime...shit..."

The word *shit* draws out. Only Ms. Vincent could pronounce a four-letter word with three syllables.

"Okay, how much do I need to know?" she asks. "And what all do you need from me?"

"I don't know the details yet," I say. "But, if I'm going down, I'm taking these bastards with me. I need you to contact Penny and tell her to expect a call from this number."

"On it," she says with a sigh. "Now go work faster." With a click, my lawyer hangs up. I take a breather while she does as I ask.

There's not much else to do in AldenSong's ICU room. There's a TV turned to the news on the far wall. It's one of the unwritten rules about hospital stay: in a patient's room, a TV must remain *on* at all times, even if it is on *mute*. Currently, there's a press conference going on at Poseidon United. I'm sure if I unmuted the TV, I could learn something. But my plate currently overflows with existing problems; adding a new one ain't ideal.

The big lug lies flat on his back with Funk Monster nestled between his heavily cast right arm and right leg. She's stayed with him from the motel until now.

AldenSong is in a medically induced coma. As much time as I've spent in hospitals in my life, I follow nothing the doctors say. Thankfully, Moscow does most of the talking. They've got the big boy strapped to so many machines it makes me think of Mrs. Lin in her final days.

No, Tanto, don't crack. Hold together, I think. I can't stop to think about what has happened. There'll be time for it.

Now is the time for war.

I dial Penny's number. Just like Ms. Vincent, Penny lights into me for not letting her know I was *okay* after the hack. She lays further into me because now I'm an *international terrorist* or something, and asks me how much of the news story is true.

"Some," I say. Silence fills the line. The only sound is her tongue clicking between her teeth, clearly deep in thought. "Penny, I need help," I start with a request and finish with the truth. "I need you."

The clicking stops.

"Go," she responds, warming my soul.

I clear my throat. "First thing I need you to do is not freak out—"

"Saying *don't freak out* almost guarantees such a response."

"There will be transactions from HydraPay using my login and password that aren't from me."

"Fine," she says. "I can stop those."

"I need you to not only let them happen, but make a note of where the payouts occur."

"Why?" she asks.

"Because I'm going to need that information as a bargaining chip," I say, intentionally failing to add that that will only work if I can find someone who never wants to be found.

"Done," she says. "Next."

"I'm going to need a team."

"As you well know, I'm a hell of a recruiter," Penny responds.

"I'm going to need engineers, coders, and someone that understands geographical and submersive interfaces..."

"You mean like someone that's worked in hydrodynamics or someone that's dealt with aquatic technology?" clarifies Penny.

Sweet, Baby Jesus, who is this woman? "Exactly."

I wait for a *no.* To hear *there's no way, it's impossible.*

"How soon?" is all she says.

"Twenty-four hours."

"Hold on," says Penny, her voice small. She's holding her phone away from her face, probably looking at something.

"Okay, I've got some prospects in my Palm Pilot..." *Of course, she uses Palm Pilot.* It might be outdated but it never hooks to a server or cloud. She and Moscow are more covert than I am. "Where do you need them?" she asks, phone back on her ear.

Moscow walks in and for a second, he doesn't see me sitting in the corner. He strolls over to Aldy. I'm prepared for Funk Monster to growl or even try to bite the Russian. Instead, she scoots over to the edge of the bed and faces away from him. Moscow takes a squeeze of lotion from the side table and rubs AldenSong's hands.

"The hands dry out faster than most believe," he says, acknowledging me. "It's the oxygen and...sterility."

While I don't exactly know what is going on here, now is not the time to muddy my waters.

"This phone is on its last use, so I'll go through the lawyer," I say to Penny.

"Okay," she says, then adds. "Speaking of which, are you okay?"

"Oh, I'm peachy," I say with a snark.

"I mean it, you dumb little bastard," Penny says, the concern in her voice belying the barb. "Are you okay?"

There's too much to unpack right now. The manhunt. Do-GoodR's death. Cyfib's revelations. Aldy almost dying.

"No," I say, being as honest as I can. "But I'm compartmentalizing."

"Oh, that's healthy…" quips Penny, a small laugh in her voice.

"It's just that…when I stop, I'll crumble."

This level of vulnerability is new to me. I put on a brave face most of the time, or at least I try to stretch one on. But, with Penny, I can tell her the full truth, not some sugarcoated version.

"And when that happens," she says, "I'll help put you back together."

Then the line goes dead. No reason to say goodbye after a confirmation like that.

Of course, all it takes to ruin this moment is Moscow pointing at the TV and saying, "Hey…I know that guy somehow…"

At first, I'm thinking that he's talking about Poseidon United's CEO Cussh. It'd make sense; that's one of the most powerful people in the corporate world. But then I catch what Moscow's throwing down: it's not about the CEO.

It's about the CITO. The Chief Information Technology Officer. Just a few days ago, my team discussed that job. How it paid $1.2 million a year. How it put a person in charge of so much info and so much power.

So, they're using our terrorist attack *to roll out their guy*, I think. *In every crisis, an opportunity.*

However, in this *opportunity,* comes heartache. I stand and walk across the room, putting my nose as close to the TV as possible to confirm what I'm looking at. I'm staring at the new CITO. He's standing there like the last forty-eight hours didn't happen.

Even without the beard or long hair, there's nowhere I'd not recognize DoGoodR.

Chapter Sixty-Four

The Bad Ones

Feudal Japan brought war to the land. Warlords or Shoguns fought and maintained their kingdoms. Depending on the war, a wealthy or influential Shogun would ally with a lesser Shogun in order to conquer a powerful rival. When this happened, the weaker Shogun would know the ramifications even before hearing an offer.

If the weaker Shogun said *no* to working together to take down the rival, he risked angering the stronger Shogun. That meant everything from enslaving to slaughtering his men then and there.

But if the lessor Shogun said *yes,* it meant something deadly as well.

There are stories about how these *Samurai Team-Ups* would take down an enemy and the alliance would gain fresh territory. To celebrate their successful siege, a large feast and party would occur, with everything from sake to pillaging...and worse. But, at the end of the day, someone must pay the bill.

That cost lay on the head, and more precisely, in the gut, of the lesser Shogun. Ultimately, a clan only has one leader. After the celebration, the Shoguns would meet in the powerful Shogun's Gakunodo, or tent, with their lieutenants in tow.

The powerful Shogun's team would be armed, and the lesser's would only have two recently sharpened weapons: a large sword called a katana and a small dagger called a tanto.

Then the lesser Shogun was offered two choices: decapitation by one of the lieutenants' katanas, or to disembowel himself with a tanto. Interestingly enough, this final act of self-sacrifice, the seppuku, was one of the highest honors that samurai could commit.

From the point of view of the more powerful Shogun, he granted his captive one last act of freedom. For me, I think, *when your head is on the chopping block, does it really matter who drops the guillotine?* But, to these warriors, it was a way to avoid interrogation and torture, protect their men from the same, and to go out on their own terms.

The Shogun would open his robe, take the tanto, and plunge it into the left side of his belly. Then, in front of this audience, he would draw the blade to the right, causing a blood flood, one that often resulted in the intestines flopping out of the body. Sometimes this very act would cause death. If it didn't, the dying Shogun would give his most trusted subordinate a command. The lieutenant would raise his katana as his master lowered his head and, in one swift blow, the lieutenant would sever the spinal cord, thus ending his leader's suffering.

Right now, I should feel decapitated by what I'm seeing on the TV. I should feel betrayed finding my *dead friend* is more than alive; he is actually a spy. He sided with the enemy shogun. I should feel decimated by the notion that this traitor was more than just family: he was our DoGoodR.

Instead, a veil lifts from my eyes. In this moment, everything makes sense. I've blamed myself, our situation, and even just plain ole bad luck, for the hack going wrong. We never had a chance. But, out of this betrayal comes a nugget of a plan on how to bring everything crashing down.

I unmute the TV. The final claps of fading applause fill the room as DoGoodR, excuse me, former Special Agent Jack Brock, flashes a smile as he reaches into his blue silk coat pocket and retrieves a speech. Without the beard, the long hair, or the dotted line neck tattoo, Do-GoodR, no, Agent Jack's freshly shaven face makes him look more like a tall baby in a suit than my cyber-Judas. I think there's a little makeup covering that dotted tattoo.

"Ladies and gentlemen, I am honored to be with you today and to be part of the Poseidon United family," he says, glancing at his notes way too much, looking like a very amateur speaker.

The poor asshole must be nervous...aww...

"While I already miss all of my coworkers at the Census Department, I am leaving one family and gaining another one."

What do you know of family? I think bitterly over the urge to vomit.

In everything that's been going on, it's been easy to forget that the Mercator Agency is part of the US Census Department.

"I'd like to thank CEO Cussh, the members of the Board of Directors, and all the shareholders and stakeholders of Poseidon United for instilling your confidence in me and what I can do to help our great company remain just that: great."

The way Do—Agent Jack—leans into the microphone and smiles perfectly wide throughout the word *great*, I wonder who trained him for this press conference.

"For the last two years, I have been embedded in a deep-cover assignment that isolated me from contact with my friends and family. Thanks to prompt government intervention, we were able to minimize a major terrorist attack on our homeland, on our soil."

Applause fills the room. Agent Jack humbly-not-humbly waits for the applause to die down, all with his plastic smile in place.

"Thank you, thank you," says Agent Jack.

Someone just offscreen taps his shoulder and whispers something.

"Um, I'm being told I am late for another meeting, so thanks everyone for your time."

Moscow hits mute and gets shoulder-to-shoulder with me as we stare at the TV.

"This bad?" he asks as Moscow studies my face.

"This bad," I confirm as a picture of Agent Jack in a different blue suit with a red tie on and the American Flag in the background fills the screen. There's no closed captioning on, so I just assume that the announcers are giving a brief play-by-play of the press conference.

"What do you need?" Moscow asks.

I answer his question with one of my own. "Moscow, do you remember when you told me that not all Russians were bad?"

"Da."

"It's time to call in the bad ones."

Chapter Sixty-Five

Dedushka

"Ah," says Moscow as he rubs his huge chin and points at AldenSong as fire dances in the Russian's eyes. "You want the man that did this to our...friend...no longer able to do things like this, correct?"

I initially say *yes*. I want, no, need Cyfib out of our hair, but something tells me he will not come after us anymore. He could've easily killed both AldenSong and me, but chose not to. "Cyfib thinks he is in the wind, but he is not the current threat." I point at the TV and, even though it is *Off*, Moscow gets the gist.

"Mister TV man is target, yes?" Moscow asks.

I nod. "I want him out of picture in the most public way."

Like a server pulling out a notepad to take your order, Moscow flips out his phone and scrolls through a list of names. "So, sniper, explosives, or something more...gruesome."

"I do not want him dead." To prove my point, I push his phone down and meet his gaze. "I only want him out of the way."

"We are saying same thing," he says and then winks.

"We most certainly are not. And do not wink at me. Do not, I repeat, do not harm this man or anyone. Do you understand me?"

Moscow nods. "You are what they call killroy—no, killjoy."

What is with people going from zero to killing? Killing Agent Jack will only make Poseidon United stronger. They'll have what they've always so desperately wanted: a powerful martyr.

Moscow's Freudian slip kicks up some dust from the corner of my brain: Kilroy. The former prisoner, fellow hackvict who helped save my ass when the Mercator Agency had us locked in an interrogation room and put literal guns to our heads. If not for him, I'd be at the bottom of an unmarked grave by now.

Some of the puzzle pieces fit together in ways I never thought possible: Cyfib, Kilroy, and their team, DISRUPT, did more than beat up the US Department of Defense like it owed them a gambling debt. One built Poseidon United into the powerhouse it is today. Another went from the first prisoner to my warden.

The last? Well, he's a paranoid lunatic with an obsession for wrapping stuff in tinfoil to prevent spying. He also holds a USB flashdrive full of classified documents, software blueprints, and administrative access to some of the most secure servers on the planet.

And he's also more hidden than Waldo swimming in a sea of candy canes.

There's got to be a way to get to Kilroy, to find him, and get that flash drive back. I don't know exactly why, but part of the key to taking down the whole damn thing lies with a hacker who has made a career of staying deep underground.

Even though I've got a little more of the puzzle, I can't see what it is. It's like I'm assembling the damned thing without seeing the picture on the box: it's certainly possible, but it is also maddening. And something in the back of my brain vibrates, like an alarm that I keep hitting snooze on. I met Kilroy during my most damaged time, when my brain and body took a siesta from each other.

What is my shit-brick trying to tell me? A deep, guttural snore comes from AldenSong. I didn't know that people in comas could do that, but it makes sense. It is only his brain that is checked out; the rest of the big guy is still fighting for his life.

A grunt enters, speaks to Moscow, then leaves.

"Moscow," I say, "is it just me, or are you very openly running our drug business during the daytime?"

"Da," he responds, like I just said something ridiculous, like *the sky is blue* before Moscow chuckles. "Why not? We own the hospital."

"You've got to be shitting me," I respond.

"I shit no man but myself," quips Moscow, though I can't tell from his tone if he's taking me seriously. "There were...rumblings about the hospital not making enough money."

And I wonder if you're the one that started that earthquake.

"So, we made an offer." Moscow's face scrunches as if he just hit his bare toe against a piece of furniture. "I feel we paid too much. Previous owners feel they got too little. End of the day, they got money, we got hospital to use for endless drug supply."

"Moscow, this goes against our *under the radar* business style."

Moscow ignores my blowfish impersonation and pulls out a pager that I didn't even know he had, checks it and says, "Your business model no longer works in our new world."

It might've been kinder to just kick me in the nuts. "You're dropping false bureaucracy and using an existing business as a protective umbrella for ease of access," I say. "What about all the licenses and paperwork?"

"Lady lawyer do most of it," he says. "As for licenses, we keep same staff. Same software. And same pharmacist, except this time he is, how you say, in on the joke."

I want to protest. This kind of exposure could lead to arrests. Specifically, Larry's and Mr. Judson's. But I stop. This is a battle for a different day. Moscow slams his acre of a palm into my back, bringing me back to reality. He pulls me close, and I smell a mix of sawdust, antiseptic, and bleach.

The kind of smells that I remember from Ron's kill room.

"I've thought about your...old home," begins Moscow. "It reminds me of my grandfather. He did not start out as a great man. Very self-serving. Full of rage. Then he found a purpose—*tsel*, in Russian."

Something tells me this story ain't short, so I grab a seat and give my legs—which have diluted into jelly following all the adrenaline spikes of late—a break.

Moscow pulls out a pack of cigarettes with Russian letters on them. He thumps the pack against his hand twice until a single cancer stick pops out. I would point out that there is *no smoking in hospitals* but, when you own the place, you make the rules. The mobster extends the pack my way, but I wave him away.

"My grandfather was one of the first to openly oppose First Secretary of Mother Russia Stalin," Moscow says as he pats at his pockets in search of a lighter. "My grandfather was a journalist and, you know the truth, that even today, journalists are not *welcome* to report the true news in Russia."

"After Stalin died, my grandfather was freed, granted...amnesty." Moscow pats his jean pockets three times before he smiles. "Then we had Khrushchev. He made some serious changes. Some call it the Khrushchev Thaw, but thawing is for ice. This triggered a mass release and rehabilitation of political prisoners. The thing was, my grandfather, he was smart man. Wise man. A watching man. He saw...opportunity."

There's something in the way Moscow says this word: *opportunity*. There's a flicker in his eyes that isn't just his; it's like it is part of him, part of his genetic makeup. It is inherited. Generational.

Moscow pulls out a lighter, flicks his Bic, fires up his cig, takes a puff, and says, "When released from prison, he asked to stay. He asked for work." Moscow exhales a plume of smoke that he wisely swats away from the ceiling smoke detectors before continuing. "Of the almost five million prisoners, almost two-thirds of them were granted amnesty, like my Dedushka. Dedushka was what I called him. Another twenty percent went to war. There will always be need for men in war. Then there were those that were too violent to release, so they went...away."

Moscow takes a drag and slowly exhales smoke that engulfs his face. "Then there were the men that went into labor battalions for the Ministry of Defense. These were the men who were not violent, but also not innocent. They'd become accustomed to working in harsh conditions."

From the little I'd seen about *harsh conditions* in the USSR from documentaries and old cartoons, those were conditions to be avoided at all costs.

"Dedushka went as high up the boss chain as a civilian could and said, *I want those men. I want those men.*" The cherry on his life-stealer burns brighter for a second. After an exhale, Moscow continues, "He knew how to work them because not only did Dedushka respect them, but he was one of them. He was a prisoner-warden. Dedushka told me the origin of the word warden was not *one who keeps away* or *one who punishes*. It can mean *one who guards*. One who *focuses*. One who *changes*. Under Dedushka's guidance, most of those men earned their freedom. He made positive out of the negative. For example, out of those men came Russia's space race, one of the only bright lights to creep out from under the Iron Curtain."

With the cigarette burning out, Moscow looks around for a place to extinguish it. Not finding one, he takes one last puff and crushes the lit cig in his hands. "That is what my Dedushka did for Mother Russia," he says as Moscow rakes the ashes and debris from his hand into a trashcan. "That energy is what I see in you. And that is one reason I like helping you."

Moscow reaches over to the bedside table and grabs a small notepad-and-pen combo. He hands it to me and says, "Write what you know, and write what you need. Give me your...Christmas list..." Then he sends me a wink and says, "I go get my red suit and reindeer."

As he leaves the room, I want to remind him I said *do not wink at me*. Instead, with beeping machines and cold, sterile air soothing me, I write. I put the beeps and the high-pitched alarms to use for more than just medical alerts.

Since those bastards have hypnotized me to increase my productivity in the past, maybe I can use some of it for my benefit.

I picture a large gold metal gong, the kind you see in Bushido movies, getting hit with a large mallet.

And then I just merely go *away*, off into some mental fog.

I put down not just what has happened in the last forty-eight hours, but also my *Christmas list*. I write every detail of what's happened that I can remember, from the little ones that might have some use from our failed hack to Rusty and her serial killer husband testing our loyalty. Cyfib's attack. My dreams. The hallucinations. My meds. It's a collection of true word vomit, and it starts as just a way to process. But something is sticking in my brain, and it comes from something the imposter-DoGoodR said.

There's key in the code.

Maybe there's something in *my* code. Something that I can use. Something that, when necessary, will save our very lives.

The smell of weak, burned, hospital coffee stings my nostrils. I never even noticed Moscow put the small, squeaky Styrofoam cup on the corner of my table. I pick it up and take a sip. It's cold. But something tells me it was piping hot when he put it down.

How long was I out? I wonder, coming out of my daze. The mobster sits on the edge of AldenSong's bed, flipping through my pages.

"Your handwriting is, how you say," starts Moscow. "Chicken-shit?"

"Chicken-scratch."

"I did not make error," he says and drops the stack in front of me. "It did make me hungry."

"Moscow, I'm sorry if my recent situation makes you want to nosh, but that's not helping."

Moscow flips through my ten pages of front-and-back notes, all the while mumbling something in Russian. I'm sure they're not flattering praises. With an *Ah-ha*, Moscow puts one of my notes in front of me and points.

I read it aloud. "A Taste of DejaVu."

I'd forgotten about that. It's from, hold on, it's from a sticker. *Where did I see it? Think, Tanto, think. Wait.* It was on Kilroy's laptop. I say, "I think it is a saying from a Hunter S. Thompson book or, worse, a Mardi Gras thing, and we don't have time to scour New Orleans if Kilroy is there."

"That is not Mardi Gras," Moscow says, and chuckles. "That is local restaurant."

And now I have my one-in-a-million shot at finding Kilroy.

Chapter Sixty-Six

DejaVu

When I find out that DejaVu isn't just the sense of unwelcomed duplication, but rather a New Orleans-style restaurant six blocks from MetroMed, I want to kiss Moscow square on the lips.

Instead, I give him my laptop, the one I used in our hack, and one order: print everything. When he asked for clarification, I repeated myself. Then I told him, "I want so many pages of code that the printer files a restraining order against me."

In a MetroMed one-piece custodial jumper and with a broom in my hand, I stroll at a faster-than-normal pace to the restaurant. The outfit is better than my black hoodie, which is all over the news, and a broom is always great cover — no one's gonna question someone cleaning.

It doesn't take me long to reach the purple-and-gold shingle-style sign hanging over the sidewalk. *New Orleans Deja Vu: Creole, Soul, & Vegetarian Cuisine.*

I want to run in and ask if anyone there knows "Leonard." However, if I'm to have any hope of finding him before getting found myself, I have to play it cool.

It also helps my impulse control that it is 10:55 a.m. and the place doesn't open until eleven. I study the menu taped to the side window near the alley. My stomach growls with each po'boy, jambalaya, and etouffee on the menu.

As near as I can tell, there are two entrances: front and alley. From my spot on the corner, just under a sign that reads November 6th Street, I have an eye on both. Every time I make unintentional eye contact with someone, I just make a few broad sweeps with my broom, and they turn away.

By the time I see Kilroy enter the alley on the far end, the spot on the ground below me is so clean you can eat off of it.

Kilroy's hair is now in a ponytail. With a backpack over his shoulder, he strolls down the alley.

Until our eyes meet.

And then he bolts.

My broom clatters to the ground as I sprint after him. He turns down the alley's exit and I struggle to catch up with him. He's fast for an old man. Hell, he's fast for a young one. Though, it doesn't hurt Kilroy that my body is nothing more than a skin bag of beaten bones and bruised muscles.

Then he does the one thing I didn't expect him to do: he runs out into the public. He darts into the most popular hotel in Memphis, The Peabody. Right where I found myself less than 48 hours ago when AldenSong and I were trying to break into that building. The last time though, I wasn't *Public Enemy Number One.*

It's not like Kilroy is living entirely above board — there's every chance he's wanted by the Feds too, so I use it to my advantage.

In the grand, two-story lobby, Kilroy fast-walks toward the elevators. I turn on my best Donald Sutherland impersonation from

Invasion of the Body Snatchers, extend my arm and pointer finger, kick my head back, and scream, "He stole my wallet!"

From each quadrant of the room, security officers in suits stomp toward Kilroy.

"Shit..." he mutters, audible over the 50 yards between us, and darts his head around.

Two security guards also rush my way, which isn't ideal, but at least I don't need to keep an eye on Kilroy anymore because I know where he's headed: the closest exit.

Before security gets to me, I dart out the exit and sprint to the far side of the hotel, bobbing and weaving between the early lunch crowd. Judging by the distance and location of security when I left the lobby, this is the best exit for Kilroy. However, there's a decent chance he's hunkering down in an empty conference room, custodial closet, or anywhere he could wait out the search.

If that's the case, I'm more screwed than a Phillips head. This was my only chance, so if I don't get Kilroy today, he's gone-baby-gone.

The first people out the door are a family of four. The parents hold a map of downtown while the kids squeak their yellow rubber duckies.

And crouched next to them, slinking out is Kilroy. He darts right down an alley.

I'm not ten steps behind him when he turns, pulls a snub-nosed .38 and aims at my head.

In his wide eyes, I bet Kilroy thinks I'm with Mercator or Poseidon. He's not going back without a fight. And that means he is about to blow my brains out the back of my skull.

I have one sentence, one utterance, to keep him from making my last thought into alley graffiti.

But that's okay, because I tell him exactly what he wants to hear.

"I know how to find Prisoner Zero."

Chapter Sixty-Seven

Nothing to Lose

There were a number of ways I'd expected Kilroy to react to my dangling Patient Zero in front of him.

None of them included pushing my back against the alley's brick wall and shoving the barrel of his gun in my mouth.

It's been over a decade since I tasted blued steel: when Agent Michelle had Mane-Eac and me seconds away from turning into collateral damage corpses. This black oxide coating is so much worse than the chipped tooth the Agent gave me; it makes me want to vomit.

There's a wiriness in Kilroy's eyes that has me on edge. I just promised Gollum his *precious*, so I best not piss off this hermit more than necessary.

I slowly point to my right front pocket. Kilroy shoves his free hand into my custodian one-piece and pulls out a folded piece of paper. He pries it open with one hand, reads the note, looks at me with narrow eyes, and takes the gun out of my mouth.

"So, you've met one devil, and have your sights on the other," he says as he levels the gun at my gut. "That still don't mean I shouldn't put a bullet in you."

"That's one option," I say before I spit saliva and gun oil on the concrete. "Ugh. The other is you give me back my flash drive and I'll give you access to a way to track Cyfib."

Kilroy flourishes the gun barrel across my face. "What's preventing me from shooting you right now if you don't give me the tracking code?"

"Because you're like me." I put my right hand on the barrel and push it down, but not away. "I have nothing to lose, and you need me as much as I need you."

"Bullshit," he mutters, thankfully returning the revolver to his pocket. "People who say *they have nothing to lose* say that to keep people from pressing." He gets nose-to-nose with me and says, "Say it again."

He's got me there. I thought I said that line with enough false bravado to sell it. I guess Kilroy ain't buying. Time to up the ante.

"I need the USB to shut down Poseidon United, to fully expose Mercator, and free my friends," I say. "And you need to go after the person who betrayed you. Whatever you and Cyfib do, that's between you. I'm going after the other guy, so shoot me now, or give me what I need. Either way, those are the only answers I want from you."

We face off. There is no western whistle heralding a pistol duel. No breeze blowing our dusters before we draw.

Nope. Only Kilroy's hand on my shoulder and a command.

"Let's you and me find a bathroom."

Chapter Sixty-Eight

All My Freaks

If you'd have told me that my morning would've started with my closest friend hulking out and dying, immediately followed by me and an army of ghosts bringing him back, and then continued with a gun in my mouth, I would've called *bullshit*. Now, as I sweep the same spot near a port-o-potty as an *actual* shit occurs, I realize that this is all pretty par for the course of my life.

Primal noises erupt from the inside stall. More caveman than human. I guess when you fill up your prison wallet, taking out a deposit means a full withdrawal.

I knock on the door. "You got a gold watch up there as well?"

Kilroy gives me a *ha ha* before he groans. "Worst part is catching the mess..."

I throw up in my mouth a little, but try not to call any attention to it. After a minute, Kilroy emerges. His sweat-soaked clothes and teary eyes tell me all I need to know.

"I go through more condoms than Hugh Hefner," he quips, before sighing. "Just not in the fun way."

In his left hand, he holds four sealed condoms. And, despite Kilroy's marginal attempt at cleanliness, they all smell like shit.

"Which one is yours?" he asks more to himself than me.

I respond, "I wish it was none of them..."

"Ah ha!" Kilroy tosses me the correct condom but I flinch away from catching it. Instead it hits my custodial outfit, sticks for a moment, and slides to the ground.

I'm not picking up something that knows Kilroy biblically.

"It's clean," says Kilroy as I doubt his subjective standard. "I mean, I'm clean too, if that's what you're thinking."

As the condom mocks me on the ground, I say, "I'm just really wondering how much I want to save the world right now..."

Kilroy bends down and picks up the condom. "Your entire generation is a bunch of big babies." He tears it open and the flash drive pops out.

This time, I catch it. I instantly recognize it as Cyfib's administrative key. Without a laptop, there's no way to make sure the tools and data I need are still on it. But I have no reason to doubt a man that almost blew my head off minutes ago. I take off my right shoe, remove the innersole, take out a single, folded piece of paper, and hand it to Kilroy.

"Paper," he says with a smile. "Classic." Then he points at my shoes and holds his nose. "You really need to clean those."

I cast a long, skeptical look at the busted rubber on the ground.

"Fair enough."

I've got a sneaking suspicion that Kilroy isn't one for long goodbyes, so I turn to leave.

"Do you really think you can stop them?" Kilroy asks.

"The difference between a hope and a plan are steps," I say, something I clearly stole from a self-help book or a vanity bumper sticker.

"And I've got just enough of a plan that hope is a welcomed byproduct." I hold the flash drive up. "You up for one final hack?"

He's thinking about it, leaning against the wall and rubbing his chin. But he shakes his head. "I've got a traitor to hunt." Then he reaches into his pocket and chucks me something else.

Unlike the used condom, I catch this toss. It's a locker key for a storage unit.

"What's this for?"

From over his shoulder, he asks, "So, what's next for you?"

Now this part of the plan, I know damn well. I say, "I'm taking a page out of Crystal Method's playbook."

"That'll rot your teeth," he says, clearly missing my band reference as he fades into the distance.

Without an audience, I still announce my plan.

"I'm calling all my freaks."

Chapter Sixty-Nine

My Homie

I'm not one for public speaking. In all honesty, getting up in front of people and baring my soul scares me more than a night in The Hole at Hackers' Haven. And I've prepared nothing. *When would I have found the time?* is the excuse I'm going with in my head.

Yet here I stand, in the cafeteria at MetroMed with a room full of people before me. I'm about to ask them to risk their freedom and their very lives on a suicide mission, and I don't even have a notecard on me.

Ms. Ingrid "Innocent" Vincent was my first call before this meeting. She said that she couldn't be there for these discussions about...*tacos*, but she agreed to call all the parties I requested for the meeting. Twenty minutes after the call, she told me who *RSVP'd* and who *Regretted*.

The first two to *regret* were Rusty and her husband. That makes sense; I'm hotter than a Michael Jordan rookie card right now. They've helped where they could.

Plus, I still have their bug-out bag, which has some useful tools.

And one that I hope I never have to use.

The second to turn me down was Mane-Eac. I don't know how Ms. Vincent contacted her, but Ms. Vincent said that Mane-Eac wouldn't be able to attend, but might call in later. She's forgiven me enough to do the hack — I think — but Mane-Eac's smart enough to do her part from Canada.

But if she's seen any news segments and knows that Agent Jack impersonated DoGoodR, I don't think there's a firewall strong enough to keep her vengeance out.

I asked Ms. Vincent if I should contact Mane-Eac directly, and the response was a *no,* followed by Mane-Eac's answer to my predicted question:

You will know when I join.

"While I'm not there, physically or even in damned spirit," Ms. Vincent says before hanging up, "my phone is always on for when the...inevitable outcome hits."

I'd take that last comment as a warning, but she's a lawyer. I don't pay her to pump me up with lies. I pay her to hit me with the cold, hard truth and that's gonna require a slap every now and then.

From the stage, clearly Larry can see the bright light bothering me, so he gets up from his seat and dims it. He's back to wearing the cornrows and gives the audience a theatrical bow before he returns to his seat right next to Mr. Judson. On the other side of Larry is Penny in a gray T-shirt with the words *Careful: Contents Under Pressure* on it.

The rest of the room contains our thugs. Well, Moscow's and Penny's thugs anyways. And, even though they sit on opposite sides of the room like a bride-and-groom wedding party, the two factions talk and joke among themselves.

Good. The last thing I need is a civil war before an actual one.

I tap the microphone, a tool I probably don't need. It sends out a high-pitched shrill squeak that closes my audience's eyes and makes a few cover their ears. I take this as a sign and move away from it to speak. Larry tosses his arms down in disappointment, but I never told him I needed it for amplification.

"Some of you know who I am. Others, well, if any of you have watched the news, you know who they want you to think I am."

Several comments about the police, the government, and what they can do to each other bubble up from both sides of the aisle.

I don't add kindling to that particular fire.

"In eighteen hours, I'm going to try to do the impossible: topple unbreakable corporate giants while also exposing a government cover-up. To most of you, this might seem like something straight out of a movie or video game. Fiction. Fantasy. But, trust me, this is as real as it gets."

To them, this is a job. To me, this is my Ikigai. My purpose.

"Does it pay?"

I don't catch the questioner until Penny turns and slaps him.

"Each of you will get ten thousand dollars for one day's work," I say. "Cash or pills."

I have that much in pills that are in storage from our *Smith & Sons* early days, but maybe not much more if the crews want to negotiate.

Silence dances through the air. *Maybe I undersold this.*

Mr. Judson raises his hand. I nod and he says, "Twenty."

The word steals a bit of air from my lungs. Noticing the shock on my face, Mr. Judson nods at me and mouths three words.

We got you.

Part of me wants to run down and hug him, but I hold on to that feeling.

"Who's the target?" This question comes from Moscow's side and, unlike Penny, Moscow stands cross-armed and lets his crew ask.

"The city."

The rumble from the crowd is more than I expected. Before it gets louder, I tap the microphone and squawk out the noise before it becomes a riot.

"Most of you are in charge of distractions," I say and point to Penny. "Your crew's focus is police and local law enforcement's attention. That means petty robbery from gas stations near police stations, contained fires near fire stations, and so on. I'll have the particulars ready in an hour."

Penny nods and winks. I want to wink back, but doing this in front of her crew might get me in more trouble than it's worth. I nod and move my attention back to the audience.

"Your job is two-fold," I say. "Depending on your background, we might use you to assemble some tech for the hack. He told me he has some engineers on the payroll."

"I've got some as well," Penny adds.

"Good," I say and motion to Moscow. "Y'all work this out."

The two mob bosses nod at each other, so I continue.

"The other part, let's call this the mischief part, will be in charge of shutting various roads and bridges," I say, my voice cracking from dryness. "I don't mean permanently. I mean, wreck two cars on a bridge to close it off, throw some tire strips so that civilian autos do the same. It's all about keeping the foot soldiers away."

Actor-thug Reggie from Larry's weeding-out-of-candidates seminar chimes in. "Do you need any particular roles filled?"

"No, wait, yes." I snap my fingers. "Do you use social media?"

Reginald kicks his head back and says, "Yes, I have thousands of followers on—"

I interrupt with, "Great. I want you to post every fire, every incident on social media."

The actor says *huzzah* to himself, then takes a seat.

"What happens if we get caught?" This question comes from someone I expected to ask it: Mr. Judson. He's thinking of his family. He has the most to lose, well, next to Penny. They're both risking a lot just being in the room with me.

"I don't know," I say as my eyes hit the floor. "I wish I did. But this time, they have zero incentive to take any of us alive. I'm sorry."

With this, several thugs get up and leave. So does Mr. Judson. He walks my way, his posture a little straighter than when I used him as a mark to enter MetroMed a few months ago.

"I'll get you the funds, but I'll only be there in spirit." He extends his hand to me. I take it. "Good luck, Vice."

"Thank you, Judson."

With a shake, my Daimyo leaves this warrior, this new Ronin, to fight his battle alone.

Both Penny and Moscow approach after our moment.

"I will have enough soldiers, comrade," says Moscow, as he yells in Russian at some of his exiting crew.

"Same," adds Penny. "But I won't be around, either."

I nod. That makes sense. Penny and the kids are in enough danger as it is.

She glances around to make sure none of her thugs watch us before she leans in and places a kiss on my cheek. "You certainly make things interesting, you dumb little bastard," she says.

Knowing I might never see her again and fearful to bare any more of my soul, I say, "I mean, we're just a porcupine and a balloon in love." I lean in and add, "what could possibly go wrong?"

Before she leaves the front, she *boops* my nose with her finger and says, "Pop." As her thugs join her in the corner of the room, only Larry remains.

"Larry, do you want me to help you put all this shit up?" I ask.

"Naw, dog," he says as he gets up from his man-spread seated position and gangsta limps my way.

Ah, no longer do I have Businessman Larry *before me. He's letting* Thugly *out to play.*

"You remember what I told you when we completed our first deal with Kingfish?"

Regretfully, I do, but I shake my head because Thugly is clearly dying to say it again.

"You're my homie." At this, Larry pulls me close and holds me by the shoulders and says, "Homie don't rat, homie don't break, homie don't run."

Everyone has their orders. However, when it comes down to the nitty-gritty, it's me and Thugly verses the world. *Out-standing.*

Chapter Seventy

A Wonderful Way

With time to kill until Moscow gets his team ready and all of my gear requisitioned and set up, I ask Thugly to drive me to the location printed on the key. Kilroy's storage locker on the other side of town.

"So, you and the Asian chick," he says, a mischievous dance in his voice. "Y'all slap cheeks yet?"

"Just drive the car, Larry."

He smiles, and the mid-morning sun flashes off one of his gold teeth. "Aw yeah, y'all did. That's my bitch there...getting it..."

"If I said *please*, would you drive the car without getting into my personal life?" I ask, knowing the answer is a one-hundred-dred-and-ten-percent chance of *no*.

"Dude, you couldn't speak for like, months, and now I've got so many questions for you. Like, is Vice your real name?"

"No."

As he rounds a turn at a very respectable speed, he asks, "What is it?"

"Nunya."

"Huh," mutters Larry as he squints and studies my face. "You don't look Dutch."

Clearly Larry is not aware of the classic punchline Nunya Business. "Why would I look Dutch?"

At this, Larry pops up one cheek and rips a fart so rancid that it waters my eyes.

"Cause you just loving this Dutch Oven, man!" he cackles.

There's the old Thugly I know and somewhat love. I try to roll down the window to avoid smelling any more of his secondhand dinner, but Larry's got the window locks on.

Thankfully, we're arriving at a six-story building that looks like your standard office complex. From the faded and rusted exterior, it appears abandoned. But through the cracked and broken windows, you can see row after row of metal sliding doors.

"Oh, this looks like one of Moscow's converted storage units," says Larry as he rolls down his window to look and probably get fresh air. "His family has done this to, like, six buildings around town."

Could Kilroy and Moscow know each other?

Larry parks the Kia under the shade of a giant oak tree, and we enter the building. I glance at the key to make sure we're at the right place.

Yep: Cooky Comrade's Storage, Unit 113.

Using the signs on the walls, we find Kilroy's unit located right next to the closest exit.

Classic Kilroy.

Larry snatches the key from my hand and is about to shove it in the standard silver lock when I grab his arm.

"What, man?"

Instead of answering, I point. Thugly follows my motion and his jaw drops.

Up in the corner, where the rolling metal door meets the frame, is what appears to be a plain brown cardboard box.

"Boobytrap," I say.

To his credit, instead of making a quip about my use of the word *booby*, Larry steps back. "Dude, is your buddy trying to kill you?"

"This is standard operating procedure for the guy," I say as I lean in to examine the device. "Truthfully, if this *wasn't* rigged with an explosive, I'd be more worried." It is just out of my reach, and I didn't bring a stepstool. "Larry, I need to borrow your leg."

"Borrow your own," he says, not willing to come closer.

"What happened to '*homie don't run*?'" I demand, hands on my hips.

"Homie also don't intentionally blow up...hold on a sec..." Larry strolls down the corridor, testing other doors, until he finds one that's unlocked. A few seconds later he emerges with an empty paint bucket. He holds it out to me, still as far from the blast radius as he can make himself. "Look, you can stand on this."

I grab the bucket, using it to get a better look at the box. It's more spiderwebs than tripwires up here. I slip my hand behind the cardboard, willing my fingers to be sensitive enough to feel for any wires. I find none. If I'm right that might mean this is a crush bomb which would ignite at compression rather than rely on tripwires or buttons to detonate.

"There's a chance this is the poor man's claymore," I tell Larry. "I think if I just remove it from its corner, it won't explode."

"Think..." says Larry taking another step away. "Or *know*?"

"Just, shit, just keep your distance," I say as I finagle my left hand on top of the box. Then I put my right hand under the package and pull.

It's stuck, which doesn't rule out a tripwire.

Maybe Kilroy set me up. Maybe he doesn't trust me, and this is the way to get rid of me.

I shake my head. No, now's not the time for paranoia.

This bit of distraction throws my balance off. The paint bucket under my feet slips and I fall.

As I do, the box teeters.

I slam into the concrete, winding myself. Dust plumes as pain fills my body.

And the box falls.

Then, like a cornrowed angel, Larry catches it.

"Oh-shit-oh-shit-oh-shit-oh-shit," is all Larry can repeat as his shaky arms hold the bomb. His eyes go wide as his brain and body fight over what to do with the box. "I didn't know I could move that fast."

"Larry...give it to me...slowly," I say. Like it's a sleeping baby, Thugly hands off the box. I keep my pace steady as I walk it as far from our exit as possible and put it near the other end.

"Man, I almost had a heart attack," Larry says, clutching his chest when I return. "Shouldn't I breathe into a paper bag or something?"

"Put your head between your legs and breathe," I say as I run my hand along the orange metal door. "I don't feel anything else."

"Are you sure—" I raise up the metal rolling shudder before he finishes the sentence. "Oh-shit-oh-shit-oh-shit..." he says, covering his face.

There's something in the middle of the unlit room behind the door. Something large and vaguely familiar, even in the darkness. I flip the light switch to my right.

"Is it another bomb?" he asks, fearing my silence.

"In a wonderful way," I respond, "yes."

Chapter Seventy-One

What Was He Planning?

What's behind the storage door is equally a gift and curse. The first time I ever saw one of these, I thought it looked kind of like those tubes where they freeze people in those sci-fi movies.

But in reality, it's a familiar tool and a potential death sentence wrapped in technological glory. Hell, I've known two lives it took.

Mystified, I take a lap around the device. It's clearly built from the blueprints that were stored on the very administrative flash drive I just recovered from Kilroy. Unlike the only one I've ever used, the one Hackers' Haven affectionately referred to as *The Coffin*, this one looks more Frankenstein-like than a prototype.

"Is this the world's shittiest time machine?" asks Thugly, standing next to me. I didn't even notice he was there.

"It's a LODIS."

"Like the insects from *The Bible*?"

"No," I say, and prepare myself to explain technology to a normie. "It's an acronym — Liquid Ocular Display Interceptor System. It stops large malware bot attacks with visual and sensory motions."

The way he stares at me makes me wish I had a whiteboard to write on.

I sigh and say, "It's a very expensive and high-tech way to make playing Galaga useful."

"Oh, I love Galaga!" says Larry as he tries to open what he believes is the LODIS's door.

"That part should be sealed because—"

Gallons of H_2H_2O, a water variant that allows for better digital refraction and reflection than water, soaks my coworker.

"Boobytrap?" asks a completely soaked Larry. I shake my head as he spits water.

With the reservoir empty, I look inside. This version of LODIS is anything but glamorous. Not only are there lots of scorch marks from haphazard soldering and welding, but the pieces are from old computers and outdated tech.

At least that liar Agent Jack wasn't lying about the government tracking computing parts orders, I think.

I take a moment and survey the rest of the room. Nothing, except for a small, soaked notepad. I flip through the wet pages. Kilroy's flight log for the LODIS.

He's got it working but, according to these notes, it's more buggy than a wagon train.

Even so, when you have so few horses, you don't look the gifted ones in the mouth.

"Have Moscow get a team here and get it set up in his warehouse. We might need it." Part of me wonders if Larry will get upset by me, the formerly mute guy, barking orders at him. I'm pleasantly surprised when he pops out his burner phone, and steps outside to get better reception.

I look at the notes again. Even though Kilroy's handwriting is as bad as mine, I follow what I think he was trying to do. He's shifted the LODIS's operating parameters to be more offensive than defensive.

What was he planning? I wonder. *More importantly, how can I use this bit of Poseidon United technology against them?*

"They'll be here in twenty," says Larry as he rushes back in. "So, we headed back?"

Before I can respond, the elevator at the end of the hall dings, and an elderly lady gets off. As she does, the combination of the chime and the elevator's rider takes me back to a time when I said one final farewell.

Chapter Seventy-Two

Goodbye

*Y*EARS AGO

A large part of me thought a scrawny teenage white boy sneaking an elderly Asian woman out of a hospital might cause a problem. No nurses questioned when I grabbed an abandoned wheelchair from the hallway. No alarm sounded when I cut off her machines, yanked the tape and needle from her IV and bandaged her wounds, or when I cut off her life-monitoring machines. And no security guards chased me as I wheeled her out into the New Orleans early evening breeze.

Granted, I think the only illegal thing we did was take a wheelchair and blanket to keep her warm. They can put those on my tab.

There was one more thing I stole, because I just wanted, no, needed the last few hours to be peaceful. And I would accomplish that by any means possible.

The cracked sidewalk outside of the hospital had lots of weeds sneaking through, fighting to live in an unlivable area. The cracks also made pushing Mrs. Lin a challenge. Granted, she weighed about as much as a case of bottled water at this point, but the chair had some heft to it. Every hundred yards or so, I'd get a wheel stuck. Nothing I couldn't get it out of, just jarring and bothersome.

"Someone, ugh, should fix those," Mrs. Lin struggled to speak through the coughing. For most of the trek, we didn't talk. I didn't because I was winded, and Mrs. Lin didn't because, well...

"It's a good thing...you always say...I fix things," I said, pushing her up a steep hill now. "How about we find some...Quikrete and you get to shoveling and smoothing...the sidewalk?"

"We haven't passed a Home Depot," she quips. "They can use my tax dollars, ugh, first..."

Mrs. Lin's swallowing was getting more difficult. It took her entire body to swallow just her saliva, like some invisible noose was tightening around her windpipe.

To get to the spot I'd chosen, we needed to cross the street. The closest crossing was a good fifty yards away, but Mrs. Lin pushed me to cross right where we were.

"But there's traffic coming, Mrs. Lin," I said.

"If they honk at us, just push me into them," she said before three cough-laughs escaped her throat. "Push hard, and get, ugh, a good payday..."

I followed her instructions, and we entered traffic. Every car stopped. No one leaned out their window and yelled. No one honked. It was as if everyone just knew.

They knew this was the last trek.

"Should we call your son?" I asked as we reached the other side. I always could tell that Mrs. Lin and Larson had a strained relationship. The way she talked about him in a way that I knew he was still alive. It was their relationship that had perished.

"Don't trouble him," she said, her voice small but set. She'd already thought this through. "He has, ugh, his own family. They will also be thrilled to get our home."

I swallowed back my grief. I was losing not just my parental figure, but also my home. I knew that I couldn't take the property for multiple reasons. One, I was a runaway minor. Two, I was no relation to Mrs. Lin but, most importantly, three, I couldn't imagine living there without her. That home would only be a house when she was gone.

The sun hid behind a cloud for the next block, only giving us slices of light through cloud breaks. Sometimes we went from shifting from a dark place into a lighter one, or vice versa. Sometimes I put my back into the push up a hill, and sometimes I had to hold the handles and dig my heels in, so Mrs. Lin didn't race off like a stunt in Jackass.

Out of nowhere, she put her right hand on mine and said, "I'm so sorry, Tanto." She started into an apology she never had to say. "I'm sorry..."

"It's okay, Mrs. Lin," I said, anticipating what she was about to say. "I want nothing that you haven't already given me."

Mrs. Lin laughed, then coughed, and, through wheezes, said, "Everything I've given, you have earned."

I shake the compliment away. "I'll find a new home..." I lie.

"I believe you, because you are...formidable," she said as her voice cracked. "I am sorry I'm leaving you alone..."

I'd only known Mrs. Lin for six months, one week, two days, six hours, and five minutes, but who was counting? I just didn't want to think about it, so I lied again. "I'll be fine."

At this, Mrs. Lin's left hand threw on the wheelchair brake. We skidded to a stop. She waited as a couple of power walkers sped past, and she turned her jaundiced eyes my way.

"Do not be brave for me, little dagger. Be brave for you, and never be afraid to ask for help from others. This life is not safe to go alone."

I chuckled and asked, "Are you about to give me a wooden sword?"

Instead of making fun of my The Legend of Zelda *reference, she kept her gaze, despite my quip. Or maybe because of it. "I know you hide your pain in your humor. Just don't be afraid to share it. It's a big world out there, but it is also a kind one. Share where you can and accept help when offered."*

I don't know how she made it through that without coughing, but she did.

With that, we pushed forward. In the distance, the park: The Oaks. It was a place where the rich in New Orleans had their fancy parties. Restaurants and bars set up there and local bands played for various charity events.

When I'd planned this, I never thought to see if the park was actually open today. Across the gate, a thick chain and an equally thick lock shut down our entry. To the side, a sign read Stay Off Lawn - Fertilization in Progress.

"Hold on, Mrs. Lin," I said, my problem-solving hat firmly on. I took a lap around the gate but found no entry. No loose bars on the fence, and no area where I could get a wheelchair through. And I wasn't strong enough to lift her over the six-foot fence.

Maybe Mrs. Lin saw the way I paced, creating and shooting down idea after idea, or the look on my face, but she grabbed me with her icy hand. When I met her gaze, she pointed to the side of the park. There the sun broke through the cloud cover and illuminated a simple green patch of lawn.

"This spot is mighty lovely," she said simply, so I wheeled us over bumps and holes.

"Get me out of this thing," she said once we got there.

I grabbed the blanket from her lap, glimpsing her purplish and swollen legs under her hospital gown. I laid the blanket across the grass, then I kneeled down and scooped her up easily. She was more of a bag of bones than the warrior woman who scared off the guy who tried to kill me in that alley half a year ago.

"Weight Watchers has really worked for you, Mrs. Lin," I say, and she slaps my back.

"Fanboy, you know I'm a…Jenny Craig girl," she said between coughs. In the distance, workers ran sprayers, fertilizing the lawn. Thankfully, we were upwind, so all we smelled was the scent of nearby magnolias.

"Mrs. Lin, I want to—" I started before Mrs. Lin interrupted.

"You've already reminded me I like to fix things," she said, tears in her eyes. I looked back toward the mowers just so she wouldn't see the same in mine. "I want you to know that you never needed fixing. You were neglected. Abused. But never broken."

I can't tell you why, but something in me shifted. I collapsed on the ground at Mrs. Lin's side and balled up. It's as if I was in a circus tent that one long rod ran up the middle and supported. The pole already had worn down over time. Now, it snapped like a twig, and all the giant tarp came crashing down.

I cried like I had never cried before. When I needed to be at my strongest, I crumpled. I didn't notice when she covered me with the blanket. I wasn't paying attention when Mrs. Lin stroked my long hair. I only noticed her when her coughing restarted.

When I finally realized what was going on, I jumped up and sniffed, then wiped away my tears and apologized.

Mrs. Lin sent me a smile as she closed her eyes, holding in the coughs. "I…heard an artist once say…Tears are just part of love's tax: they're drawn from your account…when you least expect."

"Well, I guess I'm paid up for a while," I said between sniffles. I handed the blanket back to Mrs. Lin; she wrapped her legs in it and smiled. Her eyes were darker than I remember behind those coke-bottle lenses, almost cat-like. She smoothed out the blanket and patted a spot for me to join her.

So I did.

More of the sun got hidden behind growing clouds, except for our spot. We sat there in silence for a while; me recovering from my tears and her fighting through her coughs. It was a beautiful, yet crumbling, moment of peace.

As we stared at the sky, Mrs. Lin tapped on my pocket. "Are we going to...talk about that?"

The elephant in my pocket. One syringe, part midazolam, haloperidol, and morphine. I'd kept up with the end-of-life medications that the docs gave Mrs. Lin. Before today, each one had 11%, 23%, and 21% strength, respectively. These doses kept Mrs. Lin calm and relatively pain-free.

The syringe in my pocket had the same cocktail, except at 58%, 50%, and 87% strength. Even though nurses administered this solution orally, I'd overheard several saying that, when they combined this particular strength, nurses referred to it as The Last Shot.

"I-I-I'm not ready," I said.

It took Mrs. Lin two heaves to get her arm on my shoulder before she asked me what I already knew she would. "Will you ever be?"

I shook my head and met her gaze. This time, the tears in her eyes weren't from sadness: she was in pain.

And it was time for that pain to go away.

I took out the syringe and closed my eyes. Then she said, "No," and finagled her tiny icicle fingers into mine, holding the syringe with me.

"This is not suicide, little dagger," she said. "This...this is mercy..."

I moved the needle away and held it in the sun, looking at the light going through the liquid that would end the life of the closest to a mother I would ever have.

Then Mrs. Lin extended her once-strong hand shakily and said what I needed to hear.

"Give it to me."

As if in a trance, before I knew it, she held the syringe. Mrs. Lin took the top off the syringe, flicked her nail against it, tilted her head back, and emptied the contents into her mouth.

Wincing, she shook her head and said, "Oh, it burns worse than before..." She licked her cracked lips and added, "At least my cough stopped."

I didn't have the fortitude to make a joke, or even acknowledge what she'd done.

"You know," Mrs. Lin said as she sat up. "I think that did it. Whatever was in that God-awful thing was just what I needed to cure the cancer."

I chuckled and sat up as well. "I think you're right."

"Oh, I'm always right," she said as an easiness spread through her. Her eyes seemed less yellow, less wide. It's like her muscles relaxed. Her shoulders lowered as if life's weight just up and lifted off of them.

Our little opening in the cloud closed. Now, even our spot darkened.

I scooted closer to Mrs. Lin as she stared out into the distance.

"Tanto, as much as I love to fix things, nothing stays fixed forever...unless you box it up and put it away. You can't do that with people, little dagger. Including yourself."

As if on cue, the sun broke through the cloud bank.

"You will fail. You will crack. And you will grow from it."

"I don't know, Mrs. Lin," I said, more to myself than her. "I'm not very strong."

"You don't have to be," she countered. "Strength doesn't make a fighter. The Code does."

"Mrs. Lin, if you're—"

She puts a hand up. "Stop interrupting. I'm on a deadline," she said with a chuckle as her shaky hand pointed across the green field. "This world is just so damn beautiful, and it needs all the warriors it can get. Be part of what keeps it safe."

I heard her words, but I also didn't. I was there, but I was also back in our hospital room listening to Mrs. Lin talk about her father. And the last thing he told her.

"You know what's going to happen now?" I asked Mrs. Lin.

"No," she answered, "but I'm excited to find out."

Her body continued to deflate. It's like she didn't need oxygen anymore. Her mortal coil was just holding her back. I kept my eyes on hers even as her blinks got less frequent, yet deeper. Longer. More permanent.

I pulled her close and whispered into her ear, "No matter what, it's going to be okay..."

That gets a weak half-chuckle. "Hey...I've heard that bef..."

I felt her step out of our plane of existence and into the unknown. It was as terrifying as it was magical. Now, the balloon was empty. The vessel was unoccupied. Except for the occasional twitch, which I believe was the body decompressing, Mrs. Lin's body slumped on me was no longer the person who I owed so much to.

Finally, I laid her on the ground. I wrapped her body in the blanket and waited to cover her face. Then, right before I did, I placed a single kiss on her forehead and said to her what I had never had the courage to say when she was alive.

"Goodbye, mother."

Chapter Seventy-Three

David Cones

"You good, Vice?" asks Larry as I shake my head, then nod. After we enter Larry's car, he lets me ride in silence the entire drive back. No police, no SWAT, and no Mercator Agency thugs follow or detain us. We just ride with the windows down and let the outside world be our radio. Ultimately, we make it into Memphis and back to MetroMed as the sun sets behind the Arkansas/Tennessee bridge.

"We've got maybe ten hours until the hack," says Larry as he puts the Kia in park, a little more emphasis in the word *hack* than I expected. Just like sex, no one forgets their first hack. Larry asks, "Besides sleep, anything else you want to do?"

"Okay. Five hours for sleep. Five hours for prep," I say, almost robotically. "We can grab a quick nap in empty hospital beds, then check in with Moscow. We'll have to run checks with Penny to lock in where her team will cause chaos. I can also see if Mane-Eac is—"

"Hey," interrupts Larry as he puts his hand on my shoulder. "Slow down. Breathe."

"Larry, everything I've been fighting for is about to come down to one extremely complicated hack that I don't know how to pull off."

"Breathe," is all Larry says.

I guess the universe decided that, since AldenSong is healing, I need another level-headed protector. Never in a million years did I think some Higher Power would anoint Larry as my impromptu guardian angel.

Of course, when Larry tells me to breathe, it makes me want to fidget. To argue. But then I take a beat, roll the Kia's seat back, and take several deep breaths. Larry rolls his seat back as well, and we stare at the setting sun.

"You want to walk closer to the water?" he asks.

I nod, and we leave the car. As we do, he reaches under his seat, grabs something, and shoves it in his pocket. Probably a gun. *Smart.*

An orangish hue traces over the horizon. Larry is to my left and the breeze coming off the water is to my right. The wind tickles my nose and sends a few goosebumps up my arm. It's not a big moment, but one of the small ones in life that matter.

"Last time I took time to enjoy this view," I say, "I almost got snake bit."

"Yeah, I remember it well," says Larry as he reaches into his pocket and pulls out a pint of some liquor I've never heard of: *Entrepierna Del Diablo.* "Speaking of poison..."

"What?" I ask. "No *Angry Mutt?*"

"They were out," he answers simply and unscrews the top.

The plastic pint's top squeaks when Larry opens it. Even though the liquor looks like water, it smells like paint thinner. Larry takes a pull, grimaces, and then passes it my way.

It's been a minute since I drank. It's not my favorite vice, but it's in the Top Five. I do the dumb thing and smell it, confirming it's more suited for stripping paint than human consumption. The fumes also sting my eyes, as if I don't have enough of a warning not to drink this shit.

I hold my nose and take a swig. The liquor doesn't make it past my tongue before I spray it all over the grass.

"Every bit of bacteria in my mouth just burned up!" I sputter.

"It does make your grill sparkle," says Larry as he downs another gulp. "And...everyone spits the first time."

"This may be the worst shit I've ever had, Larry."

Still, I motion for him to pass me the pint. It doesn't burn as badly as the first time, which is a little like saying *the second bullet hurt less than the first.* My throat feels like I swallowed a lit coal.

Larry studies the tequila's label. "That's actually their slogan. I think. I don't read Spanish."

"Why'd, ugh, why'd you buy this?" I ask between gasps.

"Eh, it was on sale," says Larry as he takes a swig. "Well, *clearance.*"

"I, ugh, see why," I say, then take another pull.

An ambulance roars past us. Neither of us reacts, except to watch it fade in the distance.

I wobble, the liquor hitting me faster than I thought. I'm not drunk; I'm also not clearheaded.

Larry notices and says, "Maybe we should get shit-hammered before the hack."

I laugh and take another pull of liquid funk before passing it back.

"That's gonna be the last drink I have until this thing is done. Plus, I'm on enough medication to knock out a platoon, so I can't risk getting out of hand."

As a *Devil-May-Care* haze covers my eyes, my spine relaxes.

"Suit yourself," he says as Thugly takes a tug from the pint. "I only offer this because we could totally have the David Cone effect."

"I don't follow," I say. The tequila is impacting Thugly's balance, so he leans against a nearby magnolia tree and preaches to this choir.

"David Cones was a baseball pitcher for the New York Yankees. The night before he was set to pitch, he went out and partied with the cast of *Saturday Night Live*."

"Was this with John Beluchi or Chris Farley?" I ask. "Because no one went harder than them."

"Maybe, don't remember," responds Larry as he rubs his eyes. "Anyway, Cones got blitzed. I mean, no sleep and throwing up from the time the party ended to into the ballgame."

"Wait," I say. "He was puking on the mound?"

"Look at my bitch right here, knowing some baseball terms," quips Larry with a smirk. "He puked in the bathroom. The locker room. Even the dugout."

"So, he pushed through and pitched?" I asked.

"Better," says Larry. "He threw his first no-hitter. Nine innings. The 11th no-hitter in Yankee's history."

"You're saying that if we get plastered, we might have a better chance at actually taking down one of the most powerful corporate giants and clandestine government agencies in the world hungover?"

Larry doesn't immediately answer. Instead, he stares across the water. After a minute of silence, he takes a deep breath and puts his hands in his pockets.

"We're probably gonna die, aren't we?" he asks.

We're outgunned, outnumbered, and undersupplied. We're a handful of hackers against the corporate machine. I say the only thing I can.

"I think we're going to make a difference."

Larry cups his hands and yells, "Homie don't rat!"

Maybe it's the comradery, or maybe it's the world's worst tequila mixing with my anti-seizure and concussion meds, but I join in. "Homie don't break!"

Then, together, "Homie don't run!"

We laugh. Then the laughter dies down. Eventually, only the breeze over the water and the occasional car horn in the distance are the only night noises.

"You tired?" I ask.

"Not enough to slow down now," Larry answers. "You?"

"I slept two days ago, don't want to be too greedy."

Larry chuckles and in this moment, I know he's got my back as much as I've got his. I smack him hard on the back to knock him off this lean-tree.

"Let's go piss some people off."

Chapter Seventy-Four

Blow Up Gloriously

Almost a decade ago, to keep the US government from imprisoning the real DoGoodR for life, my team and I infiltrated a government server farm. When Mane-Eac, Squirrel_Lord, and I got through the exterior defenses, we expected the movie effect for server rooms: line after line of the most advanced workstations with lights more aglow than a Christmas tree.

What we found was the reality of what happens when you outsource to the lowest bidder: outdated POS — piece of shit — machines whose cooling fans screeched more than breezed. Knowing how hard of a time the fake DoGoodR had getting us computer parts for the *S.S. Turing*, I expected a repeat of the government's server shithole.

At Moscow's warehouse, Larry and I find a setup as different from POS's as an Etch A- Sketch is from an iPad. Instead of *Desktops of the Damned*, I get *The Matrix*, the most high-tech machines I've ever seen. Twelve units all networked together. I hop on the closest terminal. Bootup is under six seconds. That tells me solid state drive storage and enough RAM in this machine to play a dozen of the most bandwidth-sucking video games all at once.

On top of one computer is a small, simple white box with a plain black ribbon. I open it, a little nervous of what I'll find. Inside is a simple notecard. *Administrator name: Vice. Administrator password: TrustDaRussian.*

I'm the guy who likes to look at the ingredients before I take a bite, so I find a screwdriver on a tool shelf in the corner. Six screws later, I'm staring at the most impressive computer I've seen in years: the hard drives are not only SSD, but Non-Volatile Memory Express, or NVME. They're the fastest on the market. The fan is uber quiet and the side-mounted video/graphics card looks badass. Down near the base, the motherboard, I notice the wiring will overclock the system. However, to combat this, liquid coolant flows throughout.

Finally, I check the RAM: Corsair. While I don't really know the brand, I flat out love the model name:

Vengeance.

And we have a dozen of these vengeful boys.

If we have this many, what kind of arsenal are we going up against? comes the joy-stealing thought.

I look closer at the setup: this terminal is not only connected to the others. It relies on that connection. I open a command prompt and dive in. It appears the system is connected through distributed computing. I heard about this because people are allowing companies to use the processing power of dormant machines for research: this type of system mainly exists in medical data and protein dynamic simulation.

"How did Moscow know how to do this?" I ask aloud.

To my surprise, Larry actually has the answer. "It's his contact in the gub'ment," he says, strolling up to a giant, ten feet long by five feet high plasma screen, and cuts it on. "I'd love some *GTA* on this bee-yotch...vroom-vroom! I think it's his brother or something..."

"Wait..." My brain itches. I know a trap when I see one. "We're trying to stay off their radar, and he got these direct?"

Larry shrugs. "When the beekeeper is guarding the beehouse, why not get your honey from the beekeeper's kitchen?"

Poor terminology notwithstanding, I get what he's saying. It's as scary as it is brilliant.

At the center of the room is Kilroy's LODIS. I check the solution tank: full. Power is on. I grab the oxygen tube, cut it on, and take an inhale. It's good to go.

Where was Moscow when I was starting out? I think.

"Oh, that's a lot of damned reading," says Larry, pointing at twelve stacks of paper four feet tall each. "You know why this is here, V?"

"I have a sneaking suspicion," I say as I join Larry and snag the top doc: it's computer code from all the files we stole from Poseidon United. "I told Moscow to print everything we stole from junk files on the Poseidon United servers, because maybe we can use it."

"For what?" asks Larry as he holds up a handful. "Kindling?"

"Just shut up and help me look," I say as I grab a handful and push it into Larry's chest. He glances at it and shoves the stack back.

"I. Told. You. I. Don't. Read. Spanish."

"Learn on the fly," I say as I spread the paper across the floor. I can't say I blame Thugly; the sequences overwhelm even this code jockey. For an hour, I dive in. I go through close to three hundred pieces of paper, looking for a clue and praying for a miracle. In the back of my head, I hear fake-DoGoodR mocking me: *To find the lies in the code, you must first read the truth in the paper.*

I don't ask how Moscow broke through Poseidon's encryption on these junk files. I just scan. Part of me wonders if I can get Larry to hypnotize me the way Cyfib did. Maybe if I went all *robotic,* I could see the answer.

Cyfib mentioned that there were changes to the hypnosis programming after I escaped. I don't know if I can exit the hypnosis the same way AldenSong did.

It's too much of a risk.

With a crash, Larry knocks off a small HD camera from one of the workstations trying to take his own picture. They're a wasted expense; no hacker wants to be seen.

In his hands it looks like a ray gun straight out of a sci-fi movie.

"Larry, what'd you find there?"

"Oh, I thought you'd know what it is," he says as he hands it to me.

It's so heavy I almost drop it. Upon closer examination, it has a classic trigger and sights. Where a safety switch for a gun would be are the words *Repel* and *Retrieve.* And along the side are the words *Drone Deterrent.*

"It's something that might just save our asses," I say and hand it back to Thugly. "We could have used one of these days ago."

I stand up and my entire body aches, the tequila hangover starting to hit. The clock on the wall says 6:20 a.m. My head throbs. My stomach aches.

What I thought was an hour of studying code was actually three. And I have nothing to show for it.

What am I missing? I take a bit of my rage out on the giant stacks of paper, kicking them around.

Larry joins in. Together, we cover the room in paper.

When we finish our mosh, a winded Larry asks, "So, why'd...we do...that?"

"Because, ugh, it felt good," I say through gasps. I toss handfuls of paper in the air.

And Larry catches them.

"Man, you actually like reading this stuff?" Larry asks, stacking what he catches.

"*Like* is a strong word," I say. "It's necessary. Let's just say that."

"Huh," says Larry in a way that catches my attention. It's not the flat *I-don't-care* tone. It's got a speck of *what's-this* in it. "So, all this stuff came from the bad guys?"

"From their junk," I say. "They were using it as a protective barrier to keep out—"

"Yeah-yeah, shut up," interrupts Larry as he hands me a piece of code. "And what's that?"

He points at the bottom of the page, an area designated for the printer. "That's the code for page printed, which printer, and all that."

"And this?" Larry shows me a different page.

"Same thing," I say and toss some paper in the corner.

"I—I really don't think so, V," says Larry grabbing two more pieces of paper. "If this code you say is for each printed stack, it should vary right? Like, have a different filename, location, and all that..."

Holy shit, I think, and grab some paper and look at the bottom areas. "They're not out of the margins," I say as a smile starts in my heart and climbs up to spread my lips. "Larry, you beautiful bastard...this is either gonna work or blow up gloriously."

Now we have less than three hours to do a week's worth of work. And, for the first time in what seems like years, I feel like we're about to bring the pain to those that actually deserve it.

Chapter Seventy-Five

From Bad to Worse

Larry and I use every microsecond of the next two hours and forty minutes. Larry is a quick learner because he's copying the code he found into everything: viruses, worms, dambusters. You name it; we put the code in it. Larry didn't just discover what I believe to be a way into the Mercator and Poseidon United network; he found THE way to do it by possibly bypassing antiviruses, firewalls, or even human intervention.

What Larry found in the code was metadata. Metadata provides information and certification about, well, certain data. It makes finding files or information easier. It doesn't explain the content; but it logs it. It clears it and says it is safe in the system.

Imagine you're a cattle rancher. Your field is next to another cattle rancher. There's one gate separating your livestock. Let's say a storm comes through and knocks down the fence, mixing the two livestocks. How do you tell which cows are yours? Through a mark — a collar, an ear tag, or a brand. But, without the mark, you can't tell whose cattle belong to whom.

The files in your system, no matter how important or useless, are your cattle. Everything outside of your system is someone else's livestock. Files branded with your metadata should be able to bypass your fence — your firewall and antivirus — without cause for alarm.

That's my theory anyway, which might get shot to shit when we attack the firewalls. We're either creating digitized missiles to launch into cyberspace...or paper airplanes about to hit a window.

The 9 a.m. alarm goes off. *Go time.* "You ready for this shit?" I ask Larry.

"Homie don't—" he starts as I put my hand up.

"Whether you like it or not, you're a hacker now," I interrupt. "And we have our own version. *Burn Bright,*" I say pointing at myself, "*Burn Fast,*" and I point at him. "Together, we say *Burn Down.*"

"Why?" Larry asks, brow furrowed.

I hang my head and mumble, "I swear I will punch you in the mouth..." Then I slightly regret taking this tone with Thugly, until he playfully punches me in the arm.

Our team outside the room is set to throw in the human element. Sometimes, that means doing something sporadic. And that works, until it comes to law enforcement and emergency response personnel. There are no better routine followers than those two groups. And that's where Penny's team comes into play: they'll cause enough disturbances to become a very unwelcome menace. Anything that is perceived as a possible threat to the general public becomes their priority number one.

Then there's Moscow's team. They'll plant enough false flags to get attention, but not cause loss of life or anything. If he follows the instructions I left for him, Moscow will add to the chaos and have more...inventive problems for the area.

For example, one of his team is currently setting fully charged cellphones along the edge of every bridge and major highway within two miles. When our hack starts, those cellphones will mimic car GPS signals. What that'll do is tell every real GPS system that the bridges and highways have too much traffic, and bottleneck the 9 a.m. crowd on smaller streets.

It's evil to mess with people's commutes, but desperate times and all that...

The oversized monitor in the middle of the room flashes the word *Visitor: Unknown*. That happens when someone joins our chat channel on the Dark Web. I click on the window, but it's empty. *Must've been a glitch*, I think.

The gravity of the situation hits me: there's no Mane-Eac. No NMH8, W8ndig's hactivism team. And no other hackers on this thread. There's no digital calvary coming to our aid.

We're on our own.

I roll my shoulders back and yell, "Burn bright!" Then I open our system's monitor: all systems are a *Go*.

"Burn fast!" Larry yells as he enters the command to load our digitized robots that will lead our attack.

I type the command to fire a salvo at Poseidon United's servers, but I wait to hit *Enter*. This is our last opportunity to back down. I mean, there's always a chance to run from a fight.

But I'm no longer running.

"Burn down!"

Fire.

Sixteen thousand bots, all loaded with various commands that include noise, destruction, and siphoning, attack the firewall. On the giant screen, we watch as our digital missiles approach their shields.

And I say a little prayer that ultimately goes nowhere as the missiles disintegrate upon impact.

"They should've made it through!" yells Larry as he tugs at his cornrows. "We put the metadata code in there and it should've breezed right through the firewall and—"

Alarms sound, interrupting him.

"We have incoming!" They just hit us with a freaking boulder of data.

How the hell did they track us so quickly? We're running a double-layered software-defined fabric through six VPNs and are as scrambled as Huddle House eggs.

The system is in recovery mode. Usually, that happens after a virus attack. We've lost four of our dozen computers.

An idea forms. I run to one of the *offline* terminals and take a risk by yanking out the Ethernet cable.

"What are you doing?" asks Larry.

"Performing an autopsy." I open a command prompt and dive. "They just hit us with a brick, so I want to know what that brick is made of."

As I type, a new alarm goes off. Larry looks at me.

"Try to move us out of the way before the next one hits."

"How?" he asks.

"Give me some magic, Houdini."

He takes my hint and goes to a working terminal, opening the software I taught him about right before the hack: Hou-Doo, a system that disconnects you from the network, scrambles the IP address, and logs you back in. It'll mess up our ability to attack but, right now, we have nothing to hit them with but bad breath.

How were they able to push through our shields? "They're hitting us with a false systems-update patch," I say, equally pissed and impressed.

Moscow sold us out, I realize. "They knew we were going to be using the same systems that they use!"

"Um, V," says Larry, a wavering in his voice. "You need to see this…"

"Not now, Larry," I respond without looking up.

Then I hear a voice that isn't Larry's, and I know things just went from bad to worse.

Chapter Seventy-Six

Far From Home

"Hello, Tanto." Those two words echo in the warehouse.

There, on the giant monitor, is Agent Jack. His perfect crew cut and clean-shaven face still don't hide my mental image of the man I once called DoGoodR. And friend.

"Agent Jack, I'm glad we can finally speak," I say with some truth. I need time to think. Like a boxer that just got jacked in the face, I'm gonna cover up until this round's bell dings.

"I bet you are," says Agent Jack, his perfectly knotted black tie complementing his crisp white shirt. "Though I don't think you're going to like what I'm going to say."

Smug, arrogant asshole.

"Clear communication is a wonderful thing," I say, working away on my command prompt, trying to decipher what component Poseidon is using to knock out our systems. "But I'd rather do this in person, if you don't mind."

"Is this so you can surrender?" Agent Jack barely contains his laughter. "Sadly, I'm at HQ and you are..."

"Not telling," I say, quick-scrolling through the code. "Also, not surrendering."

"I figured as much," says Agent Jack.

Someone enters the screen, whispers something in his right ear, and Jack nods.

"That was one creative way to try to get through our firewall. Bravo."

"You think that's impressive, you should see me naked," I say, spouting bullshit to keep him busy. A window just popped open and shut real quick on our system.

We may have a visitor...

"What I really want to know is, why didn't you turn us in when you had the chance?" I ask. "You had enough to put us all away for life."

"You think too much of yourself, Tanto," says Agent Jack. "There was an opening for CITO, I needed to serve the board a bigger fish than you. You weren't an actual threat, more like an annoying fly: a pest with a short life span. I had to turn you into an angry wasp, and no one wants one of those loose in their house. Catching and releasing you has only given you the chance to fatten up. Now, you're my own personal foie gras."

"Glad I poked the bear hard enough for you," I say. There is a thread of worry dangling at the end of his words that I just want to tug on a bit and see what unravels.

As Agent Jack chuckles, he holds up a stack of paper and scans it.

He's looking at the code just like I am. The difference is he probably had a dozen agents filter it down to a couple of pages while I have the entire encyclopedia in front of me.

"I want a face-to-face so you can come clean," I add. "You're a coder, but you've also spent time in the trenches with real hackers. Me. Mane-Eac. And I bet others. Am I right?"

"Don't try to analyze me, Tanto," says Agent Jack as he circles something on the paper and hands it off screen. "Better men than you have tried and failed."

"No doubt," I say as my screen blurs.

Someone's in our system.

"Larry, we've got a skunk in the outhouse."

"What's that — oh, yeah, on it!" he says.

He's a quick learner, but Larry doesn't speak fluent techie. Yet.

"Ah, you have a friend there," says Agent Jack. Several green lights appear on the terminals' HD cameras. "There you are..."

Without me having to say a word, Larry darts around the room and yanks all of them out of their respective terminals.

"Well, whoever you are, you are no fun," quips Agent Jack before he adds, "Just because Mister Tanto isn't surrendering does not mean you have to go down with him. If you merely type in your coordinates, I promise you will go free."

Larry doesn't even flinch when he says, "No hablo inglés, mi amigo." He whispers in my ear, "Are there other mics?"

"Assume someone wired the room," I say with a shrug.

But if Moscow did sell us out, why aren't there Mercator goons already here?

"Gotcha, I'll drown us out," says Larry as he goes over to the far wall and cuts on an old radio.

"Larry, don't use public radio—"

"You're listening to *Highway to Hell* by AC/DC with Drake and Zeke here on Memphis's own Rock 103."

I feel Agent Jack's laughter before I ever hear it.

"You're not far from home after all."

Chapter Seventy-Seven

Got You

I don't kick myself or get upset with Larry for almost giving away our position. Unless we hacked these bastards from the moon, they'd have teams ready for us all over the country. On the screen, Agent Jack gestures wildly. Even on *Mute*, I can tell he's dispatching even more teams to our region.

It's just a matter of time now...

That's about when a chat window pops up on a nearby terminal. I go to it. I can still type, but someone is typing over me. Every instinct is to shut off the terminal, to yank the power cord from the wall. But then I let the mysterious stranger keep typing, and his note changes everything.

[Kilroy] Copy metadata to folder named LoadMode and fire again.

How on earth could Kilroy know the hack was going down now?

Then I look at the LODIS. There, on the side of it, is an active camera.

I blow it a kiss and Kilroy responds:

[Kilroy] Now go f some sh up.

User has left the chat.

"Larry, I'm gonna need your magic fingers again," I say.

"That's what she said!" he shouts with glee before I show him the ended chat. Larry darts to a terminal and starts copying the code as I put these instructions on the Dark Web link that I've got for our potential hackers that are late to the party.

An alert tells me that two anonymous users have read the discussion.

We're not as alone as we were, I think, knowing damn well that this could also be a trap. I'm assuming one of them was Kilroy.

But who is the other?

I tap the mic next to the HD camera, the last operating one in the warehouse. At least, I think that. The feedback jars our listeners, and Agent Jack's eyes clinch tight. At least he might get a migraine out of this hack. Agent Jack unmutes.

He says in his best Herman Munster voice, "You rang?"

"Can you guarantee my friend's safety?" I ask because, even though we have some hope, this hack isn't working. Not yet. If it fails and if I can keep Larry safe, I can stomach what happens to me.

Or what I'll do to keep it from coming to that.

A devilish smile, one so tight across the lips it kicks the head back, crosses Agent Jack's face. "Absolutely."

His eyes shift up and to the right, the traditional *tell* for a lie. I didn't need to see it to know a traitor will always act like a traitor.

"Yeah, sell that elsewhere," I say before adding, "you've already left one corpse in your wake."

Agent Jack raises his left eyebrow in thought before snapping his fingers. "Ah, the body at the warehouse...well, you can't have killers without a body..."

"Who was it?" I ask, not able to smother the fear in my voice.

"Maybe a nobody," Agent Jack says. He leans into the camera and chuckles before he adds, "but wouldn't it be excellent if it was the actual DJ, your DoGoodR? I mean, we caught him before I took his place. How else do you think I knew so much about all of you?"

Rage fills my body. The thought of a captured, tortured DoGoodR had crossed my mind, especially in the early hours of the morning. That'd explain how they knew so much about his and Mane-Eac's on-line relationship. And how Agent Jack could infiltrate The Nameless easily as one of their own.

An alarm sounds, not on our end, but on the monitor. Then, on my terminal, a chat window pops open.

[Mane-Eac] That's my cue to light this brocha up.

Before I can type a response, a digital representation of Poseidon's firewall flashes bright across the screen. A huge chunk of the barrier just opened up. Mane-Eac has always been one of the best data sniffers and sifters I know. She just reminded me she's no slouch in knocking through firewalls, either.

"Larry, you got the code inserted?"

"Fire away, V."

I hit the command for *engage*. Thousands of search-and-retrieve bots fly through cyberspace and enter the rapidly closing hole in the firewall. They're data miners, not virus spreaders, diving into the pro-tective junk layer.

I just hope a couple make it out and back to us...

As the firewall closes, sixty bots make it out. The second they do, half of them explode.

"What the hell happened?" asks Larry. "Did they self-destruct?"

"They're using their own LODIS," I say, recognizing the pattern. "We only need one bot..."

A dozen more bots evaporate. I check our incoming data. Nothing. Not a thing. Not a single bot.

Then I get one ping. There, in our directory, is one file.

Oh-please-oh-please-oh-please.

In this file is a slightly different set of metadata.

I copy it, instruct Larry to put it on what he calls *The Nail*, and I put it on our Dark Web forum.

An alarm goes off that I very much recognize; it's a tracking beacon.

They set up a tracer, even in the junk files.

Without looking at the screen, I feel Agent Jack's words before he ever says them.

"Got you."

Chapter Seventy-Eight

Go Home

Normally, when a government agency nails a trace on you, you bolt. As hackers, we have our escape plan set and follow it within thirty seconds of detection.

But, first off, we're done running. We're staying on course until this ship plows through the iceberg or it sinks us.

And second, I not only knew this was coming; I counted on it.

The attack on Poseidon continues on the screen. I can tell that Mane-Eac is hitting the server chain located in Langley, Virginia — I recognize the names of those servers. They were vital when Hackers' Haven protected them, so their names are burned into my brain. Someone else is hitting the server chain in Denver, Colorado. My guess is W8ndig's NMH8 crew. They're not causing any damage, but I'll take all the noise I can get.

And Moscow's and Penny's teams are still keeping police and emergency fully occupied.

If they're coming to get us, it'll be Mercator Agents, not locals, that strike.

"So, you sure about this?" Larry asks as sirens sound in the distance.

"You don't ask if they packed your parachute correctly when you're plummeting," I quip and grab a pair of binoculars before peering out the door. I crack the door open and peer out. Six SUVs converge on us.

"Come on, come on," I mumble.

That's when the first one's front end explodes. The vehicle flips backwards and crashes into two of the trailing SUVs.

Larry, hearing the explosion, glances over my shoulder. "Man, your buddy Kilroy knows how to pack a claymore."

I keep silent. That crush bomb did its job: keep the foot soldiers at bay. They'll set a perimeter now, but it also means that the option of taking us alive just left the table.

"You've just committed an aggressive action toward federal agents," says Agent Jack over the monitor. "I warned you..."

Larry snatches the *Drone Deterrent* rifle and powers it up.

"Hold off until we actually see it. It only has a thirty-second charge," I caution

He powers it off. "Got the net?"

I hold the Faraday bag from the previous hack. Larry tosses me the rifle and I cover it with the bag. The longer they don't realize we have this lifesaver, the better off we are.

"You got *The Nail*?" I ask.

Larry raises his clenched fist high.

Together, we lean against the back door and wait. I crouch and study the ground. In the distance, a cup of rainwater keeps perfectly flat.

Until it starts to shake.

"Go!" I yell.

"Son of a bitch, this is a bad idea…" Larry mutters.

While I completely agree with him, I don't say so.

The harsh midmorning sun blinds us as we scan for the drone. All the SUVs are gone, which means they're out of the blast radius.

"I don't see it," says Larry as he pivots. "Maybe it's too high…"

If that's the case, and they fire while we don't see the drone, all that'll be left of us is dust and defeat.

Then a shimmer in the sky catches my attention.

"I think I see it," I say.

"Know, or think?" asks Larry.

"Screw it," I say, yanking the Faraday bag from the rifle, powering it up and firing.

A loud, deep noise blasts from the gun as a red beam heads skyward. For a few seconds, nothing happens. The drone hovers two hundred feet above us, neither retreating nor attacking.

Maybe this prototype doesn't work…

Then, as if on autopilot, the drone swivels. And descends.

When I first learned about these drone deterrent guns, I was interested in the repelling feature. I mean, one of these things destroyed my mentor, his team, and later our base. But that feature is only useful if we're running.

Besides, the last thing we want is for this drone to go home. Not yet.

Chapter Seventy-Nine

Hovering

"**A**ren't you worried about snipers?" asks Larry as his head swivels like it's a windshield wiper. I can't blame him; we're exposed in this bare field.

I keep my rifle's aim on the drone. "They won't dare risk shooting us yet, mainly because this is a thirty-million-dollar aircraft."

We're directly under the descending drone—its fifty-plus foot wingspan eclipses the sun.

The power level on the gun is dropping like there's a hole in the power cell or something going from *Full* to *Warning* in a beat.

The drone's roar is almost deafening as it lowers down enough for me to drop the rifle. Larry is Johnny-on-the-Spot with the Faraday bag and tosses it over the drone's front targeting sensor, tracking relay, and camera. Like a bucking bronco fenced in a gate, the drone fights us. It makes sense: this thing is a computer that just got cut off from the network. Of course it's going to act out.

"Quick, help me find the port," I say as Larry and I run our hands around the sleek metal and polycarbonate housing. We check the port, aft, and everywhere in between. Then Larry snaps his fingers, plops to the ground, and rolls under the aircraft. I open the hinged areas on the wings to find not just two missiles, but dual machine guns. Judging from the size of the barrels, they probably fire the same size bullets that Moscow's handheld tank killer does.

"Got it!" Larry yells as his right hand extends my way.

"It's in your pocket," I remind him, and Larry reaches into his pants. He withdraws *The Nail:*

Cyfib's administrative flash drive for Hackers' Haven.

Before I *loaned* this flash drive to Kilroy, I tried to copy it to no avail. Today, Larry and I found out we could actually load files onto the massive portable hard drive. So we loaded it with every bit of poison from my Dark Web folders: viruses, malware, and dambreakers, all laced with the new metadata code.

And the final F U to all of this: the Goemon Virus.

Plus, for good measure, we also put all the junk files from earlier, as well as the lone junk file we got minutes ago.

While it's a heavily packed crypto-bomb, it's still a Hail Mary.

"Okay," says Larry from under the drone. "I think it's in."

"Think, or know?" I echo back at Larry.

"Yeah, that *is* annoying..." Larry says with a wink as he dusts himself off. "Ready?"

I grab the drone deterrent. "We have only a few seconds, but hopefully, when I hit *Repel*, it will immediately return home."

With that, Larry yanks off the Faraday bag and the drone immediately rotates, scaring both of us. The Faraday catches on the underside of the drone, hanging on our attached flash drive.

"Shit, let me—" Larry starts, but the housing for the machine guns rolls back.

I squeeze the trigger on the rifle, expecting a red laser blast and a deep sound.

Instead, I get a high-pitched squeal and a pinkish beam that fades into nothingness.

The gun is empty.

And Larry and I are face-to-face with a hovering drone's guns.

Chapter Eighty

Don't Run

There are many Bushido stories about a warrior staring down another, waiting for the right moment to strike. There are also ones about warriors not just preparing for, but welcoming death.

This is not one of those stories. This is one of those where we either wait and pray that the drone deterrent rifle's programming worked, or duck and cover.

Larry takes a careful step right. The drone follows.

"That's not good," says Larry, Captain Obvious. Then the barrels spin on the machine guns. "Run or don't run?" he asks.

I give a third option. "Duck!"

The drone's guns pump round after round into the spot our bodies just were. The warehouse catches hundreds of rounds in seconds as we find ourselves under the drone with the rifle in hand.

"WORK, YOU PIECE OF SHIT!" I scream over the raging guns as I smack the rifle. The drone stops firing and turns its guns down on us. I slam my hand into the rifle one last time. The power gauge goes from *Empty* to *Warning*.

The drone's guns spin. I aim the rifle into the cockpit of the drone and pull the trigger with every ounce of my being.

Then, the guns stop spinning. My heart in my throat prevents me from yelling at Larry. The thudding in my ears probably prevents me from hearing him as well.

The drone levels off and ascends.

That's when the Faraday bag snags on a broken piece of metal on the ground and yanks the flash drive out.

"Shit!" I scream and catch the falling flash drive. Without missing a beat, Larry snatches it from my hand, places his left leg on my right thigh, and jumps. With his free hand, he grabs onto the side of the drone.

Unprepared for the additional weight, the drone teeters, yet keeps ascending. Meanwhile, Larry finagles the flash drive back toward its port. He misses, and the drone ascends past thirty feet up.

"Larry, if you don't drop now, you won't be able to drop at all," I say.

Larry ignores me as he keeps trying to get the drive in.

The drone continues its ascent.

Now, at a hundred feet up, Larry looks down, yells, "Shit!"

And falls.

I do the only thing I can: extend my arms as Larry flails as he falls. His upper body slams into my arms. My left shoulder dislocates as we crash into the ground. A snap like an old tree branch breaking fills the air. I think I hear myself screaming.

It takes a second to realize it's Larry: his right femur sticks out of his leg.

I yank off my shirt to tie a tourniquet on his compound fracture. Crimson covers my hands, and the smell of hot copper pennies floods my nostrils. With an *umph*, and a scream from Larry, I get the blood to stop flowing.

As we lay on the ground together, the drone crosses in front of the sun. It stops its ascent at several hundred feet up, rotates, and heads off.

I crouch over Larry. Color is leaving his cheeks as he gets whiter than normal.

There's a chance of internal bleeding. That's not something I'm equipped to fix.

"Look, we've got to get you indoors and call for help," I say. "Maybe there's a first aid kit with a splint or quick clot or..."

Larry sends me a smile as he opens his hand to reveal nothing. He got the flash drive in before he fell. As blood fills his mouth, he says,

"Homie don't rat, homie don't break..." he says through bloody teeth before his eyes close and his head goes limp. I hang my head and finish his mantra.

"Homie don't run."

Chapter Eighty-One

Devil Came to Play

I try to lift Larry, but my dislocated shoulder makes it impossible. I do what I've seen other dumb people do in movies and limp over to the bullet-riddled warehouse. After two breaths, I pull my shoulder back and slam it into the metal siding. It produces a *pop* so loud it deafens both of my ears. The impact rattles my body like thunder and shoots pain everywhere like lightning. I scream, drop to my knees, and regroup enough to drag Larry inside.

Sparks fly from our damaged machines. The drone did a number on everything. The giant monitor still displays Agent Jack and his war room, but pixelated, as if I'm playing an 8-bit video game instead of fighting for my life.

And there's a steady *hiss* coming from the LODIS that is anything but good.

I go to my previous terminal, but sparks fly from the screen. Out of all the systems in the warehouse, only two are up and running.

I check Larry's pulse. It's there, but faint. From a metal bookshelf, I grab two first aid kits and return to Larry. Once I dump all the contents on the ground, I find a shot that is part Narcan and part morphine, and quick clot bandages. First, I put the bandages on both sides of the wound, trying not to make contact with the jagged bone. Then I find a vein, clean a spot on Larry's arm, and inject him with the medicine.

His body slumps further. I don't know if it just helped or hurt, but we've only got minutes to see if this miracle actually worked.

My data shows Moscow's and Penny's teams are still keeping everyone occupied — police and emergency responders are tackling about twenty small disturbances in the area.

There's a road about a quarter of a mile from here with eight cop cars stopped. I click on the image of one of the officers' body cams. I can't get visual, but I appreciate the audio like a man in the desert appreciates water.

"Sir, move this vehicle," comes an officer's voice, followed by a frantic voice I know and love.

"Sorry, officer, but the bus just gave out," proclaims Judson. "I mean, I'm so embarrassed. I've called Triple A, but no one is answering."

A new officer's voice joins in. "I know, Judson. We already have a tow truck on the way."

I click away from the icon and smile. For someone who has to distance himself from this criminal, he certainly is helping where he can.

I don't have time to savor the support though. I still have to deal with my friendly neighborhood SWAT team somehow.

I dart over to the LODIS to pinpoint the hissing sound in the worst place possible: the oxygen tanks. I grab a bandage from the first aid kit and cover the hole too late; the meter says there is only ten percent oxygen.

The last time I went into the LODIS without oxygen, I almost further solidified its nickname: The Coffin.

If I use the LODIS, I'm probably not coming out.

"Aw, that was cute." Agent Jack's staticky voice flips in and out through busted speakers and his pixelated ass jumps all over on the big screen. "You stopped one drone. We have dozens. And it's time they all said hello."

I've fired our only shot with the drone deterrent and the flash drive. However, if I don't execute the last part of our plan, the Goemon, all we'll manage to do is piss off Poseidon's IT department with viruses.

On the left terminal, I track the drone: six miles out, closing fast. The ETA is just under five minutes.

The thing is, if it's six miles out from base, that might mean Agent Jack's flock is that close.

Or closer. I need to stall, but I don't know how.

"You sure you don't want to do this man-to-man? I'll let you throw the first punch."

Agent Jack laughs. "I'd rather put this puppy to bed." He leans back and says, "On my mark…"

I want to either scream or hang my head. We're done. There's nothing else to do stop the assault. Even if some data from this hack gets out there, it won't matter. A leak won't get the public's attention; we need a flood.

Agent Jack gives the order. He crosses his arms and stares into the camera. His eyes go wide, and several operators approach him. Then the image freezes.

At first, I think my connection dropped. Then a lone text box pops up, and I realize a familiar devil came to play.

Chapter Eighty-Two

Put a Bow on This Bitch

Almost a year ago, one of the best team hacks in Hackers' Haven occurred: a terrorist cell targeted the motorcade for David Masterson, the current U.S. Secretary of Defense. My team thought we had the *bad guys* locked down, but they almost slipped away. The only thing that caught them was a hacking technique that only one person in the world successfully pulled off: looping. For a large portion of my life, looping was a myth. In a nutshell, a hacker breaks through a firewall without detection, enters the operating system files, and creates a live copy of the system on their system. With this, one could control the system, if for only a limited time.

And that hacker just did the damn thing again. The text box in front of me equally blows my mind and gives me the fortitude to finish this.

[PT ZEUS] Work faster, dog.

Son of a bitch. Cyfib just pulled off a loop, but even he can't control the system for long. I check our drone's status: one minute until docking.

The monitor unfreezes to pure panic on the other end. Off screen, Agent Jack yells, "What do you mean, the drones are crashing?"

I watch the monitor as our destination-to-target drops from thirty seconds to twenty.

Ten.

Five.

Docked.

I wait. Nothing happens on my end. If my theory was even close to correct, then the files on the drone should've immediately uploaded without incident because the system would've marked the drone as *familiar.* That means that it shouldn't run through any anti-virus or firewall issues. It's like when you unplug your mouse from your computer, then plug it back in. Since the computer recognizes and has already used the mouse before, it immediately accepts its return to the system.

On my monitor, a window pops up. It's not of our system; it's of theirs.

We are in. The connection between the drone, their systems, and mine is solid. I enter my custom command to initiate our cyber-missiles.

Command: Lin.

On Agent Jack's screen, he freezes as everyone else around him scurries. Monitor after monitor fills with code as the Joker's laugh from *The Batman* animated series fills the speakers.

"Unplug everything!" yells Agent Jack.

One of his techs yells, "We can't! We'd have to shut down the power grid at each facility!"

Agent Jack "Do it!"

He stares at the camera with eyes of fire that narrow in like they can burn me through the camera.

"You know what?" Agent Jack says, his cool-and-collected self shot to hell. "Thank you. Thank you, Tanto, for sending that drone back and completely throwing a monkey wrench into our systems, because you just gave me a chance to reflect. I want you. Alive. And you don't need to worry about any torture because I know about the hypnosis."

Shit.

"And I know that all it takes is a little bell and a few words, and you'll spill everything. Who you work with. Where they are. And how to get them."

I rub something in my pocket, now accepting my fate instead of just worrying about it.

"And screw the perimeter," says Agent Jack. "Send a team in because I want this bastard alive to suffer."

And that's my damned cue to put a bow on this bitch.

Chapter Eighty-Three

One Last Time

As every piece of malware, family of worms, and computer-crushing virus I have access to decimates these assholes' servers, I know it is time for the final act.

From my terminal, I go to install the LODIS operating software, aka Zeus, on their servers. The application works with the actual LODIS, so I'll still have to get in the tank.

Whether or not it has oxygen.

Yet when I open the folder, I find Kilroy has renamed it from the All-Father of Greek Mythology to the scamp of Norse. "Hello there, Loki," I say as I initiate this code of mischief.

Someone way smarter than me designed the LODIS to use human instinct to repel cyber bots. The reason that the LODIS isn't purely artificial intelligence or even fueled by a neural network is because code can stop code. If someone could hack a firewall, that also means that they could hack a self-defense program.

Enter Kilroy: this recluse built his own LODIS using the blueprints on the administrative flash drive. Then he tweaked it so that this particular LODIS could attack a system instead of defending it.

I have zero idea what, or who, Kilroy planned to take down, but now is the time to figure out if it can do what is necessary.

I check Larry's pulse; it's slower than before. The bandages aren't more soaked, but he could still have internal bleeding. As his body temperature drops, I wrap him in the Faraday bag. I am concerned the plastic could overcook him, but it's all I have.

I turn and face the LODIS. The H_2H_2O liquid reservoir is full. The power is on. The neoprene wetsuit and goggles hang next to it. And the oxygen tank is only ten percent full.

I strip off my clothes and stretch into the tight, semi-foam wetsuit. After blowing into the goggles, I pop them on. Right before I step into the tank, I grab a flathead screwdriver and shove it into the wetsuit's waistband; the last time I got in The Coffin, the eject button failed, and I almost drowned.

While I'm certain I will not live to see tomorrow, I still have to get Larry to safety. He will not die for my sins.

I begin the breathing technique to steel my lungs: one breath in, four breaths out. In Hackers' Haven, I used to do this for two to three minutes before each venture into the LODIS. Time is against me, so I only do two rounds.

Hip-hup-hup-hup-hup. Hip-hup-hup-hup-hup.
Hip-hup-hup-hup-hup. Hip-hup-hup-hup-hup.

My lungs burn, then cool down during each step, preparing my body for maximum oxygen vacancy, not occupancy.

I grab the eject button and step into The Coffin. Once inside the tube, one lone button against the right wall beckons me. I smack it with my palm. The door seals, and my ears pop as a hiss of pressurized air fills the LODIS. From above me, I yank down the snorkel because ten percent oxygen is better than zero. I ignore the dangling earpiece because, like most of my bad choices, I'm going at it alone.

There's no one to pull me out of here this time, I think.

As the watery yet conductive solution fills to my chest, I put the snorkel in my mouth. When it reaches the top, a green light cuts on.

It's go time, one last time.

Chapter Eighty-Four

The Final Sleep

There's a feeling that comes over me. It's like I'm back in Hackers' Haven. Outside of the LODIS, AldenSong is making sure my vitals are good. PoBones, our resident Cajun, is handling flak, distracting the bad guys' tracking devices. Foshi_Taloa, a Native American who never speaks above a whisper, is handling dambreaking. And everything goes to plan and we save the day.

Then I remember I'm alone. This isn't the Double-H. There's no one going in but me.

And I'm okay with it. In the tank, I lean forward enough to move through ten different server directories. That's the thing about the Liquid Ocular Display part of the LODIS: it allows the user to jump between multiple screens almost instantaneously. This way, the LODIS can defend multiple avenues from attackers.

Or, in my case, attack enough to cause a ripple in the firewall's configuration. Most firewalls don't crash because of people like me. They crash because of an internal misconfiguration of their operating system.

And that's where this particular LODIS comes into play. The drone, a familiar device, docked and connected to the system. It automatically uploaded its flight data, which included our metadata-laced viruses. And all of this occurred using an administrative flash drive. Again, in theory, this is my shot to blow the lid off of these bastards.

As I lean back, I choke. The oxygen tank just ran dry. My body initially freaks out, but I calm it. Every Bushido warrior, like every one of us, faced or will face death. I may die in here, but not before I do this one last thing.

I lean into and away from directory after directory, moving. Searching. Pleading. At one point, I think I find the firewall's directory, but an oxygen-deprived spasm shoots through my body. An oppressive heat fills my chest. The only wetness in my body are my teary eyes because I will them to keep open at all times. Every blink resets the screen, and I'm out of time. To fight my urge to hit the escape button, I let go of it. As it sinks to the bottom, I instinctively claw at the tank's sides. I tremble. Shake. And then I push down the internal vibrations.

Move, Tanto, move.

I dart in and out of the directories, searching for the one I just lost. Someone shoves a hot poker down my throat as my lungs burn for air. Without a clock in here, I can only guess how long I've gone without oxygen.

If I can find the exact directory for Poseidon's firewall, I can activate the Goemon virus. However, if that shield holds, nothing gets out, and even my death will be nothing but a blip on their radar.

Spots form in the corner of my eyes. Darkness approaches. I know it'll screw up the screens, but I close my eyes as a few drops of water snake down into my lungs. I lower my head. And I push. I go through the directories as fast as my vibrating body allows.

Then I see it. And I hold. With a flick of my eyes, I activate the Goemon virus inside the firewall's directory.

You see, I named this virus after Ishikawa Goemon. Goemon was not just a Bushido warrior; he was one of the first Robin Hood-type thieves. He and his son robbed and distributed so much wealth that Japanese culture still celebrates the man through a five-act kabuki play.

Now, unlike my drowning ass, the water that Goemon died in was boiling.

The firewall still holds on the monitor that I can see through the plexiglass window. Until it doesn't. On the two surviving terminals, I watch as Poseidon's firewall collapses. Then the second part of the Goemon virus kicks in: every file, every record, just hit the web. Not the Dark Web. The actual web.

And any of them that met the boolean search that included hackers, Patriot Act, terrorists, cyberterrorists, Hackers' Haven, and a few others, just flooded every news outlet out there.

Dallas Robinette.

The Associated Press.

WikiLeaks.

The BBC.

Even local news and regional papers get blasted.

Now all I have to do is get out of The Coffin before the final sleep takes me.

Chapter Eighty-Five

All I Know is Darkness

I reach into the water after the eject button but can't find it. If only I could bend down properly. Then I do find it. However, right before I push the button, the power goes out.

That's always one of the first moves SWAT does: cut the power before an assault. However, if memory serves, they could be trying to wait me out.

And Larry doesn't have any waiting time.

I push against the door, but the pressure keeps it shut. I kick and punch, to no avail. The water in my lungs thrashes my head back and forth. Clouds of darkness overtake my eyes.

During the shakes, my right hand brushes against my wetsuit. *The flathead screwdriver!* I grab it and stab at the plexiglass. I just need a hole, a way to get air. Once I can do that, I can get out and get Larry medical help.

I stab and stab and stab, but nothing breaks through. Exhaustion, lack of air, and the water keeping my momentum and strength from breaking through keep me from doing any real damage.

This is it, I think. *I've done all I can.*

I close my eyes and relax, even though darkness and shakes envelop me. There's no sound. No coldness. Just the void.

That's when something tickles my cheek. I ignore it; it's probably the cells in my body dying. But it happens again.

I open my eyes as a stream of tiny air bubbles pepper my skin. With the last bit of my energy, I press my lips over the tiny hole in the plexiglass and sip sweet relief. Of course, my body freaks out with the introduction of much-needed oxygen. Shakes and pain flood through my chest. Even so, I sip and exhale. Sip and exhale.

When I move from the hole, I notice that the water level drops. I grab the floating screwdriver and attack the glass again, this time with air, energy, and re-found vigor.

The glass shatters and I splatter to the floor. I crawl to Larry. At first, I don't find a pulse. Then I do: it's small, like it comes from the bass beat of a car two blocks away.

I get under him and use my legs to shove his body onto my shoulders. Then I fireman's-carry him to the door. Right before we get there, I grab one last item from my jeans pocket, something I'm afraid is time to use.

I open the door to a hundred armed soldiers. Laser sights cover my entire body. I lay Larry's body on the ground. "This man was my hostage, and he needs immediate medical support," I say as I reach into the Ziplock bag with Rusty's cyanide pill. "I know you have cameras recording this, so this is my deathbed confession."

Most great warriors died in battle. Others died of seppuku, an act that meant they went out on their own terms. The tanto is the weapon used to tear open one's guts. It is a tool mostly used in the final act.

The irony of my name doesn't escape me. They won't get anything from me. This is not suicide; it is protection. This prevents them from getting to Penny, Liam, Hazel, Mane-Eac. Rusty. Dallas. and Mr. Judson.

I'm sorry; this is the only way to guarantee their safety.

As the men rush me, I tilt my head back and chomp down on the pill. Immediately, my tongue burns as poison mixes with saliva. Then my body burns as one, two, five tasers hit my chest. A taste like rotten almonds and a hint of moldy cherry fills my mouth as electricity becomes me.

I don't know if it's the electrocution or the poison that does it. I collapse, and all I know is darkness.

Chapter Eighty-Six

The Stranger

Darkness. Nothingness. The Void. Whatever you want to call it, the completeness covers me. I am shapeless. Formless. Just energy.

Part of me expects to be greeted by the ones that left me for this ethereal realm.

My father, whole and healed.

Mrs. Lin, young and vibrant.

Lance-A-Little, goggle-less.

Instead, it is just emptiness. In the distance, a pinpoint of light builds. I move toward it, not in a walk, but more in a float. Like a magnet to the fridge, the closer I get to it, the faster I move.

I leave the darkness for the light. A bright white that neither blinds nor burns. A perfect level of comfort and warmth engulfs me.

Before me is a chessboard on a black table with matching black chairs. The pieces are the same as before: one half full of Bushido warriors and the other half various computer parts. With both chairs open, I only have to choose which side to sit on.

On the one hand, technology brought me closer to people. It is how I met Mane-Eac. Lance. AldenSong. And more.

On the other hand, my belief in the Bushido Code did the same. Mr. Judson and Larry. Mrs. Lin. And others.

I take my place at the Bushido half. Upon sitting, I notice a man across from me. He wears my generic black hoodie and keeps his hands under the table. The stranger's hood rolls back the cover to reveal my false persona, Vice: a scar across the face. Oversized black rimmed glasses. Flat, dead eyes. And a mouth sewn shut with a blue ethernet cable.

The marker that designates who goes first shows white. I assume that is me, so I reach for my furthest pawn. As I move it one space, the stranger's skeletal hand grasps mine. Cold shoots through my body as *Vice's* lips tear the cable restraining his mouth. Out of the gaping hole comes a flood of digital *ones* and *zeroes* as my doppelgänger's scream echoes through my body.

Chapter Eighty-Seven

Trust Da Russian

I awaken to wetness on my face and find myself in a hospital room. Apparently, Funk Monster just soaked my sleeping face with enough kisses to be borderline *creepy*. The room looks like MetroMed, but not exactly. The space is bigger, and the equipment looks newer. Cotton balls fill my head where my brain used to exist, and my whole body aches.

"There is my dumb little bastard," comes a voice from the corner of the room. Penny puts down her hardback and strolls up to my bed. She's wearing a shirt that reads *Memphis Versus Errybody*. No clue what that means. "You've had a good slumber these last seven days."

"Where...am I?" I croak out. Someone must've shoved razors down my throat because it burns and itches. I rub on it, but all that does is make it worse. "I...should be dead."

"They had to pump your stomach, as well as give you enough drugs to make Hunter S. Thompson flinch," Penny says as she takes my icy hand in hers. "You gave us quite a scare."

"Is...is Larry okay?" I ask.

Penny nods and says, "He'll heal, but that's not what you should worry about right now."

I sit up. These doctors replaced my bones with concrete because I'm as rigid as a board. As my vision clears, I notice a dozen white roses in a vase on my bedside table. I grab the card and smile through the pain as the words comfort my soul.

For someone who believes in life debts, you sure love almost dying. Love, Cher, Timothy, Mama, and Judson.

A flash on a television on the far wall catches my attention. On its screen is a red Breaking News banner with the words *Poseidon United Exposed, Under Investigation.*

"Did...did we win?" I ask.

"Somewhat," says Penny, but her smile betrays her poker face. "I'll let one of your friends tell you more about it."

She pulls out her phone, clicks a few buttons, and then places it next to me as the voice of Dallas Robinette rings through.

"Okay, good listener, what I've been telling you for years finally happened," comes that clipped Southern accent I haven't heard in forever. "They've said I was a nutjob because I've told you the truth was coming. There are data leaks that give us news and truth. There are whistleblowers that tell their side of a story and expose corruption. And then there is this. Following the complete Wiki-Flood of ten gigabytes of secretive and illegal operations, Poseidon United, one of the most powerful companies in the world, went belly up. I'm talking full bankruptcy so bad that the Dow Jones lost ten percent of its value the very next day! You'll remember this was the same day I reported on drones falling from the sky! From this data, news sources such as the Associated Press, BBC, and yours truly have pieced together that this company, in conjunction with a clandestine government agency called the Mercator Agency, was not only capturing American citizens and forcing them into slave labor, but also silencing anyone that went against their mission. The Department of Justice has opened a full-scale investigation into this, but I've been feeding you information about this horror for the last ten years. And, let me tell you, it feels really bad to be this right about this."

There's a pause where Dallas is clearly taking a drink of water before continuing.

"Details for the algorithm for their about-to-be-born digital baby, PhauCet, show that it was set to be *the* most invasive free software ever. I mean, tracking everything from your last meal to the medicine your mother can't live without. The details are mind-blowing, and I'm still unpacking the data. Further, most of Poseidon's upper management and Board of Directors have been taken in for questioning. Except for CEO Cussh. If you haven't heard, he took his own life, apparently having hung himself after hearing the news."

Or someone hung him for it, I think.

"Ultimately, this means that what I've reported on for this long came true. So, if you or anyone you know have any information about this, or any other case, please reach out to me on the website TheSouthernEnquirer dot com. And remember, good listener, if it's weird, I want it."

Penny hits the *Stop* button and studies me. I'm blown away. It worked. It really worked. We exposed them, what they did, and what they were doing. The business crumbled. The agency is no longer hidden.

It's the victory I wanted, no, needed, but something doesn't quite fit. It's like when you go to the movies. The theater is empty. You have it all to yourself. You can be as loud as you want with a giant screen in front of you. And then the wrong movie plays.

"Penny," I say, my voice shaky. "We're not at MetroMed or Dr. Brent's Butterfield Partners Clinic, are we?"

Penny's gaze goes from me to the floor. "Yeah, about that..." she says as Penny walks over to the closed curtain. With one tug, she yanks it open to reveal my biggest fear just came true.

Iron metal bars cover the window. With strength not mine, I jump out of the bed, my IV and monitoring cables pulling machinery behind me. If my veins or muscles hurt from this, I can't tell. Or maybe my body cannot yet process this because my mental pain far outweighs my physical.

She says, "The Who sang it best. *Meet the old boss, same as the new boss...*"

I stumble to the window. For as far as I can see, cotton fields. We're in the middle of nowhere.

"I told you," comes a voice from the doorway. I turn and face Moscow entering. He is in front of me and leans down. "Good things happen when you trust da Russian."

Chapter Eighty-Eight

Welcome Home

My knees give out before my legs do. I hit the hospital room's floor in shock and disbelief. Penny and Funk Monster rush to my side.

It's Moscow who scoops me up.

"Ah, comrade, things are not so bad," says Moscow as he squeezes my beaten, battered, and be-drugged body. I push him away, yank out my IV, and dart out into the hall.

The hallway is anything but a hospital's one. My bare feet feel icky on the old, faded carpet that runs down the center. The cold air reminds me that I'm wearing a paper-thin hospital gown, not normal clothes. Every way I look, I find not hospital rooms, but hotel rooms.

That's when I notice it: blue ethernet cables running along the hallway's borders.

As the mobster's hand clamps down on my shoulder, he pulls me close enough that I can't squirm away. "You like?"

"Moscow, for the love of God, please tell me what you did," I plead.

"Better," he says as he pushes me toward closed double doors. "I show."

The weird wallpaper and trippy carpet remind me of the never-ending hallways in *The Shining*. We stomp forward until Moscow lets loose of me and grabs both door handles.

"I bet you will love this...present," he says. The last person who gave me a *present* this way hung my newest friend. With a heave, Moscow opens the doors, then puts his arm on my lower back and urges me through.

The two of us stand on a ten-foot balcony overlooking my nightmare: a fully functional and operating War Room. Row after row of hackers, no, hackvicts, type away on terminals. A jumbotron-worthy screen is on the far wall, showing several IP addresses and status bars.

Wherever we are, it's a version of Hackers' Haven.

Everything I did, everything we sacrificed for, is starting up again.

A dizziness hits me between the eyes. Moscow catches me and smacks me hard enough on the back that I see stars.

"You have questions, yes?" asks Moscow, as if my *I'm-gonna-throw-up* expression and deeper shade of paleness didn't give me away. "We talk. Come."

We return to the hallway and head to the elevator on the far wall. He presses a button and clasps his hands in front like it's the freaking Hilton and we're checking in. A ding sounds and my nostrils clear enough for me to speak.

"Where are we?" I ask. Maybe if I start with the easier-to-digest questions, I won't black out.

"Not far from da warehouse," says Moscow, as the doors open and we enter the elevator. "Tunica, Mississippi. This is one of the casinos, The Grand." He hits the button for the penthouse. "Well, it *was* The Grand. Seems they went, how you say, under, so I bought it for pennies."

The elevator moves at a snail's pace, so I ask him what I already know in my heart. "This is why you wanted all the information I had about Hackers' Haven. Why you hounded me about it."

"Hounded is...strong wording," he says as he rolls his eyes around. "Not wrong. Just strong. You know, my family did this all over Memphis. We buy property no one wants and...repurpose it."

And I'm willing to bet that he got a steal on the human beings working below when the hammer came down on Poseidon United.

"How could you buy people?" I ask.

"I bought...value," is all Moscow says as he stares at the ceiling. "And I bought it cheap, because nothing creates distressed assets worse than bad press."

The doors open to another hallway. This one looks less worn and only has a handful of rooms compared to the hospital floor.

"This floor is full of suites," he says as Moscow pushes my ass forward until we reach Penthouse 2. "My room is next to yours."

I stop our march, jerking my arm free from Moscow's grasp. "I'm not staying with the other prisoners?"

"Certainly not," says Moscow as he unlocks the door to Penthouse 2. "More will be explained. Come."

With no other choice, I enter the room. Or, should I say, rooms. With a large entryway, kitchen, dining room, living room, study, and bedroom, this penthouse room is bigger than any home I ever lived in.

Moscow goes to the walk-in closet and grabs a new black suit, pressed white shirt, black tie, black belt, and an unopened plastic bag with a pair of boxers and socks. He puts them near the king-sized bed.

Moscow says, "You can get changed and meet me in my unit," then heads toward the door. He stops and points at the bed.

On it, just like at the warehouse, is a plain white box with a black ribbon on it.

"I give you another present," is all Moscow says as he turns and shuts the door behind him.

My overloaded senses flash stars before my eyes. I'm trying not to freak out *and* pass out at the same time.

I go to the box. It's about the size of a music CD, just a bit thicker. It weighs little, maybe a pound or so. I pull the ribbon slowly away and open the box.

Inside are two things: the first, a folded note, is on top. I open the note. I read the note. Then I hit the floor.

As I do, the other items in the box fall. They make a very familiar *cha-ching* sound. One that will always haunt my dreams.

The only thing worse than being gifted a brand-new pair of cowboy spurs is what Moscow put on the note. As I lay on the floor, the note glides through the air like a falling leaf. It lands on its side, and I reread the three words that sear my soul.

Welcome Home, Warden.

Chapter Eighty-Nine

Betrayer

I don't know how long I lie on the perfectly white carpet. I just know at one point I'm dressing myself. In the bathroom mirror, I look like a shadow, a ghost of myself. I put on the clothes Moscow gave me. In them, I don't look like me.

I look like Cyfib made over. Warden 2.0.

And I'm never doing that shit. I take off everything and throw all of it in the toilet, then pull the lever. It can all flood, for all I care.

I go into the closet and check the dresser drawers. In the second one, I find a pair of blue jeans, a gray T-shirt, plain white socks, and a pair of new tennis shoes. I put all of that on.

I run water over my pale face and baldish head. Then I go to the door to leave. On the floor, the cowboy boot spurs taunt me. Their sounds echoing in my brain.

Cha-ching.

Cha-ching.

Cha-ching.

I shake my head but decide to scoop the spurs up and put them back in that box. Then I decide to bring the box with me. Not to use, but to get answers.

I enter the hallway and make the five-second walk to Moscow's door. I use the gold knocker above the walleye to knock. From inside, Moscow says, "Enter," so I do.

Once I'm inside, his penthouse room fits the same shape as mine, but not the same function. Every part has small desks set up with Moscow's thugs manning phones and working on laptops. Whatever he's working on, it's not my concern.

At least right now.

"Oh, you would've looked so good in suit," he said. "I got them in Mississippi Delta. Abraham's. Custom. You don't like?"

"The clothes aren't the issue," I say as I toss the box of spurs to Moscow. This catches him off guard, so he drops the box. My sudden movement upsets his thugs, because four of the ten men in here just dropped their hands from their keyboards to their belts.

At least four armed, and I can't discount the others, I think. *Plus, Moscow probably has his tank-killer on his hip as well.*

"I want all of those captives freed, Moscow," I say as I take a seat. "What you're doing is illegal. Inhuman. And I won't stand for it."

Moscow lets the silence hang in the air before he bursts into laughter. So do his thugs. I let them. It is the least damaging thing to happen to me in a long time.

"My friend, your instant freedom for your friends is, how you say, pipe dream," says Moscow as he wipes one of his eyes and looks away. "Would you try to talk some sense into your friend?"

"Old T is a stubborn one, I give you that," comes the voice of someone I never thought would become a betrayer: AldenSong.

Chapter Ninety

Pull The Damn Trigger

My heart hits the roof of my mouth like it just hit the *eject button*. I stumble backwards as AldenSong, complete with an IV bag, sling, and cast on, gingerly walks my way.

"Before you freak out, I did the same thing when Theodore let me in on his idea," says Aldy. Not knowing who the hell *Theodore* is, AldenSong points at Moscow.

"'Tis nickname because, in Russia, we don't do like you Americans and name people after cities," Moscow says. "It is...gauche."

"Right now, your name is Asshole, because I want everyone on the second floor free," I say as I push AldenSong away and get into Moscow's face. "Let. Them. Go."

Moscow chuckles and pops his knuckles. He smirks and asks me, "Why only the second floor?"

"Because that's where..." I start, and then it hits me like a brick to the face. "It's not just the second floor, is it?"

Moscow shakes his head.

"How...how many prisoners are here?" I ask, but this time I'm looking at AldenSong. Even though he has aligned with Moscow, there must be a reason. My friend is not gone; he's just misguided.

AldenSong keeps his eyes locked with mine when he answers me.

"Two hundred and forty-five."

The air abandons my lungs. Almost two hundred and fifty prisoners, people stripped of their rights, all right here.

And these sons of bitches want me to lead them.

Moscow gives AldenSong a kiss on the forehead and squares up to me. "Tanto, is anyone in these walls, including you, innocent?"

I ignore his question, still reeling from the last bit of news slapping the shit out of me.

AldenSong stands next to Moscow and adds, "No one deserves what we went through. We will not run that type of...operation. But we need you to lead us."

"Bullshit," I say, every cell in my body screaming to just get away. "They're not even considered human." I point at Moscow and scream, "Hell, this bastard bought them like cattle!"

"Nyet, well, yes, but then nyet," says Moscow as he snatches a laptop off the closest table. AldenSong holds it as Moscow types. A few seconds later, he shows me something that even I didn't consider possible.

It's a piece of legislation set for the next US Congressional session. While the heavily stamped watermark of *DRAFT* covers most of it, I do see that the bill deals with the same cyber terrorism bill that stripped me and all the other hackvicts of their rights.

"CliffsNotes, please," I say as a migraine needle shoots through my brain. "I hurt too much to read."

"In a nutshell, it puts back the human element," says AldenSong. "That's what Theo, er, Moscow and I have worked on. There was no way to get people, fellow criminals like you and me, amnesty or clemency. Not now. Not in today's climate. We had to take steps first. That means that, once this bill gets passed, everyone will have human rights."

"But they will have to serve human time," adds Moscow as he grabs the box of spurs. "Tanto, do you remember the story I told you about my grandfather?"

I nod, staring at the Desert Eagle on Moscow's hip. "There is no way I can be the warden," I say. "I'm a criminal, and even if I weren't, I'd never pass the background check."

"Ah, but you can be Interim Warden," says Moscow, as he snaps his fingers at me. "There is no background check for Interim."

I shake my head and say, "That's impossible."

"That's Mississippi," counters Moscow. "Mississippi's law on who can be a warden is firm, but very flimsy on Interim Warden." He pushes the box into my chest. "You can be our Dedushka."

I look at Aldensong and say, "I want to vomit and stab my own eyes out right now, Aldy."

"I know." He puts his massive hand on my shoulder and gives me a squeeze. "These warriors needs their Damn Yo."

I correct him and say, "It's pronounced Daimyo."

"No," says Aldy, correcting me, "It's pronounced *yes.*"

I lean against the far wall and say, "I am not worthy of the title, nor can I protect this tribe." I hang my head and add, "I'm not ready."

AldenSong says, "Then we will just have to all lean on each other. We have before, and we will do it again. You've spent a lifetime holding back a tide of doubt that you were never good enough. Never smart enough. I know those two things to be more than true." He pulls me close and the big bastard says, "Besides, when we're going to jump into the unknown, who the fuck else would we want holding a torch to light our way?"

As convincing as the big guy is, I have to hear this from the horse's mouth. "Moscow, when, not if, that bill passes. How long must each prisoner serve?"

"Two years," he says and follows it with one word. "Max."

Believing this deal is too good to be true, I tell Moscow exactly that.

That's when he takes out his big, black gun and hands it to me. It weighs as much as a damn desktop computer, so I almost drop it.

"Do be careful with my Desert Eagle .44 Magnum," he says with a chuckle. As confusion runs through my body, I look at Moscow as he spreads his arms wide. "But if you doubt my intentions, then shoot me."

"I've never fired a gun in my life," I say, the heavy piece of destruction slipping in my hand.

"You just pull back the slide, flick the safety, aim, and pull the trigger," says Moscow as he makes an explosion move with his hands and head. "If you doubt me, if you doubt any of this, do it. My men will not stop you."

I stare at the mountain of a skull popper in my hand, so Moscow adds, "Careful, Vice. If you don't hold that pistolet right, firing it will shatter your hand." He winks.

I can't tell you why, but everything became clear in those last seconds. There's something in the wink that sets me off, one final time. So, I take one breath, rack the slide, undo the safety, aim, and pull the damn trigger.

Chapter Ninety-One

Like Your Life Depends on It

"Jesus Christ!" screams Moscow as the gun dry fires. It's empty. *I knew it!* Even though Moscow is a gambling man, he wouldn't risk an unhinged person like me actually pulling the trigger.

In everyone else's confusion, I drop the Desert Eagle and snatch a Glock from the hip holster of the closest thug. I rack a round and aim. As I do, every thug grabs their piece and does the same thing. Except I'm the one in everyone's crosshairs.

"Now ho-ho-hold up, little buddy," says Moscow between pants. "I-I can't believe you almost shot me!"

"Day's not over, Moscow," I say, calm and collected. "I forgot something," I say and flick down the safety. "Now I'm ready."

"Whoa now," is all Moscow gets out as I toss the gun between my hands.

"The problem is, you've said everything a little *too* clean. So, here's what's going to happen. Either your men shoot me, I shoot you, or you make all that bullshit you've been spouting come true."

"Now, that's just not—" is all Moscow gets out before I place the gun's barrel to his head.

"Do not fuck with me." I'm about to die. I'm not the least bit scared. Of course, it helps that this will not be my first dance with death this week. I don't even know what good will come from it. If Moscow so much as blinks in a way his men take as an order, I'm full of more lead than a pencil. "Moscow, do you remember what you kept telling me over and over again?"

Moscow shakes as much as he can with a gun pressed into his forehead.

"You've told me what you're capable of," I start, my words even and collected. "You're a big, bad thug. You've done some good, but to get where you are, your hands are anything but clean. But my hands are dirty, too. I know that. I own that. However, those people that you say you will let go in two years need reassurances. No paperwork means no trust."

"That's not possible," says Moscow, as he turns his gaze to his soldiers.

"Wrong answer," I say as I put both hands on the gun. Moscow's men change their positions so that their gunfire will not hit each other. I think of all the Bushido stories where it came down to one last standoff. "I know that a bullet going through your brain isn't going to be enough to fix this. Doesn't mean it won't happen, but you know what will fix this situation?" I send Moscow a wink of my own.

"What?" he asks as Moscow's hands move out of my eyesight.

"Your brother," I say.

"Which...which one?"

"The one whose life I saved two years ago," I say. "The one who works in the Defense Department. The one who would've been driving the Secretary of Defense Anderson. I was the one who led the counter-hack that prevented not only the assassination attempt, but also saved the motorcade."

"I don't know anything about that..."

"Yes, yes you do," I say. "I saw it in the notes you took from me during the free writing. Tell me that it is not you who put pressure on Poseidon to sell their assets?"

Then the scared Russian shifts back into the tough one we all know and love. He rolls his shoulders back and stands. "Yes. Yes. I did just that, but getting what you want is, well, the impossible. I cannot pull that string again."

"No, you don't just need to pull that string," I say as I tap the muzzle to Moscow's crotch. "You're gonna yank it like your life depends on it."

"Are you willing to die, right now, for these people, most you do not know?" Moscow's speech is more gaslighting than anything else. Mine is as savage as the truth can get.

"I'd rather die for a stranger than live as a slave," I say, and close one eye. "How about you, comrade?"

Chapter Ninety-Two

Burn It All Down

Two hours. It only took two hours for Moscow to do *the impossible*: official US government paperwork that states the prisoners of *Location: Tunica* will be granted clemency after two years of *public service*. It's a deal with a devil, but this devil may be the only hope we have. Granted, all of this doesn't start until the legislation gets passed, especially with the recent blow-up of the Wiki-Flood, as the media is calling it. Even so, this is a battle we'll get help with. I'm sure Ms. Ingrid "Innocent" Vincent has some contacts in the legislature.

And maybe I can use some of the money I've got tucked away from MetroMed to pay the right lobbyists.

After we finish, I take the Glock and pop out one bullet. Then I hand the bullet to Moscow. "Now you have your own totem." He has a confused look on his face, but I really just did that for me.

As Penny, Funk Monster, AldenSong, and I head to the fifth floor War Room to see *old friends*, I can't help but wonder: is this how it had to end? I so badly wanted to burn it all down, to destroy the enemy beyond repair. But, to paraphrase the Rolling Stones, I got what I needed, not what I wanted. I needed to protect people. I am a

Chukanbushi, a defender of people. It's my calling. And it is anything but a curse.

The fake DoGoodR even talked about this: in Japanese culture, there is the word Ikigai. This concept combines the words *iki*, meaning *alive* or *life*, and *gai,* which means *worth*. Similar to the French term *raison d'être* or *reason for being*.

This, this here, is my reason. My tribe. My family. And I will protect them until my dying breath.

I still have the white box with the spurs under my arm when I enter the War Room. It doesn't take long for familiar faces to recognize mine, most with smiles so bright they could power the sun.

First is PoBones, who lets out a whoop and bear-hugs me. Then Foshi, who bows before me, and I return the same. Even Guard Fontana, one of the only guards to treat us with respect, tips his hat and says, "Warden," before leaving the room.

It's the old crew and a new light. It also makes me think about the faces of those who should be here with me, fighting the good fight. Quidlee. X_Marks_Da_Hot. Even Lance-a-Little. They weren't protected, but what happened to them will never happen again on my watch.

All the hackvicts face me as I prepare to say my first words as their warden.

When I open my mouth, an alarm goes off. It's familiar and, thankfully, it's one I welcome with open ears.

"We've got movie sign!" yells AldenSong, quoting the *Mystery Science Theater 3000* line that means, to us, *we've got a hacker to hunt.*

"Burn Bright!" Out of all the people to yell our mantra, I'm surprised to see it's from the always-quiet Foshi. His brown eyes scan the room, a little embarrassed by his outburst.

I glance at the box in my hand. I could use the spurs like Cyfib and guarantee that this team does its best work. Lives are probably on the line, after all. However, if I am to step into this new life, it will not be with tiptoes. It will be a with a leap.

There is one final Bushido story about capturing enemy territory. In short, it says, *to save the temple, one must be prepared to burn the temple before you rebuild it.*

These warriors do not need me to hypnotize them. They need me to help them heal. I've been going about this all wrong. I didn't need to get them out of that prison. We have to first get that prison out of them. Like Moscow's grandfather did.

I drop the spurs' box, complete with dangling price tag, in the closest garbage can. They make their final, yet muffled, *cha-ching* for no one.

AldenSong puts his arm on my shoulder, kicks his big body back, and yells, "Burn Fast!"

Finally, I cup my hands, bend my knees, and end one era, while beginning another.

"Burn down!"

Chapter Ninety-Three

Epilogue

Who Am I?

There's a series of books that Mrs. Lin and I used to read together: *Musashi* by Eiji Yoshikawa. While the paperbacks were new to me, Mrs. Lin first read these stories as a child in her local newspaper in Japan. The story followed Miyamoto Musashi, a skilled Bushido swordsman and roaming vagabond. It followed his battles with warlords and his serving the common folk with both blade and wisdom.

The thing is, Musashi didn't start out as Musashi. He started out as Shinmen Takezō, a lowly foot soldier for the Toyotomi Army. In a battle, Takezō finds himself in a duel with a warlord. When Takezō takes the upper-hand, one of the warlord's soldiers shoots Takezō in the leg with a crossbow, causing Takezō to retreat.

From there, Takezō stays on the run from "survivor hunters," a gang of soldiers intent on destroying anyone associated with the Toyotomi Army. When a hunter slays Takezō's closest ally and Takezō battles his attacker, both fall unconscious from blood loss. Ultimately, they are both saved by a young girl ringing a bell to bring help. During Takezō's recovery, his hosts tie him to a tree and leave him there for days. He suffers visions of his dead mother, his tormented father, and the life he has chosen and the deaths he has caused. In his spiritual journey, Takezō declares he seeks death, a reprieve. To this, one of his allies tells him; *to understand light, you must understand darkness. To do so, you must not only endure the shadows. You must overtake them. Only then will brightness be your true weapon.*

This was the moment that Takezō changed not just his quest, but also his name. From this point forward, he was Musashi Miyamoto, which roughly means Warrior from a Temple. I entered this world with one name and was gifted another. Then I stole a third. Now, with the option to recreate myself once again, I must ask: who am I?

Am I the scared little boy who didn't find a place in this world until Mrs. Lin discovered me in a dumpster? Or am I the mercenary hacker who took it upon himself to *save the world*, when I couldn't even save myself? Or am I an escaped-convict-turned-drug-dealer-turned-interim-prison-warden who stares more at a clipboard than a computer screen?

Maybe none; maybe all. My story couldn't get wilder if someone wrote a book about it. I mean, if you'd have told me last year I'd escape a prison, battle the evil, corporate machine and a clandestine agency, then win, just to run an even bigger prison, I'd have asked what you were smoking. In any case, I'm two weeks into running the largest collection of hackvicts in the freaking world. And, unlike my old prison of Hackers' Haven, we call this one Hackers' Harrah, partially because we've taken over the abandoned Grand slash Harrah's Casino in Tunica, Mississippi, for our operations.

But I'm getting ahead of myself. In the last two weeks, Wiki-Flood, what the media call the complete pillaging of Poseidon United's servers, has been part of every news cycle. From the smallest of memos to the actual details of the relationship between Poseidon and the Mercator Agency, it all got exposed. No secrets stayed concealed in the shadows. People who thought they ruled on one side of the law found themselves incarcerated behind the other side.

Speaking of the other side of the law, all of my residents are thrilled to discover that the change we need to get their human rights back just passed. Yep, ole pesky Section 18 of U.S. Code 2331 had an amendment snuck in at the last moment of this Congressional session that added that cyber terrorists are humans, not merely tools of terrorism. It doesn't guarantee that two years of imprisonment grants my team freedom, but it's the start we need.

Hackers' Harrah is shaped like a giant Y, with dorms slash bedrooms in the top-left part of the Y. The dorms are where we house our two hundred and forty hackvicts and ten staff. Each hackvict has his or her own room and, while they can't customize them much, the layouts are like my penthouse, if smaller. Some choose to bunk together, which is fine with me. I don't care if it's for romantic or companionship reasons, because these people deserve all the comfort I can provide.

The top-right section of the Y is where we have our gym, basketball court, medical, food, and other recreational sections. Thankfully, when I requested two point five million dollars' worth of medical equipment and staff, I didn't have to put a gun to Moscow's head this time to get what was necessary. I know Moscow is receiving funds for our hackvicts monitoring sixteen corporate accounts and four governmental, so this is probably just a drop in his big bucket. Even though we don't, and probably won't ever, see eye-to-eye, Moscow knows what it'll take to keep me running his prison: a team that supports not only the medicinal side, but also mental and psychological. Plus, hiring civilians who keep their mouths shut about working here costs. They're worth it. All of it.

As for the restaurants, we've got three already built into this new Double-H. Granted, the prisoners are also the cooks, and some of our residents have some mighty fine culinary skills.

Then, in the bottom, straight part of the Y, is where we have our tech. We have three War Rooms, each set up similar to the way we had it at my first prison. Twenty stations are set up with a giant screen in the front. The fundamental difference is there is no giant mirrored box above the prisoners. That was the first thing I had Moscow tear out. He'd followed the original blueprints, and he also thought I'd be like the original warden. I will not be some watchful, vengeful eye in the sky. I will be on the ground with my team. Again, these were some of the necessary changes and part of my signing on.

The smartphone on my belt clip vibrates. It's an alarm for my next stop-by. I'm the last person in the world to own a frequently used cellphone. As Interim Warden, there is no need for a burner phone. *Eric Vice* manages this prison while the Board of Directors is *actively* searching for my replacement. Truthfully, the world will find out who really shot John F. Kennedy way before I'm officially replaced.

And, by the time they find my replacement, hopefully there won't be a soul left in here.

As I study the vast cotton fields in every direction and sip on an actually decent cup of hazelnut coffee, I glance at my clipboard. It took me a week to get my bearings, but once I did, it allowed me to do things that Hackers' Haven never did. Case in point, I'm set to have a one-on-one with a resident that won't leave his room. It's not about pulling his weight, or even being social. He's one of the prisoners that some warden shoved too much prison into.

When Cyfib used to visit us prisoners, it was never to check on our well-being. Some of our hackvicts came from semi-supportive prisons, such as mine. Sure, we got tortured, isolated, and brainwashed, but some of my residents had it much worse.

Which brings me to Door 13. I knock, even though I have the universal key in my pocket. Sometimes the illusion of privacy is almost as good as real privacy. Of course, the moment I knock, Funk Monster barks. She's joined me on a couple of interviews, and those went pretty well.

"E-e-enter..." comes a small voice from the other side. I use my key, the lock chimes, and I push my way in.

Upon first glance, I tell FM to *stay* outside and wait in the hall. I'm concerned about her safety because the room looks a lot like the one that AldenSong threw my ass around in earlier this month. A broken TV is in the corner. Only one light functions. The sheets are stained and there are trays of uneaten food scattered about.

"Hello," I say, like I've said a dozen times since I started these sessions. "I am the Interim Warden, and I wanted to check up on you." I can't spot where my ward is, so I step over mounds of dirty clothes until I see him. He's balled up in the curtains, with only his eyes peeking out.

"Do you mind if I sit?" I ask. When he doesn't answer, I take the corner of the bed. In my previous interviews, I've had to rely on my clipboard or prisoner psychological notes that we got from Wiki-Flood. For this one though, I know him almost as well as I know myself.

I put the clipboard on the crowded bedside table and lean in slightly toward him. He pushes back toward the window, so I tilt back. Sometimes these interviews go well. Other times I'm stonewalled. And one time I got attacked, but I don't blame the guy. We all deal with Hell in our own ways.

"Some of our residents prefer to be called by their handles, and some prefer their name," I say. "Which do you prefer?"

The man mumbles something as his long, black hair falls over his face. Then the curtain pops loose, and he darts like a scared rabbit away from the sound.

"Hey-hey-hey," I say as I catch the black bearded man as he claws at his face. "It's okay. You're safe."

"Safe?" the man croaks out. "What does that even mean?"

I open my mouth but realize I don't actually have an answer. Instead, I take it back a beat. "What do you want me to call you?"

I let go of his arms and he stares at the floor as he merely says, "Do-DoGoodR."

"DoGoodR," I parrot back. "That's a really good handle."

The real DoGoodR shrugs and takes a seat on the far end of the bed. Earlier this week, Mane-Eac got the DNA results of the hair and blood samples she took from our sabotaged hack. It wasn't DJ. Rather, it was a homeless man that fit enough of the physical appearance of Agent Jack Brock.

And, while Mane-Eac could help us prove the real DoGoodR was alive and imprisoned, he is just one of over two hundred souls right here that need me. I have a family within these walls, and I must help them before I help myself.

DoGoodR slinks his eyes up from the floor just enough to say, "Go help someone else, warden. I'm too...too broken."

That's not the first time I've heard that response. I've even said it myself.

"First, don't call me warden," I say as I scoot closer. DoGoodR doesn't flinch, so I put one hand on his shoulder. He keeps my gaze, so I remove the hand and extend it. "And second, you are not broken. Only cracked. And cracks, once filled in, can make you stronger. You just need someone to help get you back to the person you were before all of this bullshit."

"Why?" he asks. "Why help me?"

Unlike the *what is safe* question, I have a million answers for this question. But only one matters. DoGoodR's eyes lighten their gaze and study my hand, as if it is a foreign object. I go to take my hand back. When I do, DoGoodR's hand moves toward mine. I hold still as he gingerly intertwines his into mine and gives it the slightest of squeezes.

I give his hand a squeeze back and put my other hand on his face. He gives me the slightest of recoils until he leans into the touch. He closes his eyes, opens them, and asks, "If you don't want to be called warden, what do I call you?"

I give him a smile as I say, "There he is." My ward sends a smile back, so I simply say, "Hello there, DoGoodR. My name is Julian, and I fix things."

THE END

Afterword

For almost ten years, this story has been a part of me. In my head. My gut. My heart. It all started when I read a news article about three employees scamming a hospital out of tens of millions of dollars of pharmaceuticals. Upon further review, I discovered only two of the three employees were ever fired, and no one was ever prosecuted.

That made me think: how did these guys get away with it, and who the hell was the third man?

Out of those thoughts came Tanto. Granted, the first iteration I wrote of this series back in 2016 was completely different from the final product before you. When life got in the way, I put the story aside until my wife and I moved to Houston, Texas, in 2017 to take care of my dying mother. It was there that I started rewriting this story into a series. From this second-wind came a character that I really enjoyed writing, though if Tanto met me in real life, he'd probably change his mind about murder. I've put our boy through the wringer, but just like a diamond forms under pressure, I feel that Tanto's heavy journey was necessary for his character development.

Finally, the character of Tanto is a lot like me, and also not. He's got some of the worst of me, and the best. He's a fighter, but it's time to put this weary warrior to rest. I hope you feel he's earned it.

Outside of Tanto's world, I currently have a standalone general thriller about an ice storm I lived through over thirty years ago. It stars Rook, a smart girl on the run who gets caught in the worst ice storm in the history of my home state of Mississippi. If you'd like to learn about it, the cover and the first chapter follow the Afterword.

From this author and from my wife and publisher Taddy, as well as our internal team and readers like you, thank you for spending your time with these tales. For more stories of ours, please visit wa pepperwrites.com, or follow me on Facebook, Instagram, or TikTok @wapepperwrites. Burn bright, my friend. Will

ONE ICY NIGHT

A THRILLER

USA TODAY BESTSELLING AUTHOR

W.A. PEPPER

Chapter One

Ax

N^{ow}

Through heavy, concrete-filled eyes, I study this madman that is trying to kill me.

Whether or not it is intentional remains to be seen, I think, as my brain buzzes along with the ringing in my ears.

"Snow don't act like this," says my whacked-out driver, Riley, who has consumed enough beer, tequila, and scripts to make Keith Richards balk.

The sleet hitting the windshield reminds me of *Star Wars'* Millennium Falcon going into hyperspace. Except *this* sleet is sticking like it is mixed with glue. The passenger windshield wiper sticks to the windshield before it snaps in two.

"It's like this weather has a mind of its own," he says, "and that mind is set on destroying everything it touches." He giggles at that. "It's God-like. I like it."

The wind smacks the side of the car, shoving us into the wrong lane of traffic. Riley overcompensates and yanks the wheel right and pain floods my head as the right side of my head bounces against the side window. Twice. At this point I'm so drunk, I either need to vomit, pass out, or keep drinking.

Instead, I try to speak.

"Shit!" I think I say that, but it could've been a thought. I try again.

"Look, I know you southern boys were raised on *The Dukes of Hazzard* and all," I slur in a jumble of nonsense, "but stop driving like you're being chased."

"You think?" Riley takes his eyes off the road and leans across the seat to look out the back window. "I bet you're right. They're always after me, always watching me."

"Who's they?" The words fall out of my dry mouth. Every word I utter tastes like cotton balls, sucking up all the saliva they can.

"They."

Well, *they* aren't going ninety-five miles per hour through this storm on a one-lane dirt road.

"Do you ever realize that every time you get behind the wheel of a car, you are a God?" Riley cackles. "You control the fate of each and every car, of each person, you pass."

"I'm sure that's exactly how they word it on the DMV exam."

Something between a laugh and growl creeps out of his throat.

"The trick is, each time, choose which type of God you are. Are you merciful..." He rocks the car side to side with quick little pulls on the steering wheel, sending me bouncing around in my seat. "Or are you vengeful?"

"Cut it out."

"Cut off the lights, you say?" He lets out a howl. "I like the way you think, girl!"

As darkness envelops our car's path, I punch him in the shoulder with everything I have.

"Ow! Quit that shit!" He flips back on the headlights and swerves around something I can't see. "See? We're fine. I'm just playing."

I would try to reason with him, but he's twice as drunk as I am, not to mention all the shit he's snorted in the last couple of hours.

A water bottle rolls across the floor and the itchy dryness in my throat burns. I grab for it, desperate for any relief.

"Don't drink that!"

Too late. I puke up my new companion's urine, adding to the smell of the world's worst tequila and beer to my ruined shoes.

And, of course, the smell and stains of the still-wet blood on them.

When I think about how the blood got there, it is enough to make me throw up again. I gag and dry heave for a minute before I shake the cobwebs from my head. I run my tongue along my sleeve like a cat grooming herself. My shirt isn't much cleaner, but I have to do something. If only my right eye would open, maybe it would help my unfocused and blurry left one. I want to put my head against the frozen-over window, just to feel the cold.

This asshole has his shitty vehicle's heat going full blast, so the windows are entirely fogged, and, despite his attempt to wipe a hole in the fog, I doubt he can see much through it.

I lean to the side, looking for something—anything—else to drink, but something holds me down. I fight the seatbelt. I yank and yank and yank, but I'm stuck.

No, I'm not stuck.

I'm tied down.

That's when I glance down and see the handcuffs holding the full-body seatbelt in.

Then I remember: those are the Sheriff's, who probably has just now figured out what I did to him.

If he ever sees me again, I'll go to jail for the rest of my life.

The roar of the defroster sounds like a pissed-off alley cat—more whirrs and screeches than warm and dry air.

The piece-of-shit car skids from side to side. With dirty fingernails, I pry open my right eye and the flash of an oncoming car's high-beamed headlights sear into my soul before I duck back down and cover both eyes.

"Shit! Ow!"

This-isn't-happening-this-isn't-happening. I'm-not-trapped-I'm-not-trapped-I'm-not-trapped.

Not again.

I claw at the release at the top of the oversized seatbelt. The latch and cuffs hold me tight.

"They designed the seatbelts for racing." Riley says this through chattering teeth. He's not cold. He's just on that many uppers.

"What are you racing in, Riley?" I snap. "The Pinewood Derby?"

He doesn't respond. Something through the small, defrosted hole in the windshield holds his attention.

"Whoa, shit! Hold on!" He yanks the wheel, and we spin on the icy road. Once. Twice. Three times. Hell, after a fourth-or-so circle I lose count. Then, like nothing happened, Riley keeps driving.

"These roads are no joke!"

I want to say that this car is a joke, or that his driving is. However, if it weren't for Riley, I might be in the local jail right now.

I've traded in detainment for possible death.

The world phases in and out. I blame the six—no, eight—shots of tequila and five beers I downed in the last, what, six hours? I'm more sober than I have any right to be; staring down the barrel of a gun sobers you up mighty quickly.

"You're kinda cute when you're not throwing up."

Prince Charming, everybody. Riley's still trying to get in my pants. Well, Mr. Driver, there's something in my front pocket, and you're not gonna like it if I have to use it.

He winks. The blood on his neck and shirt appears black in the limited moonlight. At least some of the blood is actually his.

The vehicle's defroster finally blasts air. Apparently, it only needed five minutes to warm up. As the oval-sized visibility hole melts away to give some view, I freeze. Through the sleet, in the distance, I barely make out something that shouldn't be in the middle of the road during a storm.

It's a man.

In what appears to be an orange jumpsuit, maybe prison issued.

Holding an ax.

And he's not getting out of the way.

(The Story Continues in *One Icy Night: A Rook Thriller*, out now!)

Acknowledgements

A journey of a thousand miles begins with one step" - Lao Tzu

So many steps occurred in the creation of Tanto's journey. Some I took myself, but most of them had someone holding my hand, guiding me forward. These are just a few of the people that helped lead me to complete Tanto's tale.

I believe a kind and all-powerful being granted me the opportunity to not only write, but to share my writing. I know that a Higher Power put me on this earth to tell stories that have kindness in them. For this, I am thankful.

Without Taddy Pepper encouraging me, I'd be at a loss. She's my Alpha reader, my top confidant, and the sounding board that often-times hits me with logic and feedback that I know is right, but I'm going to need a minute to mull it over. I have said this before, but this book shines because Taddy expects, no, demands great stories. Thank you, Babe.

In addition, I would like to thank the following people who contributed to this work currently in your hands:

Developmental Editor Meaghan Wagner tackled this thriller (hell, this entire series) and hit me with story-encouraging feedback. Over our years of teamwork, she's even been able to think like Tanto and helped correct my course when I went away from made our anti-hero unique and special. Our cover artist Damon Freeman and his team made all of Tanto's adventures a picturesque reality. Finally, David Sandretto's always excellent eye for details caught many a mistake as our copyeditor/proofreader (and David, I apologize for asking you to hurry because I had an injury that was going to slow me down). Thank you to this amazing team.

Our team of Beta Readers pointed out details and insights and offer suggestions that I never would've caught on my own. A big thank you to Cathy T., Josi D, Margery T., Mike I.C., Richard D. and Tabitha H.

Authors/creators I would like to thank include (in alphabetical order): Jason Aaron, Taylor Adams, Tara Alemany, Lee Child, Shawn Coyne, Scott Frank, Rachel Hawkins, Mark Leslie Lefebvre, Riley Sager, Kevin Smith, Ruth Ware.

Others I would like to thank include (in alphabetical order): Dan Alexander, Pam Burleson, Michael McGrath and to everyone who supports W.A. Pepper Writes, and Hustle Valley Press, LLC.

Thank you all!

About the Author

W. A. Pepper writes suspenseful thrillers. *You Will Know Vengeance* is his debut novel. He is an awarding-winning *USA Today, Wall Street Journal*, and *Amazon* Bestselling Author for his contribution to the business anthology *Habits of Success*. Under different names (and his real one of Will Pepper), he has published in multiple academic journals, interactive e-books, anthologies, and online. During the COVID-19 pandemic, he and his wife Taddy (plus their dog Danger) started the publishing house Hustle Valley Press, LLC.

Through it, they published four e-books that have amassed over one hundred five-star reviews. Further, the husband-and-wife team donated the first six months of revenue from the sale of each of those books to charity; this resulted in thousands of dollars raised for the reader-selected charities that support racial equality, COVID-19 relief, veteran affairs, and St. Jude Children's Hospital. He has a PhD in Management Information Systems or, as he calls it, Business Computing, from The University of Mississippi. Finally, he, his wife Taddy, and their dog Danger split their time between Colorado and Mississippi.

CONTACT INFORMATION

- will@hustlevalleypress.com

- Instagram:@wapepperwrites

- Facebook.com/wapepperwrites

- Tiktok.com/@wapepperwrites

www.ingramcontent.com/pod-product-compliance
Lightning Source LLC
Chambersburg PA
CBHW072007190726
48293CB00001B/192